GO

Also by John Clellon Holmes

Get Home Free
The Horn
Nothing More to Declare
Displaced Person: The Travel Essays

GO

A NOVEL BY
JOHN CLELLON HOLMES

THUNDER'S MOUTH PRESS

New York

©1952, 1988, 1997 by John Clellon Holmes
All rights reserved.
Published in the United States by
Thunder's Mouth Press, 632 Broadway, 7th Floor, New York, NY 10012
Cover design by Marcia Salo
Grateful acknowledgment is made to the New York State Council on the
Arts and the National Endowment for the Arts for financial assistance
with the publication of this work.

Library of Congress Cataloging-in-Publication Data

Holmes, John Clellon, 1926–
    Go: a novel by John Clellon Holmes.
        p.   cm.—(Classic Reprint series)
    ISBN 1-56025-144-1 $13.95
    1. Title II. Series.
    [PS3658.0359436 1988]   88-9751
    613´.54—dc19   CIP

Manufactured in the United States of America
Distributed by
Publishers Group West
4065 Hollis Street
Emeryville, CA 94608

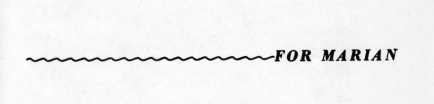

FOR MARIAN

"The days of visitation are come,
the days of recompence are come;
Israel shall know it: the prophet is
a fool, the spiritual man is mad . . ."
—Hosea, 9:7

"But whereunto shall I liken
this generation? It is like
unto children sitting in the
markets, and calling unto
their fellows,
And saying, We have piped
unto you, and ye have not
danced; we have mourned unto
you, and ye have not lamented."
—St. Matthew, 11:16, 17

"Fathers and teachers, I ponder 'What
is hell?' I maintain that it is the suffering
of being unable to love."
—Father Zossima

Literary historians share with botanists an impulse to classify, to break down the productions of any given era into taxonomies of influence, generation, group. Thus in our literary chronicles the Lost Generation—a title bestowed on Ernest Hemingway and company by Gertrude Stein—was succeeded by the generation that came of age during the Depression (one that has so far been denied a name, though it possesses a distinct identity); and they were succeeded by the Beat Generation. In such a scheme, contemporary history figures as the force that disrupts the lives of writers in their impressionable youth, sends them off to war or disillusions them, and convinces them of their essential alienation from society.

So it has been in our century. "We weren't destined to have the fate of the usual college generation," claimed Malcolm Cowley in *Exile's Return*, writing of the 1920s. "Without jobs," recalled philosopher William Barrett in "The Truants," a memoir of the 1930s, "the young were not chained immediately to the wheel of career and profession." The years just after World War II, noted John Clellon Holmes in his account of the Beats, *Nothing More to Declare*, were characterized by "a feeling of expectation without reasonable hope, of recklessness without motivation, of uniqueness seeking an image." That quest for an image by which to define the collective experience of a generation informs so many American memoirs; it is as if the very absence of a shared literary tradition prompts us to invent our own.

Still, generations do possess recognizable features, and John Clellon Holmes was among the first to reflect on the temper of the postwar era. *On the Road*, Jack Kerouac's definitive chronicle of nihilism and *anomie*, was published in 1957— the year that Norman Mailer, working the same terrain, delineated the character of "the White Negro," impelled "to live with death as immediate danger, to divorce oneself from society, to exist without roots, to set out on that uncharted journey with the rebellious imperatives of the self." But Holmes was at work on his autobiographical novel, *Go*, as early as 1949, when Kerouac had just finished *The Town and the City*, a sprawling American *Bildungsroman* that owed more to Thomas Wolfe than to any New York postwar mood and had none of the hopped-up, fast-talking hipsters who populate his later work.

Before the beats had become the Beats—that occurred later on in the 1950s, after the publication of *On the Road*—Holmes charted in *Go* their manic exploration of the unconscious, their feverish quest for experience, their glorification of crime. It was he who introduced that generation—and, in collaboration with Kerouac, the term that would define it. They had met at Allen Ginsberg's apartment in Spanish Harlem one night during the summer of 1948, when Kerouac was twenty-six and Holmes an aspiring novelist of twenty-two. At the time, Kerouac was living with his mother in Ozone Park on Long Island and used to come in to New York for occasional restorative bouts of dissipation. One night that autumn, Holmes and Kerouac were sitting around Holmes's apartment on Lexington Avenue meditating on their friends' attributes, their "weariness with all the forms, all the conventions of the world." And it was then, with "a conspiratorial the-Shadow-knows kind of laugh," Holmes recalled, that Kerouac proposed the idea of a "beat generation." The phrase made its way into *Go*, and Gilbert Millstein, who had reviewed the novel in *The New York Times*, commissioned an article for the *Times magazine* on the distinctive features of the generation it described.

That article ("This is the Beat Generation"; November 16, 1952) attracted more attention than the novel itself, and provided the earliest portraits of people soon to become famous. Readers of Kerouac or of the many books about him will recognize the characters in *Go*: David Stofsky, the voluble, wild-eyed poet whose visitations from Blake and mad babble have since become familiar lore in Allen Ginsberg's legend; Gene Pasternak, urging his friends "to live, *live!*" and rushing off to California, is Holmes's version of Kerouac; and a number of the other minor characters—Albert Ancke as the hustler and small-time underworld figure Herbert Huncke, and Hart Kennedy as the legendary Neal Cassady, whose fabled sexual charisma and pathological energy Kerouac depicted in *On the Road* in the person of Dean Moriarty—were later made notorious by Kerouac's novels. "The facts (if not the insights) there are as accurate as one friend dares to be about the inner life of another," Holmes claimed in *Nothing More to Declare*, defending his portrait of Ginsberg; and he was no less biographical, one suspects in his other portraits. Holmes's claim that *Go* is "almost literal truth" can be verified in Dennis McNally's *Desolate Angel*, John Tytell's *Naked Angels* or *Jack's Book*, the "oral biography" of Kerouac by Barry Gifford and Lawrence Lee.

But what distinguishes *Go* from Kerouac's own hectic testimony is its sobriety. Not that Paul Hobbes, Holmes's persona, is any less dissipated than his friends, any less susceptible to the blandishments of squandered evenings at nightclubs or drunken parties. But he is skeptical, conservative, unpersuaded by the ephemeral delight his friends derive from their indulgences. A solemn, industrious writer intent on salvaging his marriage, Hobbes is a reluctant participant in what Holmes elsewhere has called "futility rites"; he is a mere tourist in the underworld nightlife of Times Square dives, a realm "inhabited by people 'hungup' with drugs and other habits, searching out new degrees of craziness." Hobbes ventures into this world "suspiciously, even fearfully, but unable to quell his immediate fascination."

How different from the characters in *On the Road*, "mad to, live, mad to talk, mad to be saved, desirous of everything at the same time . . ." Yet Hobbes's very detachment is responsible for his insights: "The sense of freedom in his life, the idea of being able to control it, direct it, even waste it, of being able to entertain fancies that were detrimental or exercise a volition that was dangerous" comes to seem "a shameless illusion." Like Holmes himself, a New England Yankee from a venerable family, Hobbes is unnerved by a world where "his values are a nuisance and his anxieties an affront." He is more interested in self-preservation than in the *dérèglement de tous les sens* prescribed by Rimbaud and taken up with such ardor by the Beats. And if this reserve gives "a tinge of square moralism" to the novel, as one breathless chronicler of the period has observed, it also gives verisimilitude.

Go is the dispassionate record of one generation's self destructive rituals. Disorderly parties in squalid apartments; "hordes of chattering people" leaping into cabs and racing up and down Manhattan; the incessant quest for "weed" or "tea"—as marijuana was then called: what Holmes has captured is that state of mind evoked by Norman Mailer in a glossary he once compiled of "The Hip and the Square," a list that included "wild," "Negro," "midnight," "orgy," and "a catlike walk from the hip." But what is so surprising about Holmes's portrait, apart from its archaisms, is its familiarity:

> Now the rooms were thronged with people [he writes of a party at Stofsky's], many of them unsure just what they were doing there, but intrigued by all the talk, the smoke and laughter, and the ceaseless movement by which people at a party disguise their self-consciousness. The brighter crop of philosophy and literature students from Columbia squatted on the floors, vying for repute in that elaborate game of intellectual snobbery which passes for conversation among the young and intense. They grouped themselves (at a safe distance so as not to appear too interested) around the one or two authentic literary figures that Stofsky had managed to ensnare: a poet of cautious output, a novelist whose work had been appraised as being "not without talent," and a soft-faced critic who spoke in terms of "criteria and intention," and whose articles were fashionably unreadable. Through the rooms, like pale butterflies, flitted a number of young women, girl friends of the students, exchanging the gossip of the sets they traveled in with offhand arrogance, all the time snatching looks over their shoulders so as not to miss anything and quickly moving on.

This could be a scene from Edmund Wilson's *Memoirs of Hecate County*, the portrait of an earlier generation's rituals of decadence, or Delmore Schwartz describing a party spoiled by "the distortions of self-consciousness" in his story "New Year's Eve." There is the same inauthenticity, the same thin accomplishments made much of, the same haze of alcoholic gossip. And, like these other writers' observant personae, Hobbes is made to seem the only sentient character. Toward the end of one chaotic party, he drifts off to a corner by himself.

> dizzy from the drinking and the marijuana, and snagged in the senseless return of an old inferiority, cherishing a fond sadness as though he had perceived in all the chaos a deep vein of desperation which everyone else refused to notice. "Out of what rage and loneliness do we come together?" he thought drunkenly, certain some obscure wisdom lurked in the question.

What provoked this grim agitation, "this bleak eagerness for everything to happen at once"? In Holmes's later view, it was the prospect of nuclear war in that doom-haunted decade, combined with the restiveness that every postwar generation suffers and a rebellion against "conformist" values in favor of the "existential" (how those words have dated!). Any mad adventure, he recalled in *Nothing More to Declare*, was justified by a conviction that "something had gotten dreadfully, dangerously out of hand in our world." If a rational civilization could produce world war, the death camps, weapons of universal destruction, why not cultivate the irrational? Ginsberg—and Holmes's Stofsky—found support for this idea in Blake, but he could have found it in Keats: "Oh for a life of sensations rather than thoughts!"

The consequences of such a life are painfully evident in Hobbes's marriage, which finally succumbs to the sexual liberation of the day (another instance of a phenomenon claimed by every generation as its own). When Hobbes's sensitive, unhappy young wife goes off with Pasternak, it is with great reluctance, compelled more by some inarticulate compulsion to be of her time than by any real desire. Hobbes, in turn, must affect to be free of jealousy—another impulse that, like fidelity, is considered archaic—and proceed with a joyless seduction of his own. To be unfaithful is a duty; freedom from the social contract involves just as many obligations as obedience to it.

The other notable character in *Go* is the city itself, the backdrop against which all these lurid scenes are set. On a feverish voyage to the end of the night, Hobbes and his friends speed up the West Side Highway, while "the river-girdled length of the island slipped by them and the George Washington Bridge up ahead hung across the dark throat of the river like some sparkling, distant necklace." And on the novel's last page, Hobbes and his wife Kathryn, returning from a night of aimless carousing in Hoboken, stand on the deck of a ferry boat and gaze out across the water toward New York,

> a fabulous tiara of lights toward which they were moving. For a moment he stood there in the keen gusts that came up in the middle of the river, and searched the uptown towers of that immense, sparkling pile for the Chrysler Building, so that he might look north of it and imagine that he saw lights in their apartment.
> "Where is our home?" he said to himself gravely, for he could not see it yet.

Hobbes's desperation has a more specific cause than his friends'; his frustrated struggle to write is what really drives him out into the streets. Holmes, writing *Go* in his early twenties, had a lively sense of young writers' anguish. His portrait of the vulnerable, manic Stofsky, producing "an endless flow of half humorous, half mystical ideas, mortared with bits of poetry and insights derived from religious paintings," conforms to what we know of Ginsberg's very uneven spiritual life during the early 1950s, when he was a perplexed, awkward boy uncertain of his talent; and he has managed to capture Kerouac when he was a bellicose young novelist whose destiny had yet to be decided—before he became a legend.

Three years after the publication of *Go*, Holmes abandoned New York for Old Saybrook, Connecticut; Kerouac wandered out West; and the world depicted in the novel gave way to the legend of the Beats. But there is more of its essence in *Go* than in many subsequent records, for it was written before private experience became public myth.

—James Atlas

Introduction

R<small>E-READING</small> your first novel is like meeting a girl you loved impetuously and not wisely twenty years ago, and haven't seen since. All the things you didn't say well or do decisively then intermingle with the graphic memories that her face evokes. You recall why you loved her, but you also recognize that the loves of youth are to a large extent self-serving. It is a difficult experience, and you age a little in the process.

Certain paragraphs bring back with hallucinatory clarity the day on which they were written. Your mind flared, the words came of themselves, and in so doing memorialized forever the room on Lexington Avenue in which you worked, the drum of rain or slant of sun outside the windows, the particular smell of scalded coffee and Chesterfields. If the act of writing gobbles up and transforms the experiences about which you write ("Did so-and-so actually say that, or did I invent it?"), it also preserves indelibly the moment when a truth broke through. To write about your own life is to transfer it forever from memory to fact. The page exists to block your way into the usable past, and this is probably what keeps you forging on against your losses.

Re-reading *Go* has been like this for me. These gloomy lofts and tenements, these thronging streets and bars, these continual parties and confrontations—can it really have been like that? Did we really resemble these feverish young men, these centerless young women, awkwardly reaching out for love, for hope, for comprehension of their lives and times? Can this picture of the New York of twenty-five years ago be accurate? I can attest that it is. These were the places we lived in, the events that occurred, the way we talked, and the things we talked about. In this sense, the book is almost literal truth, sometimes a truth too literal to be *poetically* true, which is the only truth that matters in literature.

Go is, in every way, a young man's book. It was begun in August of 1949 when I was 23, and the last draft was completed in September of

xvii

1951 when I was a somewhat tougher 25. The two years of work at the typewriter were nothing but a continuation of the two years of experience that had preceded them. It is also a young *writer's* book, full of solemn gaffs, technical awkwardnesses, excesses of pessimism, and uncertain prose. It is mostly painted in reds and blacks, which are the colors of youth after all, but I think it improves as it goes along. I was learning something of my craft while writing it, and learning something of myself as well. I got a little braver as the material demanded it of me, and I got more ambitious as I grew adept.

The book is a *roman a clef* in the strictest sense of that term, for very little in it is fictionalized, and it often suffers from the blurred perspective of that *genre*. But I am amazed now to see how slavishly it hews to real events and real people. Even whole conversations are verbatim. I had been keeping exhaustive work-journals for the two previous years, and the book was more or less a transcription of these day-to-day jottings. In fact, the first draft was written with the real names intact, and several of the actual protagonists read it during its composition. The reader will have little trouble identifying the characters based on Jack Kerouac, Allen Ginsberg, Neal Cassady, Herbert Huncke and other writers and personalities associated with the Beat Generation. Nor can I disclaim that Paul Hobbes bears a marked resemblance to the young man I was then. The character of Agatson was based on a man named Bill Cannastra, and the account of his life and death is accurate in every detail. Verger was a student we all knew (now a teacher in the Midwest, the last I heard), and he is perhaps more fictionalized than anyone else in the book. The incident involving Jack Waters was based on an experience that happened to a friend of Ginsberg's, now a well-known poet, and it, too, has been exaggerated in the interests of theme. Some of the girls are amalgams of several people, though Dinah, Christine, Winnie and Bianca are as close to their originals as I could bring them. May is accurate to the young women of the time, and I went on to write about her in another novel, but in *Go* she is a type, rather than an individual.

All the pivotal events in the book actually happened, though not always in the sequence in which I arranged them. The depiction of Stofsky's "visions" was written after exhaustive talks with Ginsberg about his, and he later wrote his own account in the poem, *The Lion For Real*, to which I commend the reader for a more visceral view. Stofsky's poems are my versions of several of Allen's poems of that period, most of which have since been published in *The Gates of Wrath*. The day when Pasternak's novel is accepted and Hobbes' is rejected happened precisely as it is reported here—one of the odd coincidences that characterized my friendship with Kerouac. The events surrounding the arrest of Ancke, Little Rock, Winnie and Stofsky cleave as close to the truth as I could get, at second hand, at the time. The only completely invented incident in the book is when Pasternak sleeps with Kathryn, and this, again, was put in because it seemed thematically correct—though I am not unaware that I may have been trying to shift responsibility for my own peccadillos. As is clear, Paul Hobbes felt himself caught between the demands of an old morality and the attractions of a new, and guilt was mostly his goad.

Despite all the literalness, however, *Go* should be seen as *my* vision of that time, an honest attempt to recreate my own experience, and thereby reach an understanding of it—though of course the characters are some of the same people about whom Ginsberg would later write, "I saw the best minds of my generation destroyed by madness, starving hysterical naked, dragging themselves through the negro streets at dawn looking for an angry fix," and to whom Kerouac was referring when he said, "The only people for me are the mad ones, the ones who are mad to live, mad to talk, mad to be saved, desirous of everything at the same time." Indeed, this melling of materials has caused a mare's nest of confusion among critics and readers over the years. For instance, I once got a long, accusatory letter from a young woman, who stated that *Go* had obviously been written by Kerouac, because Hart Kennedy and Dean Moriarty seemed identical to her, and I had even introduced an off-stage character called Will Dennison—the fictional name Jack had given Bill Burroughs in *The Town and the City*. Actually, I had done this with Jack's approval, because I didn't know Burroughs then, and we all took delight in dropping these enigmatic, intersecting references into our books—as Jack did in *Maggie Cassidy* when he alludes to the mood and subject of an early, unpublished novel of mine. More seriously, it has been said in print that *Go* was nothing but a "pounded out imitation" of *On the Road*, and I suppose now might be the proper time to lay that charge to rest. As I have said, Jack read *Go* over the two years during which I wrote it, two years during which he was unsuccessfully trying to get *On the Road* on the road, and it was *after* he finished reading my first draft in early March of 1951 that he began what would be the final, twenty-day version of his own book, completed in late April of that year. I don't mean to suggest any influential connection between the two books (they rarely overlap in their material), but only to say that perhaps my rather darker view of "beat experience" was a view he couldn't share—that he found alien to his own perception—and that these objections may have provided him a needed impetus.

In any case, the two books cannot really be compared. Kerouac had found his voice and his vision when he wrote *On the Road*; I was still struggling to clarify both my craft and my viewpoint while writing *Go*. But certainly we shared a similarity of attitude based on the same experiences, and we were both trying to write directly from our own lives in those days. Those lives were occupied with things like drugs, madness, visions, booze, jazz and unconventional sexual mores, and these things surfaced in both our books in the natural course of writing. Anyone who knew Kerouac well knows that I could not have remained his close friend for over twenty years had he felt that I had stolen anything from him.

Go was first published in the fall of 1952 by Charles Scribner's, and thus it has the dubious distinction of being the first "Beat" novel to appear (the publication of *On the Road*, due to incomprehension, censorship and plain stupidity, wouldn't occur for another five years), and the fact that I had used the phrase, "Beat Generation", several times in the book, though carefully ascribing it to Gene Pasternak, may account for some of the confusion about who is properly the father of the term. Nevertheless, *Go* came out, was reviewed here and there, sold something over 2,500 copies, and then was quickly forgotten until *On the Road* appeared in 1957.

There were ironies aplenty in the publishing history of the book. Before being accepted by Scribner's, it had been rejected by A. A. Wyn, whose paperback subsidiary, Ace Books, would eventually publish the paperback edition five years later. Scribner's itself got nervous about possible censorship as publication approached, and submitted the book to a lawyer, who finally cleared it on the proviso that I make a few changes, which mostly involved a slight toning-down of the sex scenes. With considerable reluctance, I agreed to do this, but balked when I was asked to cut to *three* Agatson's *six* desperate "Fuck Yous" in the latter part of the book. "What's the difference between three and six?" I wondered. "He's not talking about sex, he's cursing the world." I stood my ground, and refused. As a result, Scribner's seriously thought of not publishing, and then suggested that if I would agree to withhold the book from paperback publication (where most censorship suits arose in those days) they would go ahead. My editor there, that good man Burroughs Mitchell, realizing that my only hope of making any money lay in a paperback sale, solved the problem by getting Scribner's to relinquish all the reprint rights to me on the proviso that nowhere in any paper edition would there be any mention of the fact that they had published the book originally. Needless to say, this didn't inspire confidence in an unblooded young author, who wanted to believe that his publisher believed in him.

The book was eventually sold to Bantam for the then-munificent sum of $20,000, only to be refused publication by them two years later (again, because of fear of lawsuits) on the advice of the very *same* lawyer who had cleared it for Scribner's. As a consequence, by the mid-fifties I discovered that I had earned ten dollars for every copy of a three-fifty book that had been sold, a book that would remain forgotten until Ace published an abridged edition in the wake of the initial notoriety about the Beat Generation in 1957. That edition, cut by almost a third, was subsequently published in England and Italy, and the original book vanished into the rare-book market where, the last I heard, the few remaining copies were going for upwards of $35.

A word about the title. The original manuscript was called *The Daybreak Boys*, which was an allusion to a river-gang on the New York waterfront of the 1840's. I felt that it was an appropriate title for a book about a new underground of young people, pioneering the search for what lay "at the end of the night" (a phrase of Kerouac's). But Scribner's had recently published a novel about public relations called *The Build-up Boys*, and rejected the title. I couldn't come up with anything else, and eventually it was Burroughs Mitchell's wife who thought of *Go*. When the book was published in England, the reverse happened. The English publisher pointed out that there was a travel magazine there named *Go*, and so the book would have to be renamed. It was finally published in Britain as *The Beat Boys*, and the circle (not to mention the confusion) was complete—in that some Englishmen still think that *The Beat Boys* is a wholly different novel than the unobtainable *Go*. But now, happily, I can state that this new edition is the only edition of the original book as I wrote it that is currently available in the world.

Any assessment of *Go* as literature is not my province, but there are a few things that I would like to add to this account. The book was a reckless attempt to dig myself out of one literary-and-life attitude and into another. It is obviously dominated by the existential perspective of those times, plus an infatuation with Dostoyevski that I shared with many tyro-writers then, who felt that extremes of spirit and dramas of conviction could best catch what young people sensed were the representative experiences of those post-war years. We were all trying to think about ourselves in a new, non-deterministic way that would hew closer to what we actually felt—which accounts for Hobbes' feeling that "though he did not know that (the Beat Generation) existed, somehow he sensed that it was there." I remember writing that line, still torn between caution and intuition, and rashly deciding to bet on the latter. More and more as the book progressed, I separated myself from Hobbes as he had lived the events, and became objective about him, and myself. I was different when the book was finished, as Hobbes, too, was different at the end of it; Hobbes who is armored, reserved, guilt-ridden and uncertain, yet the book itself continually trying to posit other alternatives to him.

When I began to write, I thought of the novel as the first volume of a trilogy that would be structured on Dante's *Divine Comedy*. *Go* was to be my *Inferno*, describing the circles of disbelief, descending from the upper world of young urban professionals, through the Bohemians, through the Beats, down into the outright underworld of criminality. As I wrote, I saw that the same hungers activated us all, and the thesis evaporated. Winnie with her unwanted pregnancy, and Kathryn with the unwanted radio, came to seem to me of equal human consequence. Ancke and Hobbes, in their different understandings, were attesting to the same perception that ego—the exacerbated persona—was an obstacle to entrance into reality. Gradually, as the book went on, I came to understand that passionate involvement in life, on any level, held out the only hope, and that lovelessness (what Ginsberg later called "tenderness denied") was the ultimate sickness of the age, and that its source was in all of us who refused to take the risk of vulnerability.

I suppose, as a result, Stofsky is for me the most successful character in the novel. For one thing, I first experienced with him the wonder of seeing a character in fiction coming to life on his own, however falteringly. He existed outside me, though I was his creator. He wrote himself towards the end, and I simply put down his words. His "earnest interferences" came to have the dignity of serious aspiration for me, and he remains the personal hero of the book to its author. He is continually more aware, more concerned, and more anguished by the consequences of action, than anyone else here. And finally, I realize, the conflict in me between one way of Being and another was resolved in the difficult work of understanding and creating this character. Stofsky alone seems capable of the future evolution in the spirit that I had come to feel was essential by the time I finished the book.

Now, in the mid-seventies, *Go* is as old as I was when I finished it. In some ways, time has been no more kind to it than it has been to me. I have passed artistic-leagues beyond it, but also I have somewhat lost the sense of urgent *zeitgeist* that it still possesses. On finishing the book in manuscript, Kerouac wrote to me on March 7, 1951: "In the last pages 'Paul' is so fine and so humble and such a gentle defense counsel in the big court that I hesitate to call anyone else in the book a greater character." Obviously, I disagree with this judgment—it was made out of the shy affection that was at the core of Jack's nature— but now that *Go* is back in the world again, I can say with some relief:

The defense rests.

—John Clellon Holmes

Old Saybrook, Connecticut
February, 1976

PART ONE

The Days of Visitation

"Last week I got the idea that the one aim of my inter-course with other people is to prevent them from noticing how brittle and will-less I have become," Paul Hobbes was writing. "I can't seem to dance without a piper. Would you believe it of me? I actually yearn for life to be easy, magic, full of love. How wonderful (and simple) it would be if we were all naked on a plain, as Gene Pasternak says. *You* probably wouldn't like him at all, but I can learn something from him because he's written an annoyingly good novel. And anyway he believes in himself, and also in life. . . . As of this moment, *I* only believe in the spring outside the window on Lexington Avenue, and in you. Is there spring up there on Riverside Drive too? Let's all go out and be naked on a plain. . . ."

Angrily, Hobbes stopped typing, surrendering to his feeling that the letter was basically aimless. He pulled the sheet out of the machine, looked it over for a moment, thrust it aside, and got up. He began to walk noisily up and down the floor. It was after five and Pasternak had been sleeping since nine that morning.

Everything in sight made Hobbes impatient: the shelves he had built for their books, the borrowed frameless paintings on the walls, the couches in need of a brush; everything that he and his wife, Kathryn, had collected and arranged so carefully in the last years. They were not enough somehow; nor were his desk, his manuscripts, and the novel upon which he had been biting his nails too long. Only the soft spring evening, which hung like some impossibly romantic water-color behind the towers of mid-town Manhattan, escaped his dissatisfaction. He was filled with that heightened sense of excitement and restlessness that spring brings to New York, when everything becomes graceful and warm with promise. A joy without object or reason rose within him, but like all such joys ebbed into frustration almost immediately be-cause he did not know how to express it.

He went to the phonograph, pulled out an album and put on a soft jazz record. He did not want to keep quiet, he wanted everything to begin; but an overly-developed sense of propriety prevented him from going into the bedroom, and waking Pasternak with cruel brightness so they could talk. Instead he sat down again and began to re-read what he had written.

But just then Pasternak shuffled uncertainly through the bedroom door, stiff with sleep. He glanced at the phonograph, then at Hobbes, and said grumpily:

"What time is it anyway? I just had the craziest dream."

"A little after five." He stuffed the letter into the pile of magazines on his desk. "There's coffee on the burner."

Pasternak nodded groggily, compressing his heavy eyebrows as if sleep was like water and could be squeezed out of his eyes.

"I got more than eight hours then," and he made for the bathroom.

This was the only anchor in his otherwise drifting days. Eight hours (any eight) out of every twenty-four, Pasternak slept grimly, insistently, impervious to noise or hunger or daylight. When he came into New York from his mother's home in Long Island City for some binge, it usually ended at Hobbes' apartment in the early dawn hours. There he would sleep on a couch until nine when Kathryn left for her job in a downtown public relations office, and then Hobbes would poke and cajole and guide him into the bedroom where he would collapse on the extra bed and burrow back into unconsciousness.

As friends, Pasternak and Hobbes were an odd pair. Pasternak was the sort of young man whose ties always seem to have a large knot in them, and on whom clothes look vaguely inadequate to contain the chunky body whose awkwardness is somehow suggestive of athletic prowess. Everything about Hobbes, on the other hand, was angular. He never filled out the corners of his jackets, his hair always needed a trim, and he had a strangely unfinished air. Even his conversation was weakened with generality and that touch of insincerity of which carefully worded speeches often smack. Like the friendships of many American youths, theirs had risen swiftly on the foundation of these differences and persisted because each felt in the other something that he lacked and envied.

Now Pasternak emerged from the bathroom with his black hair combed neatly wet, and his pensive features ruddy with scrubbing. He fixed his cup of coffee with absent-minded impatience, flopped on a couch with it beside him, and said with sudden annoyance:

"You know what I just dreamed? I dreamed about everybody I know. It was at a party somewhere. Everybody—Stofsky, Ancke, Verger, Winnie . . . even Hart Kennedy from Denver! People from years back. Agatson was there too, eating glass. And Ketcham with that girl . . . what's her name? . . . Agatson's old girl . . . Bianca." He held the cup gingerly between stubby fingers, taking voracious gulps from it. "And there were lots of others, too. . . . I honestly never realized how many people I know! Too many goddamn people. You know what I mean?"

Hobbes sniffed eagerly. "That's an odd complaint. Having too many friends! Only someone who doesn't believe it could say such a thing."

"No, but I felt like Elsa Maxwell or somebody. It was a rotten party anyway. Everyone was mad. Winnie . . . you remember, I told you about her? The big red-head, six feet tall, who used to come down to Dennison's morphine-pad on Orchard Street in the old days? . . . Well, she kept yelling across the room to some hipster, 'How about a fix! How about a fix, man!' Only real loud. And Ketcham looked down his nose at her and began whispering to everyone about 'that vile woman'!" He arched his shoulder and made a fey grimace of imitation.

"But Ketcham hasn't even met Winnie, has he?"

"No, but this is in the dream! What I mean is that it was all like that, everyone I know all mixed together and scrapping. Agatson was yelling about hailing taxis from the El, and when I looked at him he put out his tongue at me. And Stofsky kept trying to convince me he was queer, and in love with evil and all that." He moped for an instant. "You know, there just aren't any real g-r-e-a-t parties anymore . . ."

"Well, what about this one tonight at Stofsky's? Everything may begin tonight, Gene . . . And besides, that was only a dream. You're starting to believe it was real!"

"But don't you see, this was my party . . . in the dream. A celebration of my selling my book or something. And then everyone got so hungup on themselves. I tell you, Paul, I'm not kidding. I know too many people, I mean too many kinds of people. . . . And besides, Stofsky will do some real outlandish thing and mystify someone or other. You know how he is. Why, the first time I saw him, five years ago, he was scuttling along the halls up at Columbia like a mouse, no more than eighteen years old, with a huge copy of Spengler under his arm. And then when we got talking and I asked him about his mother, you know what he said? 'She's up in Madtown with the bats!' Just like that. And later I found out it was true. She is actually crazy and in an asylum. But that's the kind of thing he always does. . . .Oh, and by the way, he said he was going to drop by here after his analysis this afternoon."

They went on talking, and the warm yellow shadows of twilight slid across the buildings outside the windows. But nothing that was said could satisfy Hobbes' growing exhilaration at the prospect of the night ahead, or Pasternak's impatience at the thought of how it might turn out.

Hobbes, normally reserved and even suspicious, became more credulous and excited, but Pasternak kept losing interest and broke out every now and again: "Let's go out and have a beer! Or play some Charlie Parker records," and then "You know, all I really want is to get laid. That's what I'm really complaining about."

At this last, there was a rapid knock and David Stofsky hurried in the door like a sudden gust of wind that comes up out of nowhere. Taking a position in the middle of the room, all at his ease, he announced immediately:

"I've just seen Agatson in the White Rose Bar, and you know what he did? It was fantastic! He was already very drunk, and right while I was talking to him, he turned away, positively wriggling, and went up to a tough-looking marine and said: 'Give me a big wet kiss! . . .' the coy way Winnie used to say it to her men. Those were his exact words, everyone could hear! And I borrowed four bucks from him, Gene. For the party. Everyone's coming. . . . Oh, and you know what *else* has happened? I had a breakthrough this afternoon at my analyst's! Right at the end of the session, I had this sudden sexual urge for him. And I told him. 'Doctor Krafft, weren't you expecting identification about now?' . . . But it was very strange, because it made him furious and he refused to talk about it."

This disjointed speech did not surprise either of the others. It was Stofsky's habit to burst in full of news, for he was one of those young men who seem always to be dashing around the city from apartment to apartment, friend to friend; staying a few moments to gossip and ingratiate, and then running off again. Although he had no job, his days were crowded with vague appointments up and downtown, and for a large group of people he was the unofficial bearer of all sorts of tidings. His sources were multitudinous and his candor so infectious that it made the more suspicious of his friends question his motives. When entering a room full of people, for instance, he would pass from one to the other, shaking hands with mock gravity, then go directly up to someone he did not know, and say, eyes twinkling with excitement behind the heavy horned-rims: "You're so-and-so, aren't you? Well, I'm David Stofsky. I know *all* about you!" This was said with such eager, guileless smiles that it annoyed almost no one.

"But imagine Agatson," he went on, now pattering up and down the floor. "You know, he's not queer at all. It was just an imitation of course. But I tell you the whole bar was electrified!"

"How did you get him out alive?" Hobbes exclaimed.

"Nothing happened! Isn't it incredible? The marine was absolutely speechless, as though he was seeing a monster. He just stared at Bill, muttered something—to save his face, you know —and wandered out! I swear it's the truth. There were at least fifteen people there!" He emitted a yakking, breathless laugh, his eyes glittering.

Pasternak refused to show his amusement at the story.

"That guy's going to get killed someday, crazy son of a bitch! . . . But say, have you heard from Winnie yet?"

"No. I was looking all over Times Square for her a few nights ago, really combing it, but I couldn't locate her. If we could find Albert he might know, but I think he's still in jail."

Albert Ancke and Winnie were phantoms to Hobbes, shadowy figures that he always associated with the glaring nighttime confusion of Times Square, its unruly bars, teeming cafeterias and all-night movies. He had never met them, but Pasternak and Stofsky talked of them incessantly, along with other petty thieves, dope-passers and "characters" that they knew. The stories fascinated Hobbes, but in the three months he had known his two friends there had only been vague rumors concerning Ancke and Winnie; rumors that filtered in from casual acquaintances that Stofsky ran into during his travels about the city, which said that Ancke was serving a narcotics sentence, and that Winnie was "kicking her morphine habit" out in some walk-up in Astoria. But that was the extent of the information.

Pasternak was buttoning up his shirt, and said sullenly:

"Come on though, let's go out and have a beer or something." But then, noticing that Stofsky had wandered to Hobbes' desk and was picking through his papers idly, he added, with a worried glance at Hobbes: "Hey, you oughtn't to do that, David. Ask the guy first."

But at that moment Hobbes did not resent Stofsky's inquisitiveness so much because he might read a paragraph of his latest chapter. His chief concern was that he would stumble across the letter that was sandwiched among the magazines, for he knew Stofsky would read it aloud and ask questions with the confident belief that there were no secrets in the world.

To divert him, Hobbes began nervously: "How about your poetry, David? Have you been writing since I saw you?"

Stofsky came away from the desk to sink on the couch wearily. "Oh no, I haven't done a thing. I've been rushing around, and besides, you know I think it's bad for me. Perhaps even a symptom of disorder. Doctor Krafft was saying that I should curtail anything that might be an escape-valve, that might compete." He whinnied again in his breathless way. "He was very mysterious today, for instance. I was certain it was an authentic breakthrough, the first real sign that I'm making progress, but he told me I take everything much too lightly, and I'm not *trying*. Isn't it funny? It seems I'm not even qualified for analysis!"

"Then it wasn't a real whaddayacallit?"

"Aw, it's a lot of nonsense anyway," Pasternak growled. "Come on, let's go out!"

But as they stood outside the door, Hobbes pausing to lock up, Stofsky said with odd seriousness, that sounded even odder in one who was usually given to exaggeration and self-ridicule:

"But, you know, what could I say when he told me that? I *am* in earnest about this analysis. In a way, it's my last chance. And yet when he said that I wasn't trying, I felt like laughing, uncontrollably." He glanced with bashful embarrassment at both of them. "Remember how I used to do that all the time?"

They went around the corner and over to Third Avenue. Under the shuddering roar and sooty pilings of the Elevated there was a ramshackle, narrow bar called Mannon's where they always drank when they were in Hobbes' neighborhood. It was a grimy, ill-lit place, lacking even a neon in the window, the atmosphere fouled with the odors of urine and flat beer; and there were always a few dispirited, vacant-faced Third Avenue drunks slumped in the rear booths.

They ordered beers and sat around, saying little. The other two were concerned about Pasternak's gloominess. Like all young men, matters of the soul were the very substance of reality to them, and each one of them, in his own way, had grown surprisingly sensitive to the merest change of mood or shade of emotion in the others. Pasternak, who was usually as eager as a boy to grasp the moment and experience it fully, and in whom even angers and irritations found rude, immediate expression, now sat surveying the bar with a pinch of sour displeasure at the sight of everything.

Stofsky went after it. Sordid surroundings and inexplicable actions always created a weird excitement in him, and his tempers alternated rapidly. His moment of seriousness had vanished and the beers, the dusty walls, the doleful faces of the drunks, and Pasternak's strange mood put a gleam in his eye.

"What's the matter with *you*, Pasternak?" he began challengingly. "You look like you swallowed the monster, like that marine!"

Hobbes laughed uneasily. "He just got up, that's all."

"But look at him now," Stofsky went on gaily. "You'd think *I* was his monster! By which I mean, of course, the thing he simply can't bear to face at this particular moment!"

"Oh, you're always talking about monsters that way," Pasternak exclaimed morosely. "Naw, it's just that I haven't heard from MacMurry's. . . . Can't I be quiet if I want to? . . . They probably lost my book in their cellars or someplace. I'm just fed up with these goddamn, high-hat publishers, that's all! Did I write the book for them?"

"No, but you *did* write it, Gene, you finished it," Hobbes said earnestly, remembering his own fitful, halfhearted efforts to complete his novel. "Don't think of them. Screw them!"

"Maybe you're *their* monster," Stofsky put in with a giggle.

"Well, I've decided I wrote it because I wanted fame and money and . . . and love; not for any sterile artistries," Pasternak went on disconsolately. "I was just wooing the world with it, being coy. That's why anybody writes a book, for Christ's sake! Why should you fool yourself, Paul? I'm feeling geekish because the world isn't interested in my clumsy valentine."

"You're just depressed. Forget about it. They've only had it a few weeks. And, you know, I have the feeling that a new 'season' is about to begin. I really have that feeling."

Hobbes used one of Pasternak's favorite expressions, calculating on its effect, for it implied new strange people, disorderly nightlong parties, and fresh ideas.

"Well, I want to get married," Pasternak blurted out heatedly. "Get settled, maybe have a big farm and kids and everything. I'm tired of lurking around the streets after women, and biting my fingernails. *You're* o.k., you've got Kathryn and your pad and her salary, but hell . . ."

Hobbes could not help thinking guiltily: "Why isn't all that enough?" but he did not want to spoil his own feeling of easy good spirits by thoughts of his marriage, so all he replied was:

"Well, don't worry about your book anyway. It's a good book and good books make it eventually." But then, against his will, he lapsed into heavy thoughts.

Stofsky started to talk again, with that feverish gleam in his eye that indicated he was making an obscure point on both of them: "But, you know, Agatson got me to thinking. Of course, *everyone* has his monster, the personification of everything he really fears. A sort of Dracula in daylight! And what is analysis but the patient coming to that moment of self-truth where he can embrace his monster? And kiss the hairy cheeks without a shudder."

Very often Stofsky would suddenly come out with an idea such as this, disturbing as well as perceptive, and he would sit bouncing with infinite delight in his chair, expanding upon it. Now, without any encouragement from the other two, he began analyzing all their friends in the light of "their secret monsters."

"Now Agatson's monster would be some gum-chewing hood, with horrible checkered shirts and a shifty eye, who believed in even *less* than Bill does; who would tell him that all his wildness, his crazy stunts, his calculated obscenities (for that's what they are, you know: real calculations!), weren't tragic illustrations of the death-wish or the decline of western civilization . . . but just . . . well, 'jes' kid's stuff, man!' " And he imitated the contemptuous, oily drawl of the movie gunman. " 'Heah, go on over and plug that dame in the belly! Get real kicks!' " His shoulders quivered with strangled little whinnies. "Can you imagine Agatson's horror?"

"And with Verger, poor tubercular forlorn Verger, I'd get one of those deformed little men, with no legs, with lice, who wheel themselves around on carts and grunt for a penny, and I'd roll him into one of Verger's b-i-g serious parties one night and say: 'Look, I've brought the monster along for a beer!' . . . Think of what it would do for people! It would be better than shock treatments, having to face their own Golgothas when they least expected it."

Pasternak was laughing unwillingly, cheered up for the moment by the spectacle to which Stofsky was treating him, and unaware that several people at the bar had turned in their direction the afternoon drinker's distant, unflinching eye. But Stofsky was carried away by his idea, and turned on Pasternak:

"But, for instance, your mother thinks I'm unclean. Oh, I've known it a long time. She's nervously polite when I'm in your house as though she thought I would soil everything. Well, for her I'd get all made up in filthy rags and paint huge running sores and pimples on my face, and then knock on the door and groan pitifully when she opened it!"

Although he said nothing, this did not amuse Pasternak at all, for he was sensitive about his mother, who was still working in the shoe factory she had entered so that he might write his novel.

"And I'd be the monster with you, too, Paul," he continued with a sly, comic wink. "You know what I'd do? You know what I'd do? I'd simply walk into your place one quiet afternoon with no clothes on! ! And I'd act perfectly normal, in fact even pompous, which would shock your sense of decorum even more!" And he snickered as if the thought was deliciously sinister. Hobbes could think of no reply and covered his consternation with a grudging smile.

Now Stofsky was laughing continually at his thoughts, rocking back and forth in his seat, his hands stuffed between his legs; and the other two suddenly realized that what had begun as a mere tantalizing idea meant to entertain them, had ended up by obsessing him.

"Wherever I went, I'd bring the monster, everyone's creeping, stuttering monster! Think of it! It's the only truly saintly guise that would work in this world!"

But Pasternak, perhaps irritated by the remarks about his mother, had tired of the play as quickly as it had at first interested him. He sank back into his gloom, saying with annoyance: "What the hell would your crazy analyst say about all this, huh?"

This punctured Stofsky's pose immediately, and he flushed: "I don't know. But I guess I shouldn't mention it to him, should I! *He's* a professional monster, after all." But his downcast eyes indicated that he thought it a poor joke.

Hobbes was watching the clock because he wanted to be home

before Kathryn got back from her job, and besides, the beer was giving him an oddly sluggish feeling after all the cigarettes and the coffee.

Finally he got up, finishing off his glass.

"Look, Paul," Pasternak said. "I might as well go uptown with David and give him a hand. You have to eat anyway. We'll see you in a couple of hours, okay?"

So Hobbes left them and wandered back through the muggy, darkening street, considering fitfully the fact that, if so he chose, he could be drunk and forgetful in four hours, experiencing that illusory sense of carelessness and good will in which liquor suffused him. Somehow the thought was mildly pleasant.

He puttered around the apartment, killing time by straightening pillows and washing the coffee cups. Finally he sat down at his desk and read over the letter with dissatisfaction. Then, feeding it back into the typewriter, he wrote deliberately:

"Pardon this mish-mash of foolishness. The hazard of an increasingly hectic life. And loving you from downtown for so long, and to no avail. I find upon re-reading that I haven't even mentioned those hateful words. Well, I love you, Liza. Forgive the meditations.   Yours,   H."

Two

KATHRYN came in the door shortly before eight and caught him in the middle of a loud bop record. He took it off the machine and then kissed her.

"Where's Gene? How long did he sleep?"

"He went on up to Stofsky's about an hour ago."

Putting her purse on the coffee table, she looked around the apartment sharply, a sort of swift inspection of the premises that was habitual, and signified that she had had a grueling day.

"You did the dishes."

"Yes. But sit down for a minute, honey. Get rested, then we can go up to the Athens to eat."

But she was hurrying around, straightening magazines he had already straightened and wiping the flecks of ashes from the surface of the table. She was a small person, just five feet tall —a fact which caused her no end of torment and anger in subways and buses. Wide at shoulder and hip, she had that decisiveness of movement that seems natural and feminine in a body that verges on voluptuousness. A Navy friend of his, after looking at a photograph, had once called her "someone from far away," and Hobbes, just married to her then and separated by a continent, had thought this peculiarly apt. Her Italian descent had given her dark, luminous skin, delicate bones and a mouth that was sensual and yet somehow melancholy. It was her mouth that created the expression of slight introversion that belied her usually aggressive manner.

Hobbes always became agitated when she hurled herself into cleaning and straightening the minute she got home. He would say over and over again, night after night, "If you'd just sit down a moment, get yourself collected, you could work all night and not feel it." Though often convinced that this was sensible, she never did it. And he never fully admitted to himself that the main reason for his agitation was guilt because he had not kept the place in order.

"Did you have a hard day?" he asked, knowing the answer, but foolishly hoping she would lie to him.

She was emptying ashtrays that had only two or three butts in them. "Of course."

He drew a long face, realizing that if she had lied he would not have believed it, but would have acted as though it were the truth anyway. She watched him for an instant.

"Well, I did. That's what I'm getting paid for."

He said nothing more and let her go about the cleaning. This nightly sparring was the result, ironically enough, of their abnormal sensitivity to each other and their inverted roles in the marriage—she, out in an office; he, at home writing. When they came together in the evenings, she was completely wrung out from the frantic give and take of handling temperamental clients all day, and longed for quiet and an engrossing book. He, on the other hand, was alone so much, struggling with his thoughts and a natural laziness, that he often fell to talking to himself and, in the evenings, wanted conversation, people and excitement. Much of their time was spent in working out unsatisfactory compromises between these conflicting desires.

After fifteen minutes or so, they went out to eat. As they had only an electric burner in the apartment, and Kathryn got home so late, almost every night they had a hot meal in the same place: a tiny, overheated lunch counter up on Sixty-third Street called the Athens Food Shop. It was cheap and uncrowded, run by a large family of Greeks who cooked well and had a friendly interest in their customers. In the warm spring evenings, the walk up to this place was refreshing and, more than anything else, served to relax them.

They had hamburger steaks and coffee, and talked intermittently to one another, each contributing, without intending it, to the slight ruffle of tension. As they sat over a second cup, Hobbes glanced at the wall-clock and saw that it was quarter to nine.

"Maybe we ought to get back, honey. I have to shave and we said we'd be there by nine-thirty."

Kathryn lit a cigarette wearily, "I'm not sure I'll go, Paul. I have a hideous headache."

Dully, he realized that he had been anticipating this.

"Why not? Last week when Stofsky mentioned it, you said it sounded fine. Agatson's going to be there, and maybe even Ketcham."

"What do I care for Agatson! It won't be a good party. You know that."

"But . . . he's counting on us. And it should be interesting. We could just stay a little while."

"You can go, but I'm tired."

Hobbes sat there unhappily, sipping the steaming coffee. These last minute refusals on her part seemed to him unnecessarily arbitrary, but they did not really anger him. What angered him was the underlying sense of panic he always felt whenever they were planning to go somewhere in the evening and went out to eat beforehand. He never knew if they would get through the meal safely before she came out with it. At every mouthful, he was fabricating strategies to combat her weariness.

"What are you thinking?" he said, a question they asked each other so often that, like 'I love you' or 'Did you sleep well?' it had become a method of communication not unlike sign language.

"Nothing," and she gave him a vague look.

"That's no answer."

"I wasn't thinking anything."

"Look, I really think we should at least put in an appearance," he started, trying not to plead. "There'll be lots to drink, and it *could* be fun. We can come back early."

"All right," she replied irritably, giving in. "But I want to come home by eleven. You can stay if you like, but I've got things to do before I go to bed."

He felt an instant of buoyancy. "Okay. You know, it's just that I want to get to know these guys better. We don't know anybody else like them. Just this afternoon Stofsky had this wild idea about everyone's monster. Not a joke, quite seriously . . ."

He talked on determinedly as they walked back through the crowded streets, trying to interest her and supply good reasons for their attending the party. He knew that little of what he said really mattered to her when she was exhausted this way, but he went on just the same, trying to recapture the tremor of joy he had felt earlier.

"Are you happy, dear?" he asked finally as they climbed the stairs of their building.

"Yes," she said bluntly, then turned on him. "But you can't just ask me to turn it off and on that way! That's stupid. Why do you always ask me if I'm happy that way?"

"But are you?"

"Yes, I suppose so."

Three

STOFSKY lived on York Avenue and Seventy-eighth Street in a dreary district of junkshops and saloons. His building was little more than a dilapidated tenement with a watch repair shop downstairs in which a blue bulb burned all night. His apartment was on the fourth floor at the back; and the dingy stairways leading up to it, which smelled perpetually of garbage, were the hideouts of gaunt, fugitive cats from the neighborhood, and an occasional drunk as miserable as they.

Like cold water flats everywhere, Stofsky's place was entered through the kitchen, a small, high-ceilinged room newly painted a violent blue. Its only window gave out on a dirty air-well. To the left of this room was a cubicle not much larger, with a bed (which appeared never to have been made up), a portable clothes closet, and a few paper covered books on an orange crate. Beyond this room was the toilet. To the right of the kitchen, there was another room, more spacious than the others, which had two lofty windows hung with mouldy drapery, once long ago a rich maroon. They gave out on a stunted tree and a network of clotheslines. There was also a bricked up fireplace with a baroque mantel, now chipping and laden with books. Over this, fastened to the wall with leather headed carpet tacks, hung a cheap colored reproduction of Grünewald's "Crucifixion," which Stofsky had cut out of a magazine. But the pride of the room, and the thing which had most attracted Stofsky to the apartment, was a tremendous map of the world which covered the entire wall opposite the fireplace. It was intricately detailed as to cities, trade routes and prevailing winds, and criss-crossed with countless red meridian lines. Then there were a couple of low coffee tables, too large for the spaces they occupied before a couch and an armchair. These, and the desk against another wall, were always a clutter of ash trays, empty beer bottles, odd volumes of poetry, a few small pieces of tasteless statuary retrieved from the junkshops, and some magazines in which Stofsky's verse had appeared while he was at Columbia.

The story went that he had come into possession of the apartment when a friend of his (an older man whom no one had ever met) suddenly jumped a boat for Europe, leaving the place to him, furniture and all. It cost him fifteen dollars a month, and whenever he could collect enough cash for a bottle of whiskey and some beer he gave parties to show it off.

The party that night was typical. To it, he had invited everyone he could contact and even encouraged these people to ask others, counting on the uninvited guests to bring liquor with which to make themselves more welcome. If Stofsky was introduced to someone in the afternoon, that person was asked to come that night; and everyone, gathered in this haphazard manner, either got along or didn't. The interplay of relationships under the benevolence of alcohol was the main thing, and it was no exaggeration that if nobody else had a good time at his parties, Stofsky at least enjoyed himself immensely.

Now the rooms were thronged with people, many of them unsure just what they were doing there, but intrigued by all the talk, the smoke and laughter, and the ceaseless movement by which people at a party disguise their self-consciousness. The brighter crop of philosophy and literature students from Columbia squatted on the floors, vying for repute in that elaborate game of intellectual snobbery which passes for conversation among the young and intense. They grouped themselves (at a safe distance so as not to appear too interested) around the one or two authentic literary figures that Stofsky had managed to ensnare: a poet of cautious output, a novelist whose work had been appraised as being "not without talent," and a soft-faced critic who spoke in terms of "criteria and intention," and whose articles were fashionably unreadable. Through the rooms, like pale butterflies, flitted a number of young women, girl friends of the students, exchanging the gossip of the sets they traveled in with offhand arrogance, all the time snatching looks over their shoulders so as not to miss anything, and quickly moving on. In the crowded living room where a single light dimly shone, someone was strumming a zither the strings of which had been systematically tuned flat.

Stofsky was everywhere, perhaps the only person acquainted with them all. Like a child giving a tea party for adults, he seemed blissfully unaware that nobody was really at ease. But he found a moment for everyone, and there was something peculiarly charming about his formality and his delighted smiles;

something almost winsome in his usually wry mouth as he made graceful chit-chat or expressed interest in trifles: all of which was in bizarre contrast to the discomfort of most of his guests.

As was usual, his close friends, knowing what to expect, clustered together as they arrived and ignored everyone else. This group captured the divan in the living room and refused to budge for the rest of the evening, forming a nucleus around which the party would either coalesce or disintegrate.

There Pasternak sat, his annoyance of the afternoon changing to depression as new hordes of chattering people squeezed in the door. Nearby sat Daniel Verger, his wasted shoulders in their perpetual hunch and his thin lips drawn down in an expression of resignation that gave him the look of a young, sickly sceptic. He was talking with a girl named Bianca, who appeared to be struggling hopelessly to fasten her black, wild eyes upon him. She had a tense, full bosomed body to which she seemed absolutely indifferent at that moment, and every now and again she broke out in a raw, disturbing laugh that bewildered Verger.

The cause of her inattention was the sight of a strikingly handsome young man, who had once been her lover, and who now stood tottering against the wall map, surveying everything with that expression of private irony with which liquor loosens the features. This was Agatson, and Bianca stared at him, not out of personal remembrances (because she saw him almost every day and lived only three blocks from his Twenty-first Street loft), but for the same reason that everyone found it difficult to keep his eyes off him for long.

Agatson was one of those rare people whose reputations are in every way merited. His dissipations, and the exploits accompanying them, were near-legendary among a large group of young people in New York, and his loft was perhaps the only place in the city where a wild, disorderly brawl might be going on at any time. Once, after a week-long binge with him, a noted poet had prophecied that Agatson would be dead in three years or in an asylum, and this had provided the tantalizing aura of doom which was all that was needed to dignify the legend.

Agatson had a spare, muscular body which abuse had hardened. It was the body of a man whose drinking has become a sort of vocation, and who (unlike the run of urban sophisticates) no longer sports his hangovers like so many Purple Hearts earned in the good fight against boredom, but endures them with stoical tenacity and never complains. His dark features had that fleeting, sensual looseness that only the dissolute, just this side of slavery to alcohol, can possess. There was something mocking and remote in his fixed stares and in the curl of lips no longer firm, but not yet lax. Everything about him made even the tipsy onlooker grow alert, as if realizing that this man respected only the prodding of whim and might do anything that came into his head; and yet that all this was somehow the result of a fatal vision of the world. In fact, to many of these young men, Agatson was a symbol of that inability to really believe in anything which they felt stirring within themselves, and the craving for excess which it inspired.

Now, from across the room, his eye caught on the wan face of Verger, and he yelled: "Why if it isn't O. B. Haverton!" Lurching closer, he started to speak with winking, bleary-eyed seriousness, about how they hadn't seen each other since Harvard days, all the time referring to Verger as "ole O. B."

This was plainly foolishness, because Verger was often in the crowd at Agatson's parties and had been trying for months, patiently and vainly, to establish a friendship between them, but some streak of malicious irony had seized Agatson and he went on and on with it.

Verger, who was a theological student and whose bare, drafty flat in Spanish Harlem was filled with abstruse religious books, was, like many bookish people, flustered by a loud voice and never sure he correctly understood what it was saying.

He turned with a tremulous smile to Bianca, and said weakly: "Bill always mispronounces my name."

"You're O. B. Haverton, of course, and you used to write verse to a barmaid on Scullay Square. Do you think I'm drunk or something, O. B.? . . . We used to call him Old Bitch Haverton, you know, behind his back!"

For a moment Verger hesitated. "Well . . . well, I've changed my name," he stumbled out. "To Verger."

"Virgin! . . . Virgin!" Agatson shouted, wheeling on Bianca. "Hey, babe, ole O. B. says he's still virgin! But you used to write all about love, O. B. Didn' you do any research, hey, hey?"

Verger was blushing now for he was not successful with women, and yet often spoke seriously of love as "the one hope." But now he had about convinced himself that Agatson actually was so drunk that he did not recognize him.

Bianca tried to come to the rescue. "Oh, stop it, Bill! Why do you always act like you don't know who he is?"

"What'dya mean, babe," Agatson replied with the easy candor of a man to a woman with whom he is no longer intimate. "He's always masquerading as some guy called Virgin or—"

Verger began to cough convulsively behind his hand, his scrawny chest heaving.

". . . or somebody with tuberculosis out of Thomas Mann!"

This brought a sudden hush for everyone knew that Verger actually had tuberculosis, and knew that Agatson knew it as well.

"Hey, who's this Haverton?" somebody, who had missed this last, yelled gaily from the other room.

Verger had stopped coughing and was trembling with embarrassment which everyone but Agatson shared. "*I* am," he squeaked bravely, looking for the owner of the voice. "Only I changed my name. I didn't want to be recognized, he-he . . . And . . . and if you think I started coughing just now, Bill . . . just *so* you'd recognize me . . . for pity or anything like that . . . if you think I'd do that, or care whether you have your games with me . . ."

But then he broke off, more mortified by his own exclamation and the fact that everyone had heard it, than by Agatson's taunts. Just at that moment, Stofsky came bustling through the crowd.

"What's going on? Games? Games?"

"Aw, everyone's hungup," Pasternak growled. "What did I tell you!"

Agatson, content with himself, had turned toward the drinks with a secretive smile, but said, as he passed an overdressed, wide-eyed blonde girl whom he had never seen before: "He's an impostor, you know, babe. He's just O. B. Haverton in a clean shirt!"

Verger's dry, racking cough had subsided and he muttered apologetically: "The whiskey went down the wrong way . . . Oh, don't bother about it, David. Go back to the others! He always pretends he doesn't know me . . . And why not? Why should he?" He made an ineffectual flutter with his hand as if to wave Stofsky away, all the time clearing his throat. "Is there any beer left?" And with that he went off quickly, just as Hobbes and Kathryn pushed their way through the groups of people clogging the doorway.

"Why does he take that stuff from Agatson?" Pasternak was complaining to Stofsky. "It's crazy!"

"He believes in Bill," Bianca interjected bitterly. "Don't you know that people who can't believe in anything else always believe in Bill?"

Stofsky gave her a sharply thoughtful look before saying: "But wouldn't he be surprised if he knew he believed in his own pride even more. Poor Verger . . ."

At that, Bianca got up as a person gets up who is suddenly giddy, and went up to Hobbes and Kathryn, who had missed this exchange. She and Kathryn got along aloofly, respecting each other's distrust, but now Bianca took her hand and turned to the blonde girl to whom Agatson had spoken.

"This is Christine. She lives down the street from my building."

The girl's pale, heart-shaped face sweetened with a thrilled smile, but she seemed undecided as to whether she should get up or not. Her lips parted wetly.

The three sprawled around her on the floor. She had obviously never been at such a party before and she began to speak to Bianca in a grave, bewildered way. Pasternak had noticed her immediately, if only because her large blue eyes had flashed with panic when Agatson stumbled by.

She was getting everything terribly garbled in her nervousness, and did not seem relaxed having strangers so near her; but still, she was studying them all surreptitiously as if recalling reports about them she had heard. Kathryn took to her instantly because she seemed so helplessly out of place and at the same time eager to make a good impression. After only a few moments, they discovered that their parents had come from the same part of Italy, and they began jabbering away in what Christine called, with a shy, laughing glance at Pasternak, a "gutter dialect."

During this, Bianca leaned toward Hobbes and began whispering hurriedly: "Christine's very unhappy at home, and I felt sorry for her so I brought her along. She doesn't get out very much because Max—that's her husband, a machinist—can't get along with people. They're just simple people, you know; from the neighborhood. But she's got the sweetest little child, Ellie . . . a little elf who is tone-perfect and sings beautifully, but can't even talk yet. So tell Kathryn to be nice to her, will you, and to . . . well, sort of take it easy on her. She's really very conventional, so don't be surprised at anything she says."

Christine was saying to Kathryn in a shocked tone: "Why, that guy spends more time with that old car than he ever does with me! I'm not kidding. I tell you," and this confidingly, "I feel ashamed sometimes because he's so kinda cold, and . . . Well, it makes me feel like a who-er!" She giggled with confusion at her mispronunciation. "I can't get to sleep some nights!"

She looked excitedly about at all the people and the smoke, for an instant forgetting to cover up the fact that it was all different from anything she had ever known before. Agatson was fidgeting with the radio trying to find music, and she observed him with innocent wonder.

"Is he a queer? Doesn't he act like one though! And where did that O. B. Haverton go? . . . But maybe *he*," and she pointed directly at Agatson before she could prevent herself, "was just pie-eyed, eh?"

Kathryn made some off-color joke in Italian that sent Christine into trilling, female laughter.

Soon she was at ease, talking in excited bursts, taking them all into her confidence, and even making quick, refreshing retorts to the things they said. Every once in a while she would sneak a glance at Pasternak, who was staring at her with a preoccupied frown.

Hobbes got him aside, wondering what the trouble was.

"But what a girl!" Pasternak exclaimed, refusing to take his eyes off her. "Look at that hair! Now that's the kind of girl you never find in New York. She's like one of those chicks working in a lunch cart on the highway, a real woman. Right?"

"Well, why don't you speak up then? What's wrong?"

"Oh, you know the way I am!" he snapped back with a twinge of irritation. "I work slow. I'm *looking* at her all the time, and she knows I'm looking. What do you want me to do?"

She was talking openly now, with naive simplicity, about "that gorgon-headed husband of mine! Oh, he doesn't fool me. I know he's out cuckin' around with other women." Her eyes flashed. "It just isn't right to live the way we live, you know. Never getting out. It isn't that I like to be away from him, and be coming here without him. I'm not that way, Paul," and she turned to him earnestly. "But, would you believe it, he doesn't even want me to see anything of Bianca because I seem so happy when I come back. Now what do you think of that?" But she brightened almost immediately.

She never spoke directly to Pasternak, although she sparred warmly with everyone else. But when she glanced at him and found him staring darkly at her, an almost demure glow would soften her delicate features, and she would become distracted. Finally a few people began to dance in the space in the middle of the room, and Pasternak took her from the group without a word. She moved with him gracefully, her long, well-shaped body just a little rigid, her lips quivering, and the abundant blonde hair tumbling down over his arm.

"She's wonderful," Kathryn said. "She was telling me that she's always wanted to sing, and I'll bet she's got a voice too."

"You know, I think she's fallen for Gene."

At this, Bianca intruded with alarm: "But tell him to take it easy. She's really desperate about things, her marriage and everything . . . no matter how she jokes about it. He could hurt her without even trying to . . ."

But as if she thought this warning ultimately futile, after the music faded away Bianca told Christine she had to get home, and Christine, making an unsuccessful effort to disguise her disappointment, went with her. Kathryn struggled with them through the crowds to the door. She took down Christine's phone number, promised to call her soon, and noted the hours during which the husband could be avoided.

"What did you tell her about me?" Pasternak asked as soon as she came back.

"Nothing," Kathryn replied with a smirk. "We didn't talk about any of you. Why? . . . She's had a terrible life, you know. Now don't you go thinking she's just another—"

Pasternak was offended at this. "What do you think I am? I've known girls like that before. Jesus Christ!"

Kathryn laughed. "Don't get excited. I was just joking."

"I could even fall in love with a girl like that," and he went silent.

"Well, she likes you if that's what you want to know . . . My Lord, I told her you'd written this book and she was actually impressed. She thought you were a football player all along."

The radio was turned louder at eleven-thirty to an all night program of wild jazz. Some of the stiffness of the talk disappeared as more liquor was consumed, and somebody, obviously unused to parties of this kind or the protocol connected with them, even passed out in a corner of the kitchen, clutching an empty beer bottle.

Pasternak had gone off morosely into the crowd, Christine's early departure bearing out his forebodings about the night, when Kathryn finally said to Hobbes: "Let's go. I told you it would be terrible. That Christine was all that made me stay *this* long."

"Let's just have one more drink," he implored, jumping up before she could object and heading for the kitchen, where the zither player was sitting on the sink attempting a Bach prelude, with one or two of the students standing unsteadily around him, offering carping criticisms. Hobbes poured out two shots of whiskey, and then noticed that a girl had attached herself to Pasternak in the corner to which he had retired.

Her awkward, boyish figure was bent over toward him, and she thrust her bony face in front of his, speaking with a toothy nasality that indicated she had fled the Midwest. Her lank brown hair was clipped off crudely around her ears, and as she spoke she gesticulated with nervous jerks of her hands. Pasternak nodded every once in a while, but seemed bored by her gibbering. Hobbes approached them.

She was holding forth on the corruption, depravity and general neuroticism of modern life—the favorite topic of the tyro at intellectual parties—, and she turned to Hobbes, absorbing him into her train of thought as though he were just another proof of the contention.

"Nothing's *really* healthy anymore, and, I must confess, I'm just as glad. What a bad sign if it was! I suppose you'll think that I'm morbidly attracted to evil like the Baron du Charlus. But even he was a moralist of this new kind I was speaking about; Gene . . . Well, I don't deny it. I'm afraid I like things that are . . . oh, flushed down the drain, if you see what I mean."

Hobbes thought tipsily: "Strictly a case of self-love," and the remark amused him drily, but he said nothing.

"Well then, you oughta meet this thief I know, to see the real thing," Pasternak said. "A real thief and drug addict, none of this intellectual abstraction. Wouldn't she go for Ancke, Paul?"

Hobbes assented and drifted away, taking the drink to Kathryn. Almost as soon as he rejoined her, Stofsky rushed up to them with a shriveled daffodil in one hand.

"Where's Agatson? Have you seen him? He's disappeared somewhere, and I had this monster act all prepared for him . . ."

"Maybe he left with Bianca," Kathryn retorted. "What's the flower for?"

"But it's so early!" Stofsky exclaimed with genuine bewilderment, unable to understand why anyone would willingly leave one of his parties. "Well, you see, I was going to come up to him in front of everybody, and fall on my knees, and plead: 'Be my monster, O Guru!' You know, *really* abjectly . . . I even had this flower to present to him. And I'd say: 'I place myself completely in your hands. Be harsh with me, O Nathan!' Can you imagine it? Really grovel so he'd stop needling Verger that way . . . Oh, and you know, Verger's gone too. Yes! He was crushed —because of his pride, of course, not Agatson!"

He appeared to be vastly enjoying all this fuss, and all but clapped his forehead dramatically while exclaiming: "Oh, these egoists! You have to be a positive wet-nurse!" And he scurried off.

Pasternak, with the curious girl in tow, had wandered up, and she was still talking. With an intent expression, he held onto her arm, listening to her and yet not listening; and though she seemed aware that he was managing an interest in her physically, she went gushing on about "the purging reality of evil!" just the same.

"You can stay if you want," Kathryn stated tersely after a while. "But I'm going home. It's almost twelve."

"Just a minute, honey. I'll be right with you."

She got up decisively and went away into the mob to search for her coat. Pasternak continued smoking cigarettes and peering at the girl right through her cloud of talk, and she seemed perfectly content to have it that way. When she turned for a moment to fire a remark into someone else's conversation, he leaned toward Hobbes.

"Why the hell did Christine leave so soon? I was just getting along with her."

"She came uptown with Bianca and Bianca had to get home. We'll see her again though. Kathryn got her number."

Pasternak pursed his lips almost primly. "Well, look, this is Verger's cousin. Her name's Georgia. She's all hungup, but what the hell . . . Can I bring her to your place? Will Kathryn mind, do you think?"

"No, of course not. But we'll probably be leaving in a minute. I'll go find her."

The kitchen was stifling and filled with the students who, driven out of the living room by more confident elements, had collected there to sweat, drink and argue insolently among themselves. Kathryn was waiting at the door, glowering down her nose and ignoring them all.

"Are you ready to go now?"

"Yes. Gene's coming along too, with that girl; if that's all right."

"Anything, but let's get out of here. Where are they?"

Pasternak and the skinny Georgia were elbowing through the students toward them, and they almost tripped over the outstretched legs of the person who had passed out.

"We really ought to say goodbye to David," Hobbes suggested. "Otherwise it'll look like a conspiracy."

"Aw, forget about it," Pasternak muttered, all but pushing Georgia out the door. "He's all involved tonight. I told you how he gets. I think something happened with his analyst today, because he was even talking about going back to live with his father out in Hackensack! And you know the trouble he has with his father. He was yelling about 'a crisis' all the way uptown."

They got home and Hobbes and Kathryn went to bed immediately, leaving Pasternak and the girl moving around the living room with the radio playing softly and one warm light burning over the desk.

"What's he going to do, sleep with her?" Kathryn asked, spreading her hair out upon the pillow beside him. He turned onto his back with a sigh.

"I don't know, dear. I guess so."

They lay silent for a moment, letting the bed receive and relax them. Across the ceiling above them, moved the rushing lights of the traffic outside the window, which roared like a mindless turbine in a huge, empty shed.

"God, I'm tired," she breathed. "I drank too much."

"Do you think you can sleep?"

"Yes. I guess so." She listened for a minute, raising her head from the pillow just a bit. "They'd better keep that damn radio down though."

"Goodnight, honey," and he leaned over in the darkness to find her lips. To his surprise, she wound a warm arm about his neck and kissed him back sleepily.

"Goodnight, butch."

*   *   *   *   *

When Hobbes awoke, it was past nine and Kathryn had gone. He found Georgia sleeping on one couch and Pasternak curled up on another. There were a lot of ground-out cigarette butts and one overturned glass of water. The girl was awake and he gave her coffee.

"I hope you and your wife didn't mind," she said. "Did we make a lot of noise?" She gurgled into her cup ridiculously.

Hobbes reassured her and they sat for a while, talking absently. He wondered why she did not come out from underneath the blankets and get dressed, because she had repeated several times that she had an appointment at ten. Her conversation became more affected and obscure, and she finally lay there simply looking at him desperately, her hair disarranged and one bony shoulder peeking out.

He laughed to himself when he realized that she would not get up until he had left the room.

"I guess I'd better go then," she stumbled when he returned to find her hastily clothed. "I hope you didn't mind. It was so nice of you . . . I'll just say goodbye to Gene." She went over to the couch where he lay, tousled and sleeping grimly.

"Well, Gene, I've got to go," she said, but he refused to wake up, although his breathing indicated that he was not actually asleep at all, but merely sulking. "I hope you're not angry with me, Gene. Will you call me?"

He wouldn't say a word, and she tried to smile through her chagrin as she gave it up. "I guess he's still mad at me . . . Well, thanks a lot, Paul. I hope I see you again, you and your wife." She knocked over the wastebasket getting out the door.

Pasternak got up a few minutes later and, over coffee, he said to Hobbes in a disgusted voice. "You know what that dame did to me? She was a virgin all along. A virgin! I argued with her for half an hour, but she wouldn't give in. What do you think of that? . . . Then she got up and danced in just a garter-belt and told me about all the guys she's been 'giving satisfaction to' lately. And she's a virgin! She wouldn't even let me kiss her for an hour! I almost batted her at one point!"

"Well, what happened?"

"Oh, Christ, I let her 'give me satisfaction'! And then you know what she did? Right in the middle of it, she looked up at me and said, 'I don't know what I'm doing this for. I'm not feeling anything at all!' . . . And she laughed, she actually laughed!"

"Maybe it was funny from her position," Hobbes chuckled.

"Hell, I think she's a Lesbian anyway." He was furious just thinking about it. "You know, I'll bet I'm the only guy that's ever been turned down by a whore. Yah, that happened to me once when I was young. A whore! I've got no luck with women at all . . . Look how that girl Christine left last night, just when I was making out. And I really liked her too."

"There's always a next time, Gene."

"Yah."

After a while, Pasternak left to go back home to Long Island City, taking down Christine's address and phone number first. Two days in New York, staying up until odd hours, living an irregular life from one friend's flat to another, usually depressed him, and finally he would slip away and go home for food and sleep and the attempt at work.

Kathryn called at twelve-thirty.

"Did your friends leave, dear?" she asked with a sweet sarcasm that infuriated him because he felt helpless against it. He told her what had happened the night before only after her insistent questioning. She was annoyed and snapped out: "I don't want him to bring any of his girls to the apartment anymore. I hope you understand that. I don't like that kind of thing happening in my house."

Four

Hobbes, at twenty-five, had been married for six years. He and Kathryn had decided on it against the wishes of his divorced parents, while he was attending Columbia and waiting to go into the Navy. After his parents' separation, which had come when he was sixteen, Hobbes and his mother and sister had moved to a wealthy commuter town in Westchester, where his mother had taken a job in a real-estate office, and managed to maintain a gentility of destitution which enraged her son as a shabby sort of martyrdom, but which denoted "inherent breeding" to the townsfolk in better circumstances. He met Kathryn, who was two years older than he and had lived all her life in the house where she was born, on a morning train by which he went to the University and she to a job with an export firm.

She had had a difficult time during her girlhood, her father being an Italian and a day laborer in a town made up for the most part of advertising or radio executives and bank presidents. He had gardened, put up garages, and driven cars for most of the parents of her schoolmates, and with the merciless insensitivity of adolescents, they never let her forget it. She ran errands for her mother, hurrying along the roads alone, and engaged in school activities with defiance, contemptuous of the richer residents for the wrongs their children had done her, and a rebel among the Italian community because she would not accept their "wop habits" or the social station they took for granted.

Much of her revolt devolved upon her father, a simple, astute man whose innate curiosity about everything was hampered by his inability to read or write; and who insisted, in his pride, on presenting vegetables from his garden to all his employers. Their relationship became difficult as Kathryn got older, because though he was proud and at times even stern, he took great delight in her reading to him and explaining things his limitations denied him. This at once angered and pleased her. It brought those limitations too painfully before her, but at the same time allowed her to become more virulent and critical of them. He was secretly fonder of her than he was of his three sons (a fact which made both uneasy because it was contrary to custom) and she would rage at him for his proud display of her learning among his friends, until she had taxed that pride too much and he would harshly put her in her place.

A few months before she met Hobbes, her father suddenly died of brain fever, after an outdoor life of untroubled health. She maintained herself with stunned efficiency during all the complex funeral arrangements and the two days when the body lay, to be viewed by dark faced men and weeping women, in their front room. But when it was over, still unable to cry somehow, she abruptly got the hiccoughs, which continued for a week of misery and as abruptly ceased, leaving her overcome with a remorse about her father, now that he was dead, that shamed her more than she could bear. She felt, with that cruel perspective that death gives those it robs, that the central pivot of the family, and, more important to her then, some dear opponent and unappreciated protector of her own, was gone. She became cynical and aggressive with everyone.

Hobbes, scrambling to finish his education before being drafted, infuriated by his mother's efforts to "make a place" for them in the gossipy town, and yet feeling that an injustice had been done her by his father's abandonment (even though it had come with mutual àgreement and relief after nearly twenty years of squabbling incompatibility), established no friendships in the town, but nursed his bitter enthusiasms and his studies, writing stories and foolish poetry with a growing sense of despondency about the future. So he and Kathryn met like two dejected conspirators in an alien city, who have almost given up hope of making contact with a legendary underground. They went into league with one another against the town and shortly fell in love as if to spite the view of it both held.

They spent long autumn weekends reading D. H. Lawrence and Shakespeare together, until the sweep of forest and town through a vague haze of leaf fires from some hilltop seemed to transform these places each knew and despised into smoky images from a melancholy novel. They remained aloof, speaking to no one as though sharing secrets. Experiencing that sour exhilaration of the imagined outcast, they wrangled, discussed, and fought out an uneasy solidarity with each other. The soft, outdoor days in which they took books into the woods were crowded with blowups, gloomy remonstrances, poutings on Hobbes' part, and inevitable passion. Kathryn did not associate him with her earlier ill treatment, and thus loved and admired in him qualities which had been the object of her scorn in boys she had known in school. But her emotions, freed by his strangeness and her father's late death, soon overcame her. For his part of it, Hobbes was impulsive, thoughtless, and acted older than he was. Not pausing to wonder why she had fallen in love with him (a gangly, pimply youth in sport shoes), he often abused her feelings.

Once, while dawdling in her front parlor, he came across a page of her writing, the fragment of some journal, on which she had scribbled: "Perhaps when God takes away something, he gives something in return to make up for it. Is it only so that I'll be hurt again?" This troubled him with an unwanted responsibility, but he said nothing about it.

With spring, his mother left for Reno to get a divorce so that his father could re-marry, and during her absence he and Kathryn slept together. He had been roughly suggesting it for weeks, relying on the conflict of fear and desire that occupied her. Finally, with cold, adult resolve, they made arrangements for her to come to his empty house one day.

He watched her through the windows as she came down the lane under fretful trees that were heavy with rain—an absorbed little figure, self conscious even though alone, defiant when passing other houses, her head thrown back with lofty disdain but her steps hesitant. They sat in his untidy, darkened room, pledged to it. After a while, after awkward embraces, and excitements that were intensified because of this very stumbling, they shyly undressed, wishing they had not promised themselves; somehow unable, after they faced each other in that dim room, naked but without innocence, to draw back.

When his mother returned, Hobbes vaguely mentioned marriage to her, feeling no less discomfort than she but throwing it at her as if it were the threat of an action he would institute only if she raised objections to it. On top of his imminent draft, the thought of his marriage at so young an age dismayed her, but, sensing his indecision, she did not rebuke him and he let it ride.

Nevertheless, they were married on his leave after boot camp, and spent a lonely, passionate weekend in a New York hotel— all they had for a honeymoon. She followed him to San Diego when he was put into the Hospital Corps; she lived in a furnished room and worked in a department store. It was the first time she had been away from home, and it was like a sudden plunge into someone else's nightmare.

The grueling monotony of the five-day bus trip across the country gave way to a friendless existence in the overcrowded California city; an existence punctuated only by fleeting weekends when they built the mutual fantasy of love to shore against the horror of reality. But they could not be insensitive to the wartime chaos into which they had been thrown. All around them were the midwestern waitresses and secretaries who had come by bus or train to see their men shipped out after a few wild days of reunion, and who had stayed on hopelessly, earning enough to live but not to get back home; the teeming streets at night when hungers and loneliness reduced small town, decent boys to vandals; the abandon that seized all these young people who had been torn up at the roots, regimented, shunted back and forth across the nighttime wilderness of a nation at war; intimidated by Shore Patrols, jackedup prices and annoyed civilians; who searched in bars and movie balconies and deadend streets for home and love, and, failing to find them, forgot.

Finally Hobbes was sent back east to be permanently stationed in a Naval Hospital outside New York. Kathryn got a room on West Ninety-fifth Street, and his last year in the Navy was spent there and on duty. When he was discharged at last, and the pattern of love making and confession wedged between arrival and departure had ended, neither was prepared for that continualness of marriage the war had made impossible. The pace they had so delicately worked out failed them. Theirs was like a shipboard romance carried on beyond docking against all custom and advice. Without the heightened excitement of possible doom in which it had been born, it seemed oddly centerless.

    ❖   ❖   ❖   ❖   ❖

Hobbes went back to Columbia to "catch up with everyone else," as he put it to himself, and Kathryn went from job to job and supported them with the help of his G.I. benefits. That year was the crucial one because neither could slow down or communicate to the other the habit of isolation they had fallen into from necessity during the war.

Hobbes' efforts to reassimilate himself and find a direction were obsessive, irrational and unproductive. He crammed his schedule with philosophy courses; he read omnivorously on subways, in the halls between his classes, everywhere. He wrote pages of confused eloquence for his composition courses, and submitted fragments of wild rhetoric to his philosophy professors. It was in one of these classes that he met Liza Adler, a fiery, neurotic girl of twenty-four.

Unhappily married to an officer still in Japan, she had an integrated insolence toward everything which made her insights seem the more brilliant and audacious, and her insistence on the fragility of all human relationships profound. Hobbes was at the mercy of his thirst to comprehend "large problems" and was wandering from attitude to attitude, searching for what he referred to as a "proper, rational world-view." Liza was an alarming experience for him, a fascinating and sickly plant that thrived on the stifling atmosphere of argument over coffee and the student's tendency to analyze everything and reduce it to a "manifestation" of something else. She was, on top of this, a violent Marxist with a quick, destructive tongue and a mental agility that was new to Hobbes in a woman.

She battled with him in class, mocked him to his face, asked him openly to have meals with her, attacked him for his "unconscious fascism," doused all his ideas in the cold water of logic, and finally made a class confederate of him. After a while, he fancied himself in love with her. Kathryn was too exhausted at night to listen to his excited ravings about ideas that he was sure were changing his life, and gradually he got out of the habit of trying to embroil her in discussions, and so let off his enthusiasms with Liza. She did not encourage him but neither did she let him alone. They were comrades and (because of his confusion about everything) he followed where she led.

He mentioned his love to her, quickly appending—certain he was anticipating a carping reply—that he knew it was "all impossible." Her face clouded with irritation and she would not speak to him. He tried to explain it away, so distraught he made a fool of himself, feeling somehow that her displeasure was fatal. He abased himself and she told him that she "couldn't bear anything sticky" at that time. They did not see one another very often, but she was in his thoughts constantly; and his thoughts altered her so that she loved him in return.

Finally, she had a nervous breakdown, left Columbia and started being psychoanalysed and could see no one, so serious was her condition. Finding his outbursts without an object, he started writing to her: hysterical and moody letters of great length that had continued ever since. She rarely answered and they even quarreled through the mail. He got into the habit of writing two or three times a week, filling many pages with opinions of what he was reading, plans for books or poems, and theorizing on political or artistic matters. It became an habitual part of his life, and though he did not see her after that, she continued to exist in his frustrated imaginings, twisted by them out of her actuality and conforming more and more to his emotional demands of the moment. Whenever he fought with Kathryn and felt she did not understand him, or was depressed by the progress of his work, he would sit down and pour out to Liza all the wounds of his egoism. For the most part, she seemed to take no notice of this, writing just often enough to keep him dependent on her.

After he left Columbia, some of his poetry started to be accepted. With a growing intellectual maturity, he found that he had gained a greater facility with it. It appeared in most of the critical "little magazines"; as a result of it he managed to get an occasional book review, and even sold a short story or two. By this time, he was started on a novel, an involved, symbolical thriller that he wrote erratically, painfully and without much real confidence.

* * * * *

Their friends were mostly intellectual professionals working on newspapers or writing copy somewhere. They made up just one flippant stratum in a city full of such formations. They were liberal, slightly cynical, drank a lot and knew what was going on in the world around them. It was through one particular friend, Arthur Ketcham, who worked in publishing, that they first went down to one of Agatson's disorderly parties. Ketcham had met Stofsky there a year or so before this time, and then one day David had brought Pasternak to him with his book, hoping that one of Ketcham's numerous, if shadowy, acquaintences could give it a shove in the right places. At last, Hobbes and Kathryn had gone to Verger's one night with Ketcham to find a typical gathering of people there, and among them Pasternak and Stofsky.

At one point that evening when the chilly, sordid rooms suddenly filled with an influx of people, Stofsky gleefully took an old firecracker out of his hip pocket and set it off in a flower pot that was used for an ashtray. When the months-old buster blew up, it scattered a profusion of filth everywhere. Hobbes caught Pasternak grinning from across the room at this, and answered that smile with a consciously shrewd one of his own. Later, after they talked, and Pasternak said good-naturedly of Stofsky: "Isn't he great though?", Hobbes decided that his unashamed directness was refreshing. On top of this, Kathryn was attracted by his boyishness, and her approval always made his enthusiasms about people easier. He was intrigued with Stofsky as well, finding almost everything about him disarming, so accustomed had he become to a social manner more reserved and impregnable. Stofsky, on the contrary, began a babble of confessions the moment they met.

Through these two he heard about people who were madder and more disorderly than any he had ever known. He found that he had missed the frantic, wartime years at Columbia that Pasternak and Stofsky had lived through, before each had done hitches in the Merchant Marine. As a result of that and his self consciousness, he did not have their thirsty avidity for raw experience, their pragmatic quest for the unusual, the "real," the crazy. His quest had always seemed to him of a different order.

During his last year at Columbia, he had been at first an ardent, then reluctant, and finally disillusioned Marxist under Liza's direction. Because of the confusion in which his engulfment in the war had left him, and because of the severity with which he attacked it, he found his mind perfectly suited to the self-reflective logic of dialectics. By the time he came to know Stofsky and Pasternak, however, the fever stage of it had passed with the darkening of world events, even though he was aware that his rootless radicalism was ingrained.

The two of them often amazed and irritated him. They poked into everything; they lacked any caution, Hobbes thought; they lacked a necessary self doubt, that extroverted subjectivity that Hobbes was accustomed to and accepted without criticism. They made none of the moral or political judgments that he thought essential; they did not seem compelled to fit everything into the pigeon holes of a system. He spoke of them to others as being "badly educated" but at least not "emotionally impotent" like so many young men who had come out of the war. They never read the papers, they did not follow with diligent and self conscious attention the happenings in the political and cultural arena; they seemed to have an almost calculated contempt for logical argument. They operated on feelings, sudden reactions, expanding these far out of perspective to see in them profundities which Hobbes was certain they could not define if put to it. But they accepted him, came to him with their troubles because he would always listen. They thought of him, he decided, as a regrettable intellectual, but acted as though they believed he was not completely "impotent."

He came to know their world, at first only indirectly. It was a world of dingy backstairs "pads," Times Square cafeterias, be-bop joints, night-long wanderings, meetings on street corners, hitchhiking, a myriad of "hip" bars all over the city, and the streets themselves. It was inhabited by people "hungup" with drugs and other habits, searching out a new degree of craziness; and connected by the invisible threads of need, petty crimes of long ago, or a strange recognition of affinity. They kept going all the time, living by night, rushing around to "make contact," suddenly disappearing into jail or on the road only to turn up again and search one another out. They had a view of life that was underground, mysterious, and they seemed unaware of anything outside the realities of deals, a pad to stay in, "digging the frantic jazz," and keeping everything going. Hobbes ventured into the outskirts of this world suspiciously, even fearfully, but unable to quell his immediate fascination for he had been among older, less active, and more mental people for too long, and needed something new and exciting.

Once Pasternak said to him with peculiar clarity: "You know, everyone I know is kind of furtive, kind of beat. They all go along the street like they were guilty of something, but didn't believe in guilt. I can spot them immediately! And it's happening all over the country, to everyone; a sort of revolution of the soul, I guess *you'd* call it!"

And the more Hobbes saw of Pasternak and Stofsky and heard of their friends, and the more he found himself responding unwillingly to a disorder that he had once condemned, the more he was forced to conclude that Pasternak was right, and that something had happened to all of them.

Five

A week after Stofsky's party, Kathryn came home from work fatigued and deflated to find Hobbes furiously typing on his chapter, a perfect strew of papers, books and ashes around him, and that morning's dishes still stacked where she had left them.

So totally absorbed had he been that her entrance flustered him; and jumping up, he began hastily: "I wasn't expecting you this early. Didn't you say seven? I just had this paragraph to finish and then I was going to do them."

"If you'd do them first thing, you'd . . . but it doesn't really matter."

She sank down on the studio couch and, laying her head carefully back into the pillows, closed her eyes. Her handbag dangled over the side of the couch but she made no move to put it aside.

Hobbes quietly, almost obediently, went about taking the dishes into the bathroom where, because they had no proper kitchen, they had to be washed. At each trip he glanced at her, trying to perceive her mood, and realizing that she must be more tired than usual to be just lying there, speechless.

"What's wrong, honey? Is it that you're just tired?"

She looked up at him blankly as he stood before her holding a pile of cups in front of him like an offering. "Nothing. I almost quit today, that's all. Phone calls and shouting, phone calls and shouting all day long."

He took the cups into the bathroom and when he returned her eyes were blazing.

"What do you mean, am I *just* tired? Isn't that enough?"

"All right, I put it badly. You know what I mean. It was just a phrase . . ." He wiped the table scrupulously. "But what happened?"

"Nothing, I tell you. Just what happens every day." She passed her hand over her eyes. "Burton was screaming like a madman all day about the soap account. Actually shaking his finger! They think that just because they're mixed up with TV they have a right to tantrums. I tell you, he's crazy. I almost told him he could take his goddamn glamour job and go to hell! What right has he got to talk to me that way? You'd think I was his slave or—"

"Well, you should just ignore it, honey. Don't let them embroil you in all that. After all, it's just a job. All you care about is their money. Just be cool, and ignore it." He repeated these meaningless, bromidic phrases to sooth her, feeling vaguely that he had no right to use them.

"But what am I supposed to do? I don't even get time for a decent lunch and when I come back he's screaming before I even get in the door. I'm just sick and tired of it."

"You'll feel better after we eat."

She glanced at him and then glanced away, her lips slightly pursed. "If I just didn't know it was going to last forever . . ."

"But it isn't!" he exclaimed warmly. "Why do you always say that? Why do you always look at it that why? It's just until I finish my book, and I'm so near the end. I did a really good section today, and—"

But she had looked away and sniffed. "So what if you sell it, Paul? Let's be realistic; even then you won't make enough money. Not even if it's the best book in the world. I'll still have to go on working."

"But how do we know, after all? What can I do but try!"

He was always stymied at this point, a feeling of entrapment hedging in around him.

"That's why I say it'll be forever. Don't you see? But I just don't know how much longer I can stand it, that's all. Is that unreasonable? . . . Is it? . . . I thought you wanted me to tell you these things."

"Do you think I like it? This situation. And yet you always bring it out and hit me with it. It's the perfect weapon!"

"But it's true, isn't it? I'll be working for years. Isn't that the truth?"

He scowled and turned away, because this argument was perennial with them, always running along the same cautious lines in the beginning, always erupting at the same place and for the same reason.

"But you knew it was going to be this way for a while when we got married, and—"

"Oh, yes," she interrupted scornfully. "I'd forgotten that I'd agreed to anything, *anything!* But it's been five years like this."

"Well, what can I do? I ask you. I'm working just as hard and as fast as I can . . ." and the words stuck in his throat because he could not believe them, even in terms of the dispute. "Do you think you can just sit down and write a novel the way you take dictation or—"

The phone rang loudly, and with a mingled sense of exasperation and relief he picked up the receiver.

"Paul? This is David Stofsky. I've got to find Gene. Now I'm calling from uptown but I'm on my way down. Has he been to your place?"

"No . . . No, I haven't seen him."

"Well, I phoned him and his mother said he was coming into New York, so maybe he's on Times Square. But look, something tremendous has happened! I saw Jack Waters today . . . Do you know him? Perhaps at Columbia? . . . Anyway I'll wait till I see you. But it's one of the biggest things in my life. It may change everything for me; something weird and magical!" A cracked, exhilarated laugh seeped over the wire. "Can you meet me on Fifty-second Street in an hour? We'll look for Gene."

"Well, I don't know . . ." The phone normally flustered him, but tonight he could not seem to collect himself at all.

"Oh, come on! I've absolutely *got* to see you. And I have so little time, *time!*" The snickering, wild laugh again. "What are you doing? . . . Look, I'll meet you in front of the Three Deuces, and we'll scour the Square for Pasternak."

"All right, David. I'll try to be there."

He replaced the receiver, as if it were the final brick laid carefully in place by a man who has unwittingly walled himself into a cave.

"What did he want? I hope you didn't ask him here, because the way I feel I swear I'll slam the door in his face!"

"No, don't worry. But he sounded all excited about something. He wanted me to help him find Gene . . . He was almost hysterical," he added, half aware that he was purposefully exaggerating.

"Are you going?" It was like a leveled finger.

"I don't know. I thought if you were tired you'd probably be going to—"

"Oh, do as you please," she shot out, cutting him off sharply. "You will anyway, no matter what *I* say."

They went out to the Athens, Hobbes stuffing his hands in his pockets stubbornly and walking rapidly along because she was dawdling. Her silent bitter indifference during the meal made him anxious and uneasy. He tried to prolong a similar response in himself, knowing from the beginning that he could never hold out against her in that game. Finally he annoyed her out into the open.

"All right. You care more for your crazy friends than you do for me! No, it's the truth! All they have to do is call and you'll go out in the middle of the night to listen to them rave!"

"Oh, it isn't that. It's that I'm cooped up all day long. I go crazy after a while. And besides, I've got to experience something if I'm going to write. And what the hell, I've got to let off steam. I only *bore* you about my book and everything," he said defiantly, desperately, without remorse even when he thought of his letters to Liza.

"But why do you want to see *them*, anyway? They're just a lot of loafers, parasites! Oh, it's all very well for them to run around and stay up all night, they don't work. They can go home whenever they're tired, and sleep for three days if it suits them! They're just lazy, but you won't admit it!" She, too, was exaggerating her real feeling, and though they both knew this it made no difference and was not mentioned.

"Look, Gene's written a wonderful book, he's got a natural talent and I can learn from him. Shouldn't I take advantage of that?"

He could think of nothing to say about Stofsky, and so went on with Pasternak: "You know what stupid technical problems I have. Well, Gene can help—"

"But that's for you, not for me! What do I care about that? How long can you expect me to make excuses because of something like that?"

"Make excuses! What do you mean? Because I want to go out occasionally without you? My Lord, we can't be together every minute of the day. Why do you act like our whole marriage hangs in the balance everytime something like this comes up?"

"If that's the way you look at it, you shouldn't be married at all!"

So they went back through the streets, both silent out of a feeling of vindictiveness and futility, but carrying on the argument inside themselves. By the time they climbed the stairs, the initial issue had been lost among the thoughts it had inspired.

Kathryn changed into her nightgown without so much as a glance in his direction, and then went and sat at the window, staring out at the night and the city with lonely concentration. He fumed around the apartment, not knowing what to do, unable to let it alone.

"But what's wrong anyway? What's the use of fighting this way? You know we can't just leave it at this."

She turned without ferocity, looking at him with strange, almost shocked, intensity as though seeing something for the first time.

"Your way of thinking about things frightens me sometimes. All the things you think are important and worry about all the time. You don't think I take them seriously, you believe I think they're just 'abstractions.' But that isn't true. Just sometimes they menace me."

He went up to her, appalled and bewildered by what she had said. "What do you mean? That's a terrible thing to say. How do I frighten you?"

He put his hands on her shoulders vaguely.

"I don't know just what I meant. It was something I felt for a moment." She got up and went to the couch, but he followed her.

"But do I really frighten you? How, Kathryn?"

"Sometimes everything frightens me. The city, the life we lead, the future. Everything."

He put his face into her hair and caressed her timorously with his hands, allowing one to slide lightly along her entire length to lift her chin. "But I don't want to frighten you," he said and kissed her deeply.

She lay passively in his embrace, not helping at all, and he went on stroking her and kissing her as if endeavoring to knead something out of her body. Her reluctance ebbed away under his hands.

"This doesn't frighten you, does it?" he asked with that shy humor which always overcame him at a moment like this.

"No."

And gradually they slid, from exhaustion and wordlessness, into sex. It was as if they simply turned their energies from one thing, which had ended at a wall, into another which would bring them around it. He viewed her arousal as a kind of locked room in a clanging world; she responded unwillingly, then with a quiver of aggression, and finally with abandon. They cleaved to one another without desperation or demands, but as though the mute, natural fact of sexual difference possessed them, obscuring everything else. In the act of love, sometimes alone in their life together, they recognized and knew one another and were not afraid, but like lovers, collected strange or familiar sensations in a precious horde. It was their way of forgetting and remembering. At the end, just as the spasms were dying away, she would always laugh, a wild rollicking giggle of joy unlike any other laugh, as at a secret they would henceforth share against the rest of life. In a way it was the most sure, female thing about her. And he would lie for a moment with his head between her breasts, and feel new and raw and alive once more.

He combed his hair in the bathroom and after a moment she came in, nude and small and tingling, a wistful smile playing about her mouth.

"How do you feel?" he asked, watching her in the mirror.

"I can hardly see. I feel like your whore." She took him around the waist from the back, pressing herself to him warmly, her head nuzzling his shoulder blades. "Why don't we always think of that?"

"Because we're stupid. Do you think you can sleep, honey?"

"Ummm. Thanks to my man." She caressed him again, making those little gestures of intimacy that are always more natural and assuring after satisfaction. "But you go off and see your crazy friends. I'll let you," playfully mocking herself now that there was no more danger in it.

"Are you sure it's okay?" And he knew he could believe her because all deceits and all calculations seemed foolish suddenly.

"Of course, but give me a kiss first, to last on."

He followed her into the bedroom, and bending over her as she snuggled under the sheet he took her face between his hands and kissed it.

"Don't worry," she said contentedly, turning over.

So he went out, almost not wanting to, almost afraid that he would lose some emotion of his own if he did.

Six

STOFSKY had gotten up to a soggy noon amid the clutter of his rooms. The remains of last week's party had still not been done away with, and dirty glasses and cigarette butts lay everywhere. He had been out most of the night before wandering about Times Square ostensibly searching for Ancke or news of him. But actually some unformulated thought was stirring in him. He had found no one, however, and finally he walked all the way home.

Now he puttered around, fixing himself a greasy fried egg sandwich and a cup of coffee. The dismal light of day coming through his lofty windows depressed him, and he sat, half-dressed, flipping through the scraps of paper on which his poetry was written. He came upon one he had composed almost two years before after there had been a murder at one of Agatson's wilder parties. The stanza went:

"Some weeks ago I set in feverish rhyme
The gist of that impure morality
Ill-learned by some I often sought to mime.
And in their doubts and my fatality,
I named the farce I wrote: Mind Out of Time.
In truth, I glimpsed through the legality
The criminal but not his moral crime.
Since, I have wondered: where were we?"

No one had known Frankel, the killer, very well; he was taken for one more strange friend of neurotic, ironical Diane who had had many of them. But then one night in the midst of the most drunken disorder, Frankel had kicked her to death. Then it had come out that he was a professional gunman whom she had hired to do away with her husband, and when he had learned that she had done this out of a sort of demented irony, he had turned upon her. For a month thereafter, Stofsky had gone about mulling it, even dreaming about a symbolic figure that he dubbed "the pale criminal." Finally he wrote a series which he called "The Killer Poems," of which the one he had just read was the last. Now he found them all adolescent and obscure.

He sat for a moment, feeling he should utilize his leisure for writing, solemn as he always was when unobserved, and yet not knowing how to begin. Something about his analysis, about Agatson and Verger, and about Frankel too, was troubling him. He took a sheet of paper and started to write slowly, but after this quatrain he gave it up:

> "We waltz at waking into some delusion,
> We dance with death, we dream calamity.
> See, see! We live in an illusion!
> Peer through the glare! How rarely we are gay!"

He did not know just what it meant, and after reading it through four times he still could not tell exactly. At once, it seemed completely incomprehensible and then a series of the most foolish cliches. He threw it aside, got up, finished dressing, stood for a moment inspecting everything with annoyance, and then went down through the murky, smelly house. Checking his mail box, he found a card from Jack Waters, a friend from Merchant Marine days whom he had not seen for three months. It was almost illegible but gave a scrawled address and begged him to come there at once "before it is too late!" It had been sent the day before.

He filled with delighted anticipation because this gave him a direction in which to aim his day, and one that was attractively mysterious at that.

Stofsky thrived on such communications. They never failed to surprise and please him, because they reminded him that he existed in other peoples' thought. He solicited letters from people on the most feeble of pretexts, taking them as tangible proof of friendship and saving them in great cardboard letter boxes.

This craving for contact with other people had arisen in his childhood, of which his clearest memories were those protracted periods when he had been alone. From the beginning, he had been an intensely imaginative boy for whom the fantasy of his own thoughts had been the only pleasure. He had grown up seeing green faces at his bedside window to which he gradually grew accustomed, and every afternoon after school he would hurry to a ruined, secluded arbor near the Hackensack Gas Works (once the center of an old garden belonging to a still more ancient house that had since disappeared). There he would hide, whispering to himself amid the mossy briars and the dark shadows until the red coal of sun turned all the world to flames. At thirteen, he had become convinced that he was grotesque, a pinched little mite in other peoples' eyes. Long ago, with that childish astuteness which sensitivity relentlessly creates, he had gotten into the habit of playing this part before strangers. At one point during his freshman year at the University, he had even written a confession in a wild, almost Hebraic tone about his own "satanic monstrosity," and shown it triumphantly to his closest friends. But it was only recently, due to his analysis, that he had remembered the hazy afternoon when he had come strolling back from school and upon reaching his ugly, shingled house, seen his mother crane her neck out of an upstairs window, her hair disheveled and her black eyes wild, to scream: "The devil! The devil! Please, please help me! I must be *safe!* Oh, please help me!"

She was taken to an institution soon after that, the first of her periodic visits to "Madtown," absences from his life to which he eventually became resigned, thinking of her as off on some mysterious "higher business." His father, a respectable little man who had respectably taught high school for twenty years, never suitably explained to Stofsky just what was wrong with his mother, but Stofsky learned not to ask questions when she was gone, for his father would flush and stutter with shame and then lock himself in his study. But once, at fourteen, he heard two schoolmates discussing him, and one said with boyish gravity: "Oh, sure, David's old lady has gone bananas. You know, they say she sleeps with the devil!" And, because he developed rapidly in an intellectual way, by the time he fully understood that his mother was subject to "fits," he was already rationalizing madness in a romantic, poetical fashion and reading Rimbaud and Emily Dickinson.

Lately, however, he had become disturbed about his analysis. Though he did not mention to Doctor Krafft that he thought a medical injustice was being done him by the Doctor's refusal to consider the sudden sexual urge a legitimate "breakthrough," he brooded upon it fitfully for days afterward. After all, he told himself, the purpose of a Schachtian analysis was freeing the clogged desires so they might function naturally. Albeit his impulse had not been "natural," but still he thought it indicated he was getting ahead. His enthusiasm for the interviews fell off markedly after that, and as he hurried along to Waters' place, which was somewhere up in Verger's squalid neighborhood by the East River, he decided that his desire to write poetry that morning was a rebellion against another of the doctor's edicts and, for some spiteful reason, he was glad of it.

Waters' house was one of those ugly, narrow tenements in the Puerto Rican section of lower Harlem that is a honeycomb of partitions and tiny cubicles, in each of which lives a family of at least five. It was one of those houses that are connected to its neighbors on either side by a tangle of rusty fire escapes that are like trellises where only a profusion of washing will grow; a house reeking of the sweat of the people who exist there like so many mice, and of the red kidney beans and garlic they live upon.

Stofsky groped along the hallways peering at each rude paintless door, but he could not find Waters' name anywhere. Finally he knocked on a door under a naked, flickering bulb that hung from a wire.

A fat suspicious woman, her black hair drawn tight into a bun, wearing a faded print housecoat that contained her like a corset, opened it.

"I'm looking for Waters. Which is his apartment?"

"Who?" she wheezed, although, oddly enough, Stofsky had the feeling that she recognized the name instantly.

"John Waters."

"Oh, the crazy one! . . . Down there at the back," and she pointed with a large thumb into the murk. Stofsky nodded and turned away.

"You a friend of his? You tell him to get out'n here. You hear me? You tell him t'go and leave . . . Go aroun' walking and yelling all night . . ." She slammed the door.

Stofsky felt his way ahead, puzzled and excited by all this, until his outstretched hands met the blunt end of the hall. He could hear a voice, muffled behind a partition, speaking in a low drone; and upon feeling down the wall in front of him he came to a handle and discovered it was not a wall at all, but a door.

Indistinctly, he heard the voice exclaim: "Gentlemen, why do you persist in believing that there is time?" And at that something struck him about the voice, and he realized it was Waters.

He knocked softly and it ceased, but then after a moment bellowed: "Go away! There's nothing wrong with me!"

"It's David Stofsky, Jack. Let me in."

The door opened a chink and Waters peered out at him fiercely, his eyes glazed and bloodshot. "It really is you," he muttered abstractedly, throwing open the door and hustling Stofsky inside. To his surprise, Stofsky found that Waters was absolutely alone.

The cramped little room was filthy, with soiled shirts hanging from the cast iron bedstead, a scattering of newspapers strewn about the bureau and the floor, and a dog-eared copy of a science-fiction magazine and three empty benzidrine tubes on the chair. Beside it sat a battered valise, packed and half open.

"They're trying to get me taken away, of course," Waters began whispering earnestly, almost at once. "They come around and knock on my door, and they even tap on the walls when I talk! The idiots! What do they care about eternity!"

Stofsky was taken aback by Waters' appearance and manner. His lean, dark cheeks, once cleancut and faintly ascetic, were gaunt and unshaven. His slender, thin hipped body, almost the body of a dancer, seemed to have shrunken and stooped; and even his hands, which had described eloquent flourishes in the old days when they had recited poetry on the forward hatch of the oiler where they had met, had become bony, and wavered as he spoke. His prominent nose, once suggestive of haughtiness, was positively beaklike now, as if his features had fallen away from it. He stood before Stofsky like some scrawny, croaking bird, and he had that almost consumptive paleness of a man who is being starved by an idea that dominates him until it gradually melts away everything but his bones and his brain, and burns out of his eyes, making his face resemble ash.

"I've only been here a week, but they're already trying to get me taken away! I've been expecting them to come for me . . . In fact, I thought you were them."

"The police, you mean? But what's happened?" Stofsky fell into a whisper automatically. "Where have you been, Jack? I haven't seen you for months."

Waters was distracted by a thought, his baleful eyes darting around continually. Stofsky followed his glance from the cardboard clothes closet beside the bed to the grimy window that faced a brick wall.

But suddenly Waters was speaking again: "I've been to North Africa, Tangiers. That's where it started . . . I thought I was going crazy, but then they told me you think that on hashish in the beginning . . . I didn't see the sun for weeks . . . You know, once I actually thought of going into the desert in rags! Remember how we used to talk of a pilgrimage to Gethsemane? Remember that, David?" He touched Stofsky's arm gently for a moment. "What fools we were then! Just a couple of Byrons. I often think of those days now . . ."

"But what's this about the police? What have you done?"

Waters' eyes, like two embers, flared up again. "It's not the police, it's the bughouse boys! Somehow they know (I can't figure out who told them) that I've found out . . . about time! You see, no one is supposed to find out . . . they readjust you if you do . . . just like a watch! He-he-he!" His laugh was dry and rasping. "By the way, do *you* have a watch?"

Though bewildered by this, Stofsky exposed the wristwatch his father had given him upon his graduation from high school.

"Can I see it, David?" Waters replied in a voice that was oddly insinuating.

Stofsky unstrapped it.

Waters held it in his open palm for a moment, staring at Stofsky with a shrewd, contemptuous smirk around his sallow lips. Then all of a sudden he wheeled and, rushing to the window, hurled it out against the brick wall opposite where it shattered and fell into the abyss of backyards five stories below.

"There!" he breathed. "You see, it's only machinery."

"What's going on, Jack! Why, that watch cost ten dollars!" But Stofsky was more eager for an explanation than he was angry about the loss of the watch, so caught up was he in this inexplicable act.

Waters turned and sat down abruptly, as if the effort to keep on his feet was costing him all his energy.

"I'm living in eternity, Stofsky," he uttered wearily. "I swear I am! I'm going to, at any rate . . . Do you know what I mean? Not just poetry, or metaphysics, but really. I thought you of anyone might know what I mean . . ." For just an instant, there was something pathetic and imploring in his face, but then it vanished:

"I've been throwing things out for the last three days . . . just to illustrate, just for myself. Before that, I just sat and thought . . . You know, I went to the window day before yesterday and stood there thinking: 'Why not? Why not?' But something stopped me, some longing . . . And then I realized that death is part of time too . . ." He trailed off into feverish reflection.

"But why did you throw away my watch? What's this about eternity? . . . But you look sick, Jack!"

"It can be done! It can be! I'm destroying time, don't you see? . . . Oh, it's goddamn difficult, we've gotten so used to thinking that way. But really, it's just in the mind . . . I've found out the deep, wicked secret, that it's true what we used to say in poetry. We live in eternity now, every instant! And we always have."

He was silent for a moment, his dark brows arched.

"You know, yesterday I even thought that God was angry because I'd found out. That occurred to me . . . But then, I don't really believe in *God* either . . ."

His head was shaking back and forth slowly, he was making an enormous effort to gather his faculties, and finally he turned an almost coy expression on Stofsky.

"But, you see, I was high on marijuana for a week . . . to induce the right atmosphere. Then my supply ran out and my connection got a ship. And so I thought of you . . . Oh, I've been trying benny but it speeds everything up, it's all wrong, and besides it makes you talk." He smiled crookedly at this mundane turn to his conversation. "So I thought perhaps you could get me some tea, just a little, half an ounce would do . . ."

Stofsky's head was swarming with questions, but Waters' rapidly alternating moods gave him no chance to ask them.

"Well . . . well," he stumbled, trying to think. "I've been looking for Ancke . . . but—"

"Because they're coming for me today, you see, and I wanted to get high and try just once more," Waters went on wheedlingly. "But you don't believe me either, do you? Fool! It's in your mind, only in your mind, all this time business! *This* is eternity, right *now*, nothing changes! . . . Look here, don't you see, we judge each other, we hate each other, we suffer . . . all with the eyes of time, because we are afraid! But in God's eye, the eye of eternity, there's no more hate, no more suffering! It's so simple. I knew it all so clearly one day last week . . . And before that I didn't want to live anymore, I wanted to become nothing, I wanted to die just because of death, just because having so little time made life unbearable . . ."

"But are they really coming for you? You say, they're coming today? How can you be so sure, Jack?"

Waters' exalted expression disintegrated into a sad, somehow shameful grin: "Oh . . . well, you see, I sent papers to Harrodsville Sanitarium, committing myself . . . in a moment of fear. Yes, isn't it disgusting? Oh, two days ago . . . and telling them exactly when to come for me! I was very precise about the *time* . . ." he peered before himself darkly. "Everything is so damn symbolical . . . And, you know, the moment of doubting one's sanity is far worse than insanity itself . . . far worse . . . unbearable! You have no idea how we cling to our frightened egos! It was when I realized that that I thought: 'Why not?'"

"You committed yourself! But you said—"

Waters' eyes lit up again and shone as if wet.

"I tell you I came close . . . to knowing, Stofsky. I mean the truth of things, why we live, why we are miserable . . . For it's just the idea of time that perverts us, just the *idea!* Because of course it can't be real . . . that would be too horrible . . ."

He broke off again, his thoughts veering in another direction. "I even threw a stone at one of those clocks over the doorway of a bank. Honestly! I broke it too. Each one helps, you know; symbolically . . . And I'm almost certain someone or something is afraid because I've found out! Don't you think? . . . But there's no hope for the tea then," he added vaguely. "Not even a stick?"

But before Stofsky could answer, there were sounds down the hallway, and Waters had cocked his head with a frightened, quivering grin and was muttering: "I planned that you'd be the last person I'd see, I planned it so you'd be here! I wonder why . . ."

At that moment, there was a series of solid, insistent knocks on the door, and the gruff rumble of several voices. Waters grew rigid, his wide eyes transfixed, his fists hanging loose at his sides. Stofsky, however, did an odd thing just before the door, which Waters had failed to lock after letting him in, was thrown open. Stofsky leapt into the clothes closet, pulling the panel shut after him, and buried himself in among the sweaty suits and stiff dungarees.

He waited, his breath held in the stifling darkness, hearing the voices but unable to understand most of what they were saying. Once he heard Waters exclaim: "So it's off with my head, eh?"

Somehow Stofsky could not believe that any of it was true, and yet he was actually trembling with fear. He strained harder, but suddenly realized that he could hear nothing at all, even the voices were gone. After a few moments of that ominous silence, he stuck his head cautiously out. The room was empty, the door ajar, and only the distant sounds of life on the other floors reached him. The valise and the tubes of benzidrine had disappeared with their owner.

*   *   *   *   *

Hobbes met Stofsky, who reported all this excitedly as they stood before one of the tiny nightclubs on Fifty-second Street. His voice rose and he actually waved his arms wildly to and fro when he reached the end.

"So they dragged him off to Harrodsville to be repaired! To get his wheels oiled! As if he were some I. B. M. machine on the blink. And I jumped into the closet—as though they'd come for me! . . . Of course, he *is* a little off, I suppose, but as he said, 'Why not? Why not?' . . . There's a message in it for me somewhere." Then, as if remembering the original mission, he cried: "But come on, we've got to find Gene!"

The two young men, one continuing a perfect babble of exclamations and the other listening with uneasy silence, started to comb the thronging street. They dove into one smoke-fogged basement dive after another, waiters seizing them by the arms and disagreeable bartenders shouting "What'll you have, boys?" as soon as they entered. It was a pandemonium. In one place, bathed in a blue spotlight, a somber pianist caressed the blues before a sparse crowd of college boys in seersucker jackets and black knit ties. Next door, to the lewd thumping of a drum, a buxom redhead with purple circles under her eyes, was shaking her breasts. In the street, a blend of juke boxes created a weird cacophony, splintered by car horns and the spiel of the hawkers before each club, reciting in grating monotones the specialties of the house. Everywhere streamed the hot, eager, bored crowds: out-of-towners ambling along with gawking curiosity, like bits of flotsam that became snagged around the awning poles of each place; natty, sharp suited hipsters, cupping their butts and keeping a squinting eye out for musicians; unattached women, over-painted, underfed, who smiled mechanically and walked as if gliding down a runway, drifted with the others, waiting, waiting. Everything was framed in hot, flashing lights like a carnival boardwalk.

"But look at all this," Stofsky cried suddenly. "Why shouldn't Waters be a little off! What's the meaning of all this? . . . Remember what Eliot said?

"'We had the experience but missed the meaning

"'And approach to the meaning restores the experience

" 'In a different form . . .'

"In one of the Quartets, I think. Well, Waters has leapt right out of experience now, into pure, naked meaning! Do you see? What he was saying is the meaning of all this, this horror, this wildness, this . . . this monster! . . . but without the experience attached to it. No wonder he's gone mad! But look," and he gestured crazily down the whole teeming street, for they had reached the corner of Sixth Avenue, and turned. "Look. How many of *them* would recognize profound truths on the lips of a madman? How many? They'd put him in a cage! Out of the same fear that drove him to try, to try! And me to . . . to escape some judgment in the closet."

"After all, maybe it was the marijuana, all those ideas," Hobbes suggested hesitantly, because he had never taken any but was aware that Stofsky knew all about it.

"O, ye of little faith!" Stofsky retorted, with a snorting laugh. "No, no he'd seen through the veil, a glimpse into the truth . . . 'We live in an illusion.' How prophetic! I wrote that just this morning, and couldn't understand it then. But now, well . . . I've been looking too, you see. And I'm going to start re-reading Blake again in the light of this new, clear idea!" He kept searching the crowds as he talked, and finally erupted impatiently: "Oh, where the devil can he be!"

But though they searched all the places in which he might have been drinking, they did not find Pasternak that night, for at the very moment that they were hurrying back and forth across Times Square, he was downtown standing in the shadows of a doorway across from Christine's building, hoping ruefully for the merest sight of her.

Seven

DURING the next week, no one saw Stofsky, who sometimes vanished like that without a trace or a rumor, and Pasternak became deeply involved with Christine. She came to the Hobbes' on a Saturday afternoon, bringing a store cake and her sadeyed, plain little child; and he managed to be there. It was not easy for anyone, and Christine's rough gaiety was pathetically forced until Kathryn played some Italian records, and she began to sing softly in a melodious, untrained contralto. Ellie, a wordless and obedient little gnome, hummed along with her mouth full of cake, and got frosting on her dress and the couch cover, which sent her mother into a blushing, apologetic rage. Christine referred to Kathryn as her "Cousin Angie, that's the cousin Max can't stand, so I have to visit her alone . . .", and this became a joke among them. Finally she left, with Pasternak carrying Ellie down the stairs, and Kathryn said as she closed the door after them: "She wants to have an affair with him. She really *needs* to do something rash! I've never seen anyone so set on it, and I'm sure she's never been unfaithful to her husband before."

Four days later, Christine arranged to visit "cousin Angie" for a whole evening, and Pasternak came early to dawdle away the time until she and Kathryn arrived.

"Look," he said. "She gave me this picture yesterday in the park, and she said, 'It's the only old thing I could find.' Pretty good, isn't it?"

He showed it to Hobbes, and it was one of those stiff, somehow shabby photographs that are taken by the thousands in drafty little studios on the second floor of run-down commercial buildings along Eighth Avenue, which reduce all individuality to a Sunday-dress, harshly-lit, rigidly-posed commonplace. In it, Christine's soft, full mouth was thickly painted and tight, and she wore that expression of frozen seriousness which transforms the features of people who are never really conscious of themselves until faced with a camera they fear and distrust.

"And she kept looking around when she gave it to me as

though someone might see her do it. But all the time we were just sitting there talking . . ."

This had been the second of two afternoons in Washington Square Park where they had arranged to meet whenever possible. She was afraid that if he came into her neighborhood, even stood on the corner waiting for her to pass on her way shopping, the neighbors might see them and start to talk. Like all people who have never transgressed their own ideas of conduct, and who finally transgress them for love, actions she would have considered perfectly casual and natural before, suddenly became wicked with desire and were full of danger. She was overcome by a passion for absurdly cautious arrangements, and Pasternak went along with them because it was the only way he could see her.

"She feels guilty, Gene. She's not used to these things, and you know how people like Christine think about infidelity. When someone like her believes something is wrong, and does it anyway, you've got to expect an exaggerated reaction."

"No, it's because she's scared to death of that damned husband," Pasternak broke in angrily. "She said he got so bad last year she even thought of suicide, but couldn't do it because of the kid . . ."

He glowered before himself, with the unhappy frown of a man for whom love has become an impossibly complicated machinery of obstacles, deceptions and subterfuges, all of which never leave him a moment to succumb to the emotion which has set it going in the first place.

"I was thinking that if my book sells, I could marry her."

"Do you like her that much? I had no idea you were thinking about anything like that."

"Sure, why not? Hell, I could get a farm someplace, maybe out near Frisco with Hart Kennedy. He's still working on the Southern Pacific, you know. And I could take my mother out with us. All I'd need is a couple a thousand bucks."

"Well, be careful, Gene. I mean she'll jump at anything to get away from her husband. Kathryn says she's that desperate."

"Oh, I know. Christ, I could sleep with her any time I want. She's just wild for it . . . it's amazing! But scared too, of course. But I don't know," he said, pausing hopelessly. "Maybe I couldn't make her happy. What do you think? I'd have to take off once in a while . . . you know the way I am . . . and . . ."

But this turn of thought seemed to lead nowhere, and so he

swerved back fiercely: "But hell, why not! She's like me, she's batted around. Do you know, she lived in Pottsville, Pennsylvania, when she was a kid? Her father was a deep-pit miner! . . . After all, she's just one of those crazy, warm little girls you meet at a dance in Harrisburg, or even hitch-hiking around South Carolina. And that's the kind of girl I can understand, not these New York bitches! And why shouldn't I get married?"

"But do you really want to?"

"Sure! I guess everyone does. And besides I could make a living with chickens or something. Books don't pay off anyway, even if they do get published . . ."

"Well, that depends—"

Pasternak did not want to be dissuaded from the escape his thoughts provided: "Well, I'm sick of brooding around New York, seeing a lot of migraine-headache liberals and intellectuals! I want to get out in the country someplace, lots of land and big ranches! That's what we've got to come to again, Paul; you know that? Big families, and great steaming dinners on the table, and, well, just the seasons! Were you ever in one of those big, bumbling cowtowns in Colorado, for instance? Now, that's the kind of life I mean . . ."

So Hobbes listened patiently, dismayed by the passion for escape behind Pasternak's dream, but responding to the passion itself if not the details of the dream. Like everyone struggling to survive in the city, when the pace of things accelerated out of control and circumstances tightened around his volition like a vice, Pasternak's life seemed to turn into a battle against the city itself. But the city was an opponent, invincible because it was impersonal. It could not be beaten by a single man, and sometimes the only alternative to strangulation seemed to be to cheating it, by escaping.

"Sure," Hobbes said when Pasternak had finished. "We'll all get out eventually, I suppose. When I get my book finished, we'll probably head for Mexico and just forget about everything for a while."

"That's right," Pasternak grinned eagerly. "You can live down there on fifty bucks a month. But say, that's a great idea! It would be just like we always said. And I'll bet Christine would love Mexico."

When depressed, Hobbes and Pasternak often spoke of "forgetting everything and fleeing to Mexico." In fact, this had become a sort of prepared position to which they could retreat when things got bad—like the cute little house in Westchester around which the clerk and secretary arranged their fancies, and the five room apartment, with a Bendix, in the Bronx which enabled the factory worker and his eternally weary wife to bear the railroad flat off Second Avenue. It became a haven, the mere imagining of which lessened the wave of hopelessness which created it.

So they fell to making wild, improbable plans about taking a house in Acapulco, the four of them and Christine's child; and even began discussing the amount of money which they could spend weekly for "cervesas and digging the mambo!" Kathryn and Christine burst in fifteen minutes later and brought them back to earth.

Christine's hair was sequined with the rain which had begun to fall slantingly into the streets, and Hobbes was struck again by her glowing, natural loveliness, the kind of beauty which is vaguely suggestive of innocence of soul, and which is always somehow surprising no matter how many times it has been observed before.

She was excited almost to the pitch of delirium when Pasternak touched her arm and kissed her lips with the nervous nonchalance that always attends public intimacy. Kathryn began preparing a small supper, and Christine tried to help, unable to keep out of the way, laughing continually, her wide, warm eyes drifting to Pasternak after each remark.

"Can't you quiet her down!" Kathryn exploded with tough good humor. "She chewed my ear off all the way uptown."

Christine took this as a sign that the extent of their relationship was known and actually blushed for an instant, but recovered and exclaimed: "You know, this gorgon-head kept me waiting half an hour in the Park yesterday! That's how eager he is to see me!" And she shot a challenging, flirtatious glance at Pasternak. "But he quiets me all right. When that man kisses me I stay kissed!" Then her eyes suddenly narrowed with shame. "But you'll think I'm awful, won't you," she stumbled out. "A married woman talking like that . . ."

"As long as people do it," Kathryn snorted. "It doesn't matter what they talk about!"

She was putting dinner on the table and they all sat down, so cramped for space that Pasternak and Christine were actually thigh to thigh. During the meal, they kept up a steady stream of exaggerated talk, as people do who are helplessly attracted to each other and feel that the only way to disguise it from outsiders is to absolutely ignore one another.

"But you're right, Kathryn," Pasternak began. "Women are always right about things like that. Talk doesn't matter, as long as people do the natural thing . . . Everyone talks the guts out of life, abstracts it, perverts it . . . Like that Georgia girl." And he glanced with a nervous pinch of his lips at Christine. "But just the other day I was thinking about the sexual regeneration of the world," he hurried on. "You see what I mean? When everyone is just simple, natural . . . like so many apples!"

"Who's this Georgia anyway?" Christine asked with playful suspicion, unable to keep her eyes off his mouth as he spoke.

"Oh, just some girl we know . . . one of those 'emancipated' women who's really cold as a snake . . . No, but think of apples! Everyone's really just an apple after all. The rest is only mental, psychological. Think if we all just started acting like apples to be eaten, to be enjoyed!"

"Sometimes there's a worm though," Kathryn put in wryly.

"But you know what I mean—"

"Well, Gene, certainly if we could do what we felt was right for ourselves, without feeling guilty about it because of old fashioned rules we don't really accept privately, we'd be a lot healthier."

"But, you know, most people feel guilty about *not* feeling guilty in the first place. They're sure something must be wrong with them because they don't feel all anxious and ashamed about their real desires . . . But I think we should all just go around naked and forget the goddamn rules!"

He said this last intensely, almost aggressively, never looking away from Hobbes to Christine, who had been following everything carefully.

"Some people I could think of would look awful funny," she blurted out uncertainly, "if they went around that way!"

"No, they wouldn't," Pasternak insisted, turning to her for the first time. "They'd be just natural, *really* beautiful, the way they're supposed to be. Do you think we were made for clothes?"

His look seemed to reassure her more than anything he might have said, and she glowed again and replied with a coy smile: "You talk like one of those nudists or whatever they're called. I didn't know what I was getting into here!"

But when Pasternak took her hand and held it firmly, her face filled with that almost delirious joy that sometimes possesses people in love, when a gesture is sufficient to produce giddiness, a casual word can release the most exalted emotions, and every-day things seem lacquered with romance.

"For a couple of apples," Kathryn said, piling the plates. "You two take up a lot of room. Move, so I can get the table cleared."

Soon after this, they all walked over to Mannon's for a beer, Pasternak and Christine lingering twenty feet behind in the fine drizzle that sifted down. They held hands and leaned together whispering as Hobbes and Kathryn went on ahead.

"She says they've talked about going to San Francisco, and she asked me if I thought she should go with him."

"What did you say?"

"I told her to sleep with him before she made up her mind. That's what she's dying to do anyway, but she feels so guilty about everything—particularly wanting to—that she's liable to do something stupid. She's frustrated, that's most of it . . . But look, Paul, I don't want to get involved in it now. I mean I don't want to really encourage her one way or the other. If they want to come to our place, that's all right, but let's remain neutral about it."

"Oh, I don't think she's the type who'd break up her marriage just because her sex life is dull."

"She's just the type," Kathryn said shortly. "Mark my words." And somehow her tone made him uneasy.

Like many Third Avenue bars, Mannon's was a completely different place at night. Most of the local drunks, living on meager sums of money that went for the afternoon beers that made their days bearable, had passed out or been collected by hard faced wives by seven o'clock. A few, apparently insensible to exhaustion and liquor, held on grimly, providing a "neighborhood flavor" for the nighttime crowd. This was made up of young newspaper, advertising and radio men, all as fashionably ill-dressed as they were fashionably cynical; and the models and small fry actresses with whom they went, so delectably precise in carriage and attitude that they might just have left El Morocco, which, being right around the corner, many of them had. Anyone who ordered a cocktail gave himself away as a slummer, and the regulars (most of whom had been drinking martinis themselves in a midtown lounge not two hours before) looked away with cryptic disdain. The "neighborhood flavor," and the bartenders, paid no attention to any of them.

Hobbes found a booth and after getting their beers at the bar, they sat down.

Christine started talking to Kathryn about the possibility of her going off with Pasternak: "I could just take off with Ellie, and just leave him a note or something. What about that? It's more than he'd ever do for me. Why, he'd kill me if he ever caught up with me!"

"Don't you worry about him," Pasternak muttered. "Maybe I could have a talk with him. But, anyway, don't you worry. I'll take care of him!"

"But you just don't know him. You can't talk to him, it's impossible . . . Oh, he doesn't give a good goddamn for *me*, but he'd go out of his head if he knew I was here, he'd go wild. You know, he's a quiet boy, Paul, most of the time . . . but just sometimes I get scared of him." A frightened, tremulous smile moved her lips. "I just don't know what I should do . . ."

They sat on, Pasternak with his arm around Christine's shoulders, looking off at nothing as though trying to remember something he had never known; and a blank moment engaged them all.

Hobbes suddenly thought that in all the brittle laughter, ceaseless smoking and drinking, and vapid jocularity which constitute sophistication, Pasternak and Christine were like children whose simple absorption makes adults seem foolish. Something Pasternak had once said flashed through his mind: "You know, there's nothing like standing around with your girl in the doorways on a rainy night, trying to find somewhere to go. The hotels turn you down, the rooming-houses take one look and are filled up, and by the time you find some nook (anywhere, I even thought of a church once), you're too goddamn tired, and all the love's been beaten out of you!"

But when he looked at them, he saw only the urgent passion of their guarded looks; that first, gnawing passion, when all real joys are ahead, which finds no adequate expression in words, and is a sort of compact against the situation in which it has arisen. He remembered his own feelings of the same thing with Kathryn years ago, and was shocked to discover that now they were only lifeless memories which time had embalmed. For a moment, he longed for that first pure blush again, when even the clichés of the popular songs seemed profound, and he wondered blindly where it had all been lost, how they possibly could have let it happen. He watched Pasternak and Christine with a faint, sweet twinge, perceiving in them a kind of emotional innocence of which he was no longer capable. He had a sudden feeling that they were doomed, and that he had gained a tragic perspective on them which their own emotion would not allow. He grasped this thought with the fervor of the pessimist, recalling a sentence he had written to Liza just that afternoon in a moment of depression:

"Our marriages go wrong, our love is refused; our wives leave us, our husbands call us whores; our mothers weep silently at the sight of us, our friends sympathize for the wrong reasons; and everything seems bad, soured beyond saving, a prelude to some unimaginable catastrophe."

He was overwhelmed by a rebellious desire to help Pasternak and Christine at all costs; he would have given them anything, even fought off the husband. He did not stop to question his feeling, but acting on it, followed Pasternak into the men's room at one point and gave him the keys to the apartment: "Take her there, Gene, if you want to. We'll stay away an hour or two. What the hell! What does all the rest of it matter!"

So a few minutes later, Pasternak and Christine left with awkward explanations about a walk, as though there was a stranger present who did not know the true nature of the situation.

Immediately, Kathryn criticized him for arranging it so crudely.

"She'll probably think there's some conspiracy or other. Why can't you ever relax? You've been looking pained for the last ten minutes. What's wrong anyway?"

Consternation engulfed him. "I don't know. I got this crazy feeling . . . I wanted to help them. But look, honey, I don't want Gene to feel he's got to account to us for anything. I mean his feelings about her . . ."

"Why should he?"

"Well, maybe he thinks you disapprove of the whole thing. You said you didn't want that kind of thing happening in your house."

"I've practically pushed her into his lap, haven't I? My Lord, it's their affair, not mine! And besides, she's no Georgia. Things like this should be simple, and all this talk about running away is just confusing everything."

"Well, I never thought I'd hear you approve of marital infidelity, much less advise it!" Strong emotions invariably made him ironic. "I thought you always said that if you caught *me* with another woman, you'd kill us both?" This was something she had often threatened during their fiercer arguments.

"Well," she replied defensively. "I probably still would. But this is different. Why should Christine be unhappy just because she's too stupid to change anything? If she goes into it openly it could do her a lot of good."

"So you agree with Gene and his apple-selling idea?"

"Well, it's better than that hideous guilt of hers. Besides, why do you ask me?" There was a twinkle in her eyes and she inspected his face ardently. "What would *you* do if I wanted to sleep with some other man? Should I do it? You're always asking me."

"If you wanted to, yes. It would be better than frustration. That would eventually get back to me. Anyway, if you were attracted to a man and wanted to sleep with him, why should I be worried until after you had done it? If you came back and told me that he was better than I was, that would be one thing. I'd have to do something about it then. But if it was just pleasurable, but no better than what we have, what would I have lost?"

He warmed to the idea and took her hand across the table earnestly: "Sex isn't quantitative, after all. I get the impression most people think of it that way, as though one had only a certain amount and each time one gave some of it away. If I was worried because you wanted someone else just out of curiosity, that would imply that I was afraid of his 'know-how,' wouldn't it?"

She laughed at that because it was one of their private expressions. "But aren't you saying all this just so you'll be free to do the same thing?" she countered archly.

"No, not at all," he replied a trifle too warmly. "If I *wanted* another woman, I'd certainly have her. It wouldn't have anything to do with love. Don't you see what I mean?"

Her eyes had been dancing, for she usually enjoyed these lightly fencing talks when their relationship was smooth, but she pondered this last gravely.

"I suppose. But you'd tell me, wouldn't you? That would be the main thing, that you tell me. To find out any other way would be worse for me than your doing it in the first place. You would tell me, wouldn't you, Paul?"

"Of course, but, you know, I can't get over how sensible you've gotten about all this. Have you really stopped thinking that every time I bring it up, I'm really only trying to excuse myself?" And he said it without a thought of Liza, or the letters, or the years he had been writing them.

"No, no, not entirely," she replied coquettishly, with a delicious smile that he could have eaten. "I may feel completely different tomorrow. But tonight I'm just glad we're not beginning and afraid the way they are. I couldn't stand that again."

After another half an hour, they got up and pushed their way out of the bar, which was very crowded now and filled with that undercurrent of unrest and dissatisfaction that grows in city bars as the hours and the drinks disappear.

A curious thing happened on the way home. The rain had stopped, a damp heat choked the night, and going up Third Avenue they saw dark figures struggling under the Elevated. A few motionless bystanders had collected at a distance from two men who were scuffling violently with one another.

The chief assailant, a large, beefy man in a wrinkled striped suit, his gawdy necktie flapping, had hold of a small shouldered, shapeless fellow in a ripped white shirt, and was alternately shouting and swinging at him. A slatternly woman, heavily made up against age and obviously the cause of the fight, was trying drunkenly to intercede, and ran around them, yelling at the small shouldered man: "So you were gonna knock me down, were you? Knock *me* down!"

The beefy man swung at this, a wild, ineffectual blow before which the small shouldered man crumpled to the pavement without a sound or a whimper. As he lay gasping for breath and trying to struggle to his feet, the other man belabored him with furious, clenched-teeth snarls: "Stand up, you bastard! Stand up!"

He reached down as though into a barrel of fish, to seize an arm and yank him to his feet. The woman pushed herself between them for a moment, her face livid as she swore at the small shouldered man: "Nobody talks to me that way, you sonofabitch! Nobody," and she clawed at him.

"Leave 'um alone!" shouted the beefy man menacingly, hitting him a glancing blow. "Leave 'um alone!"

The small man staggered away toward the curb, still without uttering so much as a word, but his attacker was after him, pursued by the woman. An arm shot out and, before he could reach the sidewalk, grabbed him by one pitiful shoulder and whirled him around.

"As long as you're standing up, you're gonna fight me, you hear!" the beefy man spat out at him, then wildly commanded the woman: "Leave 'um alone! Leave 'um alone, I tell you!"

He struck the smaller man again, and the woman threw herself into the struggle, shrieking and weeping: "Why do you always say you're gonna hit me like that? Why? . . . Oh, you're bleeding, you goddamn bastard! Hey, he's bleeding! . . ."

The beefy man shoved her away ferociously: "I told you to leave 'um alone! . . . Fight, come on, fight me!"

Kathryn and Hobbes had been standing transfixed while this went on, shaken out of themselves by that wave of panic that sweeps over people when crude emotions are laid bare, deprived of their causes.

Now Kathryn cried out: "Why doesn't somebody stop him? What's he doing it for?"

Hobbes was filled with terror and nausea that he could not understand, and he dragged her away forcibly, heading for Lexington Avenue. His stomach was actually turning over.

"It's crazy!" he muttered. "Come away, Kathryn! Don't interfere! People are damned, damned . . . but let them be!"

She gave him a strange, sharp look and said angrily: "Take it easy! Why do you always have to get that way?"

"I don't know," he stumbled, collecting himself as rapidly as possible. "I couldn't figure it out, that's all . . . Who did the woman belong to?"

"What does that matter? He was killing that man!"

"I don't know . . . I couldn't understand it for a moment, that's all. It was like a nightmare . . ."

The key was on the ledge above the door, and the apartment was empty. Christine had left a note, thanking them, and saying she had to get home and couldn't wait.

Hobbes washed the fine drops of chilly perspiration off his face, and coming out of the bathroom, asked: "Well, do you think they did it?"

She walked through the living room. "I guess so. Look, the couch doesn't even look like it's been sat on, and the pillows are all straight. They cleaned up the place, trying to leave no signs."

They undressed and got into bed wearily, but his agitation would not subside. Kathryn lay for a minute, listening to his heavy breathing.

"Why do you get like that anyway? It was only a fight."

"Oh, you know," he answered lamely. "Everyone has periods. I've been jumpy all day and sometimes nothing seems to make any sense . . . But I got this horrible feeling while we stood there . . . that they were in love . . . the woman and the little man . . . and it suddenly made me sick!"

Eight

On the following Friday in the late afternoon, Stofsky interrupted Hobbes at his typewriter. Evidently he had bounded all the way up the stairs because he announced with breathless weight: "I've left my analysis . . . perhaps forever!"

Hobbes was in the midst of one of his organzied days, and as Kathryn was going directly from her job to the train for Westchester where she would spend the week end with her mother, he had been planning to get in a lot of work on his novel. Every week or so the disorder of his life would snarl around him and for a day he would carefully arrange all his activity: a book in the morning, an hour or two at his typewriter before lunch, the library after, an early evening newspaper and then more work. He was rarely allowed to keep to these ambitious schedules, for someone or something was always coming up, but so much did he rely on them that every time he was interrupted he became unusually irritable.

Stofsky stood in the center of the room dramatically as though expecting his announcement to so surprise Hobbes that all other preoccupations would be driven out of his head. And, in fact, Hobbes was somewhat startled, and trying to disguise his displeasure, hastened to ask Stofsky why he had discontinued the treatment.

"Well, in the first place I've no more money. That's one consideration. On top of that, my father won't help. He says he can't see any improvement. Who knows, perhaps he even thinks I'm incurable!" But Stofsky did not seem perturbed. If anything his manner was quite offhand, and already he was leafing through a pile of magazines on the coffee table. "I can always go back later if I want to," he added indifferently. "And besides, the main thing is that I've come to think of analysis as a sort of intellectual game—a scavenger hunt through the mind —really quite empty of emotional value. And that's what I'm after now."

"I thought you were convinced it was just what you needed? In fact, you're the only person I know who seems to get some pleasure out of it."

"Oh, that was before. I was interested, of course, and even conscientious. But my doctor took a very distrustful and cold attitude toward the Waters business . . . and there were other things, too. I've been having trouble submitting to him, and we've disagreed here and there."

This was said almost reluctantly, and yet Stofsky seemed eager, in fact, fairly bursting, to speak about something else. "It's all Aristotelian, you see, and what I'm after is a breakthrough into the world of feeling . . . I mean subjective truth . . . or . . ." He laughed nervously, moving toward Hobbes tentatively. "But these last weeks have been tremendous for me, Paul. Waters gave me just a glimpse. My whole life may be changed, and I wanted to talk to someone about it . . ."

"You've just come from your analyst?"

"Yes . . . yes, just this instant. But listen," and his eyes shone behind the glasses with a peculiar brilliance. "I must tell you . . . It's about God, you see. I've been reading and thinking and pursuing it for days, and I've decided to believe in God!"

Hobbes could not restrain his incredulous laugh. "What in the world are you talking about?"

Stofsky started striding up and down excitedly.

"What I mean is that I've come to realize that all coldly conceptual thinking—like psychoanalysis and sociology, even some religions—are just masks that give reality an intellectual order by making a selection of observations from it . . . I mean, digesting reality . . . or . . . it's so hard to explain it *this* way! . . . But all systems are just mirrors, mirrors. You look into them and you see only yourself, with the world as the dim background!"

"But what's this about God? I thought you were talking about God?"

"Well, that's just it, you see. I've discovered that if I can't believe in human knowledge anymore, I've got to believe in God . . . I mean, of course, man's *systems* of knowledge, which are really only the emblems of his fear . . . like rituals, for instance, or prayers, or even flying saucers!"

He rocked back and forth on his heels at this last touch, his eyes almost winking as if to indicate that he knew he was a clown; and yet his laughter was somewhat strained. Then he hurried on, fearful of an interruption during which his thoughts might be lost.

"There must be a reason, you see, for everything. Oh, I don't mean the beginning of the world or any of that nonsense," and he all but waggled his finger at Hobbes. "Oh, I know that's what you thought I meant! But no, I mean rather the *end* of the world! The *end!* Why must it end? Did you ever ask yourself that? It's quite fashionable to believe that it will, you know . . . But why? And why must we end either? It seems so cruel, so gratuitous that we could destroy it all, and ourselves too. Think of it! And all the hopelessness today . . . the horror . . . the suffering!"

"I must say I don't understand anything you're saying," Hobbes snapped out. "What's all this got to do with God anyway?"

Stofsky sat down, momentarily abashed, endeavoring to pick up all his threads again, and evidently confused because the discussion was proving so difficult due to Hobbes' objections.

"What I mean is that with all our knowledge, things have gotten worse, more hopeless. We know everything but the one *binding* fact, don't you see? The binding, unifying fact of human life that will make it all real, and not some vicious prank! I finally realized that so clearly. And the fact has got to be *God!*" His voice actually rose on the very word.

"Well," Hobbes said with obstinate impatience. "I don't see any sense in that at all. 'The binding fact!' God *can't* be a fact. After all, the idea of God is the greatest emblem of fear, the most subtle—"

"What I mean is the soul, spirituality, what endures! Throw out God if you must, abandon Him! . . . And why do you fall back on semantics that way? It's quite odd. But that's just what I mean! You see how a system of knowledge, like semantics, confuses the issue and introduces this false mental order into—"

"But what's this about an issue? What issue? You said you believed in God!"

"I don't believe! I don't believe at all!" Stofsky cried suddenly. "But I will! I will believe in Him! I only said that I've decided to believe in something. I must!" And he snickered slyly. "And so must you . . . But I've also decided on love, you know! How does semantics judge love? Does it approve? Does it feel love has some 'objective validity'? He-he!"

Hobbes was growing more disturbed by all of this every moment, but was uncomfortably aware that everything Stofsky was saying, even his taunts about 'validity,' was of the utmost, crucial importance to him.

"No, but listen," he was going on. "What I mean is faith, which is really the essence of God or love or . . . But, oh, pick your own word! But if there is no God, what am I? Or you for that matter? Think of that! In fact, simply because I'm incapable of grasping the idea of God objectively—I mean on the level of intellectual knowledge and rationalism and all that—I must believe in Him, or at least in the possibility of Him! Don't you see? It's all so ridiculously simple! . . . If I could think of God, and grasp Him, I wouldn't believe at all! After all, what would He be then?"

Hobbes shook his head continually during this. "But why even bring Him into it?" he began wearily when it was over. "That's what I can't understand. If there is a God, why is life the way it is? It's got to be either His Will or ours, and if it's His that makes us all fools, cogs; and if it's ours, why should we bother with Him at all? . . . No, the only God I'll ever accept is a cruel God, and I won't worship Him."

Stofsky's mouth twisted with a shrewd, somehow hungry grin: "Oh, well, if you're looking for something to worship, to grovel before . . . But, after all, isn't the whole content of modern life . . . (I believe that's the way it's put these days!) . . . Isn't all the horror and futility in itself at least a *negative* revelation of 'the binding fact'? . . . And why do you keep harping on the word God? Maybe He's only a metaphor for something else, after all . . . But think of it as a negative revelation, I mean a revelation of the *absence* of 'the binding fact'! You see! 'O rose, thou art sick!' . . . Oh, and that reminds me, I've been pouring through Blake, every word . . ."

Hobbes sniffed noticeably. "Well, that explains it."

"Yes," Stofsky exclaimed warmly, failing to comprehend Hobbes' dry sarcasm. "He's the key, an authentic prophet. And I never understood him before . . . Oh, no, I didn't reach these ideas alone . . . I've been borrowing in the Columbia Library for days, he-he! Waters baffled me about eternity, you see. I couldn't grasp it. I mean, how can we know the image from the reality? Is it just an image or is it a perception too deep for our intelligence? Because I couldn't really understand love either . . . suddenly it was only an image also, and . . ."

He went on and on, lighting cigarettes impatiently, not giving Hobbes a moment to interrupt; an endless flow of half humorous, half mystical ideas, mortared with bits of poetry and insights derived from religious paintings; all the time moving restlessly up and down, unable to keep his attention on anything outside his monologue, his eyes flashing with that almost insane brilliance. He would emit a cackling, derisive laugh every now and again, right in the middle of some comment on Melville or Donne, looking with beady, triumphant intensity at Hobbes, and then looking away to spew out more ideas in a ragged, disconnected form.

"Of course, I thought of madness at one point," he broke out suddenly, the way a person does who believes he is anticipating objections, and who makes himself almost dizzy with his own galloping perceptions into the situation. "But I dismissed it. You see, Waters was attempting to see with God's eye by means of his own. I mean, all that about eternity. Of course, it's true, I suppose, almost a mathematical certainty. But I disagree with him procedurally, all that breaking of clocks and so forth. Gestures! Gestures! It was in that that his madness lay, in the details."

Hobbes' attention was straying pointedly, and Stofsky seemed to realize that he had failed to make anything clear, and his excited expression dissolved into one of almost embarrassed chagrin.

"None of it strikes you, does it? Oh, I know something's missing in it somewhere . . . but somehow we must love, and be good . . . because, you see, I felt sickness everywhere last night. Our whole horrible, ego-filled world, sick! The spirit, sick! 'O rose, thou art sick!' . . . Really, Paul, what else could it mean?" There was something wistful about his very earnestness.

"Well, David, I can't pretend to know about these things—"

"But I don't *know* either," he pleaded. "I just feel it must be so!"

"But what must be so? You talk about God, and at the same time about love and suffering. What's the connection? If there is a God, why isn't there love? Why is there suffering? Don't you see the inconsistency?"

At that, Stofsky's face became drawn, ashen, his mouth worked slowly and involuntarily: "We have our egos, our wills, we can *will* to disbelieve . . . But actually," he added softly. "I don't really know what I'm talking about . . . although that's another matter."

He stood at the window now, staring down into the street with glassy, tormented eyes. Just then a fire engine screamed by, its sirens raising an unearthly wail until the ears grew numb with their piercing sound and the inhuman roar of the motors beneath. Stofsky turned slowly, lifting his arms to his head, his lips deformed by a stifled shriek, at once theatrical and demented.

"You see? You see? If *that* were all," and he gestured out the window wildly. "If that were all there was—motion, chaos, terror—I'd give up, right now! I'd walk out this window on the air. Just walk out and trust to luck, take my chances, die!" For one frightening instant, Hobbes thought he might actually start to climb onto the sill. "But I will believe, I tell you! I've decided to believe."

"All right, all right," Hobbes replied placatingly. "But . . . but perhaps you ought to take it easy on the reading. You know, eye strain can bring about perfectly credible hallucinations . . ."

Stofsky stood before him, frozen for the moment, as if he had not heard this, staring strangely at Hobbes, a look of pained, somehow haunted clarity on his face.

"What you're looking for with your systems," he said slowly, "is value, I suppose. The values of the mind. But I must have a reason for my being, don't you see? And an explanation of evil! And I will have it, I've decided that!" But as he said this, his distraught features grew ominously calm.

Hobbes was overcome with the embarrassment a reserved and sensitive person feels who has reduced his opponent in an argument to protestations of sincerity that have nothing to do with the issue. Though he had continually felt something obsessive, and even morbid, in Stofsky's exclamations, he was also aware that beneath them there was some avid passion that was driving him. In the face of an avid passion, Hobbes snapped shut like an oyster on a grain of sand; but like the oyster, the passion festered inside him.

Stofsky was sitting down now, leaning back into the pillows, and he had changed the subject abruptly: a somehow sad admission that he knew further talk was futile, an admission that left him nothing to do but play the guest and cause no more trouble.

He began speaking with quiet formality about a poem of Blake's which had impressed him. There was a tinge of unconscious irony in the fact that, though it was a metaphysical poem, he confined his remarks to literary angles. He spoke slowly, without emotion, and for the first time since his entrance, Hobbes did not feel that he was expected to reply. Stofsky recited the first quatrain in an even, precise voice:

> "My mother groan'd! my father weapt.
> Into the dangerous world I leapt;
> Helpless, naked, piping loud:
> Like a fiend hid in a cloud."

"Somehow it struck me," he said lazily, evidently choosing his words with extreme care, and every now and again snatching muted looks at Hobbes. "It's so economical and yet it has such true feeling, somehow childlike. I really can't account for it, because it . . . it wasn't one of those that contributed . . . well, to my idea." He was almost whispering.

It struck Hobbes as well, although he was too exhausted from the talk and his own irritation to sort out his reactions. In any case, the verse seemed particularly apt as regards Stofsky, somehow pathetic in the light of his idea, and Hobbes found himself thinking dumbly: "Right now, he looks like a 'fiend hid in a cloud.'"

But his head was spinning, his throat acrid from all the cigarettes, and Stofsky, who had grown unusually polite, got up with a strange, apologetic grimace and bowed himself out the door, saying that he could not tell when he would be around again.

"I've got so much to do, you know . . . although actually this is the first time I've been visiting in a week." And with that, and an uncertain little smile, he hurried down the stairs.

After that, Hobbes tried to rebuild the wreck of his schedule, aware that depression was moving in, thick and centerless, around him. But it was no use.

Nine

By seven-thirty that evening, Hobbes had given up all thought of work, had tried getting into a book, failed, and had even searched the newspapers for a movie. But the elusive excitement of Friday night plagued him, and like everyone in New York with nothing to do on that night, he was filled with the griping suspicion that, all assurances to the contrary, he was really friendless and unwanted. So he surrendered to the idea that to be alone would be unbearable, went out and started wandering downtown.

The bars were filling up with early drinkers, all of whom somehow gave the impression that they were simply having a bracer before going on to some smart glittering destination. The East Side restaurants exuded stringed dinner music, the hushed twitter of people who can afford any of the entrees, and that indefinably rich tinkle that results when handblown goblets and ice meet. Even the doormen, in summer uniforms that must have taxed the imaginations of their designers, were benevolent. Along the street, in a splendid parade, moved cool, laughing couples, each (to Hobbes) more handsome, gay and enviable than the last. He caught snatches of talk as he passed them, and longed even for these frivolities.

On Thirty-second Street, he went into a bar and grill that advertised manicotti and took a dark booth near the juke box, where he sat over his food and listened to Italian arias. He wanted an evening of sad songs that would remind him of a painful adolescence—a curious self punishment that often occurred to him when he was alone. And yet, he wanted people also, people that he knew and with whom he could relax. So, leaving an unnecessarily large tip, he went out.

He walked over to Fifth, and continued downtown. In almost no time, he found himself in the Twenties, where there were no restaurants, no strollers; none of the shiny evidences of a cosmopolitan spring evening. His self pity, indulgable when there had been gaiety around him to give it fuel, turned to an unreasonable desperation to see someone, do something. It was no longer a diversion, but a test.

Then he realized that he was not three blocks from where Agatson lived, and on the chance of finding somebody there, he turned down Twenty-first Street. His spirits rose immediately, inflated by the wildest expectations of parties and hordes of people.

Agatson lived in a drab district of warehouses, garment shops, and huge taxi-garages. His loft was at the top of an ugly brownstone, unoccupied but for a lampshade factory on the second floor. The halls smelled of burnt glue and bolts of cheap cloth, and the stairs above the factory floor were unlighted, narrow and treacherous with refuse. The loft itself was one of those floors-through with low windows, several grimy skylights that opened out on chimneys, and a sort of kitchen alcove at the back. It was always a fantastic litter of broken records, dusty bottles, mattresses, a slashed car seat, a few decrepit chairs from empty lots, and stray articles of ownerless clothing. Though the sort of clutter and mess that only human beings can create over an extended period of time was everywhere, the place curiously did not look like anyone's home. The thought of living in such surroundings seemed impossible. And yet, no one who knew Agatson could imagine him anywhere else.

Whereas, fifteen minutes before an amiable friend and a cheery bar would have satisfied Hobbes very well, by the time he climbed the inky stairways nothing short of an orgy would do. At the best, he would have been disappointed; and as it was, he was crushed.

No one answered his knock and he pushed open the door. Everything was dark but for a light at the back of the place. He crunched over the shards of records toward it, and discovered Agatson and Bianca sitting on the car-seat, eating cold pork-and-beans out of a can. They were alone.

Even though they were not talking, they had obviously not heard him enter, for Bianca looked up with alarm.

"Oh, it's you." She was not pleased; nor was she displeased. It was just a complication.

Agatson was in terrible condition: unshaven, red around the eyes, hands dirty and quivering. In the torn blue jeans and faded sweater, he had the look of a man who has not been out of his clothes for days. He was shoveling in the beans as if they were medicine, and said "Hello" with the painfully precise, almost stuttering whimsy that characterized him when he was sober. It was as if he was talking from a nightmare through which he was making his way on sheer nerve, for when he was hungover he always gave the impression that his faculties were spread thin and raw about him, and could be injured by a cough.

Hobbes sat down uneasily, wanting a beer, not wanting to suggest it because of Agatson's ravaged face, and seeing the fear of it in Bianca's eyes.

"S-s-she's waiting up with m-me," Agatson got out, as usual speaking of Bianca as though she was not in the room. "S-she's waiting for me to pass out, so s-she can put me to bed."

"You look like you had quite a time," Hobbes offered as inoffensively as possible.

"Oh, s-s-sure," Agatson mumbled, watching his own hands trembling, without horror but only a vague interest. "S-s-she's so sincere, you know that, Hobbes? That's her kick . . . she's s-sincere about everything. Aren't you, b-babe?"

Bianca gave him a warm, worried smile and everyone fell silent. Agatson was plainly alone in his universe of shuddering misery, and so Hobbes began to chat with Bianca, which made both of them uncomfortable.

"I thought you might be looking for Pasternak," she said finally. "He's . . . he's at Christine's tonight, you know. The husband's gone to Trenton to see his parents."

"Well," Hobbes replied, glancing from her to Agatson and back again. "I suppose I might try phoning there."

He knew Bianca would not ask him to leave. In a strange way she was too devoted to Agatson to ever send anyone away from him, and she knew him well enough never to damage his image in other people's eyes. But Hobbes also realized that she was endeavoring to get him to bed before the urge for oblivion rose up in him again, and so he got up and dialed Christine's number, having no idea what reason he would give for interrupting them at that hour, only knowing he would not just give up and go home.

Christine answered and, without identifying himself, he asked for Pasternak. Pasternak sounded puzzled and somewhat exasperated, and this flustered Hobbes the more.

"I just thought I'd call, Gene," he said in an artificially exuberant voice. "I'm at Agatson's, but I'm not staying here . . ."

Pasternak grew more bewildered, and Hobbes finally burst

out: "I've only got twelve hours or so," thinking of Kathryn's return the next day, "and I intend to keep going all night!"

"What do you mean, twelve hours? Can't you go home or something?"

"I don't want to go home. I'm going to have one more wild evening!"

"But what's happening? You mean you're leaving town in twelve hours?" Pasternak's voice rose with surprise. "You mean you're going to *Mexico* or something?"

"Yes . . . yes, that's it," Hobbes replied without a thought, only wondering if this would get Pasternak out into the night. "My bus leaves at six tomorrow morning."

"Well," and for a moment Pasternak paused as though unable to really believe it. "But that's only nine hours! But, look, you mean you're actually going? What about Kathryn? . . . Did you have trouble or something?"

"Oh," Hobbes stumbled, embarrassed by his sudden excitement at the hoax. "Oh, you understand, man! . . . But I just thought I'd call to say—"

"But listen, where does your bus leave from? How much does it cost anyway?"

Hobbes invented a plausible figure, and could not contain a twinge of guilt because the joking lie had had such an effect. He tried hurriedly to get off the wire.

"Hey, hey," Pasternak exclaimed. "Don't ride me that way! Come on, Paul . . . But, listen, man, ah . . . ah, are you going to be at Agatson's for a while?"

Hobbes mumbled something about either being there or at Mannon's, and Pasternak, caught in the middle of a quandary, said he'd try to find him somewhere later on, or at least "be at the bus."

"Well," Hobbes said. "Okay. Maybe I'll see you. But I'm going all night, so I'm not sure where I'll be," and he rang off quickly.

Though the others had not heard this conversation, Hobbes was agitated when he rejoined them. Agatson, slumped down, the can of beans still gripped in one dirty hand which no longer shook, had passed out where he sat. His mouth had fallen open and there was a curious private softness about it at that moment. Suddenly he looked gaunt and weary and tired, the way men accustomed to the bone crushing tensions of war sometimes look when they fall asleep on their feet; when the fiber of their youth appears through the unmalleable muscle to give them an expression of blind, introspective boyishness. Bianca simply sat, watching him.

"I'll help you get him into bed," Hobbes said, and between them they lifted Agatson, heavy and oddly vulnerable, all but dragged him into the front part of the loft, and laid him on one of the mattresses.

Hobbes started to unlace the weatherbeaten army brogans.

"No, no, I'll do that!" Bianca broke out immediately, moving him out of the way with firm possessiveness. "He . . . he hasn't washed for a week."

So Hobbes left them, catching one more look as he softly shut the door. Bianca was undressing Agatson with the rough tenderness women feel for men who have been hurt through folly, and he lay, sleeping fiercely, with that set, glowering innocence which children often have as they dream.

Hobbes took a subway and went home, the lust for company drained out of him. The hoax with Pasternak had been a shameless illustration of his desperation, and somehow it had resigned him to being alone. It was almost twelve when he reached the apartment, but he could not sleep and sat around listening to an all night disk jockey, smoking cigarettes one after the other. A lonely calm rose up from somewhere inside him, and he put the evening behind him with relief.

The phone rang at twelve-thirty and he was overcome with surprise and panic, for somehow he knew it was Pasternak calling from Christine's, wanting more words with him, and with the passing of the desperation, Hobbes could not think of anything to say to him. So he let it ring, thinking: "Perhaps he'll be sure I'm really going if I don't answer, and next week I'll avoid him, and everyone else too, and they'll all think I've gone off mysteriously, all in a moment, perhaps for good."

But it rang again fifteen minutes later and something made him answer, though he was actually in a sweat. He could hear music, and it was Pasternak.

"You just caught me at home, Gene," he explained immediately.

Pasternak was at Mannon's with Christine, it seemed, and they had come all the way uptown looking for him. Hobbes said that he'd just left there to come home, but appended quickly that he'd rush right over again.

Pasternak was thoughtful. "Don't hurry, Paul, if there's anything . . . well, anything personal you got to work out, you know? We'll be here—"

Hobbes realized, with a sinking tremor, that they thought Kathryn was in the apartment, perhaps listening, and that he had been arguing with her; and in his confusion he made some vague remark about "bags" and "packing."

"Well, man," Pasternak added. "I'll be going to Mexico almost as soon as you, pretty quick now! So don't you worry."

After hanging up, Hobbes stood for a terrible moment, not knowing what to do, but putting on his jacket automatically. He started down the stairs again, thinking that somehow he could gloss it over, pretend he was drunk and laugh it off or, at least, decide to "put off the trip" until Pasternak was actually ready to go, and get out of it that way. It never once occurred to him to simply confess the whole thing. Then again through all this jumble of feelings, he was perversely intrigued by the situation, and thought wildly that it might be fun to play it through and see what happened.

Mannon's was jammed, smoky, an uproar; but somehow Pasternak and Christine had gotten a booth in the back. Hobbes squeezed into it with a shamefaced glance at both of them which told him that they were stricken by the helpless earnestness that almost always accompanies the desire to be generous to someone whom nothing can help.

The three of them fell into trivial conversation at once. Pasternak kept buying beers, and saying unhappily: "You should just keep going till you hit Calcutta or someplace! After all, you can go anywhere you want now."

Hobbes smiled miserably, keeping an eye on Christine. She was completely at a loss as to what to say, and only looked at him with shy bewilderment, depending on Pasternak to show her the way.

At one point, while Pasternak was fetching more drinks, she leaned across the table, blushing and uncertain, and said: "Gee, I hope it all works out the way you want it to. I really do, Paul . . . And . . . and you tell Kathryn to call me up now, and I'll make dinner for her some night. And kinda take care of her. So don't you worry about—" But she could not finish because the painfully involved protocol of tact was absolutely foreign to her and she did not really understand what was going on.

Hobbes made increasingly feeble attempts at bravado, but could not force out of his mind the blunt, disgraceful fact that, through a selfish whim and a misunderstanding he was too weak to correct, he had utterly ruined their evening, probably one of the few they could snatch together. Here they sat, where he had dragged them by playing on an emotion he had not believed they felt for him; and the purity of their concern made his dishonesty all the more detestable in his own eyes. But something still prevented him from confessing everything.

He made one more effort to act the thing out, to be sad or bitter or relieved or whatever he would have been if it had been real, (feeling that if he could convince himself that he had convinced them some of the crime would be erased) but it was no use. Their very affection damned him.

Finally he could not stand it anymore and said that he had better leave, adding, over their objections, something about "getting at least a few hours sleep." They agreed without further argument, and the very fact that they should allow him any whim, even though it meant that they had come all the way uptown for only twenty minutes, plunged him into despair. He longed for the selfishness of which he had suspected everyone earlier.

Out in the noisy street the awful moment of mock-parting faced him. Christine, for some reason, was suddenly less constrained than the other two. She took his hand and said: "Somewhere along the way, you finish your book now. And eat and everything."

"Yes," Pasternak added emphatically. "That's all that really counts. I mean, the book. Don't mind what anyone says! And you write me when you get somewhere. Tell me where I can meet you. We'll all be waiting to hear."

Hobbes couldn't think of a word to say when Pasternak took his hand and gave it a firm, assuring clasp. Then, with Christine, Pasternak turned quickly and hurried down the street. Once he looked back, and finding that Hobbes had not moved a step, waved vaguely as they went around a corner.

Hobbes started wandering home, his mind filling with the bitterest self recriminations. His own actions seldom shocked him, for he calculated most of them too much for that; but sometimes, like now, he would find, as though coming out of a trance, that he had done something that so violated his idea of himself that he was actually horrified.

It had not happened since the war. But then, while working in the hospitals, something had occurred that he remembered now with the same sick guilt that he was feeling about Pasternak and

Christine. After his first six months of service, he had managed to discipline out of himself all useless compassion for agony that only skill could alleviate, and to view the generation of wreckage, with which he had to deal, objectively, calmly, even coldly. But one night he had been yanked out of bed at one o'clock, after a terrible day assisting in the operating theaters, to watch over a seventeen-year-old sailor who had a punctured lung.

The doctor wearily explained the situation to him before going off duty. The patient was in an oxygen tent, and Hobbes was to watch the gauge on the tank and feed him more as he needed it. He was not going to live, and if the intake rose beyond a certain degree it would mean the lung had filled up past the point where anything could be done, and there was to be no further increase after that. This might not happen, however, until morning.

Somewhat annoyed, Hobbes settled down and tried to read by the greenish night light. But the room was filled with the rasping gulps of the patient and he could not concentrate. Though he checked the gauge every few minutes, for half an hour there was no change. Once, while leaning over to read it more clearly, he glanced up and saw, through the window of the tent, the ghost like face of the boy, straining toward the feed-in. Though his young mouth was helplessly agape, he was watching Hobbes with staring, puzzled eyes.

By the end of an hour, Hobbes had given up the attempt to read and sat motionless in his chair, brutally hypnotized by the spark of life that was slowly flickering out of the boy's face. His own influence upon that spark enthralled him, it was so positively godlike. He experienced a sensation of distant benevolence for the boy, and his irritation at the loss of his own sleep disappeared. He began to speculate about the boy's life to occupy himself, all the while increasing the intake automatically. He decided he was too young to have been to college or to have known real love, and probably had not slept with a woman either. So completely did these thoughts grip him, that it was only after a few moments that he noticed that the gasps had begun to change to gurgles. Looking up with alarm, he saw that the gauge was turned as high as it was supposed to go, and that the boy's neck muscles were banded taut against his flesh, his mouth almost capping the intake valve.

But it was his eyes that snapped Hobbes out of the clinical fascination that had held him for the past hour. They were wet with the small tears of fright, and rolled wildly, pleading, pleading. For one moment, Hobbes stared into them, seeing such terrible bewilderment and yet also awareness of all that was to be lost, that the emotions he had so carefully locked away inside himself stormed loose.

He was shaken with the realization that he—detached and even irritated—was the last sight those quick, tormented eyes would ever register. In them, he seemed to see all the boy's desperate thirst for a life he had been too young to understand, and his utter unanswerable bafflement at why he should be there dying. All this swept over Hobbes, and something in him cracked discordantly and began to throb. He wanted to rush to the boy, touch him, weep, hold him perilously in life by sheer force of will, and gain one more instant to show him that someone cared that he had lived. But all he could do was clasp and unclasp his hands, and two minutes later the boy was dead.

Now the memory of that night watch stung him, and the old guilt mixed with the new to shrivel his heart. As he had that awful night, so now he longed for Kathryn; now because he had done her an injury also with his cheap lie, at least in his own mind; and because, like then, she was away from him, remote and unreachable. He remembered sadly that he had looked at the boy's chart after he was dead and memorized his name; but found that he had since forgotten it. Somehow that was the final shame, but, as always with the final shame, his loathing passed, he accepted himself with discontented resignation, and tried to turn his mind to tomorrow.

Remembering the farewells and thinking of the subway ride during which Pasternak and Christine would squander more moments on him, he climbed his stairs slowly, actually considering, for one last wild moment, going to Mexico somehow so that they would never know. But this passed too, and when he got into bed he slept.

Ten

STOFSKY sat, propped up like an invalid in his armchair, feverishly reading Blake by the early afternoon light through his windows. An intense silence actually seemed to grip the room as his eyes darted along the page and his mind swam.

"I wander through each charter'd street . . .
Marks of weakness, marks of woe."

The pitch of the day before had not let down. He was in the midst of a sort of delirium that seemed to transform everything around him. He had spent the whole day devouring, at one and the same time, Blake and Kierkegaard, although the latter had been slow and he had skipped. But he mulled each poem of Blake's, tracing his finger along every line of print, making a perfect, sharpened point of his mind so as to crack the images open. And then that morning, upon arising with a strange magnified emotion, he had found himself anticipating each metaphor, and the heart of the poetry seemed visible to him through a brilliant, and up until then, blinding glare.

He tossed the book aside, tipping over a glass, and snatched up paper and pencil, and wrote without stopping—an avid and incredulous expression transfixing his features:

"Flower of soul, flower of glare,
Stricken Rose who is so numb:
Is this shrunk impulse, like a star,
A prideful light where I succumb?
I head where dreadful wisdoms are:
Is this the knowledge that is numb?"

He sat there quivering a little, staring at the lines with a feeling of acute surprise, yet not really reading what he had just written. Moments came like this now: separated from all others, and from his surroundings, as by immense voids of meaning; and yet they seemed to be limp with light of a whiteness and power to illuminate unlike any he had ever experienced. He basked in these blank moments of entranced cognition as though will-less.

The first had glared down upon him like a million volt search-light just that morning, suffusing his intelligence in a cold white-ness, and he had had the impression that he was watching the instant of inspiration coming into being, and that at any second the vistas locked in it would burst upon him, like an explosion that is infinitely slowed down.

He got up without bodily sensation, his mind was racing so, and started to dress haphazardly, reaching for whatever lay about on chairs or on the floor. The lines seemed to stream through his head, as down an empty, resounding gallery:

"Love! sweet Love! was thought a crime . . .
And mutual fear brings peace,
Till the selfish loves increase."

He wandered out of his apartment and found himself in the street with the book still clutched in his perspiring hand. He stood there for a moment, a laugh fluttering in his throat, realiz-ing he had never been so worked up before. He decided he would go up to Columbia to seek a more complete edition of Blake's work, and started for the crosstown bus; once having made his plans, forgetting about them immediately.

An odd thing had happened the night before, although he had not recognized its oddness until after collapsing on his bed and snapping off the light. He had been reading Blake for over an hour without once looking up, even, it seemed, without blinking. When he came to "Auguries of Innocence," he sat there after the first four lines, his mind snagged and unable to continue. The light shone translucently on the page, and the print seemed large and black; but gradually as he looked at it, almost through it, in fact, he saw it grow—thick with ink—until it stood out coarsely, wetly, as though embossed there. His mind would not move forward, and though he was only fixedly gazing at words without meaning, he was aware that he was thinking of the objects of the words in the letters themselves. Gradually, as the ice white, eye-numbing glare seemed to flood toward him, he saw (or thought he did) the flower represented in "Heaven in a Wild Flower," a large black and white rose which soon shifted its in-tensities, changing shades, and became an extravagant red, a bloody fist of a blossom that he glimpsed, not on the page but through it, or rather through the words themselves. He sat there, immobile, as though in an hypnotic rapture, his eyes unable to move, looking, looking, breathless lest it should fade away.

Then, without a thought, he stumbled into bed. The darkness made his vision flame instantly. He had a remote sensation that his eyes were giving off pools of red light that changed to white and then faded palely away. And then, as the darkness filled in around him, and his ears seemed to become attuned again and he heard the infinite rattlings and shiftings and breathings of the house, he had thought that what had happened was odd.

These thoughts occupied him on the way to Morningside Heights. He moved mutely from bus to subway, thinking of the experience and trying to remember the peculiar living softness of that rose's curved, red petals. He was brought out of this when the train reached the One Hundred and Sixteenth Street Station, and he had to scramble to avoid the closing doors. Crowds swarmed down the stairs into the subway, and he stood at the top, suspended in this unwilling trance. An angry elbow in his stomach snapped it, and he moved out of the way and started walking downtown.

He crossed Broadway and went into the Columbia Book Store, a large irregular room with textbooks stacked everywhere and book-crammed alcoves in which customers dawdled. He had always liked the place: it was large and well-stocked and the clerks—most of them students themselves—did not keep alert eyes peeled for book stealers as they were ordered. It was possible to slip thin volumes under one's arm or mix them with class books or, in winter, stuff them beneath overcoats.

He meandered past a table, reading titles, only after five or six realizing they were books on economics and politics. He turned and worked deeper into the store, flipping absently through pages, unfolding jackets and inspecting bindings vacantly. After finishing each table, he would glance guardedly around, a sly squint of irony on his mouth and a laugh bubbling in his throat. All the time he was conscious of this, as though his responses had converged near his mouth in the giggle that he must not let out. Lines kept on pulsing through his head and, when staring at a page, before his eyes as well:

"The look of love alarms . . .
The weeping child could not be heard . . .
And her thorns were my only delight . . ."

Then, without warning, it happened for the first time. Aware of a sudden flush of warmth, he looked up over the edge of the book he was holding, out into the store and back through its whole length in the direction he had been working, until his gaze reached the door. It seemed a terrible distance. But everything was different, doused in that same all revealing glare of whiteness, and yet also as it normally was. He seemed to have gained a sort of X-ray perception, and he peered through the stacks of books and the browsing students as though the surface of reality was some kind of film-negative. He was at once startled and paralyzed as he had been the night before.

A student, moving lazily toward him with idle interest in his eyes suddenly seemed to be contorted with fear; his features, as he gazed inflexibly into the book before him, twisted with a crude, animal terror. The book in his hands, and indeed all the books, seemed to be vibrating with invisible shivers, and he heard, or thought he heard in the somehow shocking silence, a soundless commotion all around him. As he watched, consumed by the subtlety of his emotion, everything—books and students and walls—appeared to equalize itself, and the whirring in the air seemed to come from everywhere. And yet, all around him he felt a chemical, piercing fright. Everything was buzzing with the same energy, a kind of cohesiveness within the substance of all things that spit in and out and around the room like a band of electricity, an impersonal, yet somehow natural love, cementing the very atoms. He gaped at the student, now almost in front of him, into the wide, flat face still, in his eyes, rigid with that cloying fear as it perused the book.

Just then, however, the face raised itself to his and abruptly dissolved into an alarmed sneer:

"Well, whaddya see?"

Stofsky ran out of the place, shaking with wonder and apprehension. He walked without a thought of direction, pushing through crowds of students, his mind snarled with thoughts and images.

A vision! A vision! The words kept stinging into his consciousness like quickening waves of fever. As he went on, almost running now, he found himself haunted by the odd uprush of pity and rage that had taken control of him during the moment in the book store. It was love! he cried inside himself. A molecular ectoplasm hurtling through everything like a wild, bright light! And they were afraid, afraid, almost as if they all suspected. He had seen it clearly, in an instant of pure clarity: the chemical warm love that swam thickly beneath their dread!

How he got home he never remembered. He ran or walked or flew the whole way. The streets melted and blurred with one another, the dank hallways swung by drunkenly. He burst into his apartment and seized a piece of paper, numbly aware of the huge fatigue that caught up with him a second later, as he wrote:

> "See the changing dolls that gauge
> The changeless lull of dancing glare!
> As if they lolled beyond their stage,
> They dance around the world in fear.
> These are the dancers of the Dance,
> Their strangled acts, its only proof.
> Their arms are crude to all but chance,
> And every move is stiff with Love."

*   *   *   *   *

He slept deeply, oppressed by a sensation of heaviness of which he was conscious even through his sleep. He raced to contain eight hours in the three he actually lay among the tangled sheets. In his dreams, he watched himself gnawing on unconsciousness while the other 'he' floated in a tepid neutrality of emotion.

He fixed himself coffee when he got up. He was not certain of the hour, but it was dark through his windows and the buildings across the way were squared with blocks of damp light. He felt a timorous elation inside him, thinned by regret, because though he could remember the moment in the book store (and the total significance of every detail amazed him), he could no longer feel it.

He was alarmed by what had happened because he recognized, with a trembling guile, that it was not a mere invention, a projection of his own longings into all else, but an unwarranted unasked-for moment of "visionary comprehension." His dreams had never terrified him before because he had always known them for dreams, and, like a clown of infinite sagacities, had only been pretending with himself to the contrary. The certainty of this "vision," however, gave him a momentary qualm about his stability. And yet his whole nature, down to its minutest inclinations, seemed drawn to it. There was a reckless craving in him to believe in it, as though some ceaselessly revolving wheel inside his head would be set at rest by what he had seen.

He got up and put away his dishes, and his pallid face, mounted by the heavy spectacles, was drawn. He went back into the living room, which was still a debris of clothing, books and papers, and sat down on the couch, picking up Blake again. He thumbed through the pages without really looking for anything special, but trying poem after poem as if they were the key.

> "To find the Western path
> Right through the Gates of Wrath
> I urge my way . . ."

He read the rest with a conviction of the literal factuality of the words which astounded him. He skipped to another, feeling strangely that it was starting to happen again, the gradual flooding of warmth through him, but slower this time. He did not look up, but went on reading in a terror of expectation.

> "Ah, Sun-flower! weary of time,
> Who countest the steps of the sun,
> Seeking after that sweet golden clime
> Where the traveller's journey is done."

By degrees, he became aware of a voice that seemed to be reading along with him. At first he dismissed it as a sort of mental echo, but then it increased in sonority, intoning the lines slowly with gentle benevolence. He tried closing his eyes, delighted that all his faculties had remained with him. And the voice went on.

> "Where the Youth pined away with desire
> And the pale virgin shrouded in snow
> Arise from their graves, and aspire
> Where my Sun-flower wishes to go!"

He raised his head warily during this and stared before him. There was no incandescence this time, no suffusion of whiteness. He seemed, in fact, to be witnessing the phenomenon, instead of feeling it emanate from within him. He looked into the center of the massive world map which covered the opposite wall, looked right into Africa, and listened to the voice, which sounded from there, as though he was receiving instructions.

It stopped and there was a weightless still in the room. He

had retained some of the warmth and a sweet glow of placidity flowed through him. He could not account for the voice, although he thought, satirically, of what Hobbes had said about hallucinations brought about by eye strain. But this thought ambled through his mind, leaving no mark and arousing no anxiety. He was serenely content to hear the echoes of that deep, gentle voice in his intelligence, for that is where it had sounded more than in his ears. It was the voice of Blake himself, he thought wonderously. And it was all literal and explicit! *He* was weary of time and the horror of the world, and Blake had spoken to him out of eternity. And then he laughed for the first time, cautiously and yet with gladness.

He got up, held in a tranquil objectivity that made him consider taking his pulse and respirations. But behind this whimsy were the cracklings of the energy that raced through everything, all inanimate objects; and he glimpsed it as though through a veil. He could record no distrust this time, but rather he was filled with a hesitant anticipation, sure that something more was about to happen. He went to bed without a thought.

It happened again while he slept, as though he had come upon a sly snake in a dream field, only to find it real and grinning at him. He woke suddenly, pulled upright on the bed, with no idea of how much time had passed. The room was pitch black, although through the kitchen he could see a faint glow from the living room. The air was murmurous again, and it was with surprise and fear that he found his mind in a turmoil. He was wringing wet, his naked body clammy and hot, and all about him the fathomless darkness was charged with immediacies, intimations, as though the shadows were whistling shrilly just above the pitch of his ears. He sat there, frozen with dread, listening to this vast hubbub, to the vibrations of numberless, unformed voices that seemed to be sternly commanding him.

Then he felt that he was tottering on a slippery, bat-thronged chasm, invisible in the murk, being powerfully urged on to take some wild, irrevocable leap. There was an impulse, dark within him, to hurtle himself through the air, as though by so doing he might rend the wall he sensed all about him. He sat there, his body tensed to the point of agony, and suddenly seemed to be drowning in spasms of bestiality that shook him, a great pulse of carnal ecstacy whose only expression could be a groan. He wanted to gibber and rock and scream, and for an instant he remembered the first moment of blind fear in his life, when he had sat, a wordlessly horrified boy, during a scene in the movie, "Doctor Jekyll and Mr. Hyde," in which the actual transmutation took place.

But now they were calling to him, those flickering, disembodied voices out of time! The old, gaunt poets; the insatiate thinkers, hungry for light, who had pushed on out of the world; all imprecating him to leap through the wall! And terrified, he recalled in a flash of hideous indecision, a paragraph of Melville that went:

> "For as this appalling ocean surrounds the verdant land, so in the soul of man there lies an insular Tahiti, full of peace and joy, but encompassed by all the horrors of the half-known life! Push not off from that isle, thou canst never return!"

And in the din, he was tormented because he could not decide whether he was entering the "insular Tahiti" or leaving it. The whirr increased to a wail and he was shuddering with his desire to leap blindly, thoughtlessly, into the vortex of that sound. But he knew that if he let go, and fell into that violence of relaxation, he would shriek, flail his arms, and howl as the animality within him erupted.

"I must go mad!" he thought. "They are asking me to whirl, like Waters, into truth, but first I must pass through the fire and babble like an idiot!" And he could not, but sat rocking and panting, sobbing to himself, and then clapped a pillow over his head, pressing it down upon him.

He tried to scream or bawl or shout into the smelly bed-clothes before it was too late, but nothing would come. And it was a race against Time! Time! he whimpered inside himself. But he could make no sounds under the stifling pillow. When he raised it, the droning swept back with increased turbulence, and he felt the scream, palpable and welling in his throat.

Then he thought that if he let it out he would rouse all the neighbors, shatter the silence of the house as though it were glass, and so held back fearfully, and would not pass, shrieking, beyond the wall. Finally out of an ingrained, hateful timidity (whether because of the neighbors or the voices he did not pause to decide), he staggered out of bed and stumbled about his apartment, flicking on lights and throwing open windows. He ran about, gasping and weeping, and finally put his head under the cold water faucet in the kitchen.

He walked up and down the creaking floor trying to tiptoe, muttering to himself: "Why do we suffer? What have we done? Why? Why?"

And then as he passed the mirror, he saw himself in it, tousled and feverish, like the reptilian specter of his dream; and suddenly he laughed out loud, and screwed his lips into a buffoon's grimace, and protruded a waggling tongue at himself. He stood there for a moment, giggling like a demented child with a doll it thinks is live.

Then a new desire seized him. He wanted to tell others what had happened to him. He had had visions! He knew, at last, what his mad, forlorn mother, "who slept with the devil!" had tried to tell him. He had had revelations! And suddenly he was frightened of being alone, as if exercising a last, failing perception on himself. It pained him mortally that he should be alone now, and some of his usual selfconsciousness returned. Nobody cared when a man went mad, he thought nonsensically, sadly; but as he threw on his clothes, he laughed and laughed. And he hurried, thinking that before he could get out of the apartment another visitation might prevent him.

He rushed down the stairs, trying to be quiet but making a fearful clatter, and ran into the empty street, pulling up sharply. The crisp, tart night air quieted him, and he stood looking up into the sky, as though casting about for a place to go. Another giddy thought took him: "Die! If thou wouldst be with that which thou dost seek!" Shelley had said. And another: "Why fear we to become?" All of it, every word, was truth and all these years he had read it blindly, without understanding. All of literature seemed new to him then, a vast untapped vault into which he had been given admission.

A car whizzed by, and when he looked he saw, across the empty street, the neon of a saloon buzzing steadily, and the sidewalk before it stained red and green. He could call from there.

He pushed through the doors, noticing that it was two-thirty by the circular, dust-faced clock above the bar. It was a dismal place, garishly bright, and in a corner a few workmen slouched and talked. Stofsky paused, an absurd, wild-eyed figure, staring at them gravely. He wanted to shout to them: "I've just had a vision! Look, look, God is *love!* The world *can* be redeemed!" But they gazed back at him pitilessly, and then averted their eyes, and he ran for the phone booth instead.

He stood inside it and could remember no numbers. Then

Doctor Krafft's home telephone in Ozone Park clicked out of his memory, and with his dime, for that was all he had, he called him collect. As he waited, fidgeting, his every thought was vivid, brilliant it seemed, and he inspected each one carefully so that his account would be graphic and coherent.

He heard the operator ringing the number, and then Krafft's voice answering angrily. She told him from whom he was receiving the call and he paused for a moment, trying to come awake.

"It's Mr. Stofsky, Doctor," he interrupted. "I've just—"

"No . . . no, operator, I won't accept the call," Krafft snapped, slamming down his receiver and breaking the connection.

Stofsky flushed with mortification and bewilderment, but went on dialing numbers madly. He called Hobbes but there was no answer; Pasternak, although he knew the hall telephone in his building was shut off after twelve. And after failing with them, he called others; people he had not seen for weeks, others he scarcely knew. But no one answered.

He left the booth and the bar with a tight, mournful indignation in his heart. "Nobody cares when a man goes mad," he repeated bitterly to himself. "Nobody cares behind the wall of fear!"

He stood again in the street, a slight cool wind on his neck, and an objectless rage coursing through him. He wanted to shout to somebody, to reach them even if he had to pull down the mute city, stone by resisting stone, to run into apartments, bars and hotels, trumpeting his news, telling them all of his sad revelations. But there was nowhere to go, no one who would see him. He might have been only an idea in somebody else's head, somebody who now slept. With a twist of self pity, he went back to his apartment.

The "visions" and the night air had not changed it, but the rooms were drafty from the open windows. He felt somehow disillusioned, without strength, and he took off his clothes once more, turned out the lights, and sat at his windows, musing down into the yards below. The stillness now was absolute but for the elusive snatches of far off traffics crosstown. He was burned out with his exhilaration, his insides felt dredged and dry as from days of marijuana. He lit a cigarette and looked up over the flat, uneven rooftops into a sour, reddish sky, streaked with the reflections of lights that banked off the cumulous cloud formations.

He was centered in a moment of calm distant loneliness, without traces of fear or jubilance. These first reactions had passed without his noticing, and he sat like the only living thing in a ruined, derelict city, condemned to face an immensity of impending space, contemplating the desolate sky through his thoughts.

That sky was furled with shifting clouds that exuded a faint scarlet shimmer as if in globules. He thought then that the beast of the universe, that malign, scoffing monstrosity beneath all nature, was sick or sickening. The clouds seemed to be feeding on themselves like huge, carnivorous plants; and human unconcern, the refusal to understand that he had seen in the faces of the students and heard in Krafft's voice, was part of that sickness and that self consumption. He watched these thoughts string themselves out against the night, with evil fascination.

"As if God were mad! As if we were not alone!" he whispered aloud, imagining the entire sky as a great, inane eye gazing balefully down on him. Oh, the unspeakable horror of that thought! It was as though the very pumping, physical heart of all humans was being remorselessly atomized by the machine of a gigantic mind, over which hovered the sky, a dumb mushroom-head of smoke.

Then *this* was the sick rose, he thought! This, the heart itself, was the dying blossom through which love drifted unheeded, and which hung, as the clouds hung in that night, lifeless and rotting on a wintry vine.

Sitting there, naked and chilly, he longed for something certain and close beside him, for the love that he wanted to cry out to everyone lay just below their trembling masks. He was like the ancient, saddened mariner, who wandered, like a night without hope of dawn, from land to land with a strange power of speech. A heaviness sank upon him at that, like a responsibility or a fear that was so much his that he could not even *fancy* shirking or escaping it.

He felt as though tears were about to drop, heavy and wet, out of his eyes, because he was rewarded and damned. And he remembered when, at fifteen, he had looked in a mirror after getting slicked up for his first high school dance, and had sobbed and laughed at what he saw. But now the tears did not come.

PART TWO

Children in the Markets

"THERE hasn't been a party for three weeks, so *we* have to give one, eh?" Kathryn said with mock horror as they walked down Sixth Avenue toward West Third Street. "A lot of people staggering around breaking glasses and cluttering up my floors! And besides, Mr. Ketcham, what guarantee do we have that you'll be there?"

"But of course I'll be there. What do you mean?"

As always when Kathryn joshed him for his unreliability, Ketcham laughed with easy surprise, and replied innocently or in kind without offending her, she who was quickly offended. Hobbes had always felt that Kathryn got along better with Arthur Ketcham than he, but he was also grateful for the fact.

"I always come when contracted. How about Friday night? Is that all right? I'll help you make out the guest list."

"Will it be that kind of party? It sounds hideous, but all right, Friday night."

Hobbes was pleased by her willingness, and credited it to the large, tasty meal they had just finished at the Normandy, a cheap French restaurant on Ninth Avenue. Then also, she had been feeling better lately. He had slept through the persistent jingling of the phone when Stofsky called late the night before, but Kathryn, whom it had awakened, had not moved and had finally outlasted it obstinately. When she told Hobbes about it the next morning, he was surprised that she had not awakened him to share her anger.

They were on their way to meet Pasternak, who had called Hobbes during the afternoon to say that he was supposed to meet Christine in Washington Square at three o'clock, but wouldn't be able to make it. Would Hobbes, if she phoned, tell her that he was sorry and would get in touch with her? They had arranged to meet at nine that evening at Freeman's, which was a Village bar. Though Hobbes had seen Pasternak once since the night at Mannon's, the latter had tactfully made no mention of Mexico, probably concluding that "the trouble" had been worked out.

Just as Ketcham arrived at the apartment that afternoon, Christine called, and she sounded aggressive, although she made no reference to the Mexico incident either.

"That guy never turned up, Paul! He left me standing there like a goddamn fool for two hours!"

And then after Hobbes had explained: "Well, he could have reached me somehow. That makes the third time!" There was a pause and a catch in her voice. "Do you think he's getting tired of me or something? Tell me right out, won't you? I never been with a person like him before, and after I've thrown myself at his head and all. . . . ! Has he got another woman?"

Hobbes tried to placate her, but he was not good at subterfuge for other people.

"Well, my God, I'm risking my baby's future for him. Doesn't he care that Max's getting worse and worse all the time? I think he even suspects. What can I do, Paul? I'm in love with that gorgon-head, that's all . . . But I didn't think he'd treat me like this . . . Then I suppose I deserve it for what I've done with him!"

But now, walking down Sixth Avenue, Ketcham was concerned about something.

"Does Gene feel I'm critical of him, I wonder? I haven't seen him for over two weeks. You see, I told him he should cut his book a little before he gave it to MacMurry's, and you know how irate he can get, in a kind of way. But I was wondering, has he been avoiding me?"

Hobbes enjoyed his desire to explain why Pasternak hadn't been around, even though he did not know the actual reason. He liked it because it placed him in a mediatory position with Ketcham, whom he envied slightly because of his orderly bachelor life, and the impeccable taste which was as evident in his conduct in relationships as it was in his books, records, and the decor of his apartment in the West Eighties, which Hobbes liked to think of as 'The Firebird Suite.'

There was but one flaw in the order of his life, and though everyone knew of it, and sometimes Ketcham himself would make references to it, it was never discussed, because like all people who are reticent about themselves, he gave other people a feeling of uneasiness that only extreme delicacy on their parts could annul.

This flaw was Bianca. It was well known that they had been engaged just before she met Agatson. With Agatson, that engagement and Bianca's feeling for him had gone out of his life. He had no other women, still visited her regularly once a week, and, though he was an intellectual, modern young man, allowed himself the old fashioned virtue of being true to her despite everything, uttering no reproaches, and even endeavoring to get along with Agatson, whom she continued to adore even after he had thrown her out.

But now Hobbes set Ketcham's mind at rest in a light, bantering tone: "You know how Gene is. He gets all involved in these things and they have to run their course. Christine will probably come to the party and you can meet her then."

"I don't think she should come," Kathryn said. "She wouldn't like it at all. She's not used to the kind of people who will be there. Look at the way she was at Stofsky's party!"

"What do you mean?" Ketcham asked suavely. "She can't be more attractive than you." His charm was natural, and he was always thoughtful and attentive with women.

They met Pasternak in Freeman's and he was standing alone at the bar among the throngs of Lesbians that habituated the place. They ordered beer, and the thick, tense atmosphere was so contagious that they stood watching everything, unable to concentrate on each other.

The Lesbians were in couples, the "men," brutal, comradely, coarse; wearing badly cut business suits and loud ties. The "girls" were carbon copies, except for long hair and dresses. The bar was filled with raucous jokes, back slapping and the suck of cigarettes. A few graceful, shoulder swinging homosexuals glided in from the street, mincing, chirruping and trying to rub up against everyone.

"Christ, let's get out of here!" Ketcham exclaimed with unusual heat. "It's horrible!"

They went and the trance passed from them, and Pasternak started talking excitedly.

"Say, you know, I found Winnie this afternoon. That's why I couldn't make it in to Christine's. She's holed up in a pad out in Astoria throwing her morphine habit; just like Verger said. He gave me her address . . . It's out in a huge, stinking tenement section, and there was this Tristano record going the whole time I was there. She *lives* to bop!"

"It sounds horrible," Kathryn interjected.

"No, she was lying on the bed when I came in. She'd had ropes on herself last week. Imagine that, she'd tied herself down! And we talked and then her boy came in. This simpering little guy, some petty thief or someone, who brings her milk and a Danish every day. His name's Rocco Harmonia, or something like that; but they call him 'Little Rock' Harmony! What do you think of that? And he said to me the first thing: 'You know, man, Win's just about got the Chinaman off her back!'"

"What does that mean?" Ketcham inquired, fascinated by all of it as long as it did not come too close.

"Coming off junk! Isn't that mad? She was throwing the Chinaman off her back!"

He was still talking when they wandered into the Santa Maria, an old Italian bar that was now the hangout for crackpot painters, writers and a few miserable existentialists. The flat lighting gave everything an underdeveloped look. The place was filled with nasty arguments. Bitter, cracked voices were raised on all sides. Lonely, soft chinned young men stood around in couples, watching everyone else, and a girl at the bar was berating two boys for what she called "the lust for absolutes." There was contempt in her voice, the same scathing contempt that rolled back and forth across the room. The boys, ill dressed bohemians who wanted to talk about art, had been involved in the subject of "absolutes" against their will and sat sullenly, only half-listening. Everyone seemed to be watching everyone else.

Fortunately, Pasternak was oblivious to all this.

". . . And I got this big letter from Hart too. You remember I told you about Hart Kennedy! Well, he's driving east with a buddy of his and should be here next week."

Kennedy was a wild young man Pasternak had met on one of his previous trips to California. He had regaled Hobbes with fabulous stories of marijuana parties and crazy driving in the mountains around Denver where Kennedy was originally from. Hobbes thought of him as a sort of half-intellectual juvenile delinquent, but had never been able to get a straight impression from either Stofsky or Pasternak.

"He might be here in time for the party because he drives like a madman—absolutely the greatest driver in the world!—and he says he's got a new Cadillac. He wrote me all about this tremendous orgy he was at with a lot of Negro bop men and hipsters—"

Ketcham, though amused and interested, wanted to move on

again, because the Village always irritated him. They strolled through the streets, just as a fine, sifting rain began. The bars were overflowing, music struggled with laughter. Angry people were trying to pick fights or get drunk. Young oily toughs were standing around in leering packs, watching the girls go by and hooting obscenely. Everyone traveled ceaselessly from street to street, dive to dive.

Washington Square, the trees already laden with rain, the arch hazed by a thin mist, was deserted but for a few couples sitting on the benches under umbrellas, thrusting with one another. Lonely, stoical old men, their worn corduroys soaked, crouched under the trees with sorrowful, lined faces.

They walked on and on, stopping here and there for beer, doing what they used to call, in the old days, "the grand tour of the Village"—now somehow unpleasant. Only Pasternak's enthusiasm carried them:

"And I'll get Verger to bring some weed to your party. He's gotten an oz. from a passer up on One Hundred and Twenty-fifth Street."

"Good," Kathryn said with exaggerated approval that caused the others some surprise. "I'm sick of drinking anyway. Do you think you can really get it?"

"Verger'll bring it along if you call him up."

"You do that, Paul. I've always wanted to smoke some, haven't you, Arthur?"

"Maybe it's the new taste sensation we've been looking for . . ."

They went to another place, a basement room with candles and war trophies, which was fashionable with an uptown crowd, and was now filled with motionless women in cool frocks and their inattentive companions. It was very much like a sad and unsuccessful cocktail party that had given up and moved to a working-class bar in the hope of inspiration.

"Why did you stand up Christine, Gene?" Kathryn asked brusquely. "She was phoning about it earlier."

Pasternak bunched his eyebrows, disliking the turn. "I told you, I was out seeing Winnie. I couldn't get in in time. But listen, you get Verger and his tea, and I'll see if I can round up Stofsky somewhere . . . I don't know where the hell he's gone this time! . . . But we'll have this mad, vast party on Friday, eh? The greatest party! . . . You coming, Art?"

"Certainly, but you're not going to bring this Winnie are you?"

"No, she'll still be on the bed. Besides, she's laying low these days. This character she's with, this Little Rock, he's got her all itchy about things. But I'll bring Christine, how about that?" He looked from Kathryn to Hobbes.

"Sure, Gene."

"I don't think it's a good idea at all, if there's going to be tea! I'm afraid she's going to get herself in trouble with that husband anyway, the way she's going."

Pasternak sulked. "Christ, she's okay. Why do you always dream up these things?"

They let it drop and stood having beers silently. Pasternak's joy at having found Winnie and hearing from Hart Kennedy, who was a very important friend to him, would not be dampened, and when they broke up for the evening on Eighth Street, heading for different subways, he said:

"You remember, Paul, you said you thought a new season was about to break? I guess you were right!" And he ran off through the puddles.

"Now, Arthur," Kathryn said firmly. "You be at our place at nine, or don't you come at all! I don't want you coming in dead drunk!"

Ketcham replied evenly: "What do you mean? I never get drunk," which was not true, but this was a standard game they played. "Besides, I want to see *you* get drunk. You're always saying you're going to, but then you go home!"

Kathryn was decidedly affirmative.

"I'm going to get stinking drunk and let the party take care of itself!"

"That's the only way," Ketcham laughed, although he was always worried for days before he gave one. "Just let yourself go."

Two

It was a night when no manner of arrangement or calculation would have helped the party at all. As if an announcement had reached them by messenger, the young people gathered together, boisterous or hesitant upon entering, and thereafter touched with joy or expectation as the telephone pealed through the records and the talk. Some parties are like a ritual in which all the guests take part, and this was one.

To Pasternak, who had called early in the evening to say that he had picked up "three crazy Raskolnics" and was bringing them, the party was a sort of communal act, and being in a good mood he ran around between the groups, officiating. To the Raskolnics, who turned out to be indifferent young tea-heads, the attempts of others to mix and be genial demanded a rebuff as proof of initiation. One of them, Samson, a bohemian version of the muscle man, brooded by himself most of the evening, reading books or studying bop solos, while his girl, a toothy, serious child in sandals, feasted her dilated blue eyes upon him.

And to Verger, who surrendered to the feeling of importance that possessing marijuana gave him, the party was a secret riddle to which he had supplied the last line; although he was somewhat deflated by the Raskolnics because they also had tea, and acted belligerently casual about it as though they always carried "a few extra sticks."

Georgia had been telephoned by an impulsive Pasternak and came, wide-eyed as a naughty child sneaking out to meet a neighborhood gang of roughnecks. "This is going to be stimulating, I know it!" she exclaimed when told of the marijuana. "Who's coming? . . . And who's *that* person?"

Like a strange ambassador whose higher knowledge makes him absentminded, Stofsky arrived late, drawn and yet serene, and smiling loftily at everyone. He settled on a couch, a watchful mouse among blind cats, and when he went unmolested for a while, got up with an introspective frown, and just as Christine entered the door, looking as though she were coming from an unfashionable cocktail party, he climbed on a chair and recited a new poem which began, "I shudder with intelligence," and to which no one listened.

Pasternak introduced Christine around during this and matter-of-factly got her seated. When the poem was over and Stofsky, with a wistful smile, surveyed an indifferent audience bent on other sensations, and returned to the floor, Pasternak drifted away from her, back to the Raskolnics who were staring down their noses.

A few begrudging comments were made concerning when the marijuana would be smoked. "Let's go! Let's go!" Kathryn kept repeating, her cheeks flushed by the whiskey she had been drinking. Then she fastened onto Verger with impersonal persistence, until finally he pulled a slender cigarette out of his breast pocket, and acting unaware of the expectations of some and the apprehensions of others, he carefully lit it.

It was passed around by Pasternak, who gave instructions on how to "pick up" to Kathryn, and all sipped deeply. Hobbes, changing records in a fluster, avoided it that first round. But Georgia, who had never had any before either, started to jump about to the whirling music as soon as she exhaled the acrid smoke, believing the effect to be immediate.

"Is that really mary-juana, Paul?" Christine asked, speaking in a shocked hush. "Gene wants me to try it, but I don't want to take any *drug!* I didn't know you had any friends who took anythink like that! Gene's not . . . he's no addict is he?"

"Go ahead, Christine, it's harmless. It's not really a drug at all." But he left her so she would not see the timidity in his own eyes. She went into a corner and fell into conversation with an observing, speculative girl no one seemed to have brought, named Estelle, to whom none of the gigglings and foolishness of the party appeared unusual.

Kathryn was gulping whiskey and sucking the sticks of tea, and Hobbes, across the now hazy, crowded room, watched her getting drunk. The party lifted off the ground. Three or four anonymous, corduroy-jacketed students arrived to talk monosyllabically in a little clot and eye the others darkly. A fat Chinese poet by the name of Anton filled the door once, ogled all the girls and immediately began to dance awkwardly with Georgia who was, by this time, in a sort of ambulatory swoon.

The room filled with an almost invisible smoke; Pasternak had insisted upon closing the windows so none of the tea would escape; and within the tapestry of voices and the turbulent rise of the jazz, there was the sipped inhale of many breaths as stick after stick circulated. Pasternak, holding one to Hobbes' lips, shouted at Kathryn: "Stop drinking that whiskey! They don't mix!" But she kept gaily on.

Once Samson approached Hobbes furtively and said: "What do you do with your roaches?"

Hobbes' head was spinning. "We can't get rid of them. We've tried every—"

"No, I mean your butts!" His thick, phlegmatic face pinched with disgust. "Your butts of tea!" And he held up a sorry, shriveled stub. Hobbes got him a dish to put it in, mumbling in his confusion, because he had not known that all the remains were assiduously saved to roll more cigarettes. Samson went away and smoked with cynical nonchalance and would not even lift his eyes from the page he was reading when a stick was passed in his direction.

Christine, with alarmed eyes, moving uncertainly about among the babbling congregations trying to find a friend and staring crossly and sadly at Pasternak who went on and on, rushing from group to group with cigarettes in his hand. She huddled with Kathryn for a moment, as though believing her disapproval was infectious, but she did not find a dissenter there.

To Hobbes, who took more and more of the tea after the first drag or so seemed to have no effect on him, there was an illegal and surreptitious air about everything that thrilled him. He threw away whatever hostly compunctions he might have felt in the beginning, and wandered about after the cigarettes. A detached, pleasant pulsation set up in his head and the weedy taste disappeared from his mouth, and his personality seemed to flow away from him without damage. He watched, unmindful, as glasses were overturned by dancing feet and piles of books swept under tables. An hysteria of stimulation seethed in the room and everyone's voice rose imperceptibly in pitch. The phonograph was turned louder, and Hobbes stood near it, laughing happily to himself at what others were doing, considering it very revealing, and yet aware that his thoughts were segregated from one another, and any consecutive train gone. There was only a restless elation.

"What's wrong with Christine, Gene?" he asked once.

"Don't talk to her! You know, she's mad, and I swear she's

turning into a bitch. What the hell is wrong with tea anyway? Just let her alone for a while."

Ketcham finally arrived, with a quizzical, scrutinizing expression on his face, bringing the wife of a friend of his, Janet Trimble who was pretty, somehow feathery and in a flurry of vexation as she took the drink Hobbes brought, and turned her level eyes on the cavorting people as though they constituted a menace.

The noise and smoke and exhilaration seemed to have risen like freed balloons, carrying everyone with them as though they clutched unseen mooring ropes. Any worried helpful efforts that had been made to keep things going ceased, and after a while Pasternak disappeared with Christine. At which Kathryn whispered breathlessly to someone: "He's taking her to the subway! She's mad as hell, just as I knew she would be, and I even heard him tell her to shut up. Ugh! These filthy, tense relationships! . . . Where's that last stick?"

More people came up the stairs and were so immediately lost in the crowds that they might have come, stayed an hour, and gone away again without their once being noticed. During this, Hobbes found Ketcham at his elbow, saying: "My God, Paul, where did all these people come from? Who are they? You'll be getting a reputation for being Agatson's Uptown!"

And Hobbes whirled away, groggily pleased by that because Agatson and Agatson's parties were symbols of something after all (he could not quite remember what), and in his joy he tripped over the feet of one of the Raskolnics, who only grunted and moved out of the way with disdain.

In fifteen minutes, Pasternak returned, his face shiny with the rain that now pattered down into the midnight streets.

Kathryn pinioned him in the hall. "Is that the way you treat women, Gene? Football player! . . . She's just a stupid wop, and so you only take her to the subway, eh? What kind of a man is that!" She threw her arms about his neck wildly, and went on and on in this vein.

Hobbes came up to them, and she turned around at a dark look from Pasternak. Staring past Hobbes at someone else, she declared suddenly: "You can have him, Estelle! Look what I've got! A football player!"

Hobbes wheeled about and found Estelle beside him, her shoulders thrown slightly forward out of the draped green dress, poised perfectly, as she gave him a vague smile of understanding. He took her by the windows, which had been opened into the drizzly night, and talked foolishly out of his confusion. He heard her speaking with calm abstraction, but found he could not keep his attention from wandering.

"Why do I always choose impossible people?" she asked no one, although he thought wryly that he heard calculation in her voice.

Kathryn was kissing Pasternak now, and as Hobbes put on more records, he thought that she wouldn't be able to reproach him about flirting anymore. And then he forgot even that.

"It never happens this way," the girl was saying, looking at him with full, deep eyes. "Usually, it happens differently, the *other* before this. That's maybe what made me arrange it this way."

Hobbes had no idea what she was talking about, but like a missionary with an eloquent savage, he covered his failure to understand with smiling silence. He drank down a fumy glass of whiskey and turned up the phonograph again.

A deep, steady and yet languorous movement seemed to pervade all the people and their shadows on the walls and the walls themselves. Hobbes was blandly amazed by his ability to peer at it all, as if through some cloudy mirror, with no particular feelings. Everything seemed to glitter darkly, flashes of wild light bounded off glasses, the chatter and the laughter fused into a strangely languid buzz; Georgia's gestures became more angular, comic and somehow dear to him in their hypnotized release; and he fancied that he saw Kathryn slide into the bathroom with Pasternak, a block of light welling out the door, but he could not be certain. This added a sorrowful justification to his general inattention.

"The surprising thing is that you haven't kissed me yet," he heard Estelle say, as though he had suddenly broken in on some odd telephone conversation between unknown people. He looked at her artfully, not believing what he heard. She was smiling lazily at him, and that gathered his faculties.

"Should I? I can't really hear you, there are so many people."

She simply smiled more palely and waited. Kathryn—he could just see her through the smoke and the dim lights and the figures which thronged through both—had gotten into someone's raincoat and slipped out the door with Pasternak. Hobbes laughed idiotically at that, taking Estelle's small hand and pressing it hotly. He sat there in a blurring dizziness that would not turn to the cynical bitterness he longed for, looking out at everything through strange, clear eyes, all thought of consequences and perspectives vanished from his mind.

"I'll walk you to your bus," he said for no particular reason, wanting to put his face into her dark, short hair but feeling the eyes of Ketcham and perhaps the Trimble woman upon him, and realizing that they did not look down from the same cottony plateau as everyone else.

He pushed into the bedroom where the coats were and found Verger and Georgia lying on the bed, whispering to one another like improper children. Excusing himself with a formal word, he searched through the thick pile and found Estelle's plaid overcoat. Throwing it over her shoulders, they hurried through the bunches of people, stepping over two prone Raskolnics in the hallway. The disconnected phrases, the mechanical groaning of the record which everyone ignored, the creaking of the floor under gay abandonments, all muffled away when he closed the door.

The halls were damp and somehow neutral in their silence. Leaving the furor farther behind, Hobbes counted the stairs as they went slowly down, both suddenly constrained, aware that now they did not have the noise and confusion to bring them together.

Hobbes took off his glasses in an awkward gesture as they moved across the last landing, and then he put Estelle up against the wall crudely and, catching a tremulous, near-frightened hint in her eyes, he kissed her. When he came away, she stood there watching him with a fleeting, almost shy warmth. He muttered some words about such things being difficult to do gracefully for someone who had to get off their glasses first. At that she took his hand decisively and led him back into the darkness of a dusty corner where light never reached, and against another wall he kissed her some more. She didn't utter a sound, and both, as though struck dumb by some remembrance or trepidation or desire, thought of the actions of the other as proof of some elusive worldliness. Hobbes went on and on without real excitation, mildly astounded by the dream-like ease of it all and by his former muted worryings. Estelle melted against him with an almost impersonal resignation, and for some reason that pleased him.

After a while they went down into the street, which was full of the murmurous rain and the echoing whirr of cars. Everything was wet and lonely and close in the night streets, and the gesture which Hobbes had been dreading, the one that would detain her, came effortlessly and went. They walked amid the puddles toward Third Avenue, as if in this wet, harsh universe of the city their hands clasped together between them were the only warmth, and that city's dismal, rainy hostility reason enough for their mutual response. They went into a bar where Hobbes was not known. Later he remembered figuring it out with swift, passionless interest.

In a dark booth, he talked to her aimlessly and kissed her whenever he felt like it, and filled with gentleness toward her when she sat, speckled with silver drops, waiting and watching him. Occasionally she would talk mysteriously, and he never knew what she was saying but listened to her words as though their very sound was a source of joy to him. Every once in a while, she would put her hand against his chest lightly, with wonder, and then reach over and kiss him. He talked on and on, about nothing, as though observing some ancient, unbroken rule he could not question, and she paid no attention.

"What do you feel?" she asked finally.

"What should I feel?" He had not stopped to think, as in the vanishing of his self consciousness he had not stopped to push his rumpled hair from his forehead or lower the collar of his soggy jacket.

"Well, you should want to sleep with me for one thing."

"I guess I do," he answered with foolish seriousness, and after that they went back to the slow, wonderous explorations and were content not to speak.

He was feeling high and wonderful when they emerged into the desolate night once more. He took her arm firmly between his fingers and led her across the street under the dripping, shadowy pilings of the Elevated, and all he could think to say was: "You're strong, something strong I can feel. I'll bet you're a tennis player."

Failing to find a bus, he walked her to the subway on Fifty-third Street, and turned her around at the stairs, moving her whole full length against him. She looked at him with childlike obedience, her pupils wide, and reached for his hand and with a frightened tremor, held it against her breasts and then kissed his open palm that was spotted with rain, and then ran off down the stairs.

He hurried back, running in spurts and then walking slowly. He passed a few hooded people whose leashed dogs hesitated, like incontinent drunks, beside lamp posts or fire hydrants. 'If they only knew what's going on at my place tonight,' he conjectured happily. But even that made no difference somehow. He recalled Kathryn and Pasternak idly. Where could he have taken her after all? He did not know and so dismissed that idea as well. He bounded up the stairs, stepping gingerly over a spot where someone had vomited; and looking at his watch, he was surprised to find that he had been gone for over an hour.

     ✦   ✦   ✦   ✦   ✦

Everyone but Stofsky, Verger, Georgia and the Chinese poet had gone. The lights were out, an all-night bop program hummed out of the radio, and a single candle made a quivering finger of light on the table. The room seemed full of dusky subsidings, a shambles of butts, strewn glasses and books, the sad mementos of a carouse that had swept on elsewhere. Everyone who had remained was gathered around the table in a laconic group, rolling new cigarettes out of the collected roaches. The room, so suddenly emptied of its raucous life, rose dark and silent about them and when they spoke (which was rarely because the party's end had left them stranded in their own preoccupations), it was in low whispers.

Hobbes went into the bedroom with a sly wonderment in mind, and turning on the light he found Kathryn asleep in a crumpled heap of bedclothes, still dressed. He stood watching her heavy breathing dilate her nostrils, and in this unguarded moment thought of her abandoned behavior as an ironical tribute to his own ideas. She lay, as though held unwilling in the grip of sleep, and he rearranged her blanket, but she did not stir.

In the darkness of the other room, Georgia now lay beside a weary Verger on one of the couches, bundled among pillows.

"Kathryn passed out after she threw up," she said dully. "We carried her into bed. Is the radio too loud?"

He shook his head and sank down beside Stofsky, who sat cross-legged on the floor, trying to read a book. And as though the gloom and the silence had brought back such meditative things, Anton lay bulkily on the other couch, sipping tea and muttering something about Browning to himself, while his dark eyes rolled up and down and his belly quivered with tiny snorts of laughter.

"You didn't smoke tonight, David. How come?"

Stofsky gazed at the ceiling with airy mysteriousness.

"I've got something else now."

Hobbes knew vaguely of Stofsky's investigations of drugs, knew he had tried them all with eager experimentation a year or so before, and had even filled two notebooks with records of reactions and imaginings while under their influence. But now he wondered what it was he "had."

"God," Stofsky replied with a significant pause, pointing above him dreamily, his eyes somewhat sardonic. "And I've had visions, you know!" He laughed with embarrassment, ridiculing his remark, because no manner in which he told of his experience could contain the awesome feeling he had been holding in all evening. "That poem I recited—'I shudder with intelligence'—was written soon after them. It was an attempt to evoke mystical phenomena . . . or . . . But, you see, I've been thinking about death for a week, and I've come to a few conclusions . . ."

"How did it go again? The poem?" Hobbes answered, trying to fasten onto one of the fragmentary thoughts that drifted through his mind, and thinking of "visions" as more of Stofsky's exaggerated vocabulary.

"It's not one of the best, although some of the lines have pivotal images I'll use again . . . But it ends like this," and his voice was soft and sing-song:

> "I shudder with intelligence, and wake
> Beneath a deeper stare,
> To hear a beast we cannot slake
> Devouring without mind.
> Impossible to me, that glare,
> And mortal, watching there,
> Before the cosmos spins the eye goes blind!"

Hobbes nodded absently when it was over, for actually he was wondering where Pasternak had gone and how long Kathryn had been away with him. But Stofsky was not dismayed by his indifference; in fact, he did not seem to notice it at all.

"I went out to Hackensack, you see," he continued eagerly. "I called everyone up, but no one was home . . . Where were *you* when I wanted to talk to you about salvation, eh, eh? . . . But anyway I was frightened and I didn't want to be alone—like a wise man with tidings no one can understand!" And he snickered in his confusion.

But it served only as a short pause for he was dying to tell someone about his experiences, though fearful of a reproach if he seemed doubtful of them himself, so without further interval, he gave Hobbes, an unresponsive companion, a disconnected description of the "visions" and his days in Hackensack.

He had hurriedly written a note to Doctor Krafft which he posted before catching an early morning bus. It said simply: "I think it has started to happen. I have had extra-sensory experiences." As was typical of Stofsky, he did not mention, and barely thought about, the doctor's rebuff over the phone, and considered his failure to do so a tactful response to another's indiscretion.

When he got home, he announced to his father that he had had "visions," and when this brought forth little more than a psuedo-literary reaction, he appended, reckoning on its effect, that he was afraid he was going mad. His father rewarded him with the same sort of hysterical outburst that had seized him when, after several weeks of hesitant feelers, Stofsky had confessed his homosexuality. The two had an uneasy relationship anyway, at the bottom of which was mutual distrust, and when they were together they invariably squabbled over philosophical matters or Stofsky's "evil companions of the city" (as his father called them).

Roused by what he considered his father's bigoted shock at homosexuality, Stofsky had said: "But do you just want me to shut up shop sexually? Help me to get over this 'horrible sickness,'" and he savagely aped his father's tone. "Should I become a stuffy schoolteacher in a small town and strangle in Rotary affairs?"

"Yes," his father had screamed at him. "Yes, sublimate, sublimate! Anything's better than . . . than seducing little boys!" That had ended the discussion.

Now his father talked heatedly to him again about his "wild life and his malady," and they bickered once more, one threatening and the other protesting, about the validity of the "visions." Stofsky was frightened, but his father's antagonism soon led him to defend the "visions" wildly.

He sat most of the first day, staring at a peeling wall in his tiny bedroom. He went over the experiences minutely and, as he brooded and speculated, attached further levels of meaning to them. His father came knocking at his door every few hours, shouting and pleading: "What's this? What's this? Why won't you come out and eat like a normal boy? . . . Damn your mother! Do you hear that? Damn the day you were born!" Stofsky ignored him and sank deeper into his thoughts.

The next morning he called Krafft at his office. The conversation was short:

"Did you get my letter?"

"Yes."

"Then may I see you?"

"I don't feel it would have any value at this time."

The very brevity of it lessened the impact of the refusal, and Stofsky went back to his books and his musings with no anxieties. He had ceased to *fear* the doctor, he instructed himself, and thus he did not *need* him any longer. His father kept questioning him, scolding him, begging abjectly for him to "come to his senses," but finally he left him alone. After two days of this, a card from Pasternak inviting him to the party gave him the impetus to leave.

He told of all this with an agitated tone of self-derision which did not disguise his earnest sincerity.

"You see, I've decided that death is only the end of the dream, but more important . . . suffering is just the moulting of the ego! Do you see? The monster disappointed to discover he's only a runny-nosed little boy! But mainly, it's love, you see . . ."

Hobbes hardly heard any of this because, during Stofsky's report, he had been overcome with sleepiness and was using all his attention to contend with a somehow undesirable, but powerful, fatigue.

". . . And I came to many more remarkable decisions about what I should do next . . . a sort of campaign platform in fact. I've even formulated a mystical slogan for myself!" He tittered at the thought, watching Hobbes closely. "The way to salvation is to die, give up, go mad! . . . To suffer *everything* to be! To love . . . well, ruthlessly!"

When Hobbes gave only the vaguest of laughs at this, Stofsky broke off and then said: "But . . . but now, we'd better leave, eh? Don't you think?" And he got up with the playful civility of expression that signalized his mockery of himself. "We'd better go and let you get to bed. Look, it's almost five. Well, well! . . . We'll go on up to your place, Verger, or to mine if you want to . . ."

He roused the others, herded them out of the door, and said to Hobbes with gentle finality: "Thank Kathryn, will you? And give her a message of friendship from me."

The last human remnants gone, there only remained the dolorous atmosphere of dead smoke and stale air. As Hobbes passed through this into the bedroom, he tried to piece the evening together into some continuity so that he might remember it the next day. He did not pause to wonder why Stofsky had waited so long to speak to anyone about the "visions," a thing which, in the light of later events with which he was connected, was to seem decidedly odd to him. As he lay down, he tried to remember what Estelle had looked like, what he had felt when with her, anything about their time together. But it had all hazed over and seemed even more unreal somehow than the things which Stofsky had been raving about. Upon realizing that, Hobbes felt a certain respect for the marijuana.

Hobbes woke up groggily at eleven to find a dismayed Kathryn surveying the fantastic disorder of the apartment which, in the harsh glare of day, assumed a chaotic spontaneity that only hours of the tipsy comings and goings of many people can create.

"Where did you go?" she asked guardedly, as though the wreck was too complete for any comment to cover.

"After you and Gene went out, I took that girl, Estelle, to her subway and then walked around for a while. My head was spinning. How do you feel this morning?"

"Horrible. But not hungover somehow, sort of empty." She was pale and shaken with the morning and tried to elude his gaze. "I can't remember beyond a certain point. I had on somebody's coat and then—"

"Tea doesn't leave a hangover, that's probably why. Do you remember vomiting on the stairs?"

"Yes, I'm mortified. What will everyone think of me? Everything blacked out right after that." She poured coffee and lit a second cigarette. "But then there was no one here? For Ketcham and that Trimble woman? . . . God, I'll never be able to face them again!"

"Why? It was a good party. Everyone seemed to have a fine time, and Ketcham even said that it was getting like Agatson's uptown."

"Was I very drunk, Paul? I kept smoking those cigarettes, but nothing seemed to happen . . . Never again! I can still taste them. Do you realize that's one of the first times in my life I've ever thrown up?"

"That was the whiskey. Don't worry about it."

She went about the cleaning without the usual anger. She did not blame him for the mess, feeling herself too guilty of it for that, and sweeping and straightening methodically, as though it were a kind of penance. As was their habit they discussed the evening, comparing impressions, both unsure somehow until the composite picture had been built. When Hobbes mentioned seeing her go into the bathroom with Pasternak, she was surprised.

"I did not. I don't remember that at all."

He recalled his dizziness and the people who had blocked his view.

"You were pretty drunk by then," and at further denial from her: "Well, I can't help that, honey. I saw you. Christ, it doesn't matter, does it? You were having a good time, that's what counts."

"Yes, but I still don't remember it," and her glance was more apprehensive. "Gene was funny though. When we had drinks over at Mannon's, he kept saying, 'What's going on around here? Why are you here with me?' He was awfully confused, but he bought me another whiskey."

Hobbes said nothing because he was still amazed at the film of detachment which fogged around him.

"What was Estelle like? Did she have a good time? I didn't get a chance to talk to her."

"I guess she did. She had a lot of tea and so I took her to Fifty-third Street." It was not really a lie, he thought, for now the moments in the bar and the rain were no longer the least bit logical or important to him.

"What shall we do this afternoon?" For once the long, purposeless hours ahead, which she always felt had to be filled in some previously arranged-upon manner, were a harmless topic.

"Anything you want, honey. A movie or something."

He owed Liza a letter, and now there was much to write about and he would not have to sit, inventing splenetic or weighty sentiments to present the postman. But he felt no interest even in that.

They languished about in the dingy expanses of the afternoon lull, talking fitfully, as people talk who cannot say something they feel must be said. In another mood, Hobbes would have put on a light to combat the damp, dreary glow that filtered through the windows as the day muttered away. It cheered him usually, and expecting Kathryn to protest the waste of electricity always provoked him. But he was content to sit silently, letting his very immobility sustain the revolt of his body over the extra glass or cigarette and the too few hours of sleep.

"But what's wrong?" she asked once, almost pleading. "Is something the matter? Are you angry?"

"Nothing's wrong, honey. I'm just quiet, that's all. You know how I am after drinking a lot. Why? What do you think could be wrong?"

She was annoyed by the grandeur of his innocence. "Nothing, I was just wondering. But you haven't said anything for twenty minutes."

They sat, idly hinting, evading, pretending; wearying each other with feints and silences. Kathryn saw his every word as a hidden reprimand, and though Hobbes recognized that this made her hopelessly defensive, it was not until another hour had passed that he would give up the game.

"Look, do you think I'm angry about you and Gene? Is that what it is? You know me better than that. Don't you believe me when I tell you that things like that have nothing to do with marriage or love? We had a talk about infidelity, didn't we? So you were kissing him. I mean it, it doesn't matter to me! It's normal for you to be attracted to other men. It made me happy last night because you were acting freely, naturally. Now, is that what was worrying you?"

"Yes, I guess so. I was just wondering." It did not entirely set her at rest, although it assured her that he was not angry. He noticed this.

"I really meant it, honey. You don't want to be neurotic about such things . . . like Christine. And you know how much I like Gene."

So they talked about Stofsky, and laughed uncertainly together over his "visions," both feeling that in knowing such people and having such parties, new and unknown changes were entering their lives.

Four

Three days later, in another early summer dusk, Hart Kennedy arrived at their apartment with an eager entourage made up of Pasternak, Stofsky and a fellow called Ed Schindel, who had driven from the coast with him.

Hobbes had learned of their arrival in New York earlier that afternoon with a call from Stofsky:

"Yes, yes, they came around but I was out, so they left a note . . . Have they gotten in touch with you? I've been calling madly everywhere. They were at Verger's too, leaving notes . . . You see, I haven't seen Hart for almost two years, and now notes, notes, phantom notes and that's all!"

Soon after that, after Hobbes had tried to get back into the chapter he was retyping, and when that failed, to get off a letter to Liza which had still not been written, Ketcham had called to say that they had been at his place the night before; Hart, Pasternak, Schindel, and Hart's first wife, Dinah, whom they had picked up in Denver on the way from San Francisco.

Then Stofsky had called again, on his way to Agatson's to check there: "If they come or phone you, hold onto them until I get in touch with you. It's very important! Bye-bye," and he rang off to continue his restless search in all the various places in which his hopes located them, finally to meet them accidentally on Columbus Circle near an automat they had all frequented when Hart had lived in New York two years before.

When Kathryn got home, Hobbes excitedly told her of all this, and because her day had been relatively uneventful, she said with amusement: "Don't be so jumpy. They'll come here soon enough as it is. Don't worry about that!"

But, nevertheless, everyone stumbled during the first, awkward moments, except Ed Schindel, whose rangy height and flushed boyish face contrasted oddly to the small, wiry Hart, who moved with itchy calculation and whose reddish hair and broken nose gave him an expression of shrewd, masculine ugliness.

"Say, this is a real nice place you got here," Schindel said politely, shifting his Redwood of a body easily. "Yes, sir!"

"What do you think of all those books, Hart?" Pasternak asked, with an exuberant grin.

Hart nodded briefly, shrugging muscular shoulders. "Yes, yes. That's fine."

"My mother fixed us a big dinner, Paul," Pasternak went on, refusing to sit down. "That's where Dinah is now, washing clothes and stuff like that. You know, they drove all the way from Frisco in four days!"

"Christ," Hobbes replied uneasily. "That's terrific time. Was it a tough trip?"

"Oh, you know, man. We got our kicks."

Hart was the only one, but for the secretive Stofsky lounging in a corner, who was not blundering into uncertain formalities, but he kept moving most of the time, looking out the windows, reading book titles, tapping out clusters of pattering beats with his foot.

Hobbes put on a bop record, hoping it would relax everyone, and after only a few seconds of the honking, complex tenor sax, Hart broke into a wild eyed, broad grin and exclaimed:

"Well, yes, man, yes! Say, that's great stuff!"

He stood by the phonograph in a stoop, moving back and forth on the spot in an odd little shuffle. His hands clapped before him, his head bobbed up and down, propelled, as the music got louder, in ever greater arcs, while his mouth came grotesquely agape as he mumbled: "Go! Go!"

Hobbes wandered about nervously, feeling he should not stare at Hart, but when he saw Stofsky looking at the agitated figure with an adoring solemnity, he stared frankly with him, remembering Ketcham's description:

"This Hart is phenomenal. I've never seen such enormous nervous energy, and Gene gets just like him, in a kind of way. Hart and Dinah kept dancing and smoking and playing my radio all night. I didn't get to bed until six, and I was sure the neighbors were going to complain."

Pasternak sat next to Kathryn, both feeling a slight tension which led him to speak haltingly and without intimacy, and Kathryn to josh him boldly to cover her consternation. Each looked anxiously in Hobbes' direction, though talking about Hart.

"Really, he's tremendous," Pasternak said with dark belligerency. "Really . . . You know, at these bop clubs, Hart sits around and yells 'go, go!' at the musicians, but all the people around him are yelling 'go!' at Hart!"

"Sure," Ed put in with a meandering drawl. "He's real hung up on music. Everyone knows him around Frisco."

Hart was suddenly impatient, came up to Hobbes decisively, put an impersonal hand on his arm, and started talking rapidly.

"Now, we came over tonight, you know, to meet you and everything—Gene told us all about you—, but you see, we've got to get ten bucks somewhere to keep going. You understand, for food and things. Now if you can let us have it, that'll be great! Ed, here . . . Ed Schindel," and he reached for Schindel's arm without shifting his gaze from Hobbes, "he's getting a check, see. Back pay on the railroad where we were working in Frisco. Positively be here by Friday. So you'll have it back in just a couple of days. We've been everywhere, all of Gene's connections and everyone, but we couldn't raise it."

"Well . . . ," Hobbes stumbled.

"It's just a loan, see. We're just borrowing. You know, I've got my first wife along, and we've got to get located. You understand."

Pasternak had turned to Kathryn. "My mother gets paid on Friday, so we can get it back to you by then."

"All right," she said evenly. "We were broke just yesterday, but I got my check this morning."

"That's great!" Hart said, a brief, easy smile relaxing his lips. "Now, look, man, we ought to be cutting out," and he swung on Pasternak. "See if we can pick up Ancke on the Square. He's out of jail, isn't he? Isn't that what you said, David? Maybe he could get us a connection for some weed."

Stofsky slid into the conversation like a department head making a report at a board meeting.

"Verger saw him two days ago, right after the party, in fact. Ancke came in about four one morning, slept on the floor, and then stole fifty dollars worth of Verger's books. He said he hadn't had any junk for three months."

"He stole Verger's books!" Hobbes exclaimed.

"Yes, like a Tartuffe in rags! Two Oxfords of Dryden, and a complete set of Calvin and Luther . . . the English ones Verger got at school . . . He's probably lurking somewhere on the Square, Hart, trying to set something up . . . I've absolutely *got* to get hold of him."

"And that's a friend of Verger's!" Kathryn interjected with crisp candor.

"Oh, he's not angry with Albert, just sad about the Calvin. Ancke doesn't like to steal from friends, so he must have been broke and desperate . . . I once told him all about his stealing, I mean the real inner drama of *why* he steals, but he didn't take any heed. I guess I'll have to have another *long* talk with him!"

"Well, come on then," Hart said hurriedly, and with such impatience that it brought everyone to their feet before it was hardly out. "Now, we'll go down there and find him, see. Dig all the bars and that Riker's he used to hang out in when he was peddling. Maybe he'll know some real great pad we can get, too . . . Say, why don't you come along, man?" and he looked at Hobbes sharply. "Sure, come on. That's fine!"

Kathryn didn't seem to mind; in fact, she hoped that causing him no trouble about it would still her tiny remorse about Pasternak, who had remained at a distance from them both since their arrival, and so Hobbes left with them.

Hart drove the new Cadillac with a reckless precision, manipulating it in the sluggish midtown traffic as though the axle was somehow attached to his body. He talked steadily and yet managed, while cutting in and out of the snarls created by less agile machines, to lavish his attention on whoever else spoke up. While Stofsky amplified the news about Ancke, mentioning the robbery with serious concern, Hart's mouth widened in an intense smile, and he wagged his head violently, saying over and over again:

"Sure, sure . . . I know, man! . . . Yes, of course . . . That's right! That's right!"

Whenever they paused in the thronging light of street crossings, he would doodle on the dashboard with both hands, beating out little rhythms, his eyes continually sizing everything up. Pasternak would take up the beat on his end of the board, varying it somewhat. Hart would respond, the action seeming no longer just a time-killer but something secretly edifying and communicative. He would lean across Stofsky, who sat with coy confidence between them, and his round, sharp eyes would burn hotly at Pasternak and his hands pound on relentlessly. They would increase the beat, bouncing up and down in their excitement until the car rocked and people in neighboring ones craned out toward them curiously, and Hart would yell at each crescendo: "Yes, yes! . . . *That's* right!"

They cruised slowly down the block between Broadway and Eighth Avenue, and as they passed a Riker's, Pasternak leaped out of the moving car, shouting: "I'll cut in and look around and pick you up at the corner." He disappeared between two parked cars and was lost among the streaming crowds that flowed along in front of brightly lit movie theaters and amusement arcades.

At the corner of Forty-second Street and Eighth, Hart said: "I'll get it parked and we'll search the bars." They all piled out and he drove off.

Stofsky glanced absently around the busy corner with a strange, benevolent satisfaction in everything, sympathizing with all the rush and hurry, but not approving of it in his present seriousness. Ed Schindel gazed every which way, not afraid to gawk, as though this was the axis around which all else that he had ever known actually swung. And Hobbes stood nervously, looking up and down.

Pasternak hurried up to them, his head lowered furtively: "I couldn't find him. Where's Hart? We can try the Paradise."

And so, in a straggling group, they walked up the street to a large dark bar where they began many of their journeys in quest of one or another of their "underground" acquaintances; people who wandered around Times Square in its crystal night-time hours as though it were their preserve, their club, and their place of business rolled into one.

But Ancke was not there, and the five of them stood about, eying the collection of swarthy individuals who filled the place and drank and smoked with an indolence which somehow suggested a temporarily relaxed stealthiness. Everyone seemed to be observing the five of them with idle, professional glances, and Hart moved about the bar, as though efficiently inspecting some shady merchandise.

"Order just one beer," he said, and Hobbes did so uneasily. "Say, that cat's got tea!" he went on in low tones. "In the booth, with the fairies," and they all looked guardedly toward a simpering young man in a turtle neck sweater, who sat tightly squeezed between two other young men very much like him.

"Sure, man, that cat's *real* high on tea! Look at those big, staring eyes. Get that! Dig those hands. Why hell, man!" He was all but licking his lips with a kind of hungry, giggling anticipation. "Catch his eye, Gene . . . No, no, look, I'll cut back past him to the can, see. If he doesn't pick up on me, you do the same thing! You got it?" Like a harried but understanding manager, who inwardly feels he must do everything himself and takes a certain pride in the fact, Hart rattled out these instructions and then darted off.

Sure enough, after Hart passed him the young man in the sweater edged out of the booth and ambled toward the back of the bar in the direction of the men's room into which Hart had disappeared.

The bar was filled with the drone of low conversation, and while they waited the beefy bartender waddled crossly up and down behind the counter mixing drinks for newcomers. Hobbes looked apprehensively toward the doors, outside of which flowed the myriad, flashing lights of the street; the gay, cool groups of chattering high school girls, and the constantly preoccupied, nattily dressed little men, inevitably sucking on cigarettes as if their last, and padding along, hatless, on guard.

Those doors swung with quick, oiled swishes and anyone might walk through them. But once inside, the hazy dimness, the jukebox which (as though part of a wry satire) ground out the same optimistic show tunes that spun in other bars, and the blank barrage of dozens of calculating eyes: all this bespoke some deeper, more essential community of those who drank and waited here night after night, than could be found in neighborhood bars elsewhere in the city. Snatches of aimless talk between two slick haired drinkers, the affected gibberish of a dwarfish fairy who could barely reach his glass atop the bar, or the occasional surly snarl from someone who would have been considered merely drunk elsewhere all seemed heavy with hidden meanings. While waiting for Hart, the other four peered about, like children who have been told not to stare at a relative's eccentricities.

Hart was back. "Let's cut out. No, he didn't have any left. Oh, he was high, okay . . . and he said a friend of his is coming in later—his connection, I guess—but, hell, we can't wait around for that. He wants two bucks a stick! What a drag! He gave me the address of a guy that peddles goof balls, though, but kee-rist, who wants to get hungup that way? Hell, no, man, none of that goof for me! Not any more! But, come on, we'll dig Lee's for Ancke . . ."

Moving down Forty-second Street in a restless platoon, they darted into bars and coffee stands and penny arcades, Hart deploying them with quick, enthusiastic commands, and pausing often to comment joyfully on the sad ragged drunks who wove weary figurines down the pavement; or the flushed, wet mouthed old men, who stood quivering, heads thrust avidly downward, before stereopticons they painfully cranked, as though unaware that others gaped at their lewd contortions with amusement, or uncaring if they were. The whole surging street glittered brightly with its countless, gaudy neons, as though it was covered by some vast roof of white light. Beneath it, the five vainly searched and finally wandered into Lee's, the huge, teeming cafeteria on the corner of Broadway, where steam tables fouled the air with a wild conflict of smells, and servers, presiding over them like unshaven wizards, imprecated the shuffling crowds indifferently, while the greasy, beardless busboys, like somnambulists, moved among the littered tables mechanically.

They got coffee, which Hobbes and Stofsky paid for because Hart did not want to break the ten, and then they gathered around one table against a sweating wall. Hart could not keep still and he and Ed jumped up and down, talking excitedly, digging everything. Stofsky drifted off with stern aloofness to get a frankfurter, leaving Hobbes and Pasternak fidgeting over the cups, unable to talk.

To Hobbes, whose gaze roved ceaselessly, the place looked like some strange social club for grifters, dope passers, petty thieves, cheap, aging whores and derelicts: the whole covert population of Times Square that lived only at night and vanished as the streets went grey with dawn. To all this crowded room, there was an underground urgency, as though it was some limbo in the night's wanderings, an oasis which all these people inhabited at one hour as part of their shady, secret routine. Hobbes recalled the early, golden dusk out the windows of the apartment, that had been alive for him with as yet unknown excitements. And now he sat, not sad though oddly unnerved, thinking to himself that here, two scant hours later, he was watching some confraternity of the lost and damned assemble. And yet somehow he was not repulsed, but rather yearned to know it in its every aspect, the lives these people led, the emotions they endured, the fate into which they stumbled, perhaps not unawares. He longed to know it all, and for a moment hated his own uneasiness while sitting there.

Pasternak was still moody and would not take a cigarette when Hobbes offered him one.

"I was depressed for three days," he began abruptly, not looking up but obviously very serious. "You know that, Paul? I sat for three days at home, thinking about friends, and why I was a writer, and even why I was alive and everything. And about death and other enigmas."

"David must have told you about his visions."

"Sure, isn't that crazy? Hearing Blake that way?" And he gave a perplexed laugh, shaking his head slowly. "But it was really Hart who got me out of it. And my own pride. You know, I brooded about it for three whole days. Why, I even wrote big dialogues in which I asked people what it meant—"

"What what meant?"

"Oh, life and everything. You know. This whole thing with Christine got me thinking. But in these dialogues I ran around yelling: 'What are we going to *do* about it? We've got to *do* something!' Like some silly Myshkin . . . But I said, 'What am I trying to write for? Why do I think I can win love that way?' It's just another justification I'm attempting . . . for myself, for my existence. When I wrote the book I was bitter, full of concern and everything. But you know, Paul, all that's hassles, complaints we make about life, which is really magical and crazy and nothing more."

"Well, the writer's job is to find out why, isn't it? There's nothing wrong with that, it's decent work."

"But that's another bitterness, a complaint, 'finding out why'! I think death is the only important problem, and it's really no problem at all, just a grisly amusement. You know what I mean? . . . So I've decided that life is holy in itself, life itself! All the details, everything. Just loving all things, all ways! . . . It took me three whole days. Oh, I wouldn't have committed suicide or anything like that. My pride always told me, what does it really matter? Only the holy details of life matter! Do you see?"

Hobbes bent forward eagerly, and yet also fearful lest Pasternak see his eagerness and draw back. "But what made you so depressed, Gene? I know exactly what you mean, but what caused it?"

"Oh, you know, I get like that every once in a while, everyone does. And, well, Christ, MacMurry's turned down my book, the bastards! After almost two months, they send it back with a rejection slip about paper costs and the risks of first novels! What do I care about all that! . . . But, you know, when I ran up to Hart, asking him, 'What are we going to do about it?' . . . Not the book, because that really doesn't matter, I've decided I wrote that for myself, my own soul, a sort of plea and nothing more . . . but death and the unsolvable mysteries of life . . . When I asked Hart that, do you know what he said? He said, 'Don't worry, man! Don't worry about it. Everything's fine, and life is only digging everything and waiting, just waiting and digging!' . . . And that's what he does. Look at him! Everything's perfect for him . . . Oh, he has his miseries, worse than ours sometimes, believe me . . . But he knows everything is perfect, and so it is . . . You remember Kirillov in *The Possessed?* The guy who couldn't stand ecstasy for more than a split second? Well, Hart's Kirillov, only he can stand it all the time, and all of life is ecstasy to him!"

"Well, forget about MacMurry's. Keep sending it out. You're going to get it published, and just because a few editors can't seem to understand a really honest book, don't you lose faith in it."

"Oh, I don't really care about it any more. Last night I told myself, while I was watching Hart, that I'd have to choose between the drawing rooms full of Noel Cowards and the rattling trucks on the American highways, that's all. I can't have both, and I might as well get used to it."

Amid the whirl and stir of the cafeteria, they sat talking of such things, alternately earnest and silent. Each was touchy lest the other might, at any moment, make some reference to the party or Kathryn, and each wondered how they might convey to the other that it did not matter, that it was to both (although they did not know it) a simple occurence, nothing more, and need create no void.

Neither saw, as they conversed, that Stofsky had attached himself to a ragged, shivering old man, whose soiled alpaca jacket hung around his shoulders like a shroud, and whose wispy hair straggled over a lean sorrowful countenance. His eyes wandered pitifully and so drunk was he that he did not know what to make of the intense, grave young man who ran back and forth between his table and the counter, bringing cups of coffee, guiding them to his quivering old mouth, talking all the time with words of encouragement, and occasionally laughing to himself. But Hart and Ed, who had covered the place thoroughly, did notice and came up to him.

"Say, look, let's cut out of here. Ancke's not coming and nobody's seen him. I talked to a guy over there but he didn't even know he was out of jail. He used to peddle with Ancke out in Chicago. Imagine that! A real beat character!"

Hart, once more bent on getting things organized toward a

common objective, was not curious about the old man on whom Stofsky had been fastening himself. "Come on, we've got to get some *stuff*, man! Don't you know anybody who might have some? How about that cat up in Harlem? Or this guy Verger?"

"Ask Gene about Verger. I don't think so. Go ahead, I'll be right with you." He leaned closer to Hart eagerly, whispering so the drunk would not overhear. "This old man's a beggar, you know that! And he knows a-l-l about grace! Do you know what he just said to me? 'Everything's getting better all the time!' Just like that . . . But go ahead, I'll be right over . . ." And he turned back to the confused old fellow, and exclaimed weightily: "Grace is come by works and deeds, though . . . But then, of course, *you* would know that. Would you like a cruller or a Danish or something?"

Pasternak was sure Verger would have no more marijuana and they all stood about mulling the problem, Hart making endless suggestions with such restless energy that Pasternak seemed loath to point out that they would lead nowhere. Hobbes, who cared little whether Ancke was found or tea procured, watched Stofsky saying goodbye to the bewildered old man.

Then he rushed up to them excitedly: "Gene, Gene, that's what we must become! Beggars on Times Square! As soon as I saw that man I knew he was on the bottom, looking up, noticing the sky at last! I asked him, 'What does it feel like to be Job?' and he said, 'Everything's getting better all the time!' "

He could not resist the snorting, feverish laugh that beat in his throat, but then, seeing that the others were disinterested, he checked himself for a moment, and then began in a totally different tone:

"But there just might be a chance, about that tea, that is if you want to cut up to Columbia. I've still got a mailbox in my old dorm, and Will Dennison—you remember old Will Dennison from New Orleans, Hart—well, old Will Dennison wrote me a big letter last week and said he was sending along a can of Orange Pekoe and he hoped I'd enjoy it . . . So we might try up there, although he's never sent one before even when he said he would . . ."

"Well, come on, man! Why didn't you say so before? Yes, that'll be fine! We were going to stop in and see Dennison on the way across, see, but we didn't because I thought he'd be in jail or retired or something, you know? But come on, let's ball up there and take a look in that little box of yourn!"

They roared up the West Side Drive at eighty miles an hour, anticipation bringing silence. The river-girdled length of the island slipped by them and the George Washington Bridge up ahead hung across the dark throat of the river like some sparkling, distant necklace.

At one point, Hobbes asked Pasternak if he had seen Christine since the party, and Pasternak tightened, as at an unpleasant reminder, and said "No." Hart was curious about her.

"So you're getting a steady piece now. Well, that's fine, man! There's nothing like a big dull routine stretch of laying once in a while, you know what I mean?"

Presented in this light, Pasternak, who had been half afraid that Hart would disapprove, laughed nervously and agreed.

The streets around the University were soft with night and quite empty, and the car rolled smoothly through them to the dorm on One Hundred and Fourteenth Street where David had his mailbox. He got out without a word and vanished into the building.

They sat, itchily waiting, Ed watching out the rear windows. They joked irrelevantly, as though on some underground mission too crucial to be spoken about. There was a party going on in one of the dorms, and they could hear shrill laughter and dance music, and so peered up at the windows that were gay with light. Once a pretty little Negro girl rushed by the car, crying: "Bill! Ah, Bill, whyn't you come on back inside?"

Hart craned his head out after her, with a wide, appreciative grin, and called: "Listen, honey, I ain't Bill, but I'll do!"

"Here he comes," Ed drawled finally. "Yes, I do believe he's got a parcel. Yes!"

"No! . . . No!" Hart shouted with disbelief jumping up and down with joy and with his effort to see Stofsky coming; searching for a term to express his relief and excitement, and finding only a negative one strong enough.

They looked at the package while they sat there, but they did not open the Lipton's tea box in which the weed had been sent. It felt like almost two ounces, enough for a long time.

They whirled off, heading for Stofsky's place to smoke it. They flashed across town, cutting down one way streets, beating the dashboard and bursting into exclamations or song at every traffic light, like children released to the nursery after the ordeal of holiday relations.

"If you can let me out on Lexington, I'll grab a subway,"

Hobbes began. "I really should get home."

They all tried to inveigle him into coming along, but he was firm.

"O.K.," Hart said, assuming a smooth suavity again. "We'll cut on down to Fifty-ninth and drop you. Hell, you should come along though and blast with us! Sure! . . . But this way, there'll be more for us, right?" And he laughed at his own frankness, and then went on as though clearing up a loose end. "We've been all excited tonight, man. You understand! I'm not coherent anymore; I mean, in any intellectual way, see. But I dig you, I dig you going home and all! Yes, sir!"

Stofsky twisted around to face the back seat as they reached Hobbes' corner. "I'll be down to see you in the next couple of days, Paul. I'm thinking of looking for a job, you see . . . I'll be a big d-u-l-l working man, maybe on a newspaper or something."

Everyone was surprised.

"Yes, you see, I'm going to pay Verger back for those books," he announced to everyone. "I introduced him to Albert, after all, and Verger doesn't understand about his stealing. But it's really my debt."

Hart jumped out of the car with Hobbes and said, flashing a smile: "Sure, we'll be seeing you over the weekend, and we'll blast some of this tea, okay? We'll be around!"

And so Hobbes climbed his stairs, half regretful that he had not gone along, knowing that the new season had indeed arrived for all of them.

Five

"HART will get parking lot work, at which it seems he is very adept, and Dinah has experience in soda fountains," Hobbes wrote to Liza three days later. "They've moved in with Stofsky for now, and intend to take off for New Orleans in a couple of weeks. Over the weekend of the Fourth, there should be a big time and enough drinks etcetera to bring an end to dreaming." It was a long letter, describing them minutely and laden with his comments and reactions; an effort to transcribe his feelings of discovery which somehow failed, and so he wrote on and on about "this beat generation, this underground life!"

It was almost five when the phone rang. It was Christine.

"Gee, I'm sorry to bother you again, Paul." It was the third call in as many days. "But . . . but would you talk to me for a while? Could you? . . . I'm baby sitting at my cousin's, and I just got this awful feeling—"

"Sure, sure, what's wrong?" he replied, as if he meant 'Oh, no, don't; I've had such a good day so far,' and knew she would bring this illusion, so necessary to him, to an end.

". . . felt as though I wanted to kill the kids! Ellie's sleeping right here, and my cousin's little boy, and I feel like I want to kill them! Oh, Paul, what's wrong with me do you think, what's wrong? . . . I've been feeling so horrible—all dirty and confused—, and I haven't seen him for a week, he hasn't even called me or written! . . . But I don't care if I never see him again after what he's done!"

"Take it easy now, keep talking. What's happened?"

"He got me pregnant, Paul. That old gorgon-head. And when I saw him, I told him, and he said it wasn't him! What does he think I am to go around inventing? . . . So I told Max and made him believe it was him that did it, but—"

"You told him? What have you done about it?"

"Oh, I took something and it's okay now, but I haven't seen him, even once, since then. But what am I going to do? I want to put this pillow over my baby's mouth! Am I going crazy or something? . . . God, Paul, I never would have done this horrible thing if it wasn't for him! He doesn't realize what he's done to me. I can't understand what's happening . . . something *awful* must be wrong with me! What did they ever do, my little baby, and little Joe? What did Ellie ever do to me? And look what I've done to her . . . and now I want to kill her so she'll never know!"

"Relax, don't talk like that. I'll talk to you till it's gone. Just make yourself comfortable and tell me everything you want to." The drama of the situation seized them both at that. "Now look, do you love Gene, Christine?"

"Oh, I don't know, Paul. I thought I did. But I knew I was doing a sin. And I'm going to pay for it now! I deserve it all for what I've done to my kid and Max."

"Stop talking that way. If you were unhappy, unsatisfied, and had a chance to change it, why shouldn't you? Why? Why *shouldn't* you be happy? You mustn't ever look at it as though you've done something wrong."

"But it was, Paul. I hate myself now, and I hate him too. You can tell him that I never want to see him again. I wrote it to him in a letter, but you tell him that when you see him, all right? I want you to tell him how miserable he's made me, and that I don't *never* want to see his face around here again."

"Okay. But the important thing for you is to take it easy, and think it out calmly. You've got to try to remember and stop judging yourself. Listen now, wasn't it what you wanted . . . then? When it happened, I mean. Look at it that way."

"Yes, yes, I wanted that more than anything else, but—" She was shaken by the intensity of her own reply, but was driven by the weeks during which she had carried her emotions inside her, unable to speak them out to Pasternak because of the shy guardedness which love had brought her, and constantly fearful lest her husband suspect. "Oh, it was all right, but I was wrong to do it. Just for that. Now I feel unclean, cheap, like a damn who-er!"

"But what's happened has happened. It was what you wanted then and now it's over. It happens every day, Christine. Is it wrong for you to want to be happy, to take the chance, no matter what it costs? . . . If you've decided you don't love Gene, forget about it. What Max doesn't know won't hurt him. Look at it that way."

"Ever since that party, he was different, Paul. I think it's that mary-juana. How could I want to go with a boy that takes stuff like that, and thinks about things that way? And he hasn't even *written* me since then, not once! But you tell him I don't want to see him, that's all!"

"Look, Christine, you shouldn't believe all those things."

"Well, that's just the way I am. I tried to be like he told me, but he's just wild and childish and I don't really want to be like that. All I want is to get back to the way I was before I ever knew him. I want to stop hating myself for what I did, throwing myself at him that way."

"But don't tell your husband, you wouldn't gain anything by that."

"But I can't go on like this! All I do is think about it, I can't sleep. I think I'm going crazy or something. And I almost told him last night—"

They were like a distracted father and the child who, under neglectful eyes, has suddenly grown up into trouble but must trust him out of desperation. They spoke on, neither really believing that the condolements, the accusations, had accurate, dispassionate meaning, but listening for the other's answering voice.

"Listen, Christine, don't tell him a thing. Why cause yourself trouble that you don't have to go through? And think of what it'll do to him."

"But I can't stand having done this behind his back! Oh, he's quiet and unaffectionate and everything, Paul, but he's a nice boy. He can't help the way he is! And he don't deserve having this going on behind his back! I want to tell it to him, to confess it . . . Oh, I know he'll probably kill me or something, he gets crazy, but I deserve it! I knew I'd have to pay."

For the first time, Hobbes recognized how alone she was. She did not have the understanding friends whose values would condone or justify her actions when her guilts arose, nor was she possessed of that intellectual self sufficiency which would enable her to rationalize and prevent them in the first place. She had been going about her household drudgeries, her outward routines unchanged for the brief affair that had perhaps meant for her all childhood dreams of freedom and love and hope come true, all bitter desires for an end of the inarticulateness of her marriage, the graceless apartment unlit with tenderness, the grief of her few thwarted years. But inside her, ravaging like some pet surprisingly turned monster, these soured dreams and yearnings had been loose, and now she could only ask questions to which there seemed no answers in her narrow knowledge of life.

"But you don't think there's anything serious the matter with me . . . my mind or anything, do you? I was awful afraid last night that I'd start screaming it out to Max. I couldn't help it! I didn't know what was wrong. I didn't know what it could be! . . . But, oh damn, here comes my cousin now . . . I'd better hang up! You tell him, Paul, will you? And don't think I'm awful! I was just afraid I'd do some horrible thing. Don't tell Kathryn about it, please! . . ."

And she rang off with a tiny sob.

"Damn her, damn her," Hobbes thought, feeling he had been cautiously playing her on the end of the line, and had, after an almost even struggle, lost her through some fault of his own. "Why does she have to be that way?"

Her refusal to see 'reason' seemed to signalize to him a deficiency on his own part, and he kept muttering as he strode up and down the room: "Why does she have to be so stupid, so goddamn stupid about it!"

Without realizing, he found himself sitting at the typewriter again, facing the unfinished letter which he had written, like so many during the last month, without a thought of Liza, but rather out of egoisms that needed a convenient release. The agitation Christine had unknowingly caused addressed these self centered thoughts to Liza once more, and he yanked the sheet out of the machine and stuffed it away in his desk with the other letters, like this one, that he had written but, gaining perspective because of some delay, fortunately not sent.

Kathryn heard his account of it with an almost maternal shake of the head.

"She'll tell her husband before she's through, you wait and see. Remember, I told you she wanted to suffer."

"But why does she have to be so foolish? She got something from it, that should have been enough! But I just couldn't explain it to her for the life of me!"

He wanted to escape, only incidentally for Christine, from the inevitableness of Kathryn's view, which she offered to him with such casual, womanly surety. Before it, as at the recollection of a past guilt, he, as a man, felt suddenly prey to all fleeting, mannish pretensions—a barren Adam confronted with his rib's fecundity.

"Well, she *is* a fool," Kathryn went on, like someone who is hardened and resigned might speak of a younger, tormented sister in whom they find too much of themselves to ever be gentle. "How could she change her whole life? Even if she wanted to. And I don't think she ever really did."

Hobbes lapsed into silence, angry that such things should disturb him, and remembering that he had good reason to feel at last out of reach of other peoples' troubles because of the recent end of one of his own. For the day before, he had typed out, in final copy, the last chapter of his book and it lay on his desk in a neat white pile; the product of the germinations of more than a year ago, the reckless initial outbursts on paper, and then the slower, labored hoardings of further weeks and months until it stood, a wobbly, awkward structure, enough distorted in its separate parts to need a still slower, and more difficult, second draft.

The joy he had expected to feel, the sudden realization of freedom and the end of guilty worrying at idle time to which he had become habituated: all this failed to appear. He had not finished in one last, swift push to the summit and then over, but rather at a slogging, inching pace, only to look up, as it were, and see that there was no more to be done. But he could not manage to imbue himself with a sense of completion even when he walked about the room, the heap of papers clutched in his hand, hoping to derive from its very weight the import of the moment through which he was passing without what he considered proper emotions. Finishing the book released him to no indulgence, no time-killing that he had not given in to while writing it. But he sat down to Liza's letter, feeling he should take advantage of the leisure he had earned, even if he did not want to. And now, he told himself bitterly, Christine's phone call had ruined his first day.

Six

PERFORMANCES, assortments, resumés: the weekend of the Fourth was made of these. Everyone's enthusiasm rose continually during the two days, as if they all cherished in their heart's privacy some extraordinary memory of the holiday, long since considered infantile but still capable of evoking for each the hot, lost forenoons in all their American hometowns.

Then, the box of fireworks had been carried out into the street to be set off in a lavish squander, which consumed everything before the day lengthened into green afternoons and parades, and forced them to be content thereafter with what hungry ecstasy could be gained from the detonations of others.

These buried memories rose in everyone's mind, and as though each was secretly intent on recapturing or reducing the recollection, the simplicities of noise and chatter invested them, and they became as babbling and foolish and imaginative as children.

There was something fortuitous in their gathering, without previous arrangement, on the fretful, rainy Friday night when they tore up to Verger's in the Cadillac. Hart dashed about, helping Kathryn into her raincoat; and then grasping Dinah about the shoulders gruffly and ogling her, he exclaimed: "Lotsa weed tonight and crazy music! You dig that, woman?"

She laughed with an intimate twinkle in her large blue eyes, with a glance that assured him of her appreciation of his attention, but his words meant nothing to her; in fact, neither of them believed in words, and only used them to hint at some inexpressible thought. Then Dinah turned to Kathryn, establishing a secretive, womanly air as easily as she had just acknowledged Hart's masculine joy, and said:

"You fix up your hair like that all the time? It looks real cute on you. But, you know, I feel all funny in this ol' dress. It's all we brought along though. They kidnapped me out of Denver without giving me even a chance to pack anything!" Then they were off into the wet lights and snarlings of the midtown streets.

Verger's damp, bare rooms were permeated with his feeling

of exclusion from possible celebrations that were going on elsewhere. He lay, sprawled weakly on one of his cots, among bookish refuse. The others with him, Ketcham and a brittle, arrogant girl called May who lived next door, could not raise him from his depression, and, as if to remind them of their continuing failures, he would cough raspingly every few minutes, hunching his thin body and then falling exhaustedly into the pillows again, and say no word.

The sudden influx of Hart, Dinah, Kathryn, Hobbes, Pasternak and Ed Schindel who, because of the excitement of the dash uptown, did not recognize his mood, brought him to his feet with a self conscious, hacking laugh to rustle among plates and tin cans in the kitchen for glasses.

The radio was turned on, angular shadows danced in the top corners near a chipped place in the ceiling through which the ribs of the building shone whitely; laughter echoed, then filled the crowding silence.

Kathryn sank down beside Ketcham, who said: "Thank God, you've come! It was getting awful and I was just about to leave. She's been insulting him for an hour, and he wouldn't say a word. He's like a lovesick schoolboy with her. Yes, with May! . . . But you know, I called you two yesterday, thinking the three of us could have dinner, but I couldn't get you in." His relief made him unusually warm.

Dinah stood, between kitchen and living room, eying not so much the furnitureless apartment with its creaking, worn floors and its dreary unpainted walls that were scarred with old holes in which decades of portraits, calendars, snapshots and saints' pictures had hung, but surveying with watchful, pleasant interest the first clusterings of the others. Hart, who somehow usurped the hostly functions wherever he went, was speaking excitedly to Verger at the encouragement of Pasternak, while Ed, who dwarfed the room, smiled with self effacing benignity nearby.

Dinah, a slim, fresh, pale eighteen, was pliant and yet fragile, a self-possessed bluebell of a girl who gave those around her a certain intangible security by her presence. She had a comradely, direct gaze that was bestowed impersonally on all but Hart. She seemed a wise child, without confusions, utterly wrapped in the moment's developments but distrusting analysis of them, and aware only of the look and gait and mood of others. Her oval face glowed with a feeble, girlish flush, and her wide eyes calculated upon life attentively.

Now she chatted with the affected May, who answered in a shrill voice:

"Oh, yes, I'm living next door with a girl friend, you know. I really don't mind the neighborhood because I think everyone should have their year of bohemianism—although, of course, my mother would be horrified if she knew I was living in Spanish Harlem. But I suppose all mothers are that way, don't you think?"

"We're looking for a place," Dinah replied with an affable calm as though she had somehow evaded May's affectations. "Do you happen to know of one? We're staying with David right now, down on York Avenue . . . David Stofsky. But we can't stay in his pad permanently. I've got a job in a Rexall's starting on Tuesday, so we'll have enough cash."

Verger brought whiskey, which Dinah declined sweetly with this: "Oh no, thanks, I never drink any more. Two years ago I was real lush and drinking a quart a day, but I don't pick up now. I even tried to kill myself once." It was no confession, no effort to impress, but simply a friendly remark as she said it. Verger hovered near May for a moment, watching her with sad tenderness, blind to her foolish words and flighty gestures, a patient sorrowful adoration on his face which she ignored expertly.

At that moment, announcing themselves with a muffled rumbling through the halls, Agatson and a disconsolate crowd appeared, only half of them coated against the rain. The others were soaked and Agatson, in the tattered, shrunken pair of blue jeans and turtle neck sweater, looking as unshaven and fierce as a thirsty Portuguese fisherman, shouted: "Is everyone drunk around here? Who are all these people? Who lives in this joint? . . . Ketcham, what are you doing *here* of all places? Bianca was asking about you just last night, yes, yes! I told her to shut up and stop being sincere! . . . Is anyone real drunk? . . . I just walked up the street on the car-tops, and hit only one convertible!"

He was with a Village crowd which, like so many others that night, had come together accidentally and set out restlessly wandering to find themselves in Verger's desolate neighborhood by the river. Now they straggled in and out of his rooms, poking suspiciously into everything, grabbing unguarded glasses and going at the liquor.

Verger was overwhelmed, and as nervous as he always was when Agatson was around, and sat on the floor amid the feet, drinking and coughing. Then, pushed into a corner by their comings and goings, he huddled with an old, rusty long-sword which leaned there like the emblem of some deflated ideal he was reluctant to finally bury. He stabbed at the floorboards with an ironical fervor, not caring how they cavorted among his precious books, but only peeping at May occasionally and, finding her intent upon the tousled and raucous Agatson, returned to his chipping with renewed introspection.

Time withdrew and their excitement flourished. Hart gathered Hobbes, Kathryn and Pasternak together and herding them into the bathroom with Dinah, extracted a stick of marijuana from his hip pocket.

"O.K.," he exclaimed as though someone had ventured a question. "We'll pick up in here, see. There isn't enough for anybody else so there's no use broadcasting it, is there? You dig what I mean? Just cut back in here once in a while and we'll light up real cozy, okay?"

He lit the cigarette, giggling and laughing and talking between puffs, then held it to their mouths one after the other. Dinah closed her eyes ecstatically and sucked deeply three long times, holding her breath after each.

"Yes!" Hart broke out. "Yes, yes! Again, baby! Go ahead, another one! That's right!"

Outside, May was being pulled about by Agatson, his eyes burning viciously, in a formless dance. The music came from the same all-night program of wild jazz that midnight unleashed to all the city's hidden, backstairs pads where feverish young people gathered over their intoxicants to listen and not to listen; or hipsters woke, like some mute and ancient dead, to have their first cigarette of the "day." The night hours vanished before this music's bizarre imagery, until it finally evaporated into news reports at dawn like a demon turning into a tree.

Across the room from where Hobbes sat on a cot drinking, Kathryn drifted into Pasternak, who was bobbing regularly to the music.

"My God, Pasternak, don't you ever get tired of this noise?"

"What do you mean? Listen, that guy's actually *laying* his horn! You don't listen to it!"

"How the hell can I help but listen to it!" and she laughed scornfully and had some of his drink. They lingered together awkwardly, unable to speak in any but crude, sparring words, yet perilously joined by an unwilling curiosity and awareness concerning each other.

But now Hart and Dinah had started to dance, she clinging about his neck lithely with both bare arms, her head averted into his shoulder. He gripped her hips with large hands and moved her to him and away as though he had tapped a world of grace and abandon inside her and could direct it at will. Their feet hardly moved, but the rest of their bodies weaved rhythmically; she, lidded, trance-like as though in a swoon of dreamy surrender; he, unyielding, compulsive and yet also precise as he pressed her against his chest tighter and tighter.

The room's attention pivoted to them: Ed and Verger watching complacently; Agatson as though it were a clever diversion; Kathryn and Pasternak with an intent, yet somehow dispassionate interest.

May, however, frowned with disgust, shaking her head, and muttered: "Good God!" She searched the faces of the others for agreement, sure they would feel that the mysterious antagonism between the sexes, which she found exhilarating and necessary, should not be so willingly and simply dispensed with.

When it was over, and the others resumed their shuffling about in the weird light, Hobbes found Pasternak beside him, saying eagerly: "Isn't Hart terrific? And he's like that all the time! He doesn't care about anything! He yells 'go!' to everything, everything!"

"Sure, Gene, but the word for *that* is 'come!' not 'go!' Haha! . . . Come!"

If this was the wrong sort of answer, Pasternak gave no explanations, but lurched immediately away.

Time withdrew before the tide of saxophones that taxed the radio, now rising over the lunging drums in banshee screams which brought shouts from the dimmer corners, then skittering pell mell down some slope of melody as the rhythm broke on a wild, hard phrase. Trips to the bathroom and the weed, which never seemed to run out, made all sensation more fragmentary, bizarre, grotesque. People lay knotted together grimly, while others danced in stumbling gaiety, or fought their way to glasses. Talk capsuled into exclamations and laughter; the sense of having watchers around vanished from everyone's mind, and they wandered about, paired off, retired to corners, started conversations and abandoned them unfinished.

Hobbes hovered alone by a wall, dizzy from the drinking and the marijuana, and snagged in the senseless return of an old inferiority, cherishing a fond sadness as though he had perceived in all the chaos a deep vein of desperation which everyone else refused to notice. 'Out of what rage and loneliness do we come together?' he thought drunkenly, certain some obscure wisdom lurked in the question. 'Don't you ever ask yourselves why?' And he fancied, through his dizziness, that he was speaking aloud.

"What's wrong? Are you feeling all right?" a voice said in the din, piercing his monologue. "Is anything wrong?" It was Kathryn, face flushed with a half smile, half frown. "You've been scowling for hours, and I'm drunk as all hell!"

"Oh, *you* know," he replied thickly. "The ridiculous questions. What about me! How do I fit into this! . . . Humph! You know."

"Jesus Christ, why do you always have to get like that?"

"Well, go away then and have another drink. Go ahead. Where's the end of the night? That's all I was thinking. The whole long night! But go have a drink."

"We can leave whenever you want, but I thought you were having a good time. It was your idea." And she went away with irritation, before he could say that that was not what he had meant at all. So he sat there, knowing that the thoughts had risen in his head because he was dizzy and felt like vomiting, but not realizing that he had skilfully prevented both of them from recognizing this fact.

A commotion suddenly broke out near the windows. Verger, risen from the floor where he had been immobile most of the evening, stood, like a wheezing Golem, brandishing his sword wildly, and was methodically pouring the only remaining bottle of whiskey out the window into the rain. Agatson leapt up from the mattress where he had been thrusting with a disheveled May, and tried to rescue the bottle; but Verger, who endorsed temperance when he was drunk, let it go and there was a distant explosion of glass in the backyards below.

"Now why did you have to do that?" May was moaning thickly. ". . . very childish when you get stinking that way . . ."

As if to fight away some Calvinist Satan of his imagination represented by the tottering figure of Agatson, Verger started swinging the sword crazily, eyes aflame and a strange laugh twisted on his lips. Somebody roared above the radio, laughter screeched in the darkness somewhere, like the mocking of sharp beaked, unblinking birds; and then, at a furious swing which

Agatson made no effort to keep away from, the sword crashed through the window nearby, throwing Verger off his balance. As though a trap had been sprung, he thudded stiffly to the floor among the shattered glass, still weakly clutching his rusty weapon.

"O. B.! O. B.! O. B.!" Agatson chanted over his prone body, making a wild sign of the cross.

"A window's broken," Kathryn yelled in the kitchen. "Let's get the hell out of here before the cops come!"

And, as if this charade had brought something to an end, Hart gathered them all together around the sink and said: "We're out of liquor and weed, see, but there's this friend of Ketcham's here that knows a connection up in Harlem, so we'll cut up there to this after-hours joint he knows!"

So they all slipped away, joined by Ketcham and his friend, Ben, a smiling fellow with a smell of benzidrine about him, who loped down the stairs with them, making vague jokes in a midwestern drawl. As they went through the halls, the indifference of the colorless doors and the emaciated cats they found on every landing, and of all physical things, to their very presence, drove them farther into their hilarity.

❋　　❋　　❋　　❋　　❋

As though they were the creations of that night, it drove them, drunk and sober, towards the dawn, through a jumble of dreary streets to still drearier precincts, conglomerate with derelict houses where no light showed, that were fronted by bent iron railings, crusted and awry. The steady drenching of the rain made this Acheron of tenements appear more miserably squalid, and the car careened onward, Hobbes muttering, each time Hart swerved around a torturous corner: "Go! Go!"

They jerked to a halt just off One Hundred and Thirty-eighth Street and, leaping out, Ben leading the way, approached a darkened brownstone no different than its neighbors, where, gathering at the top of the stairs, they were greeted by a large, grave Negro, who smiled distantly as he held the door wider for them to enter, saying: "Good evening, gentlemen. Step right inside, just through that door . . ."

Beyond a room of sofas and ash-stands which had once been the front parlor, was a high ceilinged, drab hall, its windows tacked over with dusty black velvet, a bar built on one side and a scattering of circular tables filling the other. The room was crowded with people, mostly Negroes; the single drinkers at the bar, the parties squeezed around the tables. In the heavy yellow glow from a dim, crystal chandelier—a light as flickering and unreal as if it had come from tapers—an opulent Negro woman was singing, accompanied by a grinning guitarist in a sports shirt, and by an intense pianist, whose cocked head seemed tuned in on some wild poetry within the music which his dark fingers, spidering along the keys, endeavored to draw from the prosaic upright.

Amiably, Ben collected four dollars, managing to edge into a space at the bar, and ordered four drinks, all they could afford. No one seemed to notice them; the faces lining the walls were hot, placid, distracted.

The singer, stamping her foot three times, led off into a fresh burst of song, raising her arms in graceful supplication. "All of me-ee-ee . . . Why . . . not . . . take . . . all of me-ee-ee!" She started sliding between the tables, head thrown back, pausing at each with her hands expressively outstretched in appeal. The guitarist shuffled along behind her, muttering encouragements. Her dusky eyes leveled knowingly at each customer and, as though each saw there and heard in the music the memory they all must have attached to this rebellious and wistful American jazz which was somehow most expressive of the boiling, deaf cities and the long brown reaches of their country, at every table a dollar was pressed into her hand, and with a swing of generous breasts she would move on.

Hobbes, caught up in the living music, gravitated to the piano she left behind. At every fresh chorus, the ascetic Negro there released greater ringing chords, as though the increasing distance of the voice brought the inner melody closer to his poised ear. Hobbes, leaning toward him, was, through his giddiness, suddenly possessed by the illusion of emotional eloquence and started to chant softly, improvising broken phrases. The Negro glanced up for an instant, nodding abstractly, long gone, and with no resentment at the intrusion.

It was a room which day, and the things of the day, had not entered, perhaps for decades; and everyone there was aware of where they were, and of the illegality of it, and yet because of this and the sensual voice of the woman, still moving like some buxom priestess among them, they were caught up together.

Pasternak, against a wall where he and Kathryn stood close sharing a drink between them, exclaimed: "But it's all the same!

Everything's the same as everything else! Every *one!* . . . Bay-do-baydo-boo-ba! Can you hear it? . . . But look, look at Hart go!"

The singer was moving across the open space toward the bar and Hart, his head bobbing up and down and his eyes narrowed, was shuffling to meet her, stooped over and clapping his hands like an euphoric savage who erupts into a magic rite at the moment of his seizure. She watched him coming toward her, with dark experienced eyes, and for an instant sang just for him, her shoulders swinging on the deep strums of the guitarist who tarried behind, watchful and yet also appreciative. Hart stopped before her, bobbing, ecstatic, and then, falling down on his knees, he cried: "Y-e-s! Blow! Blow! . . . You know who you are!"; for this was his offering, all he could give. And, as if she accepted it in lieu of money, with a wave of her head, a bright wink at the crowd, and a great display of heaving bosom, she strutted on.

Dinah was smiling faintly, all this and much more being usual for her, allowing him to have it without a word as proof of her commitment to him at that moment. He could say nothing, but laughed hoarsely and took her about the shoulders. There was one more prolonged, incredible chorus, and with a last smile, the singer disappeared and the music was over. Having no more money and having come to some consummation, they all straggled out and into the car again.

Ben's connection had not showed; the sweet cologne fragrance of benzidrine about him and the discoloration of his lips suggested that there may have been no marijuana connection at all, but somehow that did not matter. Continuance was what concerned them, and where to go next. After a number of improbable ideas (places that would not be open, people who would not be up), they settled on a friend of Ben's, who lived on One Hundred and Twenty-third Street and Amsterdam Avenue, who would "surely have liquor." Although at another moment this would have seemed unlikely to them all, now they believed it with bland innocence as though all discord in the universe had been resolved by their harmony, which, in any case, did not depend on such details.

They rode as in a sunken city whose life is frozen in watery silence, they alone capable of breath and words, and finally pulled up before another dead house on another bleak street. But as if a morning premonition had touched them, and all felt for the first time a slackening, they groped down a long corridor in a centerless throng. They reached the end of it and went down a treacherous stairway into a dismal backyard, empty of all but garbage cans collecting rain, up two more steps and then, like movie spies taking absurdly circuitous routes, through a window with a broken sash, to find themselves in a chilly, enameled kitchen where people were blankly sitting, drinking coffee. Sensing hostility and leaving the amenities to Ben, they dispersed into the dark echoing rooms beyond, which were filled with incongruous furniture (the rightful refuse of country attics), and where a battered, caseless radio was buzzing softly. Refusing cold coffee coldly offered, Kathryn and Dinah locked themselves into the tiny bathroom, while Pasternak and Hobbes crouched outside. Hart and Ed, wordless and wet, played darts down a narrow hallway connecting these chambers, and finally, with only Ketcham and Ben feeling any embarrassment, they trooped out the window again, Hart calling back from among the cans:

"Sure, we understand, sure. You know, we just thought you'd be up, that's all. But say, if you see his connection, see, get an ounce or so for me. We'll cut by again!", all the time sniffing and chuckling to himself, until his words seemed almost a taunt.

They headed for Ketcham's, and the night and the rain had gone. Hobbes and Kathryn left them there, without excuses, withdrawing from exhaustion, while the others went on to the Magnavox, the quart of beer Ketcham hoped might still be there, and a continued resistance to their own sweet fatigue.

The wisdom of their search for some end of the night (the night that was a corridor in which they lurked and groped, believing in a door somewhere, beyond which was a place from which time and the discord bred of time were barred), the wisdom of this seemed to Hobbes, whose mood had changed again, one answer to the reason for being on which Stofsky had once impaled him. But his avowal, even of this strange thought, was motiveless and without intensity.

On the subway, Kathryn slept unashamedly on his shoulder as they sat among the denimed workmen with lunchpails and fresh newspapers, the hurrying, brisk little secretaries who would get their coffee and a Danish downtown and come fully awake only then, and all the other early riders who opened offices, relieved night porters and prepared machines for the first great, groggy wave of the rush hours.

At Seventy-second Street, a merry troup of Girl Scouts, on a hike that would bring them to a picnic's joys, filled the car with their eagerness and their starched scamperings from seat to seat. Some sat, large eyed, hand in hand; others chattered, craning about, open legged, reading all the advertisements to each other; and a little white socked Negro girl was laughing happily as she fiddled with her neighbor's pigtails. In his almost pleasant dullness, Hobbes thought suddenly:

"To be like them or like us, is there another position?"

Seven

At Ketcham's, at nine that evening, the center shifted. It was a night of conversations and accidental comminglings.

Everyone sprawled about the apartment, intent, like Ed, on a folio of macabre drawings by Otto Dix, or without interest for the moment, like Pasternak who slumped moodily in a chair, half listening to the Prokofieff Hart had put on the Magnavox with an experimental chuckle. Ketcham and Dinah cleaned the table of the dishes out of which they had just divided a lone can of oxtail soup. Hobbes and Kathryn, phoned by Pasternak when he awoke, arrived and were absorbed once more.

"You want a strip, Hart?" Ben asked genially as he carefully wadded a piece of benzidrine-soaked paper in a chunk of chewing gum. It was the last of his second inhaler of the weekend, each of which had contained eight strips. "Please go ahead, have one. I'm going out and get some more anyway. The druggist up on One Hundred and Fourteenth Street is getting really worried because I've had this bad 'sinus trouble' for the last two months, but he gives it to me just the same."

"No thanks, man," and Hart laughed firmly, clapping Ben on the back with a knowing grin. "I can't even stand the smell. Ugh! . . . I was real hungup on it two years ago, you understand—coked most of the time—but it drags me now. I get too jumpy, see, can't function on the stuff. Just isn't my kick . . . You remember, baby," he called over his shoulder. "Out in Denver? I was real flipped!"

"Sure, why he almost killed me one night, he got so angry and all," Dinah replied, wiping the table with a dish cloth. "But that was on the pills, wasn't it, Hart?"

"That's right. I was taking about twenty a day. Whew! But hell, things go too fast on benny, you know? For me, that is. I get *real* mean and nasty on it everytime."

Ben drifted away, somewhat dampened, to help Dinah.

"Give me tea anytime, slightly green tea, you know?" Hart went on to Hobbes, fishing in his pockets for his supply. "You get a perspective on everything. Everything just drifts along real s-l-o-w!"

"I noticed that music sounded wonderful last night. I never heard such piano. It just couldn't have been as good as it sounded though."

"Yes, yes, man! That's right! You got it! But *everything's* great on tea! Everything's the greatest. That's the point, you see? You're just digging everything all the time. Hell, when I was on benny, two years ago or so, I got all mean and . . . compulsive, you know? Always worried and hungup. Sure. I was a real big serious intellectual then, toting books around all the time, thinking in all those big psycho-logical terms and everything," and he giggled at the thought. "You know: inhibitions and complexes and complaints! I was getting deep psychopathic kicks all the time! Why, damn, I was stealing cars then . . . compulsively!"

He was rolling a stick while he told of this, bobbing up and down as the words tumbled out, tinged with an almost modest humor.

"A compulsive car thief!" Hobbes laughed. "You mean you didn't want the cars? You were just taking them for . . . for kicks?"

"That's right, man! Why, I must of stole about a hundred cars in six months that year. I hooked up with this real beat hipster who'd been on benny since the army, see. I was just about eighteen, you know, and I got hungup on the habit myself. We were beating our way from Denver down into Missouri, stealing the cars the whole way. We'd pick up some slick job, drive it a hundred miles or so, sell it and grab another one. It was real kicks in the beginning."

"But didn't you ever get caught?"

"That's what I'm coming to, see. We were coked up all the time, making crazy mileage on the cars because we didn't have to sleep, and we got to this little beatup old town—I don't remember, Boonville or someplace—and we were in shooting pool in this place, and when we come out right there is this shiny new tan Mercury, not two thousand miles on it. Why man, I got itchy just looking at it. All chrome and whitewalls . . . We'd gotten so hungup taking them that we'd never grab one at night or anything easy like that, we'd snatch 'em right under the owner's nose! Well, both of us looked at this Merc and the same thing hit us . . . Why man, we had a bran' new Studebaker parked right down the block, we'd just grabbed it the day before—"

"But you took the Mercury."

"That's right! Yes! We just climbed right into it, without a word between us, like it was a plan, and started off. I was driving and out the mirror I see this guy crossing the street from a beanery and waving his arms, and right away a couple of cars start out after us. We didn't have more than half a block on them! . . . We scooted around a corner, pulled up sharp behind a beer truck in the middle of the block, and beat it into the nearest house and out the back into the other street."

"Then they didn't get you?"

"Hell no, man, but I got scared! Yes, sir! Not because they almost nabbed us, but because of me, you see? I wasn't getting any kicks out of it. It was just taking the cars, just getting away with it, just chances, you know? But that's benny for you, you get all worked up, so compulsive you can't see straight."

"Is tea any different?"

"Why sure, man, you know that! You're just high, that's all. You're just digging everything! You're . . . well, you're perceptive . . . But hell, you can't explain it; all this intellectual terminology drags me now. It isn't that really. Gene tries to put it into words, see—about some guy in Dostoyevski—but it's nothing you can explain that way. It's just getting your kicks and digging *everything* that happens. Like everything was perfect. Because it really is, you know?"

He laughed hastily at these words, ridiculing them for some inflexibility in them that he alone perceived.

"Well, I suppose so," Hobbes put in. "From that point of view."

"No, but *you* understand . . . Now, everything was perfect on the trip. That's an example. *Everything* happened right on schedule, except we didn't have a schedule, you see! We caught all the great bop—they were blowing the greatest the nights we were in town, everywhere!—we dug everything perfectly; you know, women, tea connections, money . . . we got great kicks all the time! That's what I mean. *Everything* happens perfectly for me because I know it's going to! I expect everything, everything is kicks! . . . You know, David talks about visions and God and going crazy and everything . . . well, that's okay, that's the way he sees it. I mean, it's the same thing really; he's right on his level . . . It's just that *everything's* really true, on it's own level. See?" And he waggled his finger excitedly. "You get what I mean? Everything's really true. I mean, the same as everything else. Now on benny or psychology or something like

that, you get hungup on one thing, you don't just accept everything anymore. You know, you get compulsive like with those
cars! Why man, that isn't getting your kicks and having your
life! . . . Now on tea, everything slows down, everything's interesting and real profound, and you realize that everyone really
knows everything, but just doesn't see it, you understand? . . .
See, you and I *know*, really, that everyone's the same; I mean,
they know the same things that we do actually, about life! And
on tea you get so you're digging all of this happening, everyone
trying to cover up and keep their systems; but you dig, all the
time, that it's *all* really true, even the covering up! All of it! But
kee-rist, man, you know what I mean!" And he hit Hobbes in
the arm. "*You* understand!"

He lit the cigarette hungrily, taking great, sucking puffs, and
darting around to everyone, holding it out of their lips, urging
them on, as though after smoking they would know something
too complex or too simple to be explained by the sort of talk
in which he had just been engaged. Hobbes did not "know," and
felt annoyance at the ideas, because to him "everything" was
not really true. There were some things, and some ideas, that
were seriously false.

The phone rang and when Pasternak answered, it turned out
to be Stofsky, wanting them to pick him up at York Avenue. Less
than a week before, with the help of the employment service
at Columbia, he had gotten a night-boy's job with the Associated
Press, and he had to be at work at ten-thirty.

"We all stayed up here last night," Pasternak was saying. "No,
they went home . . . Yes, they're back now—"

"Here, let me talk to him," Hart said, taking the receiver.
"Sure, man, yes, we're cutting right down there now . . . Oh
. . . And he's going to be there all night? You want my key
. . . Yes, yes . . . Hell, don't worry about it! . . . No, not here,
but we'll make out . . . Well, you know, we'll get fixed . . .
Okay, we're cutting right down . . . Yes, man, right this instant!"

Stofsky was standing in his doorway when they roared up and
he scooted out to the curb, his hands stuffed down into his pockets
and an odd, secretive twist about his lips.

"Waters woke me at six. He'd just gotten off the train from
Harrodsville, and he's got to go back tomorrow. He's upstairs
now, sleeping. And, you know, they gave him shock treatments,
and when he told them about time and eternity, they put him
on a lock ward . . ." This bubbled out rapidly and then he peered

around at them as the car rolled down a darkened cross street. "But didn't you tell them about Waters, Hart?"

"Well, no, you see I didn't think everybody knew him. Hell, I didn't know who he was, man. Where's he been anyway?"

"In a sanitarium; over a month ago he committed himself. I was up at his place just before they took him away, you know . . . And he's real quiet now, Gene, with a sly, deep gleam in his eyes. Oh, lots has happened!"

While Stofsky succumbed to the questioning of Hobbes and Pasternak and the curiosity of the others, Hart was preoccupied, noticing that the gas gauge was alarmingly low.

They swept down the East River Drive, a dark, imperturbable breadth of river beside them, and a sprinkle of headlights moving steadily past them from downtown. Hart gunned the motor as they slid under the outflung, straining arch of the Fifty-ninth Street Bridge, and kept looking down each turn-off with sharp, efficient jerks of his head. But it was an ambiguous neighborhood of renovated Georgian houses in tidy, regular rows, and great cavernous garages, their folding doors welling with white light. At Forty-ninth he swerved off the parkway and headed into the floodlighted, vacant rectangle of a filling station.

"We'll cut in for gas."

"How about a quarter from everybody then," Pasternak started.

"That's okay, man. Just keep your eyes open."

The others went on talking, unconcerned with such matters when not pressed into them, all but Ed who unfolded his length and got out with Hart.

The pumps were untended, and inside the crowded garage-shed the mechanic lay prone under the chassis of a touring car, his feet protruding toward them motionlessly. Ed, with a look in that direction, ambled up to the air pump, uncoiled a stretch of hose and started filling the tires lackadaisically in plain view of the garage, pausing every now and then to check the pressure.

Hart, the car between him and the garage, had the hose off the nearest gas pump and, without a look either at the engrossed mechanic or the trickle of traffic that buzzed by not twenty feet from him, was calmly filling the tank. After every two gallons, he would flip the meter back to zero and continue.

Hobbes, sitting in the front seat and not really listening to Stofsky's enthusiasms, could see Hart in the rear-view mirror, and sat, with a sudden incredulous chill, watching him while he did this eight times.

He shook the nozzle neatly so no drops would spill, replaced it on the pump and climbed in beside Hobbes, whistling to himself. Ed kicked the rear tire, recoiled the air hose and, after he slid into the front seat, they pulled back onto the highway smoothly. The mechanic was just crawling out from under the touring car as they dawdled at the corner for the light, but he didn't even see them.

"That was real slick, yes, sir!" Ed burst out proudly. "How much did you get?"

"Sixteen gallons, man! Almost a tank! That's the most yet . . . Yippee!"

Dinah, who had been smoking and talking interestedly during the whole operation, laughed as if she had been waiting for the verdict, and said: "We got fourteen outside St. Louis that time. After we slept in the car, remember? . . . Isn't he awful though!" This, to the others.

"Didn't you pay him?" Kathryn exclaimed. "You mean you didn't pay him for the gas?"

"Now she realizes!" Hobbes erupted nervously. "I suppose that's the acid test, if *she* didn't even know what you were doing! . . . What does it matter, honey? He didn't even look up."

"I don't like that kind of thing, Paul. I don't like it! If you want to go to jail, all right. But next time let *me* out, I'd rather walk!"

"Oh, we had the money between us anyway," Pasternak interrupted with a mixture of placation and peevishness. "We *could* have paid for it."

Stofsky was staring at Hobbes and Pasternak with strange displeasure. "Why do you both turn on her, for *her* nervousness . . . What odd gentility!" And he laughed with sudden amazement.

❂   ❂   ❂   ❂   ❂

But it was not forgotten when later Kathryn and Dinah chanced to talk. Hart had surrendered his key to the York Avenue apartment when they dropped Stofsky at Rockefeller Center, and their very lack of purpose after this had brought them to Times Square, as if all quandarys ended there, all quests began. They had cruised around looking hopelessly for Ancke, for when on the Square they always searched him out, believing him, night and day, (some watchful Ariel of hipsters), always elusively there among the lights and hurry. They had soon given it up, and at Ketcham's silence and Hart's guarded suggestions, gone to Hobbes'. There, in the dimness and the bop which was put on the phonograph, Dinah said assuringly to Kathryn:

"You mustn't mind Hart, honey . . . about coming here and the gas and all. You folks are so swell that he just wants to keep going. Do you really mind, just this once?"

"Far be it from me to mind!" Kathryn replied, glaring across the room at Hobbes who was watching Hart and Pasternak roll cigarettes. "I just don't want to get thrown out of here because of the noise and that tea. Is that too much to ask?" There was some defiance in her expression. "I don't like stealing, that's all I meant in the car. I don't like to have anything to do with it. I know I'm probably a *prude* or something—"

"Oh, 'course not. I understand. I'm always telling him he'll get caught the way he does it. But, you know, once when we were living back here, when we were married, I had to tell him the police were looking for him about those cars just because I wanted to get away from him. Why, he even hid up in New Haven and grew a moustache and everything. And then I went back to Denver and got annulled. I know how you mean, about the gas, all right. Why, I couldn't even leave him then without telling him that story about the police. He does all these crazy things all the time, but you can't stop him short of scaring him. But you shouldn't worry about it."

"I don't want to get arrested! It's not my gas! . . . But why did you come back east with him anyway if you felt that way about him? He's married to someone else now, isn't he?"

"But *I* introduced him to Marilyn. And she's a real sweet girl, graduated from Bennington and everything. That was when he followed me back to Denver . . . But, you see, I married Hart when I was fifteen, I was real stuck on him, but it just didn't work out right. I swear we almost killed each other lots of times. Why, he used to hold a revolver on me all night sometimes and follow me around in the streets because he thought I was cheating on him. That was in the beginning."

She laughed confidingly, almost with nostalgia, glancing fondly at Hart's gyrations over the music. "Oh, he's still in love with me . . . but it's really all over for *me* anyhow. I just couldn't take it, I mean caring about him and living with him too. When I went back to Denver and he married Marilyn was when I got to be a real lush. I drank a quart or more each day. I had this boy, a friend of my brother's, who would bring it up to me in

my room . . . I still love him, you know, but I don't want him
or care any more. You can't *care* for him, it gets to be too awful
and unbearable . . . Now I'm having fun with him again. It's
been so much better this time." She leaned closer in her confidence. "But, you know, I won't stay with him long. Oh, no,
not this trip! And he knows it, and that's why he's always as-
serting himself . . . like over the gas and with other girls. But,
I swear, it just doesn't bother me any more like it used to."

"Well, I couldn't live that way!" Kathryn exclaimed with
shock. "It would be better to be alone and thoroughly miserable!
You're a fool!"

"But all *that* doesn't matter the way we are now, honey. He
says he'll kill me one day, even though we never really fight any
more. But I won't be around that long. You see, it's that he's got
to 'go' all the time, he's got to be leader, have lots of people
around him all the time. I understand all that, sure. It doesn't
matter to me. And you just can't stick close to him if anything
matters to you."

"Well, he certainly has an effect on everything! Nothing's been
the same since you people came. And Gene acts just like him
too."

"Well look, I told Gene, honey, that he shouldn't think Hart's
so terrific and crazy that way. Gene tries to play up to him and
imitate him, like you say. I told him that he shouldn't let himself in for all that. But that's just the way people react to Hart,
they always have. Everyone does at first. You watch out for your
husband now. I know, I've been through it."

"But you stay with him and take this trip, even though his
wife's your friend! Why? I can't understand that at all. If you
say you don't care for him anymore."

"But sure! He's the best boy for me in a way. I'm still stuck
on him really. But it's just that someone's got to care and someone not. Why, I've always had more fun with him than with
anyone. And he's real nice now that he's not so sure of me. . . .
Marilyn was going crazy trying to live with him anyway, she
used to write me all about it. She isn't the kind of girl who can
take it for too long, there's something soft about her, you know?
Oh, he'll go back in a month, you remember what I say! No,
I just thought the trip would be a lot of fun."

She smiled easily, with such candor or such consummate irony
that Kathryn was speechless.

"Oh, by the way, did he give Paul back the ten dollars? Ed

got his railroad check and I told Hart to pay it right back to you all, you've been so swell."

Bewildered, Kathryn said that it had been returned the night before.

"Well, you know," Dinah added almost drily. "You got to keep tabs on those things with Hart, or he'll manage to forget them somehow. Even with friends."

Hart was darting around with a cigarette, exclaiming: "We're out of paper! Isn't that a drag? We got enough weed for two or three more, but we'll have to get some paper somewhere. How about it, man?" he said sharply to Ed.

Ed was up, a faint, shiny smile on his broad face, and gone in a moment, without pause or thought or reluctance. Hart dragged Pasternak to the window, cackling and leaning far out of it into the night.

"There, down there! Look at that big bastard go!"

Down three flights in the empty corridor of the street, Ed, who had shot out of the entrance of the building as though running for his life, was streaking uptown, arms pulled in at his sides, and his thighs pounding like pistons.

"Dig the head, Gene! Dig that head, all pulled down, see! R-e-a-l streamlined, you know! . . . Look, he's going to beat that light!"

The lone runner, now in the street, now on the sidewalk, sprinted wildly through crossings, was momentarily lost to them behind overhanging neons, and finally vanished entirely in a dark block, going full speed uptown on his crazy mission.

While they waited in the darkness, for the light had been extinguished and there was only the glow of the city through the long windows, Hart drew Dinah upright and they started to dance as they had the night before. She shot a sympathetic, amused glance at Kathryn over his shoulder, as if in corroboration of all she had said, and then put her face down into his throat to stand, wound about him, while he held her against him and moved tensely to the bop beat, as though somehow aware of his inability to make any point on her.

While they were dancing, Stofsky phoned, having a period with nothing to do and wondering what was happening. Hobbes, who had fumbled for the receiver in the blackness, found himself asking Stofsky immediately about his odd last remark in the car. It had irritated Hobbes, for he was sure it disguised some presumptuous and lofty judgment of him.

"What did you mean anyway? About my nervousness? And that crack about gentility?"

"I don't know. What did I say?"

"You said, why was I criticizing Kathryn for *her* nervousness; and then you said, 'What gentility!' Just like that. I suppose you think I disapprove too, about the gas. Isn't that what you think?"

"Well, don't you disapprove of stealing? There must be some big, rational morality about that. I just got this funny reaction, to your reaction, and I thought of you as some anxious Socratic straight-man . . . he-he! . . . like Euthyphro. After all, he was really a liberal type, wasn't he?"

"What's that got to do with it?"

"But that's exactly what I meant by my remark. Don't you see, Euthyphro wanted to kill his father for killing a slave that he (Euthyphro, I mean) didn't really care anything about. That's essentially the whole genteel pathos of liberalism . . . ideas being more important than men."

"How did I suddenly get to be the representative of liberalism? And what's gentility got to do with all this?"

"Well, Kathryn said what you were really feeling all the time. I mean below your shrewd smiles and your Machiavellian agreements." He laughed, but so odd a laugh that it did not seem to rise from what he had just said. "Don't you think people know you're mocking and judging them? Although that isn't the important thing about this—"

"But actually *your* reply was much more of a gentility than what I said if you'll remember correctly," Hobbes sniffed angrily. "How do you *know* that I disapprove, after all? Why should I? It doesn't matter to me what Hart does! But Kathryn *does* think it's wrong, and yet you, who don't at all, criticize me! Whose is the hypocritical gentility? I really don't approve or disapprove of it . . . My own standards apply only to—"

"But you don't accept! You don't accept it! Secretly you're always judging, really very snidely, because you don't come out with it. And then you attack Kathryn when—"

"I didn't attack her, for Christ's sake!"

"But you can't seem to just love her the way she is, everything about her! You don't just accept her. You always squash her in the name of protecting her from other people . . . that's what you think you're doing at any rate, that's how you justify it! But that's really apologizing for her to everyone else. And you shouldn't be ashamed, Paul . . ."

"Oh, now I'm ashamed! This is rich, very Stofskian and weird! But I suppose one mustn't ever ask a prophet what the hell he means!"

"But you did ask me."

"Well, what makes you so superior? Why do you people always assume that you can understand me so well? And, moreover, act so goddamned concerned about me, as though all your condescension was for my own good!"

"Is that what you really think? That I'm being condescending?"

"Well, aren't you? I *don't* judge any of you. Why the hell should I bother? But how can I operate when you've typed me right off the bat? Don't you think I know what you think of me?"

"Well, Paul, I've always thought of you as an . . . an evil intellectual; by which I mean someone who hates charity, the charity of the heart . . . more to the point, really fears it because it's not rational or sensible in all circumstances, or something real irrelevant like that . . . You see," and he gave another nervous little snort that seemed to clog in the wires. "You see, I never really loved you, I never could . . . until right this minute, now that you're being honest at last. You always nod your head so insincerely and appear to agree with everything everyone does, whereas actually you don't agree at all. In fact, you look down on everyone in a secretly patronizing way, like a mass observer who never forgets his job even when he participates. That's why I never loved you. But now when you mock me I see your . . . your confusions, you know? After all, why should you be afraid of confessing?"

"What do you mean! Why should I confess to you, in heaven's name?"

"Perhaps everyone should confess to everyone. The rest is probably only pride. But, you see, I really can love you now . . . actually because you've been savage with me. Just because of that."

"Okay, okay. Let's forget about it. And I didn't mean to be savage at all. Why did you say that?"

"But you should, if that's the way you feel. You really should . . . with me, at least!"

"Well . . . well, in any case, it's not important. It's nothing world-shaking . . . And, besides, here's Gene, he wants to talk to you . . ."

Hobbes thrust the receiver at a surprised Pasternak, and left him with it with relief, at once annoyed and hurt by the conversation and hoping, for some reason, that no one else had overhead.

The night seemed to have slipped by unpropelled by any event or aim. At one point, Ed rushed in breathlessly, holding the packet of papers in an enormous hand, and puffing and grinning with triumph.

"I ran seventeen blocks and back," he gasped proudly. "What kind of time did I make?"

No one knew.

They rolled more cigarettes, sat about smoking them idly, and, when they were all gone, drank three quarts of beer that were in the refrigerator. Ketcham and Ben slipped away finally, whispering 'goodnight' to Kathryn, and disappearing before the others could notice. Everyone remaining got quietly high, growing speculative and drowsy, content to drift. Kathryn got tired and moody and went to bed with aloof looks at all of them, but no real anger.

It was arranged that Hart and Dinah would sleep on the couches, having nowhere else to go. Once faced with the direct request, Hobbes, still troubled by his talk with Stofsky, could not think of a way to refuse.

"I'm going to keep going," Pasternak replied when Hart asked him what he would do. "Come on, we'll go down to Agatson's. Hell, it's only three-thirty."

But Hart was bent on other things, and Pasternak started talking about the hundred yard dash with Ed. Eventually, taking the remaining bottle of beer with them, they wandered off down the stairs and out into the street once more, but not before Pasternak had said to Hobbes with some exasperation because he wouldn't come along:

"What the hell did you talk about to Stofsky? You know what he said about it? 'I've been baiting Paul's hook.' And then he said that I should tell you not to worry, that he's really just a 'fishmonger.' Isn't that strange? He's talking like a mad Hamlet these days."

Hobbes was dizzy and nauseated from the beer and the marijuana and, leaving Dinah to arrange the spare blankets, he went into the bathroom to make himself vomit as was his habit whenever he was too drunk or sick to sleep. A line of Blake kept running through his head, the line that Stofsky had recited to

him: 'Like a fiend hid in a cloud! Like a fiend hid in a cloud!"
It had occurred to him while listening to Stofsky's distant, intent voice over the telephone.

While leaning over the toilet getting up his nerve, he thought that the moment before making yourself throw up must be very like the instant before suicide. You are almost content to bear the sickening headache and the torment in your stomach rather than go through that moment. But the prospect of relief made you foolhardy and you jammed your finger down your throat.

Only after it was done, and he stood gasping over the washbowl and looking blankly at himself in the mirror, did he seriously think of what Stofsky had told Pasternak and ponder on it.

Eight

A T nine-thirty the next morning, Stofsky went immediately to Verger's from his job, not even pausing to eat. He mounted the long, dark flights slowly, at once relishing and restraining the eagerness that filled him.

He slipped into the apartment, finding the door open and Verger sprawled on a cot beside the shattered window. The rooms were damp and Verger had obviously not been to bed at all, for his shirt, ripped on one shoulder and soiled, was deeply wrinkled, and beside him on the floor were three bottles of beer, two of them empty and the other half gone. He looked up wearily, unshaven and pale, and there was in his wanness a kind of resignation through which no surprise, if he felt any, could penetrate.

"I've just come from work. Actually this is my first call of the day . . . What happened to your window?"

Verger explained briefly, omitting any reference to Agatson's part in the window breaking. He would pause every few minutes to take a painful, determined pull on the remaining bottle, which would leave him gasping and coughing. He seemed to derive some bitter pleasure from these fits and would smile thinly and sadly to himself when they had passed, and then continue as though uninterrupted.

"I've been lying here since some time after one," he added finally. "Reading the Pensées. Cah-cah! I finished up to five hundred and one and then I stopped." He reached down into the pillows beside the wall and brought the book up with him, held it for a moment, and then let it slip to the floor.

Stofsky was somewhat irritated by all this, and stared out of the broken window, considering how he could most effectively come out with his urgent news, for his relationship with Verger was elaborate.

They had been close friends as undergraduates when their academic thirsts had, for a period, coincided. Verger had proved more scholarly than Stofsky, and less creative; lacking that restless ability to improvise which had seen Stofsky through examinations for which he had not studied, and made him an enfant terrible among the group of shy, intense students that invariably plunge into literature and philosophy rather than dare the uncertainties of football, dates and dances. They had started as conspirators, nursing their wild ideas together, but when Stofsky had begun going about with a crazier, less intellectual element on the campus, they had seen less of each other.

Now Verger lit a cigarette without looking up, and said with a peculiar lassitude: "The last one I read . . . cah-cah-cah! goes like this. 'First step: to be praised for doing good and blamed for doing evil. Second step: to be neither praised nor blamed!' . . . A sort of ethical relativity." And he giggled under his breath. "Quite an heretical idea to read at six o'clock in the morning."

"Oh, well, heresy! Of course, every idea's heresy to someone," Stofsky exclaimed impatiently. "But look, I don't want to discuss Pascal! I've come here, you see," and he brightened up and continued with suppressed delight. ". . . to your abode, that is, with gifts. Well, not gifts exactly, not gifts . . . But, you see, I'm getting my affairs straightened out and I wanted to settle up all debts the first thing."

Verger was watching him with weary attention, unable to keep his mind on such gibberish, yet not really annoyed.

"Now," Stofsky went on with an evidently delicious gravity. "I have here my first pay check . . . for my vigils in the interests of American journalism, and I have come here, to your pad, as I said, to give you part of that check—ten dollars is what I can spare—in partial payment for the books! Now, next week I can give you the same amount . . ." He took a ten out of his wallet with a flourish and held it forward.

"What books are you talking about?"

"The Calvin and Luther, and what were the other ones? The books Ancke took. He wouldn't have slept here that night if it hadn't been for me. And, of course, he'll never be able to pay it back, so I've taken on his debts . . . Believe me, I have my own reasons."

Verger snickered weakly and pushed himself up on one elbow. "I don't want your money, you fool! Cah-cah-cah! Do you think I'd take your goddamn money?"

"I'd buy the books for you if I had the time. I have my reasons, I tell you—"

"All right, all right, I'm sure you have . . . But why do you make this gesture to me? You were always making gestures to impress me in the beginning, but, Christ, I don't want your money! Cah-cah-cah! Cah-cah!" He doubled over with the series of quaking coughs, and for a moment he appeared to be laughing. "The books don't matter to me. I didn't care anything about them . . . Besides, the set of Calvin is unobtainable."

"But of course you cared about them! You got your Bachelor's on The Ninety-five Theses! They were your favorites. But it isn't because of the books, at least not entirely. I have my own reasons, as I said. And it's *not* a gesture at all, not really. At any rate, if it is, it's only for myself . . . A gesture of charity for myself, he-he! . . . But that doesn't concern you . . . Now, you mustn't be foolish about this! And why don't you get that window fixed, it's like a crypt in here!"

He would not stand in one place, yet seemed unwilling to sit down, and so he walked up and down with some agitation.

"As far as the window goes, I suppose the landlord will fix it eventually. I don't really care, and I won't have to worry until next winter. Now, it's air-conditioning . . . cah-cah! It doesn't matter . . ."

"But you *will* take the money?"

Verger took another drink. "Of course not."

"But it's very crucial to me!"

"I don't want the money! I tell you I don't care about it at all. You know that! Cah-cah-cah! . . . Have you got a cigarette?"

Stofsky handed him one, dropping it on the floor in his confusion. "Why should I have to beg you? It's crazy that I should have to beg you to take it! It's ridiculous . . . a game you're always playing . . . Oh, yes, I almost forgot. You don't know what's happened. Waters turned up last night . . ."

And he proceeded to relate the entire story, changing the subject in the hope of discovering another way of approaching the matter. He laughed nervously, hurrying on and explaining earnestly each new development. Verger listened with the same lethargic interest, making an occasional ironical comment or asking trivial questions. Stofsky's account got more incoherent as his failure to arouse Verger persisted.

"And you know what he told me? About visions and eternity and madness! A very strange, sacramental thing. 'The trick is to act just like everybody else!' That's exactly what he said, all the time leaning over and whispering behind his hand, just as if someone might be listening . . . the F. B. I. or God! 'The trick is to act like everyone else, as though you were in church. Watch the other people and do what they do!' Isn't that mad and really almost saintly? I mean, a saint incognito. He's very profound and chastised, you know? Watchful! He kept going to the window and peering out of it!"

"I suppose that's what they mean by adjustment."

"Oh, and he asked about you, real strange things. It was very weird what he remembered . . . but I've forgotten most of it. About your lung and your love-life. He-he! . . . But then there may have been no connection at all." He knocked over one of the empties in his excitement. "Oh, by the way, how's May? Gene told me she was in here Friday night. Do you think she'd be up? It's not too early is it? I'd like to say hello."

Verger glanced at him sharply with a sallow flush.

"No . . . no, she's not there. She . . . she went down to the Village last night, I think, and . . . cah-cah-cah! I didn't hear her come back. She's probably staying over with Bianca or . . . I would have heard her, I'm sure I would . . . if she'd come back. And anyhow," he said hurriedly, raising himself to a sitting position for the first time. "Anyhow I've got to go down to the corner for some more beer. What time is it?"

"It's ten. Let me go down and buy it. Where do you go? That little Puerto Rican delicatessen?"

Verger fished about in the papers and books on the table. "I've got enough for two quarts. That'll last me. Here."

"But aren't you going to eat? You mean that's all the money you've got? . . . Really, it's so foolish, it's senseless. I tell you I mean to give this money to you! It really isn't a gesture! Why should I make a gesture with you?"

"You've got your reasons I suppose."

"Then it's just some kind of subtle pride on your part, isn't it? Some private pride you'll never speak of, and that you're probably ashamed of!"

"That's completely absurd! What are you talking about? You know, it's too goddamn early for—"

"Don't be proud," Stofsky exclaimed earnestly. "You know how you pretend to despise all that! You think of yourself as someone who's above such middle-class considerations, such egoisms —for that's what they really are, I've realized it recently . . .

And yet inside you're filled with an injured pride, like . . . like some fallen gentleman in Balzac!"

Verger's apathy, at last, had been pierced.

"It isn't true . . . cah-cah-cah! You know it isn't! What kind of game are *you* playing? Ever since those visions you've been like the devil's advocate with me! . . . But this is childish!"

"It doesn't matter what you say. You certainly understand how important this is to me. It's all right if you make jokes about 'my reasons.' But there couldn't be any other explanation for your refusing me, except pride . . . wanting to keep the upper hand with me! I didn't realize you cared about such poses. And you mustn't, you know, because you really can't believe in them! Now, here take—"

"All right, all right! Leave the goddamn ten bucks! What do I care! If you must be stupid, leave it. But it isn't pride, David. How can you think that? I mean it, all that's *really* foolishness! Cah-cah-cah! . . . I don't care. I insist on that! Why should I be proud? Why? . . . No, you see, you can't answer that! . . . But if you want to throw away your money, I'll take it because you want me to, because of that, you understand! It doesn't matter one way or the other to *me*, I insist on that!" And he got tiredly to his feet, looking more pale and thin than before.

Stofsky beamed with hidden victory. "Now, let's not talk about it anymore. You should go down and have a real sumptuous meal, some crazy Spanish soup or something. Don't you think you should eat after all? You can tell yourself it's on me. It'll be the first time I ever bought you a meal! . . . And I should be going, of course, I've got to sleep sometime."

Verger shuffled around nervously, running his hand over his sunken cheeks and avoiding sight of the ten that Stofsky had laid on the table. "Okay . . . Cah-cah! Thanks . . . Yes, that's right, you've been up all night too, haven't you?"

As Stofsky backed himself out, not exactly reluctant to leave, but somehow uneasy about the outcome of the interview, Verger said distantly: "I think it's probably true, what Waters said . . . about acting like everyone else. And yet *you* don't believe it at all!"

He closed his eyes and giggled with embarrassment.

"Goodness me!"

Stofsky fled without any comment.

Nine

AMONG the numberless marquees and neons, midway within that tent of light that is Times Square, was The Go Hole. You passed a shouting, bereted Negro in a blue jacket with gold epaulettes, went down a series of stairs and landings, paid one dollar at a little booth where a brunette named Margo made change apathetically, managed one more flight of steps and emerged into a darkened, shadow-thronged cellar where a maitre d'hotel separated the eaters from the watchers; the later being pushed behind velvet guide ropes to a clutter of folding chairs at the back, and the former allowed to enter the club proper.

The dense crowd, shuffling in the dimness, fidgeted while waiting for the music. Groups of young men, Negro and white, stood three deep at the bar, waiting for chairs in the bleacher section as a squad of bartenders pressed them with drinks, or moved them on. When a seat was vacated, there was a scurry among those standing in the back to capture it. Those already sitting, concentrating on this game of musical chairs, shifted restlessly from one to the other, trying to get nearer the front. People squeezed together, craning over the rows of heads to get a look at the bandstand, which seemed unreal and remote, limned with pink and yellow spotlights.

Among the crowd there was a predominance of sharp pin-striped suits in Hollywood cut, black horn-rimmed glasses, long lapeled soft shirts, and suede shoes. Their wearers (mostly Negroes, Italians, and Irish kids from First Avenue), acted as though they had never been in a Broadway night club before. They studied each other ceaselessly, drinking very little, smoking with pinched lips, and deciding who among new arrivals was "hip."

Like hired ushers at a revival meeting of hicks, the hurrying waiters and bouncers herded these young roughnecks about with annoyed competence. Though all the employees were dressed very much like the customers, they were evidently contemptuous of the music, and intent only on cramming in as many people as possible.

When the music began, silence swept the room as if by command. As the sound built slowly from an eerie, hesitant geometry of ensemble phrases to the wild tumult of some tenor sax solo, the hushed attention of the audience would be split by the thud-thud-thud of stamping feet, an occasional "go!" would signify approval, and finally, during a piercing trumpet chorus, two enthusiasts in the rear would become totally "gone" and start to babble and laugh.

These restless youngsters, finding a passion in this music that belonged defiantly to them, were part of a spectacle that was offered for curious outsiders, come to experience a new diversion. The faithful themselves, jammed like immigrants into a cattle car, closely watched by the angry bouncers, laughed at by those who could afford drinks and tables, were oblivious of this, however, and they became willingly transported when cued by the musicians, who played only to them and remained bitterly indifferent to the noisy parties at the tables in between.

The Go Hole was where all the high schools, the swing bands, and the roadhouses of their lives had led these young people; and above all it was the result of their vision of a wartime America as a monstrous danceland, extending from coast to coast, roofed by a starless night, with hot bands propelling thousands of lonely couples with an accelerating, Saturday-night intensity. In this modern jazz, they heard something rebel and nameless that spoke for them, and their lives knew a gospel for the first time. It was more than a music; it became an attitude toward life, a way of walking, a language and a costume; and these introverted kids (emotional outcasts of a war they had been too young to join, or in which they had lost their innocence), who had never belonged anywhere before, now felt somewhere at last.

It was a Friday night a week later, when Hart hurried them all down the stairs, leaving the paying of admissions to Pasternak, to stand in the entrance, already jiggling to the music. Even Ketcham and Ben had come along out of an ironical interest. Dinah, who had been working as a counter girl at a midtown Rexall's for a week, but had somehow made no adjustments in their disordered life because of this and had maintained her cool willingness to do anything and go anywhere in spite of it, had been picked up at her job just half an hour before, changed her dress in a ladies room, and now glided among the scramble of chairs with a pensive, almost wise glow of recognition on her pale face.

They could not find enough seats together, and Kathryn, Hobbes and Ketcham were wedged in behind a pillar, while the others seized seats up near the railing as they became available. Kathryn, who had only consented to come after they had stopped for a meal which no one else wanted, peered about with irritation at the excited, sweaty crowd all around them.

"What a bunch of low-foreheads!" she exclaimed to Hobbes crossly. "It's what I've always said: this is hoodlum music!"

Ketcham smiled at her sympathetically but made no verbal agreement. Hobbes moped and did not answer. He continued to watch everything, unable to get rid of a feeling that he too had, that he was uncomfortably out of his element, but not wanting Kathryn to see this.

He marked it down to what had been a fatal week for him. Confusions had descended on him like an avalanche. Hart, Dinah and Ed had stayed two nights, because Waters had not left Stofsky's on schedule. And although Dinah had done dishes, made beds and swept the floor, and Hart had been, in his own way, remarkably cooperative about turning in at a decent hour and keeping the music down, Kathryn had become more and more resentful and antagonistic. In bed, she would complain loudly to him; she was sullen and cold when with the others, and their placid determination to ignore her hostility only made her angrier.

"I don't care *where* they go! They're only thinking of themselves, you know that! . . . Then why shouldn't I? After all this is *my* place. Why should I have them here if I don't want to?" Feeling like a referee whose function it is to stand between two opponents and absorb the punishment of both, Hobbes had managed to mediate and there had been no outbreaks.

When they had finally gone back to Stofsky's, Hobbes had hoped for a few quiet days in which to digest his unsettlement and establish a new routine to replace the one which the "season" and the completion of his book had destroyed. Circumstances gathered to prevent all this. The day after they left, Hobbes had timorously called up a slight acquaintance, who worked in the editorial department of a large publishing house, and had arranged to deliver his novel for their consideration. Then at the last minute, he had gotten panicky, and spent a whole night doing rewrites which had seemed so unsatisfactory to him the next morning that he had thrown them all away. After leaving the manuscript with his friend, he had wandered around, feeling unpleasantly committed and lacking even the barest confidence in the book now that it was finally out of his hands. Upon arriving home, hoping for an hour or two of quiet reading before Kathryn got back from work, Christine had called and plunged him into further complications.

"Well, I told Max, that's what's happened. I told him everything. I just felt I'd never be able to live with myself until I did it. And I feel much better . . . like I could breathe again . . . Oh, he almost killed me all right! I thought I was finished, I really did. He called me horrible names . . . but then I deserved them. And once he even held my head in the stove and wouldn't talk to me for hours. He made me tell him everything that happened, and he near broke my arm the way he was holding onto me."

There was no terror or desperation in her voice as she said this. She sounded, if anything, chilly and oddly self-satisfied.

"But you feel better about it? How did he take it? Is he going to throw you out?"

"Oh no, I begged him not to, and I admitted everything. He was awful hurt . . . Oh, it was painful to see. He was going out to kill Pasternak, but I calmed him down. And I feel so much better. See, I was right about it, wasn't I? I knew I should tell him . . . Oh, he'll make me go through hell now, but I don't care. I deserve it for acting like a two dollar chippie! I'll have to pay for it, but it's better than feeling like you can't breathe . . . And, of course, I haven't heard anything from Mister-High-and-Mighty since I wrote him that letter. My God, how I could ever have thought that anybody like him was worth my time, I don't know! But I told him what I thought of him all right. Did he mention my letter?"

"No, Christine, but after all, it's none of my business. But listen, you don't think that Max'll do anything to you, anything serious, do you? He must have guessed that Gene got you pregnant."

"Oh, no . . . You see, I didn't say anything about that. I just told him that we, you know, fooled around, that we didn't *actually* do it. And really, it's the same thing . . . Oh, no, I didn't tell him what we actually did."

Hobbes, if he had been less weary, might have been amused by the inconsistency, but he only exclaimed: "I thought you told him everything! But why did you tell him at all then? What was the sense of that?"

"Well, I knew that if I just was honest I'd feel better. I couldn't stand all the horrible lies and sneaking anymore. I'd just as soon suffer with a clean conscience."

There had been a pause at this point, during which Hobbes had exhaustedly decided not to pursue it any further.

"I can't help it, I'm not saying you all are wrong, you understand. It's just my opinion. But I can't be like the rest of you. And I'm really glad it's all over. Some people can lie and deceive and everything, but I'm just not made that way . . ."

Soon after that she had hung up, after making clear, without ever saying it, that her coolness and disapproval now extended to all of them. She had called precisely to tell him that it was all over, and he knew she would not call again. A day later the incident was still bothering him, because it had not turned out as he thought it would. He felt no sympathy for her as he had after the other calls, but only a blind rage at himself for having assessed her wrongly. And in this rage she had no existence. Some trust in him had been violated by her reversal, an obstinate belief in the possibility of an impossible situation. People never proved to be either as noble or foolhardy as he wished them to be. His bitter, fond dreams of them always fell apart like the makeshift self justifications they were, leaving him feeling sorrowfully faithless.

Now he sat, taking as an assurance of the attitude Christtine had rejected, Hart's excited unbuttoning of his shirt to the waist. That Hobbes felt discomforted and alien in The Go Hole arose, he was certain, from an imperfection in himself, some failure of the heart; for Stofsky had set him wondering. In his despondent mood, such lacerations were sweet to him.

Ben had brought a pint of whiskey in under his jacket, and was drinking it through a straw in his buttonhole. During numbers when the lights were suddenly lowered and a hundred flushed faces were breathlessly upturned out of the massing shadows, it was passed back to Ketcham and Hobbes, who sipped nervously. Kathryn derided everything with devastating sarcasm.

She became particularly acid when, the third time, along with the bottle came Christine's letter to Pasternak, which he had been showing everyone in front. It was an awkward, ambiguous attempt to shame him, which his action in letting everyone read it indicated had not failed. She ended it with this clumsy reproach: "And you'll never be a writer either, because you don't believe in God!"

Dinah laughed coldly when Hart said of this :

"But that's the greatest, Gene! Most girls when they bawl you out, you know, yell about how you didn't do the dishes or you've been screwing around or you don't give 'em their kicks, but this piece talks about God! Don't you see how really *great* that is?"

Dinah stared at him, a fierce and sullen smile moulding her soft lips, and then pointedly turned away.

At the intermission between sets, Hart disappeared in the midst of fresh mobs that loitered around the bar. Everything he saw overjoyed and excited him beyond words, and he could not sit still for a moment, but must note everything enthusiastically as if it was the first thing in the world.

Kathryn had endured it as long as she would, Ketcham said wryly that he "had had enough," and Hobbes acquiesced with a martyred air which did not reflect the tinge of relief he actually felt. Leaving Pasternak explaining the music to a tipsily interested Ben, and Dinah and Ed sitting with that blank patience of most of the other spectators, they gave up their seats to the crowd of those who were waiting, and started up the stairs.

They found Hart at the admission booth, making snickering arrangements with Margo, with that winsome, glowing charm of which he was sometimes capable. Hobbes made their excuses, nodding in Kathryn's direction and whispering: "You understand, man!"

Hart returned to his single-purposed assault on Margo, who was married to a jobless drummer addicted to barbiturates, and who watched the nightly pilgrimage of furtive, nonchalant youngsters with the bemused indifference of the initiate. She listened to Hart's frank sallies without a word, but eventually she became intrigued by his coquetry. And proving himself no ordinary hustler, he overcame her by slipping a stick of tea into her palm with a wink, at which she leaned closer and muttered something in his ear.

Ketcham, Hobbes and Kathryn hurried off a past-midnight Times Square, that was blown with fragments of torn paper and echoes of muffled music, to a drugstore on Fiftieth Street and cups of sour coffee. Ketcham's interest in the evening suddenly struck Hobbes as being merely kindness to him.

"But what do you think has caused this cult, Paul?" he inquired smoothly. "I mean the whole thing is really a ritual in a kind of way, isn't it? The shouting, the clothes they wear, the talk . . ."

Hobbes' dismayed attempts at explanation were little but an intellectual gloss over his sense of treachery, for he did not feel that he could understand Hart and all the rest of it through the invocation of merely fashionable social or psychological analyses (he felt these attitudes for the first time somehow too narrow), but he fell into them from habit. Kathryn and Ketcham discussed it easily, relishing their judgments, while he sat forlornly smoking cigarettes.

"Oh, and you know what happened," Ketcham said at one point with gossipy confidence. "Ben was over at Stofsky's last night, and they were all high, and at about five o'clock, just before they all went to sleep, Hart came out of the bedroom and told Ed to be sure to wake Dinah up at eight-thirty so she could get to her job on time. 'You get her up and drive her down, that's the most important thing! Don't let her oversleep now!' Then he went inside again and didn't wake up till twelve himself. And she'd been up all night, taking tea and drinking beer with Ben."

"Sure," Kathryn said sardonically. "He doesn't want to lose her salary. Oh, he cares about those things, no matter what he *says!* But does he get a job? It's been two weeks and I'll bet he hasn't even been looking. That's the *beat* generation for you!" And she looked at Hobbes.

"He's been to the parking lots he used to work on. Gene told me he was out most of yesterday . . . but this is a bad time of year . . . After all, it's summer," he added hopelessly.

"Well, I notice *she* found something."

"And it's so amazing the way Ed runs Hart's errands. Have you seen that? He's like a Boy Scout, Paul, don't you think?"

"Well, *she* won't do it forever," Kathryn interjected with certainty. "She's always getting me aside, and don't kid yourself, she doesn't think he's any rose. One of these days, he'd better watch out. You know, she's really tougher than any of them."

She parted from Ketcham with the warm laughter of acquaintances who have abruptly become intimate through suffering boredom or irritation in common.

Walking home through the empty, tepid streets of the east side, Hobbes could not help but think of all things as being unaccountably illusory. He could not even keep his grudging acceptance of Hart and Dinah, as amoral, giggling nihilists, from degenerating into a suspicion that they were wound in the same petty conflicts that fouled the life he knew.

As if sensing this, Kathryn said with evident relief:

"God, it's good to be alone again, back in our own life. And we *don't* have to see them so much from now on. After all, we're *not* like them, and they'll just have to recognize that fact. Right? Don't you agree?"

And Hobbes assented out of another habit.

Ten

"So naturally, I cut up there this afternoon. Of course, she's real cool and everything, but what a body! And, man, did she pick up on me the other night!"

Hart was telling a drowsy Stofsky about his afternoon. It was past five, Dinah was not back from work yet, Ed was off somewhere on one of his wide-eyed, private jaunts, and Stofsky, just awake after too few hours of sleep on the couch, lay exhaustedly smoking.

"But listen to this for a drag. See, she told me her apartment number the other night, but I forgot it. It's this brownstone on Ninety-fifth Street, and I was pretty sure it was something like Five-B, you understand? So I'm there right on time, all slicked up, even got my tie on . . . like I'm making an important sale or something, you know!"

Stofsky snickered and narrowed his eyes in the smoke.

"That's right!" Hart went on, treating this as a favorable response. "And I'm real excited just thinking about it! Because I haven't banged anybody, not *anybody*, since we picked up Dinah, except her, of course, and this Margo is real cute . . . So I get there and I go up and try her door, and there's nobody home! Get that! There's nobody home after I've been making these plans, and telling Dinah I'll be out looking for a job so I can't pick her up after work . . . and everything!"

"Serves you right," Stofsky replied, getting up stiffly. "She stood you up on your first heavy date in New York! For a sailor perhaps." His laugh was edged with a vicious playfulness; and looking at Hart, to whom he was so attracted and with whom he liked to play the confounding oracle most of all, he wondered why he felt glad for a moment.

"But listen, man! You don't know how I was hungup. I've got nothing to do, so I cruise downtown digging the park. You know, sailors wrestling on the grass, dames rowing in the lake, kids with pretty nurses! Everybody is getting their kicks but me! I'm almost ready to pull up and start jacking off, when I remember

I've got her phone number, and that I wasn't sure of the apartment. So I call her up, and I was knocking at the wrong place the whole time! You understand! . . . I was down on the wrong floor! It was Six-B, and she's been waiting. You know, in a negligee, with Scotch and soda, Billy Eckstine records, and everything! And she gets all hungup being *angry* with me! Dig that! . . . Well, I'm all set to cut back on up there, when she says her husband's just come in. But she goes on cursing me out till my dime runs out. So for the whole afternoon, I'm nowhere! . . . Now, what about that for a drag!"

Somehow the story tickled him with its irony, though it was at his own expense. He rolled about in his chair, so convulsed that he failed to see Stofsky's equally ironic, but not as good humored, pleasure in the outcome.

"Well, that's what you get for philandering around while your little wife's out working. That's just justice! Do you mean to tell me *you* don't believe in justice?" Stofsky deliberately said this in a sham-serious voice, smiling vaguely all the while and wagging his finger, but something more was on his mind and he was only trying to frame it by this.

"But you know, Hart," he began with sudden gravity. "I don't approve of your deceptions . . . I mean, you aren't just . . . well, just straight with everyone. Why do you think you have to deceive Dinah? I mean, it is a deception, really it's very crafty of you . . . when you know how you can hurt her."

A tiny quiver around the eyelids and the immobility of the rest of his face indicated Hart's surprise and annoyance. "But why are you trying to put me down, man? That's the way women are. They get all hungup on those things. You and I know that! That's their level. *We* understand all about that."

He took down the Chinese tea-box from the bookshelf and started rolling a stick of marijuana, turned from Stofsky.

"But it's so wrathful . . . your own particular, sly kind of wrath, I mean . . . to be that way with Dinah of all people."

"But you know the way she is. And *you* understand all that, *why* she is and everything!"

"But that's why it's actually, deeply wrathful and egotistic on your part. What's the sense of getting away with all these deceptions, just for getting away with them . . . when you love her really and you know that she's just waiting for a last provocation . . . and when you yourself aren't really, I mean spiritually, that way at all . . ."

Hart was lighting the stick, but turned at this, letting it go out, to stare blankly at Stofsky. His strained gaze seemed to be measuring the confines of some prison of an idea, stubbornly refusing to admit that it had no flaw.

"Aw, come on," he mumbled after an instant, relighting the cigarette. "Why do you want to bring me down, man? You know about these things. Here, blast some of this! It's that real green weed Ed picked up in Harlem. Come on now, you don't want to get hungup on all that!"

As Stofsky sadly declined, abandoning his questions in the face of Hart's resistance, Dinah and Ed, carrying two quarts of milk, came through the door into the kitchen to unload butter, coffee, cans of beans and tamales, and five potatoes from their pockets.

"We bought the milk," Ed beamed proudly.

They stole most of their food to save money. The first day in the neighborhood, they had scouted around for a large, under-staffed grocery store. Dinah would engage the storekeeper in conversation at the front counter, feigning girlish shock at the prices, insisting on a comparison of brands, and thus snagging his attention by her indecision. Meanwhile, Ed and Hart would loiter among the stacks of cans and vegetables, as though waiting for her to finish up, and systematically fill their pockets with all they could carry. After a few minutes, Hart would take Dinah's place, and while he haggled over a pack of cigarettes, carefully count-ing out his pennies, she would drift toward the back of the store to load up. Finally they would buy milk, bread or some other item too bulky to secrete, and leave unhurriedly and in plain sight of the proprietor. It never failed to work, and the very fact that variety in their meals depended upon their own nonchalant skill was enough to make them embark on the operation with eager gusto each time.

Dinner was wearily prepared by Dinah, while Stofsky hovered about her asking about her day, and nodding sympathetically at her replies. Ed put plates and silverware on the low coffee table, and they all sat down around it.

Hart devoured his portion of beans and tamales, smoking be-tween mouthfuls, fiddling with the radio meanwhile, and talking continually about any chance thought that came into his head. Ed guffawed at all his exaggerations while shoveling down his food.

"You'd better eat, Dinah," Stofsky said, noticing that she was only picking at her plate. "Here, have some more milk. You really should, you know."

"That's right," Hart added to this with a sly smile. "You see David's worried about you, honey. You got to put some meat on your bones! See, he's real concerned about your health! Just like he was your old man!"

Dinah glared fixedly at him for a moment, and Stofsky flushed while he filled her glass.

"Well," he spluttered. "She . . . she doesn't eat enough . . . And why do you jeer at me that way?" He was confused, and glanced shyly at Dinah and then back at Hart. "Sure, I'm worried about her. She's . . . she's my girl friend, after all. That's right, isn't it, Dinah?" He laughed awkwardly and kissed her cheek. "We're thinking of going steady."

"That's right, David," she replied defiantly, with the haughty look of a hurt little girl in Hart's direction.

When they were finished, Ed announced that he was heading uptown to look up a girl whose address a friend of his in San Francisco had given him. Stofsky, who seemed unaccountably excited about something, leapt on this and said: "You're sure you've got the address straight? You wouldn't want to get all the way up there and not find her in."

"Why, sure. I got it right here on this slip of paper."

"But what a *drag* that would be! Right, Hart? Just the difference of one number for another! You could be pounding at Five-B, and all the time she'd be just upstairs, waiting eagerly for you! . . . In a negligee! . . . Is it Five-B or Six-B now? That makes all the difference. Isn't that right, Hart?"

"Aw, hell," Ed said, perplexed, studying the paper. "It isn't either one. It's apartment forty-four. Probably a real classy building too. What are you talking about anyway?"

"Go ahead. You cut out, man!" Hart interrupted sharply. "But fill up the car on the way back. And see if you can bend her for a couple of bucks!"

After he had gone, Dinah asked, as she piled the dishes:

"What's all this about Five-B or Six-B, David? You got him all confused. He's liable to think about that all night. You know how he gets hungup."

Stofsky watched Hart light a new stick of tea.

"Nothing. It was nothing at all. Was it, Hart? . . . It doesn't really matter."

Hart considered him blankly, and then, as if taking up a challenge, started to laugh and babble. "Sure, honey, I got all hungup this afternoon. Wait'll you hear this for a real drag! David got a laugh out of it!"

And while he heaped dishes, embraced her gruffly, snickered or hopped about, he told her about the experience with Margo exactly as he had told Stofsky. Every few moments during the account, he would shoot a glance at Stofsky and cackle triumphantly.

"What do you think of that? Isn't that the craziest!" he finished, dancing all around her, dragging loudly on the cigarette, and giggling with wide, wild eyes. "I mean that's a real hassle, isn't it, baby? . . . Here, have some of this!"

"No," and she washed the top of the table with a rag.

"Come on, come on!" he exclaimed with a tinge of irritation. "This place is like a morgue. Hey, we didn't have any dessert did we? But how about some cool weed with whipped cream on top! How about that?" He kept thrusting it in her face, but she would elude him, and went about the dishes lethargically.

"Oh, come on, baby," he wheedled angrily. "Leave them, for Christ's sake. What's the matter? Listen, I've got enough so we can *all* get high, and Ed says this guy's supply is unlimited. He's got a greenhouse out in Hoboken or something, you know! Hiss-s-s-s!! And, man, this is real *wild* tea! Come on . . . David, dig some of this!" He stood in the middle of the room, sipping and exclaiming, sweating profusely. "Oh, for pete's sake, you two are psychological! Hell, I didn't *have* to tell you about it, did I?"

Dinah turned and stared coldly at him. "You didn't tell us if she was a good lay for you."

"What'dya mean! I didn't even see her! I told you how I got the wrong address. That's the joke!"

"Oh, stop it, Hart," and she took a cigarette from Stofsky and slumped down in a chair. "I know you too well for that, remember."

Hart retreated into an air of injured patience. "Do we have to go through all that again? Why shouldn't I tell you if I banged her? What does it really matter? . . . But I didn't, that's what's so crazy about it! I didn't even get to see her. Isn't that right, David?"

"That's what he told me, Dinah," Stofsky said earnestly, regretting the outburst with Ed that had begun it.

"Sure. You see? Besides, why do we have to get all worked

up? What does it matter anyway? *You* understand about these things."

"No, I don't," she answered calmly. "I don't really understand anymore. And I won't pretend to just to make you feel better. So you take your *new* understanding, I'm stuck with the old one."

"Oh, for God's sake! This is like some big, serious Hollywood drama! You know, David? With Bette Davis . . . You're my woman, baby! I didn't even bang her. Why I didn't even get near her! And so what? You act like Kathryn Hobbes or someone . . . Now, why don't you pick up. See everything through big wide eyes, right? Look, I'll make a bomber, a big thick one just for you."

Dinah glanced at him briefly, as though he barely had a place in her thoughts. She fiddled with her garter while he was rolling the cigarette, but there was something about the compression of her thin lips that worried Hart, and his talk became more and more excited as a result.

Suddenly she started to speak, her face strangely pale and her voice slightly choked:

"You're telling yourself that I'm being jealous and crazy . . . for no reason. You don't even think that I've got a reason! But all these women are a fact and your saying they weren't or aren't doesn't eliminate them. You say that all you care about is facts. Well, they're a fact! I won't list them, all the ones two years ago and since, you know them, or maybe you've forgotten them . . ."

"But why are you getting hungup? What do they matter? Come on, have some of this tea, will you? . . . And what about all the times I made you happy, huh? What about all that? You know I love you but you just forget it when it's convenient!"

" 'The times you made me happy!' You're the one who forgets! Oh, I know all the women didn't matter to *you!* You could forget them all right. And 'the times you made me happy!' That was only when I was completely deceived! And you knew that, Hart. Even when I said I believed you! That's what you never understood, for all the talk about understanding."

"But, you see, that's only *one* level," he said, gesticulating nervously. "You know that. All this suspicion and jealousy and all the rest of it. That's the way the squares get hungup, out of fear. I thought you *knew* that, baby. I picked you up in Denver, didn't I? We came all the way up from Tucson, just to pick you up, didn't we?"

"*I* never told you to pick me up! I thought I was finished with you. Sure, it was dull and nowhere up there and I jumped at the chance to get out, but that's because I'd forgotten what it was like with you. But that certainly wasn't your fault. Two years ago I didn't guess I'd ever forget it . . . But you know we never really had anything together, surely I never did. There wasn't even anything to talk about after a while, you know that. Your only interest was you and your kicks. So you hid out behind your tea and your music and tried to figure out how to get an afternoon off to go bang somebody else! . . . Don't lie to *yourself*, Hart! That's the way it always was . . . But now I never want to watch you lie around and masturbate and think of other girls and other things again. It's all just too much of a *drag!* I can never even pretend to believe you anymore. I can't even pretend for your sake. And even right now you lie."

"But I'm not lying! I didn't even get to see her!"

"This isn't Marilyn or one of your cheap pick-ups. I know you. Do you expect me to believe you ever again? Why should I?" She smoked on with an ominous calm, and there was an impregnability in her replies that made him wilder. "Why should I?" she repeated evenly.

"Because, you bitch, it's the truth!" he broke out in a wild bewildered laugh. "It's the goddamn truth! That's what's so crazy!"

"A couple of years ago I would have trusted you, and believed everything you told me . . . But all that doesn't matter!"

"The hell it doesn't! . . . Just cause you're tired and everything, why do you have to light into me? Don't *you* understand why you're doing it? Don't you see, baby?"

"Yes, I do . . . Oh, not on your level, I suppose! You can believe that it's my fault, that I'm just square and a drag. Go ahead, that's what you'll do anyway. And it doesn't really matter about *this* girl. Believe what you want to about that. I'll just stick to my 'square' ideas!"

"Well, this really is a comedown. What do you think of this, David? You see, I'm real high now and I can get *everything* that's happening! *Everything!* Look at her bitching about Margo, and me standing here apologizing and getting all worried! Do you dig all that? Isn't it the craziest thing yo uever heard of? When I didn't even get to lay the dame!"

"Oh, sure, call in the reserves. He'll agree with you probably.

He's on your side, he believes in you, and thinks you're a big shot! You've *fooled* him! But you can't see, Hart, that it doesn't matter about this girl. It really doesn't matter at all. It's your whole way of doing things!"

Hart stood in front of her, grown rigid, studying her with a strange, twisted scowl on his lips. "Now, okay, you've shot off and we've listened. I remember how you used to run around in Denver. Don't talk to me about running around. And you were just a kid too. Don't be bitchy with me!"

"I don't want to talk about it, Hart. You only care about looking good in front of your friends and yourself. All your insults and the cheap lies don't touch me anymore. They don't touch me at all! I like them, do you hear that? I like you to say everything to me."

She rose to her feet, infuriated by some new thought, as though she had, for the first time, become somehow aware of the collection of small miseries that made up her position in the situation and was stunned with anger and self pity by the sight of them.

"Go ahead! Play the leader of the gang! But I like it, I like it, because it keeps my loathing for you alive!"

"But what rights have you to go over me? And talk about lies; what about that time you told me the cops were after me just to get me outa New York? Was that nice? What about that? . . . You think *I'm* lousy, you think *I'm* trying to impress other people! You go crying around about how tough things are for you, about how I'm always giving you a hard time. And then you'll smile like an innocent lamb when I'm looking! Who do you think you're fooling? . . . I married Marilyn just because of you, just because you were a lush and playing games with anybody who came around! How do you think I felt about that after I came all the way out to Denver looking for you? . . . But this time thought you understood everything, that you knew what it was between us and the way it had to be! . . . But, man, what a lot of crap this is! What are we doing anyway? What in the world are we doing? . . . Isn't this the craziest, David? He-he! . . . For nothing, I didn't do anything this time. And *you* know it! You know that's only an excuse to get back at me! What for?"

Dinah was standing in front of him, her eyes wild and brimming. "Maybe it is! It doesn't matter! I told you that. But you can only listen to yourself talk all the time. And call me names!

But go ahead, I love them, they don't hurt me anymore! They make me hate you, Hart, hate you!"

Hart turned with a desperate malice to Stofsky. "Dig this! The kid is feeling s-o-o sorry for herself. Playing the virgin, playing the injured highschool girl! It's really insane, you know."

Dinah slapped him across the face, a stinging, crazy blow.

"Shut up! Shut up! Don't you ever get tired of it? Of everything!"

Hart's eyes were glittering and strange. "You stupid little bitch, you'd go all the way for anybody with a bottle of whiskey when I married Marilyn. You were nothing but a mascot for the football team when I met you, for Christ's sake . . . But I understood that, didn't I? It didn't matter to me! It never mattered to me!"

She hit him again, tears starting from her eyes.

"I was a kid when you met me, just a kid. Just a stupid little girl who wanted to be popular! But you really fixed me, fixed me, fixed me! Didn't you! Admit it. Admit you fixed me for good. And I'll never forget you for it!"

Hart started to laugh right in the middle of her next slap. It was a gutteral, grating sound that was buried inside him, and seemed only to echo of a laugh.

"Bitch! Bitch!" he muttered at her. "Look at the little bitch!"

Her pale, drawn face was streaming with sudden tears that fell from her cheeks in large, shiny drops onto her dress. She hit him again and again, wildly, without thought or aim, screaming all the time:

"Why have you done this to me, Hart? Oh, I wouldn't have believed it! How could I ever have met you? How could I ever have married you at all!"

Her hands quivered before her, clenching and unclenching into little harmless fists, and her sobs made her words almost unintelligible: "How could I have met you! What *are* you!" And she kept hitting him uncontrollably and saying it over and over again: "What *are* you! What *are* you!"

Stofsky had risen with alarm, even pain, evident in his face, just as Hart lashed out and struck her viciously with his fist on the forehead. She seemed to collapse before the blow, and, still weeping pitifully, fell to the floor in a heap.

Hart stood gasping and staring at her oddly. He had gone suddenly white and the hand hung limply at his side and then jerked and trembled spasmodically.

"What are you doing to each other!" Stofsky was crying out. "Stop it now! Stop it immediately! . . . Oh, look, look, she's bleeding! Dinah, Dinah, can't you get up? . . . She didn't mean it, Hart! You knew that! Didn't you understand? . . . Help me with her! Look, she's bleeding where you hit her . . ."

A cut had opened on her forehead and blood was, indeed, pulsing out of it, mingling on her cheeks with the tears. She was sobbing softly, moaning to herself, but not, it appeared, from the pain of the wound.

Hart was suddenly beside her, helping her up, caressing her with the limp hand, half laughing and half crying as he looked into her face.

"Baby, honey! Are you all right? Baby, look what we did! Dinah, Dinah! Put your head back, honey. Oh, look what I did to you!"

She wound weak arms about his neck and let him comfort and caress her, still sobbing inside her stomach. He was kissing her forehead, babbling through the kisses, and Stofsky stood back from them, watching them as though they were children who thought themselves alone, an agitated, crestfallen flush on his features.

"Are you all right, baby? It'll stop in a minute. Look, look, honey! I broke my thumb on you. See it!" and he waggled the bruised hand before her eyes, laughing and grimacing with pain. His lips were stained with her blood, and she stared at him with bewildered wonder. "I think it's broken!" he cried out, putting it to her mouth roughly. "I broke my thumb on you, baby! See, see! Can you feel it? . . . And I kept praying you'd keep hitting me! I actually prayed you'd get me mad enough to smack you! Isn't that awful, baby? Isn't that crazy! I was praying for you all the time!"

Stofsky had a wet towel and tried to get Hart to release her so that he might put it on her forehead, but they would not be separated and she clung to him desperately, cooing and moaning: "Hart, Hart, poor Hart! What a foolish baby you have! What was I doing! . . . Oh, David, what can we do? His thumb feels just like rubber . . . I'm sorry for saying those things about you, David! I didn't mean those things."

"But keep this on your forehead, Dinah! . . . Is it really broken, Hart? Are you sure? But don't move it! Don't touch it!" Stofsky was almost wringing his hands as he went from one to the other with his feeble ministrations. "That's right, there's a hospital down on Seventy-fifth Street. Come on! You've both got to go there right away! . . . Can you get up, Dinah? Can you lift her, Hart? . . . But don't move the thumb! Do you want a sling? We can be there in a few minutes . . . Oh, Ed's got the car! . . . Well, no matter, we'll walk. Come on! Come on!"

They raised no objections, as long as they could be together. Each kept comforting the other, laughing, confessing their feelings, but every once in a while Dinah would start to sob again silently, and moan: "I knew you were high, that's why I did it, and now you're not high any more! And you've broken your thumb!"

They huddled together, aiding each other, but for the most part silent as they walked through the dark, stifling streets. Stofsky flitted around them, fearfully distressed and helpless, and looking more shamefaced and guilt-stricken than either of them. He herded them across side streets, talking all the while and trying to raise their spirits, but only managing to sound somehow apologetic, as if everything was his fault.

At one point, he started capering around them as they walked, turning out his pockets in search of something, and almost shouting: "But I forgot to tell you! I've been getting big, formal letters from people, who conclude that I'm 'intolerable' . . . and 'disordered.' Those are the very words! Isn't that weird? Look, I have them right here! I've been carrying them around like spiritual credentials!"

He waved two crumpled, soiled sheets of paper before their faces, and giggled with embarrassment.

"I went up to see Ketcham the other morning . . . Well, I didn't go up there to see him exactly, but I happened to be at Columbia and dropped in on him. And we had a long talk about philosophy and other matters, during which he kept nodding his head and smiling at me. You know how these people nod their heads! And then this morning I got this letter. Listen to this, Hart . . . It should really be read with that calm, measured nod of the head . . . like a rector! But listen: 'David, I do not mean to be unkind, but I must ask you not to come to see me again. For reasons of my own, I don't feel that I can take your kind of disorder at this time. Don't feel offended. Arthur.' . . . You see!! He had his own reasons *too!* I must have terrorized him . . ."

He grinned wildly at both of them, and went on immediately, thinking somehow that it might amuse them: "And there's one from Verger too. In fact, he was the first! His is more tortured, you might say . . . and considerably longer, but there's this at the end which turns a nice phrase: 'Your eternal gesturings and confessions (such a waste of time!) have become intolerable to me . . .' My eternal gesturings are a waste of *time!* I think that's very apt, and secretly true, of course; although he probably didn't mean it in that sense! But he, also, requests that I don't visit him again. Isn't it fabulous though? I feel something like a . . . like a contagious disease! But think," and he seemed to grow sad at the thought, "think of how terrible for them! You know what they're both like, reserved, always hiding in their own ways. Think of how difficult I made it for them, even though I was right . . . No, not right, I guess . . . but sincere! I *was* sincere, Hart! You must believe that much anyway! . . . But perhaps they don't even realize yet how terrible it was!"

A desperate gleam came into his eyes, and he laughed idiotically again: "And there'll be others, others coming! I know it. And I'll save them all . . . like you save rejection slips. He-he! But these will be of the soul!"

Later, at work among the clattering machines and the listless night time activity of the news office, after he had left them at the hospital, still wordless and enrapt in each other, silent as a kind of penance, each to each, for their naughtiness; later, he wondered, in some privately naïve fashion of his own, about the justice of their dispute. Through the curses, tears and violence, he could see no right and wrong on either side, but only their ill-starred obsession with one another. The rest seemed only issues, fears, blindness that disguised their similarity, their secret lovelessness. They were the same, and perhaps everyone and everything was the same in that sense! No mere squabble could efface that! So ran his thoughts.

Sitting at the desk, mulling them, Stofsky knew the horror of his own perception. 'Suppose it is true,' he thought giddily. 'That there is no right and wrong, but only this creatureliness that I saw in the bookstore!' The idea fatally attracted him; he went to it like a childhood haunt that is rediscovered and found to be redolent with simple, moving remembrances; and yet it horrified something more worldly in him.

Thinking again upon Dinah and Hart, he wrote out on a piece of yellow copy paper:

"Why do finite angels fly
Away from their infinity?
All that they know, they knew as men;
What was so, is so again.
Oh, when will human vanity
Give up vain inhumanity?"

Then he stuffed the verse into his pocket with the two letters, telling himself that what it might reveal to Hart and Dinah had been revealed to them already; and choosing to forget his own fear at the sight of it.

But Dinah, if she had seen it, could not forget or forgive, and though she and Hart slept tenderly together in an older, speechless innocence that night, and laughed together about their wounds the next day, on Friday, when she received her salary, she went from her job to Times Square and took a bus for California anyway, telling only Ed.

Eleven

On the following Monday, Hobbes and Kathryn came back from a meal at the Athens to find Pasternak, Hart and Stofsky waiting for them in the Cadillac. What they had thought would be a quiet, sweltering evening at home turned out to be a night they would not soon forget. Quite suddenly, as they were led to believe it always happened, Hart had decided to start back for the coast sometime the next day. Ostensibly this was the reason for the visit, and as it seemed a good one, even Kathryn did not resist the intrusion.

There was no marijuana and so they fell back on beer. During the ensuing hours, someone was always absent as they took turns going downstairs for more. All new bottles were immediately opened, spread about the room, and no one seemed to notice that the small quantities procured each time, and their quick consumption, made constant trips necessary. The next morning Hobbes was surprised to find twenty-two quart bottles littered on the table and under the couches, even though by then he had more important things to think about than this arithmetic.

That week the heat had settled down savagely, and even at night, though robbed of its blistering source, it lingered on in the streets. It lay over the city like an invisible siege, and gave everyone a discomfort in common. But that evening, with the beer that spread a cottony thickness through their limbs, the group forgot it temporarily. They sat about in shirt sleeves, perspiring easily and drinking, and all got pleasantly tipsy, the temperature adding potency to the beer. This combination lent everyone a feeling that composure, as it was impossible, was also somehow superfluous. They all simply gave in to themselves.

All but Hart. The difference in him would not have been immediately noticeable to someone meeting him for the first time, as Estelle did for instance when, after an hour, Ed rang the bell and came in wordlessly with her tagging behind him. She could not have recognized that Hart was strangely (for him) gloomy and disconsolate.

Of course, he frankly announced that Dinah had disappeared, and even said to Hobbes with a dispirited smile:

"We got all hungup over Margo, and that's how I busted the thumb . . . poking her. It was a real drag, ask David!" But he cared more than this confession would indicate.

Somewhere at Stofsky's he had found a water pistol (the remnant of some masquerade of David's in the past), and he brandished this all evening, now going through impersonations of cowboy actors, the irony of which was somehow deceptively innocent, and then filling the chamber with beer and squirting it down his throat. When Estelle was introduced, as though recalling who and what he was in the eyes of the others, his face filled with vast, mock approval, and he leveled the gun pointedly from his hips and clicked it repeatedly in her direction. Later, however, sitting on the floor with Hobbes among the glasses and bottles, he took to putting it to his head and firing it, laughing scornfully, and pretending to fall dead.

Pasternak exclaimed immediately upon coming in:

"Yah, I'm taking off with Hart. What the hell! I gave my book to Carr & Horton's three weeks ago, but they'll reject it just like MacMurry's did. And why should I get hungup? All this writerish worry and care is really unnatural, you know? And maybe I'll get me a job on the Santa Fe for the fall, and then go up and play roulette in Butte! You have to live, Paul, *live!*"

He displayed boundless anticipation about the trip, and a touching warmth for both Hobbes and Kathryn. He seemed to be bursting with a boyish good feeling that overwhelmed all means by which he could express it. Alternately, he would beat pots and pans to the bop on the radio, turn while doing this, to shower Kathryn with eager, trusting smiles and clumsy kisses, and then, after the record was over, lie on the floor under a full bottle of beer and wriggle gaily as he drank it. Once he tried to do everything at once, and splattered himself, only to rise licking at his forearms as he took off his soaked shirt. He flew from Hobbes to Kathryn, and back again.

"Don't worry," he said earnestly once to Hobbes. "I'll come back sometime when I've had my fill of this crazy country! Who can say when? But I'll come back when I know, Paul, when I *know* all about the good life!" And because of the rumpled, embarrassed grin that accompanied this, Hobbes realized that it was no mockery of him, but only Pasternak's own crude assurance.

With Kathryn, Pasternak strutted like a high school athlete, who is arrogantly nervous about the fascination he creates. Her quizzical objections to his enthusiasms disappeared when he took her by the shoulders, shaking her with rough tenderness, and roared: "*Let* me spill beer on your floor! Let me! Just 'cause I'm going away! And relax! Here, here, you spill some too!" And so pleasurably taken aback by his directness was she that she spilled a little with a wanton, devilish snort.

As he got drunker, he talked more warmly to her, in grander, more extravagant tones which she could not really deride.

"You're pure!" he cried once. "I swear you're pure as snow! But I under*stand* you, Kathryn. I've always understood pure women. You're really motherly, not one of these scared, brittle, intellectual girls who pretend to know everything, but never even blink, not even one girlish blink at *anything!*"

She leveled a slightly suspicious, imperious eye at him and retorted: "Nonsense. I'm just a dumb little wop and you know it."

But his flushed face filled with joy at this, a joy which could not be suspected: "Sure, that's right! But not dumb in *that* sense! It's just like I'm really only a Polak, just a damn Polak millhand! You see? I knew you understood all that."

Observing this and acting on the daring that it gave him, Hobbes approached Estelle as she sat placidly on the couch where Ed had left her for a few minutes. Oddly enough, she was the girl whose address he had been given by his friend in California, whom she had known briefly while in college, but she hastened to add: "I came along with Ed just to see you both again. You never called me after the last time," this with a friendly, though reproving and somehow intimate smile.

"I like Ed, don't you? But he's a real Midwesterner. Do you realize he tried to borrow money from me the other night?" And she laughed elegantly. "He's awfully cute looking though, isn't he?"

Her self-possession was at once terrifying and intriguing to Hobbes, and he sparred with her uneasily. It seemed she was a secretary in a midtown export firm, lived with her family on Ninety-eighth Street, and was not at all interested in saying any more about herself. She answered all his chatty questions in an off-hand, precise manner, all the while inspecting his face and eyes with calculating, challenging glances that bore no relation to the conversation. Her relaxation was impregnable, and it flustered Hobbes, who fell back on an attitude tinged with cynicism under which familiarity could be safely hidden. But her wide, rational eyes disarmed him, and he was relieved when everyone gathered in the bathroom where Hart had begun writing epigrams on the walls.

Pasternak gigglingly insisted on adding to Hart's scrawled caligraphy "Paul cons Kathryn" and "Gene cons Christine." Underneath these, he laboriously spelled out: "David cons God!" After her immediate horror at these defacements, Kathryn seized the pencil from him and, with a sparkling, assured smirk, crossed out "Christine," and wrote in "Everybody!"

Estelle, who had followed Hobbes, only laughed at these announcements, treating even Stofsky's writing of "Anyone who cons anyone cons themselves!" as the most casual and innocent party-fun. Taking strength from her acceptance of all this, Hobbes pressed her arm at the door, when soon after it she left with Ed, and suggested: "Maybe I'll call you at your office. We can have lunch . . . or something." To which she only smiled mysteriously and, as she went down the stairs, winked at him capriciously.

Stofsky, in an unusually excited and affectionate mood, sat on Hart's lap a good part of the evening. His frivolities while there seemed somehow in dreadful earnest to the others, and they treated all his actions as commonplaces, as though recognizing his real intent, although this was not the case. Hart himself hugged him, playing his role in what was only part parody, and being accommodating to cover the depression he considered a "drag."

Stofsky, for all his writhings and laughter to the contrary, noticed everything. Once when Hart said to Hobbes, pointing the water pistol menacingly at his head, "Well now that you're in my boat, man, shall we rock it together?", all the time nodding at Pasternak and Kathryn across the room who by this time were bent confidingly together, agreeing volubly, and Hobbes replied that it was all the same to him, Stofsky broke in heatedly: "That's right. Don't worry. We'll all feel repellently ugly together! We'll crouch here like three inhibited cockroaches!"

When Pasternak and Kathryn, unable to drift away from each other, trapped in an awareness both had tried, right up to the last, to dismiss, slipped out the door together, Stofsky beetled his brows and laughed the louder, as though trying to discreetly drown out something, and leaving Hart bobbing dully to the music, he came up to Hobbes, his blushing embarrassment failing to cover the conflict of motives that was boiling up in him. Screwing his mouth into an almost desperate, yet timid smile, he said shrilly:

"I'm here, Paul Hobbes, to make love to you!" and he snickered at his own effrontery. At Hobbes' surprised but effective parry of this, he asked, without vexation: "But have you ever had relations with a man since you grew up?"

"No!" Hobbes replied without moving. "But I'm perfectly happy, David. And *you* mustn't worry. I don't judge anything. I really don't! Why should I? Beyond a certain point everyone is on his own!" And Stofsky, though near enough to the window to see that the Cadillac was no longer where they had parked it, smiled apologetically and hurriedly tried to change the subject.

"I've been thinking seriously of plans to save Verger! The worst thing that could have happened to him right now *has* actually happened! May . . . you know, Verger's May . . . has been abducted by Agatson! It's just some whim of his, a joke probably, but somehow he got her to move in with him! . . . I have all this, quite by accident, through a friend . . . This could ruin Verger now, he's sick anyway of course, and he's not the type to just forget her. He might have put her entirely out of his mind if this hadn't happened . . . She's really a rather shallow girl after all, but now he'll waste himself away to nothing out of unrequited love! . . . He's . . . he's the kind who'd give his own *wife* away to . . . well, to feel like a martyr! He-he!" At this he positively blushed, and quickly went on babbling and fluttering his hands nervously, as though to distract attention, peeping at Hobbes every few seconds, bashfully expecting anger.

But, though Hobbes too knew the car was gone, and the failure of Stofsky's crude tact had not been lost on him, he exhibited and felt no real anger. Strangely there was only that relief that attends the clarifying of a touchy situation, no matter in what direction. He thought, drunkenly, that it lay with him to be cheery now that most of the party had disappeared, even though everything about Pasternak's and Kathryn's departure was still in doubt. It was somehow easy for him, and he became more animated than he had been all evening, displaying what he was sure was a winning amiability and ease. He went farther: he became expansive on everything that was brought up, cultivated Hart in his depression, would allow no one their low spirits, and chattered away even when both Hart and Stofsky made little effort to respond. Aware of the turmoil within his laughter, and yet somehow attracted to the position in which he found himself, he became actually light-headed, as people are when suddenly released from an intolerable tension. In fact, he was truly sorry when they rose to go, and tried to discreetly suggest that it might be best if they stayed away from the apartment on York Avenue for a while, guessing that Pasternak and Kathryn might be there.

Hart, morose and introverted, only wished for a change, but Stofsky, with sad understanding, stood for a moment, meekly sympathetic and said, touching Hobbes' arm: "We'll go over to the Paradise . . . Maybe we'll run into Ancke, Hart, or another wizard of the night! . . . But why don't you come with us, Paul? We'll have humble, loving conversations together. We've never really had them, you and I . . ."

But Hobbes declined, somehow aggravated by Stofsky's sincere concern, feeling it intruded upon the sanctity of his situation; and, as Stofsky perceived and accepted even this, they left him to what turned out to be a lonely vigil.

❋   ❋   ❋   ❋   ❋

Kathryn came back at four o'clock to find him still dressed and lying quietly on a couch, smoking. As soon as she entered the room, she became extremely nervous, as if he had put her in an unfortunate position simply by his presence there. Nervousness always made her seem preoccupied and impenetrable, though this was far from her actual state of mind.

"I hope you didn't come back alone, honey. At this hour."

"Oh, no, Gene drove me back in the car all right . . ." After standing hesitantly for a moment, she finally sat down and lit a cigarette, and Hobbes recognized, through the preoccupation, her intense embarrassment.

"Why didn't he come up? Why does he run away like that? I seem to have made everyone terribly uneasy tonight. Even David and Hart went away soon after you two left. What does everyone expect me to—"

"I didn't want him to come up," she interrupted suddenly. "It's late and he's still drunk . . . and besides . . . I've seen enough people for one night."

Hobbes sniffed brusquely to himself, as if she had unwittingly made a joke. "Hart and David didn't break in on you did they?" he asked then with measured delicacy. "I tried to hint that they'd better not go back there for a while, and they said they were going over to the Paradise, but you never can tell . . ."

"Why shouldn't they have come back? You didn't have to do *that!* What'll they think!" She was almost irritated, pursing her lips and flicking the cigarette ash away repeatedly, but then, remembering her position, she began again falteringly:

"No . . . no, they weren't back when we left. We . . . we just started out for a drive, you know, because it was so hot, and then Gene wanted more beer and we went to a lot of bars, and got drunk, and he said there was whiskey at David's so—"

"You don't have to account for it," Hobbes insisted easily. "Really. Just relax . . . Don't you think it's cooled off now though?"

This seemed to distress her. "Why shouldn't I tell you about it? Who *would* I tell about it?" Her look implored him, and she began once more: "So we went up to David's, and Gene was so funny. He kept talking about you, and asking me if I thought you disapproved of him."

"Well, certainly you understand that."

"Of course, but he was really worried about it. He thinks you're wonderful, but he can't make you out; you know how he is. And then we kept necking and everything, just sort of playfully, and drinking. He kept filling my glass, and after all that beer—"

"You shouldn't mix whiskey and beer like that, you'll get sick. But you don't *seem* drunk."

His solicitousness seemed contrived to keep her at a distance. "No, no, it went away . . . But I'm just trying to explain—"

"But you don't have to, sweetheart."

"I want to, I want to tell you about it! Why won't you let me tell you? . . . Well . . . anyway we got very drunk sitting on the floor, and he was telling me about Hart and Dinah . . . and I got . . . dizzy for a while, and—"

"You had intercourse."

Pronounced so calmly and distinctly, it shook her, although, of course, she had been leading up to it herself, and so, while answering, she would not take her eyes off the floor.

"Yes. It was silly actually, I suppose, but we were so drunk that—"

"Why was it silly?" he replied with aggravation. "Really, Kathryn, you don't have to say all that on my account!"

"But it *was!* . . . It was, you know, sort of childish and . . . awkward . . . in that messy apartment and everything. And he kept whispering to me, and then he wouldn't say a word."

"What do you mean, whispering? What did he say? Is that when he was telling you that he thought I was wonderful? You mean he was whispering sweet nothings in your ear!"

"No, no! You know what I mean. He didn't really *say* anything, just foolish things, like how I was 'pure.' You know, just drunken things. I didn't mean that he said anything in particular . . . I was just trying to tell you how sort of stupid it was—"

"But why do you say that?" he exclaimed peevishly. "Don't you see how hypocritical that is? You shouldn't distort things like this afterwards . . . just because you feel guilty or something like that!"

"But I'm not distorting them. It *was* silly. Oh, you know, what I mean! It . . . it didn't *mean* anything! That's all I'm trying to say. It was just . . . just sort of ordinary and awkward!"

"Well, that's really my fault, I guess," he laughed somewhat bitterly. "I should have warned you about that. I mean, you're really romantic. You know, you have a movie conception of these things. And there's always awkwardness . . . It can't be helped and you shouldn't judge Gene because of *that!* I mean there are arrangements that have to be made after all. The appropriate place; you know, going from living room to bedroom, taking off clothes . . . and the other things! People always expect everything to happen by itself, to be easy and smooth. And why should they think that these essential practicalities take anything away from the experience? I've always felt that—"

"But I didn't mean . . . those things so much!" she broke in, mystified by this outburst, and sure something more relevant lay beneath it. "It was just . . . really nothing. I was sort of surprised and I felt like laughing."

"But listen, Kathryn, you've got to get this straight for yourself. You mustn't regret things you wanted to do just because of anybody else. Don't you see how foolish it is? You didn't feel guilty at the time, did you? I mean, it was just something that . . . that happened, wasn't it?"

"Yes, I suppose so. But I really didn't *feel* anything. That's what I'm trying to say. I mean, I was sort of amused by Gene, and we were having fun—"

"Exactly. As I always said, you're attracted to him and he's attracted to you. Is there anything wrong in that? I ask you, isn't that normal after all? People can't eradicate these things just because it would be neater and easier if they did. And why should they? Why? It's so stupid when you think of it. But the important thing is that you don't lie to yourself afterwards. That corrupts the experience, that distorts the reality of it. *That's* what causes neurosis, all these ridiculous guilts and fears that people impose on experience, when they didn't actually feel them at all when it happened. Don't you think that's right? Don't you *really* agree with me?"

She was confused by much of this, and kept looking earnestly at him trying to decipher hostility behind his remarks. "Well, I guess so. But what I'm trying to say is that it wasn't important somehow. I mean it wasn't particularly . . . pleasurable . . . I was drunk and we were just sort of . . . fooling around . . . and he wanted to. It wasn't in *earnest!* Don't you see what I mean?"

"Certainly. But you shouldn't be so on edge about everything, honey. Relax." And he began to chuckle. "I didn't mean anything by that. I wasn't reproving you. You know how I feel about these things. I was just asking you . . . well, if you'd had a good time!" A distracted, enigmatic laugh broke from his lips. "Like your father would ask you!"

"Well, as long as you understand," she said with a disappointed pout. She sat undecided for a moment, sure it wasn't really all settled, looking at him surreptitiously as he became involved lighting a fresh cigarette from the stub of the one he had just finished. Trying to make the move appear careless, she came and sat down beside him, with a faint-hearted weary smile as though he might send her away. "I'm exhausted," she breathed. ". . . and it's . . . good to be home."

He put his arm around her with subtle magnaminity, and she snuggled closer into his body, trying to find shelter in it. He could feel the heaving of her breasts against him, and he stared for a moment at her lidded eyes and the wide, tremulous mouth. He was surprised to find a heightened awareness of her within him, as if she had been transformed in his mind and was suddenly new and unopened. The warmth within her, some thick female electricity, brought a tingle from his flesh where, unknowingly, she touched it, and for an idiotic moment he felt an old clogged desire to *know* her physically, and feel her, quivering and aroused, beneath his own weight. He forgot the tangle of ambiguities, his involved lonely thoughts while he had waited for her to return, and taking her trembling half-smile into his mouth, he kissed her deeply, with strange, aggressive ardor, as though he was trying to exact some inexplicable surrender from her lips.

But then he drew back abruptly at a new idea which had occurred to him, and laughed almost hysterically.

"But, you know, you weren't the only one! Oh, no! I wasn't entirely abandoned. Would you believe it, I have my admirers too! Stofsky came up to me and said he wanted to make love to me! Wasn't that nice though? I think he was almost fainting with excitement! Ha-ha! . . . But *I* refused him, of course. Maybe I was being too prudish, do you think?" He laughed feverishly at her baffled expression. "And then later he said that I was trying to give my wife away . . . well, he didn't actually mention *me,* he pretended to be speaking about Verger . . . but it was too apt to be a coincidence. What do you think of that? How would you like Stofsky for a rival? Ha-ha!"

She didn't find this funny at all, and sitting up, she frowned petulantly. "I don't like him when he gets like that! He scares me! Why is he always saying things like that?"

"Well, I'm sure he never said them to *you!* You're just not his type!"

She refused to be sidetracked by these wild jibes.

"But you should be more cautious, Paul. You don't want to get mixed up in that kind of thing, even though you—"

"You don't think I'm a latent homosexual, do you! I mean, there *are* limits to how far justification should go! I was sure it would give you a laugh! To think that at the same time . . . And he was just trying to be kind in his own way. In fact, I'm sure that you're the cause of it, ha-ha-ha! That is, you and Gene! David thought I was lonely, he just wanted to comfort me. In his own cautious way!"

"All right, all right, if you know what you're doing."

"And speaking of caution," Hobbes began suddenly. "I don't know how to bring this up. I suppose there's some form that should be followed, and I'm not trying to make it difficult for you, but . . . well, I hope that certain awkwardnesses, or perhaps better, certain practicalities were observed by you and Gene . . . if you see what I mean."

His modesty, because it was a pose, was offensive to her.

"Of course! What did you think!"

"But you're sure," he insisted. "I mean, I don't care about the rest of it, you know . . . I think it's fine, in fact . . . But I don't think I'm overstepping myself to want to know about—"

"I'm absolutely certain! . . . What do you mean, overstepping yourself?"

"Well, my position as . . . as cuckold!" and a wry, shrewd smile defaced his mouth.

She was crushed again, but also infuriated, and her reply was despairing: "See, I knew you really cared about all this! I knew you didn't really believe everything you're always saying! Why won't you tell me what you really believe?"

"But I have," and he seized her arm as she rose. "Don't run away," he said firmly, laughing lightly and pulling her to him again. "Really, I was just kidding. I should be allowed to at least make a joke shouldn't I? You said that all of it was really funny, so why should *I* have to be so serious about it? Ha-ha! Really, I was just joking with you!"

She turned her face to him, and her mouth trembled again with her earnest desire to believe him so that her own feelings might be clear. "Are you sure? It doesn't make any difference?"

"Of course it doesn't make any difference. I know it sounds ridiculous, but you see, my trouble is (socially, that is) that I really mean what I say. I really mean it! But *nobody* believes me, Gene doesn't even believe me! They think I've got some deep scheme or something. And I've always got to assure everybody that their guilts don't mean anything to me, not *anything!*"

She kissed him with fatigued submissiveness and they undressed and got into bed. She lay in the crook of his arm in the darkness, half expecting him to make love to her and half wanting him to; unable to convince herself that everything was all right, but not mentioning it for fear it would irritate him again, and thinking that if she acted as though it were all right eventually it would become so. For a long time, as he lay there silently beside her and made no move, she restrained herself, but then she asked him, having to have some verbal pledge:

"And you do love me?"

"Of course. Don't be silly any more."

And she accepted it because it was reasonable, even though it did not set her doubts at rest, and turning over, she said, more to herself than to him: "Well, I'm glad *that's* over with anyway!" and she did not mean the two hours she had spent in Stofsky's apartment or their discussion of them, but something else that had started farther back in their marriage.

Twelve

Soon after Kathryn left for work the next morning, Pasternak called and, after some hesitation, told Hobbes that he, Hart and Ed were leaving for the coast about nine that night. He said that he would be busy most of the day "borrowing money," but asked if he could call at seven so they could get together. Hobbes immediately agreed to this.

He had been busy sorting out his reactions to the incident of the night before, and had half concluded that Pasternak would leave town without getting in touch with him. Although nothing had been mentioned over the phone by either of them, Hobbes felt an excited expectation about the meeting because of his changed position with Pasternak. He realized there was a similar change with Kathryn, but had not yet decided just where he, himself, stood in that quarter. Immediately after their talk, he had felt a twisted relief, interrupted with moments of jealous irritation. Estelle had entered his mind, and he had even suggested to Kathryn over their morning coffee that they see more of her, mentioned it almost as an illustration of their new position. But after Pasternak's call, and the strange expectation that was his reaction to it, he began to experience the emotion of self righteousness, combined with a feeling of the martyr's power over those who have sacrificed him, and he found himself relishing his own guiltlessness in comparison to Kathryn, and to preserve this sensation he drove Estelle, and the possibility of sleeping with her, from his mind.

But something happened that afternoon that robbed him of these emotions and indirectly affected his interview with Pasternak. It began when Ketcham dropped in on him at two, wondering if they could have a few drinks together. He had just come from a "courtesy lunch with a client of the firm," and now he wanted relaxation. Hobbes was genuinely happy that he had come and was glad for any company, so they took the subway down to the Village where Ketcham had to pick up some manuscripts, planning to drink after that.

It was a humid, oppressive afternoon with occasional, desultory showers clearing the streets, and after concluding Ketcham's business, they started roaming from one small, nearly empty barroom to the next, having a few beers at each one, trying to ignore the baseball on the television, and talking of books, concerts and mutual friends, as was their habit.

Eventually, after scurrying up Sixth Avenue when a gust of warm rain caught them unawares, they found themselves at Haverty's (Agatson's favorite bar), and were surprised to discover Verger crouched in one of the booths. Getting their own beers from the bar, they joined him there.

He was huddled in a corner, like a spider, with seven empty glasses before him. He wore the same filthy, torn white shirt and ripped trousers as when Stofsky had visited him nearly two weeks ago. He was unshaven, gaunt and positively swaying over the table in a drunken trance. His lips were rigidly compressed in an effort to prevent their trembling, and his glassy, large eyes wandered behind his spectacles, unable to settle for very long on anything. On one pale cheek, over the bone, there was a bluish discoloration and the rest of his face was streaked with dirt. He coughed wearily every few minutes, and his voice was thick and rasping when he spoke to them.

"You've just this minute come from Agatson's, haven't you?" He made a wily, crooked smile and shuffled his feet under the table. "Well, why shouldn't I sit here? . . . Oh, I know what he told you all right! But it has nothing to do with either of them, my sitting here; nothing at all. Please note that I said that."

"What do you mean? We haven't seen Bill," Ketcham began hesitantly, snatching an apprehensive, but also amused, glance at Hobbes.

"You mean you haven't come to demand that I stop 'haunting' him? That's the very word he used to me; you know, I'm sure he thinks that I believe in ghosts . . . But you haven't seen him? Paul, is that true?" He started to cough but, so excited was he by something, that he swallowed it, and gripped Hobbes' arm suddenly: "Is that really true? You can't deceive me, you know. I've been here the whole time, waiting and . . . drinking."

"No, we really haven't seen him," Hobbes replied uneasily, eying the glasses. "And it looks like we're way behind you."

"But haven't I a right to be here? How dare he conclude that it's because of him . . . or even her, for that matter! Cah-cah-cah! Doesn't he think I have better things to do than . . ." He shuffled his feet again, his shoulders shivering as though a chill had run through him. "But it's infuriating . . . when I understand him more than anyone else. I really do . . . Are you sure he didn't send you to find me? There's no need to make gestures with me . . ."

"Of course not," Ketcham insisted with tight lips, humoring him. "What in the world has happened to you?"

"I'm just waiting for May, that's all. Why should I hide it? I suppose it's utterly foolish, isn't it? It's really the same as abasing yourself, at any rate that's what I thought last night in the Square—"

"You mean you slept in the Square?" Hobbes broke out.

"Oh, I didn't sleep. But it *is* revolting, isn't it? This hanging around, waiting, 'haunting' them this way . . . I haven't any pride though, I don't care about all that any more . . . And, you know, she's really too brittle for him, that's why I'm waiting. She's really too frivolous, and he'll get tired of his little plot . . . or she'll get scared. And there's no one else to wait, so . . ."

The rain, now splashing steadily on the plate glass window, caught his gaze for the first time: "Oh, look, it rains! On field and tree. And how does the next line go? . . ." Then that seemed to slip away from him also. "But did you ever think of Bill as an elephant? Really, as an elephant."

Ketcham laughed derisively.

"That's what he is, an elephant who always forgets. But he won't go to the graveyard, you see, he refuses to go and die in solitude. Do you see the connection? . . . Giants should creep away when they start to get senile, like elephants . . . I mean, great people who stand for something, people that other people believe in . . . you know, heroes. Agatson used to be a hero, after all, to lots of us; at least he believed in himself and that's always convincing. But now that he's repeating himself, going through the old vaudeville routines, he should disappear, don't you think? . . . Or is all this sentimentalizing, to think of him this way?"

He laughed earnestly, reflectively, but he had forgotten the original point of his speech.

"But the more people who see him losing his grip, and see him merely chuckle when some envious existentialist breaks a lily over his head (do you know that actually happened the other night, right in here!) . . . when they see him just ignore that, the less people will be able to believe in him. Do you see what I mean? I had it all so clear last night, but now I've . . . Well, am I being sentimental about it? . . . But what if all Prometheans are condemned to end in chains? I mean, if that were some natural, immutable law! Think of it a moment!"

Ketcham was at once diverted and annoyed by this rabble.

"You're taking him too seriously. Don't you think you're considering him to be more significant than he is? Bill is just a college boy who never grew up, and all that's happening is that his act is getting tedious and not drawing the crowds it used to in Cambridge. It's pathetic, not tragic. He simply refuses to admit that the beer is running out and that no new guests are arriving."

"No, no! It's *other* people who have deluded him, formalized him. Think of that. His trouble is that he creates biographers wholesale! Do you see what I mean? All the Midwesterners in his coterie insist on getting Boswellian. And he's always read his own notices, you see. That's my point. He used to be a way of life, and now he's degenerated into . . . into a state of mind!"

He paused, reaching for Hobbes' beer absently.

"What he should actually do is go up in a puff of smoke, or vanish into the Syrian desert in rags, never to be heard of again! That way he might become part of the culture, a kind of black prophet, his apartment something of a shrine . . . instead of it all turning into a playful joke, something to be hawked to every new crop of Villagers for a dollar-ninety-eight, an aging clown . . ."

"Well, don't worry about May," Ketcham said with a strange touch of scorn for him. "That's Bill's stock in trade. He's got to ruin a woman every few months or lose his opinion of himself. You're not the *only* one! Look what he's done to . . ." and he swallowed, "to Bianca. We're quite a fraternity. And you shouldn't care about it!"

Verger cringed before these harsh words, his face gone chalk-white under the beard, and his large, blank eyes misty and hurt like a small animal's. His hands clutched vaguely on the table, and he began to sob softly, coughing and crying at the same time.

"But she loved me . . . she *would* have loved me if he hadn't come around. She would have, I tell you! It's all very well for you to say 'don't care' . . . but, but she was the first for me

. . . I've, I've never had a girl, never! Isn't it comical? . . . Oh, I know," he wept, sniffing but not trying to keep back his drunken tears, "she thought I was stupid, even ugly . . . But I didn't care about that, I would have loved her selflessly, I would have done anything . . . Listen, she wouldn't even kiss me, cah-cah-cah! . . . Why do they think they have a right to hurt me this way? Why, why, I ask you why!"

He ground his head down into his arms violently, sobbing terribly and writhing about in the booth.

"I don't mind her going off, if it was just to see . . . what he was like. I understand, but . . . but she wouldn't even kiss me! I told her that she wouldn't catch anything. You can't pass the germ that way. I told her over and over again! Does she think *that* was easy for me? And . . . and I'm going to die soon anyway, I feel it! Die, die! . . . She could have *pitied* me! She could have at least pitied me! I wouldn't have minded even that, I would have clutched at even that! And now it's . . . it's—"

He lost all semblance of control, and could not even speak any longer. His frail chest was so shaken by the deep sobs that it seemed about to shatter like a window in an earthquake. He beat his head against the table feebly, his sobs so depriving him of breath that all that came out of him were terrible, shameless groans.

Ketcham looked helplessly at Hobbes, who was stunned by all of it but managed to exclaim:

"What'll we do? We ought to get him out of here! Feel him, he's soaked through and he's so drunk he'll kill himself if he wanders in the streets this way."

"But where can we take him? . . . Daniel, it'll be all right! Stop crying now, you've just had too much to drink . . . There's no one but Agatson down here. It's just three blocks."

"But should we take him *there*? I mean—"

"Why not? We've got to get him out of here. Why not take him there? . . . Bill will let him stay, have no fear! Bill will love it, in fact! It's irony, remember?"

They took the doubled-up, gasping figure between them and somehow got him out into the rain. There he seemed to find his feet and staggered between them speechlessly, still possessed of the heavy sobs that thrashed inside him like a demon in his breast. They hurried through the streets pulling him along, increasing their gait every time huge soundless coughs would stagger him the more. Once he broke away from them wildly, crying out:

"No, no, no! It's *not* vicariousness!"

He stumbled a few steps, his arms thrown up into the drizzle like a demented evangelist, and then he fell all in a graceless heap in the gutter, his legs grotesquely awry, and his sockless ankles looking absurdly spindly and naked in the dreary light.

Somehow they got him to Agatson's, soaked, nearly unconscious and unable to walk any longer. They had to carry him up the narrow, stale smelling stairways, but after this awkward ascent, they pushed into the dark loft and laid him on one of the mattresses, sweeping beer bottles and a pile of dirty laundry out of the way.

The place was the usual filthy litter, the small windows shuttered, everything in complete disorder, and at first they thought no one was there. But after a moment, Agatson wandered in from the kitchen, only half dressed in a pair of spotted blue jeans, an inquisitive glint in his sunken, tired eyes. His lips quivered slightly, and the skin on his face seemed tautly pulled across his cheek bones. He was obviously suffering from a bad hangover.

"I'm sorry we had to burst in on you this way, Bill," Ketcham said, with sudden impatience at the sight of him. "But he was wet through, completely drunk and coughing badly. There was nowhere else to take him. I think we ought to get him undressed and warmed up. And maybe he'll go to sleep."

Agatson peered curiously at Verger as he lay, breathing with difficulty, on the mattress.

"Sure, he can lie there. Isn't he dirty though! Has he been falling downstairs again? And look at that bruise . . . Did I do that to him? I was drunk last night and I can't remember . . . we were wrestling . . ." He swung about and shrieked into the kitchen: "May! Hey, May, your beau from uptown has come back again! Come out of there! We have guests! Ha-ha-ha! . . . She won't come out though."

There were movements from the darkened kitchen, and vaguely they saw a dim head peer out, a grey blob that disappeared immediately. This seemed to amuse Agatson.

"She refuses to see anybody. She's been hiding in there for days now! . . . May, for Christ's sake, stop being bitchy! . . . You know, I think she's frightened of the ghosts . . . Come out here, you whore!" he screamed gaily. "Gentlemen, I want you to meet the worst goddamn tramp in New York! . . . May, hey May!" But she would not budge from behind the door where she had taken flight.

Agatson was now bent over Verger, eyes flashing with some new idea. "You hear that, Verger? The worst tramp in the whole country! What are you crying about? . . . Hey, May, now he's crying for you. Come out here and do a dance!"

Ketcham stood looking at Agatson pluck at Verger's shirt, and his face was clouded with disgust, as though suddenly everything in sight had become insufferable to him.

"Stop blubbering, Verger. You don't know what I saved you from . . . None of you know what I've always saved you from . . . 'Through my fault, my most griev-ious fault.' Ha-ha-ha!" After one beady glance at Ketcham, he continued to pluck at Verger, vindictively patting him on the cheek, and squeaking:

"Why don't you stop coughing, for Christ's sake! Getting germs on everything! Don't you know how unseemly it is?"

Verger stirred, although his eyes had been open for the last few minutes, and were glazed as they stared up at the disheveled figure that stood over him.

"He's alive!" Agatson cried. "Why don't you just go off and die, Verger! Instead of coughing all over everybody! I told you you were only a ghost."

"My God!" Ketcham exclaimed in a shocked whisper.

"That's what you should do, Verger. Crawl off like a spider and die. No one's going to fall into your web any more. Think of how *that* would impress everyone! If you just died! Think of how everyone would pity you *then!*"

Verger was staring fixedly at him, coughing a little now and then and squirming under the insistent fingers.

"Don't cough on me!" Agatson cried wildly. "Oh, he's gotten his disease all over me!" and he leapt back, feigning revulsion, striving to keep the insane laughter buried in his chest. "But I'm your friend, Verger. I'm your only friend! I pity you, I bleed for you! Cough on me if you like! Go ahead, if it'll make you feel any better. Spit on me! . . . But, no, I'll be St. Francis, and I'll embrace the poor leper!" And he came toward Verger with his arms outstretched in a merciless parody of pity.

Verger raised himself weakly and looked at Agatson with such strange, hurt eyes that Agatson stopped short, the laugh dead in his mouth.

" 'Why am I condemned to believe in you for an eternity,

Nikolay . . .'", but after this Verger stopped also, as though remembering that the quotation was hateful to him. He fell back on the grimy mattress, coughing again, and mumbling, his face constricted with shame:

"How horrible everything is! Cah-cah-cah! Horrible! But I'll forgive you even for that, Bill . . . But just let me rest and catch my breath . . ."

Agatson was pulling at his leg, shrieking with sudden idiotic laughter again: "I don't want you dying here! I won't have it! . . . May, hey May, get off your rump and help me throw this leper out of here! He's going to die on my bed!"

Ketcham rushed at Agatson, pulling him away.

"For God's sake, leave him alone! Can't you see he's *really* sick! . . . Bill, come away from him! Look at him, he's coughing blood. He's *really* sick, can't you see that?"

Ketcham was in a paroxysm of alarm, his eyes distended with horror, but Agatson, at these words, stopped yanking Verger's inert leg and stared at him, as though he had been shaken out of a fit which had possessed him.

"Well, Jesus Christ, why didn't you . . .? For Christ's sake, why does he come here . . . if . . . if he's really sick . . . I mean, he's been here off and on for days, so how was I—"

Hobbes had stood through all of this, unable to move for some reason, but as Ketcham and Agatson covered Verger up and wiped his face with an old shirt, Hobbes discovered that May was hovering in the dimness of the kitchen door, watching everything strangely.

Her hair was uncombed, ratty, and there were puffy circles beneath eyes that fear had brightened. She wore a torn yellow kimono and her face was drawn and pasty looking. She clutched at the sleeve of Hobbes' jacket, keeping a stealthy eye on the others, and bending toward him, whispered:

"Quick! While they're busy. What can you tell me about this person?" Her nod indicated the sobered Agatson who was tucking in the blanket. "What's he *really* like? You've known him for years. Tell me, quick, tell me!"

Hobbes was too surprised by this, and still too stunned by everything else, to make a coherent answer: "What do you mean!"

She glared at him then with intense, mad suspicion, even loathing, on her sickish face. "You're just like the others! You're not fit to wipe his shoes! I know what you think! But *I* didn't ask Verger to keep bothering us. Why don't you all leave Bill to me, he wouldn't do these things if you'd all leave him alone, and stop coming here! . . . He likes Verger, but he does these things for the rest of you! . . . Oh, how should you understand! Why don't you leave him alone?"

She actually spit in his direction, almost shouting these last words, and then she fled back into the darkness, the yellow kimono slipping over her bare shoulders in her haste.

But now Verger had begun to speak, still coughing, but looking up at them earnestly: "No, no, no, I'm all right . . . drunk . . . and dizzy that's all . . . Stop tucking me in that way, Bill. It doesn't matter. Cah-cah-cah! . . . If I can just rest for an hour or two . . . just to get my breath, cah-cah!"

"You can stay there . . . if you want to," Agatson replied hoarsely, shifting his weight from one foot to the other. "I don't mind, Daniel . . . I'm sorry about—"

"But don't you want a doctor?" Ketcham asked. "I mean, don't you think you should have one? The blood—"

Verger laughed faintly. "Don't worry, Arthur. This happens all the time now. But . . . but reach in my pocket and get my wallet. It should be in the hip pocket, cah-cah-cah! Take the ten dollar bill and give it to Stofsky, will you? I probably won't see him for some time. Give him that ten, you understand? He started all this . . . ca-cah-cah! I mean, my part of it . . . this foolishness! But don't tell him that, don't say—"

"But it's all you've got! Don't you have any more money at home?"

"Don't worry. Please do this for me. Give him that ten," he entreated. "But don't say anything about this!" He uttered a pitifully weak laugh. "It's all too hateful and foolish! What games we play with ourselves! Cah-cah! And the Gods fall anyway . . ."

He made a wry, childish face at them. "I should get over quoting other people's bad epigrams, shouldn't I? For the first time, I see how ridiculous it all is . . . everything . . ."

He even managed a soft little giggle, and then he turned over, his eyes closed, and pulled the blanket up about his neck.

"Good-bye," he breathed suddenly after an instant of silence, and then he seemed to fall immediately asleep.

Thirteen

Pasternak called on the dot of seven, and though that morning this would have struck Hobbes as indicative of what he could expect from their meeting, the events of the afternoon had left him too gloomily disturbed to think of himself as being safe, because he alone was innocent (he believed) of what had happened between Kathryn and Pasternak. More subtle consequences than those originally implied by his position had become apparent to him.

Pasternak was at a cafeteria three blocks away, and wondered if Hobbes would meet him for coffee while Hart was across town getting the gas and oil checked. Nothing was said of Kathryn, and it impressed Hobbes that she was relieved at not having to go. A moment of cruel whimsy had seized him when she had gotten home from work and started to take off her clothes to be more comfortable. He had begun to suggest that she stay dressed so as to be present when Pasternak came. But recognizing her wish to avoid him, and remembering May, he did not pursue it.

The cafeteria was large, harshly lit, invariably the haunt of people who had nowhere else to go and ate meager, indifferently cooked suppers there or simply drank coffee. Among them sat a frowning, thoughtful Pasternak, making obvious by the awkward way in which he watched everything (as though it bore out some new, sad insight that had come to him) his inner disturbance.

"So you're off," Hobbes stated at once, quelling his own nervousness by immediate reference to the ostensible reason for their meeting.

Pasternak made some sort of answer to this, one equally beside the point that was lodged between them, all the while probing Hobbes' face with worried and yet purposeful eyes.

"But, you know," he added quickly. "I planned to take off a couple of weeks ago. Oh, more than that even! Before Hart ever came—"

"Certainly. I know. Heavens, do you think I disapprove? I kind of wish I could come along. But, home and wife . . . It'll probably do you good, though, getting away from everything. And besides, I suppose you'll get a chance to write sometime."

"Oh, don't worry, man!" Pasternak reassured earnestly, breaking into an unhappy smile. "I'll write you a big letter from Tucson or somewhere, tell you everything about it. Sure. And, hell, I'll be back in November at the latest."

"No, no . . . I meant your work."

As though this misunderstanding was painful for both of them, they looked away from each other simultaneously, studying the shabby groups of men with embarrassed discretion.

Pasternak seemed also vaguely disappointed about something, and began again manfully: "Well, everybody's different, I guess. I wouldn't say how it should be for everyone. But I *have* to get away; and anyway New York isn't *really* America. I mean, everything here is actually just an unreal social swirl!"

"It's no more unreal than anywhere else, I imagine."

They talked on, almost indifferently, sipping the coffee regularly, and then they were silent, brooding before themselves. Once when Pasternak looked at Hobbes to find him staring absently at the sleezy waitress collecting dirty dishes, he broke out:

"No, but I mean I was thinking last night . . . well, about everything. Why should I get all hungup on writing and all that! Or *you* either for that matter. I've decided it's really unnatural, biting your nails and writing books. What did I ever get out of it? Three years sitting up nights, scribbling, and being unmarried and mad! It isn't real . . . But then you know all that."

He lapsed into a morose silence as though all further attempts on the inarticulateness between them would prove futile. His brows gathered with hopeless desperation, and his eyes wandered from the steam tables to the piles of dirty trays.

"Well," Hobbes said suddenly. "Don't just creep away like an . . . well, like some elephant!" and he made no effort to suppress the private sniff, only making sure it sounded vaguely cynical. "You'll get some other idea for a book, and you'll be just as unmarried and just as mad again . . . And, after all, it's decent work."

"What do you mean by that anyway? Creeping away! And about the elephant, what the hell was that?"

Hobbes was somewhat confused, but said hastily: "I just meant that I know you'll go on working no matter what you do. What did you think I meant? . . . I wasn't being pontifical, it was just an opinion . . . Who am I to tell you what to do?"

"Well, it's just that you're always locking horns with me," Pasternak replied lamely, staring down his nose, evidently convinced of some obtuseness of his own which the uneasy conversation was dangerously highlighting.

"What in the world do you mean?"

"Oh, you know well enough. Like last night . . . You were constantly looking at me out of the corner of your eye, when I spilled the beer and wrote on the walls. Oh, I know you laughed! But, hell, I'm no fool, Paul, and even though I was drunk . . . And I really *was* drunk . . . I feel that you're always trying to put me down, or you're suspecting me—"

Hobbes threw his hands despairingly into the air. "What are you talking about? How do I give people this impression! . . . I wasn't looking at you in any way. Can I help my face! And why should I be doing this, for Christ's sake?"

"Oh, you know what I mean. About Kathryn . . . and going away on this trip and everything. And Hart and the gas, for instance!"

"What do you mean about Hart? Have I ever thrown him out? Have I ever been unfriendly? You know very well what I think of him . . . I like him, I really do, because he's no pale Basarov, he's not just negative like some Village Agatson . . ."

"Well, I didn't mean only that. It's that whenever Kathryn's around I feel that you're locking horns with me, like we were Indians wrestling . . . I don't want you to throw your wife at me!"

Hobbes flushed and was genuinely taken aback.

"But I'm not! Why is everyone saying this to me suddenly! And, Gene, I don't care about *those* things, I tell you! You know what I mean . . . Why don't you believe what I say? Isn't that what Hart's always telling you: 'Why get hungup?' Well, *I* mean it. Kathryn likes you, and that's fine. I'm glad of it. If she has a good time, I'm glad of it! Why not? I love her, don't I?"

Pasternak gave him a long, astonished look, still suspicious and not trusting himself to understand this last.

"Well, I was *drunk*," he blurted out. "And those things happen . . . and they don't—"

"I know, that's just what I'm saying. Kathryn's self conscious, you can see that, and that's why she's aggressive and sometimes makes trouble. She's convinced that people don't like her, and that even when they're nice they have huge plots and hidden antagonisms. I'm always telling her that it isn't so, that she should just relax, but she insists that— But, anyway, what I mean is that I'm really glad when she . . . when she gets less introverted, and has some fun. That's the only thing that matters to me."

Pasternak continued to frown blackly, sitting mutely under these words as though they were incomprehensible to him.

"Well, all I mean is that I feel you're trying to . . . well," his hands gestured impatiently, "get me all involved!"

"Good God! The way both of you act you'd think *I* was at fault for something! What the hell did I do? I didn't say anything about it, did I?"

Pasternak hunched his shoulders heavily, refusing to look up. "But that's it, you were just observing, watching. And I want you to know that I'm not trying to . . . get away with anything. I'm not . . . well, I'm not in love with Kathryn . . . or anything like that. That's what I mean."

"Of course, you're not. My Lord, who suggested such a thing!"

"And I don't like all that. I mean all that free-love stuff, that liberal bohemianism, between friends! It isn't right, or straight, that's what I think!"

"But what's that got to do with it! What do you mean liberal bohemianism? I'm not trying to sell you anything."

"I just don't think it's right between friends. I mean, it makes you feel like a criminal or something. You're looking at me right now, like you think I'm some real, greasy Judas. I know all that."

"Am I? How, for God's sake? I told you it didn't matter to me! Really, you're getting paranoic as a bedbug! Kathryn had a good time, she and I didn't have any trouble. The reason she didn't come along tonight is because she's tired . . . But really, she doesn't hate you and everything's fine between us. What do you want me to do, apologize to you or something?" He snickered excitedly. "Wouldn't that be funny though? Everything considered?"

"That's just what I mean," Pasternak countered with despondent irritation. "Things like that. You're always jeering at me, in that real secretive way, trying to . . . to shame me."

"But I'm not, I'm not! I didn't even want to talk about all this . . . Hell, I don't know," he said suddenly, seething with injured bewilderment. "You'd think I was a regular leper, I seem to infect everyone just because of what I believe! . . . But how is it different from what everyone else *professes* to believe? How is it any different? . . . And it's no ironical illustration of anything, the way I act! It isn't, Gene! I'm not trying to prove anything about 'liberal bohemianism'! Really, would I go to such lengths out of irony? Would I?"

They talked on this way, Hobbes becoming more and more excited, Pasternak less and less so. Finally Pasternak offered him a cigarette, holding out his own as a light, and his guilts, which had inhabited him like a haunted house, vanished so abruptly that for a moment he doubted their reality. They took with them the dark scowl, leaving only a rather timid, sheepish smile.

"Well, you know, Paul," he said falteringly. "I just didn't pick up on it, that's all. I'm sorry . . . about everything. I didn't want you to think that . . . well, that I was sneaking around or anything. We understand each other all right. I was just getting it straight."

And thereafter, he brightened uneasily, as though Hobbes' heated reassurances had not alone set his inner fears at rest but had reduced the whole level of their conversation to irrelevancy in his eyes. Laughing and glancing at Hobbes almost shyly every now and then, he started speaking eagerly about the trip. Hobbes, himself, said nothing more, but listened and agreed with everything perhaps too volubly, continuing the debate in his troubled thoughts, however. Despite this, they managed to convince each other, through this warm, trivial talk, that everything was settled, before Hart came back.

They stood in the street beside the Cadillac and said embarrassed 'goodbyes.' Hart, all the depression of the night before swept away by the prospect of being off again onto the road for which the cities at either end, and the kicks they offered, were only, after all, a necessary excuse, clapped Hobbes on the back, saying:

"Well, man, we'll pick up on each other again. You'll cut out to Frisco, or I'll be back, you know! Sure! It's been great kicks! Take it slow now!" And he hopped into the car, gunning the motor with anticipatory ecstasy and jabbering to Ed who was already half asleep in the back.

Pasternak said, as he got in: "So, everything's okay now, Paul? . . . Keep plugging at it, and I'll write you a big letter from somewhere . . ."

And suddenly they had pulled off into traffic to make the light at the next cross street, waving out the windows gaily, and leaving Hobbes standing there with that hesitant awkwardness of a blind man in a crowd, who always seems to be living an instant behind everyone else.

≈≈≈≈≈≈≈≈≈≈≈≈ Fourteen

"Love that is doomed possesses me for some reason," Hobbes wrote to Liza a week later, the first week in August, in a fit of lonesome self pity. "I think of you and me as the doomed lovers we never were. We walk in some autumn's continual rain in my dream, and grasp at one another, as though each moment was the moment of parting, drinking in every feature, every change of expression. Each thing then becomes the last, and we wander down deserted streets, without touching, and are aliens wherever we go. Life is a perpetual defeat for us. We found each other reluctantly, allowed ourselves passion at the expense of sadness, opened to each other only out of irony. We said goodbye when we met the first secret time. We have no eagerness, no ecstasy, only the likeness of this sense of defeat. We come together rarely and then like two infected lovers in some contagious ruin, we lie down together only so that we might die warm. Each stolen moment is like a withering rose caught at the superb beauty of its decline, death already dreadfully kissing it. This is what I am thinking these days: of doomed lovers (you so rare and dark beside me), living a trapped life in a city set for destruction. How many beds we will get into tonight, apart; how many silences endure and how much longing will remain sweet and prisoned in our limbs without escape! Doomed lovers in buildings that will be ruins! Just part of my dream of you these days . . ."

But he did not send the letter, knowing it would only anger her, and put it in the growing sheaf of those which he had not sent, but saved as private documents of something. It was a rainy Friday, Kathryn would go from work to take a train to Westchester and her mother for the weekend. He faced two days dedicated to lonely, monkish idling, but walking up and down the apartment, snarled in a spiteful purposelessness, he had suddenly felt the uprush of self pity, like the maudlin but secretly cherished tears that one allows oneself while listening to that lovely, shallow music that dignifies adolescent memories, and he sat down and poured out all this in the letter, which, when it was finished, he could not even send. He was torn with a sense of his own lovelessness, like the suspicion of a hidden disease which has no symptoms, and he thought enviously of Kathryn and Pasternak.

Finally he called Estelle at her office, with the reckless audacity of a man who has resolutely decided to make a fool of himself. She seemed glad that he had called, and her voice was purring and confident at the other end. As though she was tuned in on his thoughts, she gently goaded him into asking if he might see her, and then told him (for which he was grateful) to meet her at six-thirty when she got out from work.

He walked across town in the rain, starting too early and having to dawdle. He realized that he did not know her, and had no idea of what the evening might hold; and among the scurrying summer crowds and the splashing taxis, he moved listlessly toward her, trying to expect nothing, and yet full of foolish, eager hopes.

When he saw her at the entrance of her building, unworried, calm, watching people that passed her with a strange, blank consideration of their existence, he realized that he must look like some dripping spaniel, his hair straggling wetly across his forehead, his selfconscious swagger giving away the awkwardness he actually felt.

She knew a restaurant on Fiftieth Street and took his arm firmly. He tried to get a cab, standing in a puddle waving his arms, cursing himself as inept for not being able to flag one down, although all of them were taken. Finally they walked, scampering from one awning to the next.

Over drinks and the eventual sauced scallops, it was better. He sat, feeling a vague sense of isolation that he could not describe even to himself, while she talked easily and at some length about her job. He carefully noticed the abstracted way she lit a cigarette in the middle of a word, and the direct gaze with which she listened to the few polite comments that he made, as though she could not hear them. When she said nothing for minutes on end, and seemed content to merely look at him without any particular meaning in her looks, he made sporadic attempts at amusing chatter, in which she would helpfully participate with everything but her eyes, which were intent elsewhere.

After more drinks, he experienced panic again when he realized that they must go somewhere else. He could think of no place to take her and would have been abjectly grateful if she had insisted on a movie in which he had no interest, but her very willingness to do anything he wanted terrified him. After a few aimless suggestions, he mentioned The Go Hole with a flippancy that was calculated to keep from her his own preference. She assented immediately and, as it was only a few blocks west, they walked. The rain was letting up, and Times Square was a huge, damp room with a red ceiling, and warm showers falling through great arcades of light.

They sat at a table at the back of the club in a half darkness. The place was nearly empty and the musicians played forlornly to the cluster of chairs in the bleacher section. Estelle observed everything silently, and even her enjoyment was indestructibly placid. She would nod her head when Hobbes explained the music and its devotees to her, giving him her attention as if it were a rare thing and reserved for him alone. But once, when he was quite unaware that he was staring at her profile as it was clearly cut against smoky light, looking at her face and memorizing it impersonally, she turned to him with her large, somehow intimate eyes showing no surprise, and putting a cool palm on his cheek, turned his face back to the music with a small laugh of playful remonstrance.

While they were there only one thing aroused his curiosity enough to distract him from her. It was a party of three that took a table nearby during one of the intermissions. He had been half-heartedly trying to explain to her what was suggested by the term "cool," as hipsters used it.

"When the music is cool, it's pleasant, somewhat meditative and without tension. Everything before, you see, just last year, was 'crazy,' 'frantic,' 'gone.' Now, everybody is acting cool, unemotional, withdrawn . . . What can one designate the moment that comes after 'the end,' after all? I suppose it's complete passivity, oblivion . . . But, look there, the guy coming to that table is 'cool'!"

And it was true. The man he indicated so perfectly epitomized everything that might conceivably be meant by the term that for ten minutes Hobbes could not take his eyes off him.

Wraithlike, this person glided among the tables wearily, followed by a six-foot, supple redhead in a green print dress, and a sallow, wrinkled little hustler, hatless and occupying a crumpled sport shirt as though crouched in it to hide his withered body.

The "cool" man wore a wide flat brimmed slouch hat that he would not remove, and a tan drape suit that seemed to wilt at his thighs. The stringy hair on his neck protruded over a soft collar, and his dark, oily face was an expressionless mask. He moved with a huge exhaustion, as though sleep walking, and his lethargy was so consummate that it seemed to accelerate the universe around him. He sprawled at the table between the redhead and the other fellow, his head sunk into his palms, the brim of his zoot hat lowered just far enough so that no light from the bandstand could reach him. He became particularly immobile during the hottest music, as though it was a personal challenge to his somnambulism on the part of the musicians. His passionless trance denied their very existence, and every now and again his head would literally drop to the table, and he would sit, snoozing like a peon in a cowboy film, his body folded down upon itself as though woven in an invisible cocoon in the air.

The tall girl paid absolutely no attention to him, watching the musicians, tapping long fingers and idly lighting cigarettes. She swung her broad shoulders languorously, letting her eyelids flutter closed when the tenor played a throaty ride, her teeth inside the full lips grinding together deliciously. The hustler, on the contrary, kept turning toward the "cool" man, with a slight, sardonic twist on his mouth, hunching forward. Every once in a while, eyes glowing over the unhealthy cheeks, he would whisper something, receiving no answer, and then he would run a swizzle stick inside the "cool" man's ear, tracing its contours; or devil it, under the hat, along the ridge of his nose, but he could raise no glimmer of life.

In the absurdly soft hat and the extreme drape, the "cool" man looked like a caricature of a petty hood, but if there was viciousness or depravity in his heart it could not penetrate through the thick torpor. Everything had dragged him so much that he no longer dug anything at all. One imagined that if a waiter had come up and requested him to remove the hat, he might have slowly, with weary irritation, reached to the holster under his arm and fingered a chilly automatic. Some night, in this very spot, when he had sunken to the abysses of his droopy lassitude, he might have pulled out his rod and sullenly shot up the place out of sheer ennui.

Estelle was intrigued by Hobbes' fascination with these three, but when he said, "You see, it's really the end of feeling, through feeling too much. Look, he's not even interested in the girl . . .

or in anything! Even sex is a drag because he's gone to the end of it. He's gone to the end of everything!", she replied:

"Then let's get out of here, all right? He's so cool he's not even there, and that's too cool for me tonight. It might be catching!"

They went to an empty, paneled barroom on a nearby side street. It was almost three, and they sat among the deserted booths, with a soft juke box humming somewhere, and every once in a while the affable bartender would put down his newspaper and bring them more martinis. Hobbes suddenly had the feeling that the rain and the night had rejected them, driven both of them to a corner out of the turmoil and noise of the city, and their presence in that night was forgotten, unknown to anyone. It made him warm to think that, and he turned to Estelle, certain that everything she would do from then on would have a mysterious significance to him.

Without hesitation, peering into the large brown eyes with the clear flashes in them, he began to tell her about the "beat generation," tell her that though he did not know that it existed, somehow he sensed that it was there, tell her things which he had never thought out clearly himself, things the "cool" man and his own heightened concern about the evening had thrown into relief in his mind. He talked steadily, gravely, about the war and how it had wounded everyone emotionally, using the "cool" man as an example. He spoke of Hart and Stofsky and Pasternak and Agatson, of their faithlessness and his recognition of a similar discontent inside himself. For the first time in many months, he allowed himself the luxury of voicing insoluble questions, allowed himself to feel that desperation of disbelief, that bewilderment in the face of experience that he seemed cruelly incapable of comprehending, that had always soured the conclusions he had sought so terribly to believe.

Finally he ran down, and her presence across from him became evident again, their difference, their separation from each other became clear once more, and he was suddenly overwhelmed with embarrassment. They sat for an instant and he dared not look at her but could only mutter wildly: "Say something to me!"

But she would say nothing, and only leaned across the table, like a wise little girl listening, for the first time, to some female voice that a man can never hear, and bringing his face close to hers, put her moist lips against his with that intent preoccupation in the act itself that always amazed him.

Immediately, he became nakedly aware of her. His abstract

desire for someone toward whom to fly his arrows, in whom to find a comforting, pleasing picture of his effect: all this vanished, leaving her sitting across from him, her eyes wider than before and shining as if wet; her shoulders curved slightly forward until her breasts were no longer taut but seemed about to quiver with her breathing, as though experiencing some infinite voluptuousness heretofore only fanciful. He realized that his attraction for her had never been localized before, but now his eyes filled up with her image, and she saw it there, and drew back as though his eyes, themselves, had caressed her passionately.

They talked on as if this had not happened. The idea of her, as possible for him (and this is how he had thought of her before), evaporated into a longing for what she could give him, that gentle, demanding thirst of her female heart. The evening, suffused in his thoughts with this almost fatal awareness, became an hour-glass in which the rainy streets, the taxis, the meal, and all faltering, outside arrangements, seemed to narrow down, like a cone, to this moment. And beyond it everything opened up with a delicious, intimate excitement. He thought of the late streets emptying, and the whole city, standing silent in showers, as being theirs to prowl in.

And soon it was almost four, the bar was closing, and they got up to leave. After he had paid the check, he went out and found her standing quietly in the doorway, looking out into the dim wetness, waiting; and he knew that she must come back to the apartment if he was not to lose his emotion in frustration. But he did not know how to bring it about, and was somehow conscious that, although nothing had been said and there was no tacit arrangement, they had reached a point of arousal where she would not help him anymore, and that bungling on his part, just because he was out of practice, would drive her away.

They started walking toward Lexington Avenue, and he made a small joke about taking her to the subway. She said nothing to this, but when on a corner waiting for the light, he kissed her with hungry clumsiness, she let him. They walked on. Park Avenue was like a long, echoless movie set, all the hotels and smart shops dark above street level, and the occasional, empty cabs cruising by the only sign that they were not wandering in the deserted ruin of his letter. He did not feel, giddy with worried expectation, the emotions he had written about, however, but rather that he had triumphed over them. He filled with something inexpressible.

How to tell her that the whole night had become tender and propitious to him; no casual transgression of fidelity, but a reprieve from lovelessness! How to tell her that he wanted her utterly at that moment; not merely a wordless, selfish contact, but a sensual knowledge of her secret female existence! So ran his wild, inappropriate thoughts.

They walked up Lexington and before the entrance to his building, he took her arm and said:

"Let's go up. To get dry. You're soaked and we could have a cigarette. You don't have to worry . . . I'm tame."

She hesitated for a moment, considering a deeper question of agreement than that he had set before her and one no man could really fathom, and then started up the stairs ahead of him. He felt suddenly that she was taking him at his innocent invitation, and that still nothing had been assumed. This affected his offhand unlocking of the door, and after she had gone in silently, he dropped the keys out of consternation.

He took off her coat and she sat on the couch, her long legs folded beneath her, waiting for him to light her cigarette. He sought in her slightest action a sign of approval, but finding none that he could rely on, he kissed her anyway, and she lay back in the pillows, her eyes closed, her lips wetly parted as he traced his fingers over her body. Her head was on his chest, her dress about her thighs, and she lay so quietly against him that he knew she had placed herself, for that moment, childlike, in his trust. This made him draw back, and in the close darkness of the room, he said:

"I can help you only so much, and then I've got to help myself . . ."

"Kiss me," she whispered impatiently, almost as an assurance.

Her mouth opened softly on his, receiving his tongue, and she clutched his neck. They clung together, and when his hands found her thighs, and they parted, she sank beneath him blindly, taking his mouth between her teeth with thrilling avidity, all of her length tensed and ready.

Then it suddenly occured to Hobbes that his erection was gone. It was like waking up, getting to your feet and finding that one of them is still asleep. You stamp it on the floor, you walk about, you know the foot is touching the floor and that you are walking on it, but you cannot feel it. It hit him with tremendous surprise and embarrassment, but he was sure, at first, that simple consciousness of it would correct it.

He concentrated on her soft body straining against him, her legs hooked about his thighs, holding him into her, and then he heard her strange, small voice near his ear, gasping:

"What's wrong, sweetheart?"

He kissed her with increased desperation and bewilderment, and could not answer, hoping momentarily to feel the flush of warmth in his loins. But it did not come. From then on he struggled hopelessly to disentangle himself from what was paralyzing him, but whatever it was clogged numbly somewhere in his pelvis and would not free itself.

His hands strayed to her dress and he unbuttoned it, feeling that if she took it off he might become aroused in the necessary way. She got up and, almost obediently, went into the bedroom to undress, with a sudden modesty he could not have imagined in her. He thought that watching her remove her clothes would help him, but did not know how to suggest it, and only stood near the door waiting. She came out, naked but for a black, lacy slip, looking up into his face wonderingly. Her hair fell on the wide, bare shoulders, her breasts swung deeply in the cups of the slip. On the couch again, he became aware of his own clothes and stood up to take them off, feeling it graceless, but now seriously disturbed by the dullness spreading through his body. As he lay down, she pulled the slip up to her waist and drew him into a wild, urgent embrace. But it was useless.

"Damn, damn, damn!" he cried out incredulously. "I don't understand it! It never happened before . . . But how about you? . . . Let me—"

Without a word, she seemed to assent for a moment, guiding his hand in blind abandon, but then, with remarkably sober decisiveness, she lay back passively, running one finger along his naked arm, and watching him as he stroked her thighs despairingly, knowing she had given it up. Then she looked down at herself, as he was, and, as though her desire had passed so completely that it had not been real, she crooked her leg again and again, silently considering its length.

Thereafter, he was haunted by the bitter ache of his failure, and she retreated into a distant, though slightly warm preoccupation. They lay together for a while with cigarettes, Hobbes fighting the apologies he could not bring himself to utter, and then they got up and dressed.

When he went to the door to see if anyone was in the halls before they descended the stairs, he found that it was locked, but remembered that he had forgotten to do it when they had come in. He turned to her, standing in her coat near him, and for an instant, her locking of the door before they had begun (such a confident, knowing gesture) exhilarated him, and he took her to him and kissed her. She squeezed his hand affectionately, but then he was flushed with shame again because it was another sign of his inadequacy.

They walked to her subway silently; it had stopped raining and dawn was chilly and grey behind the dead buildings. Their faces were drawn, ashen in that light as they looked at each other, without the anxiety or mystery of hours before, and she too plainly had knowledge of his failure to become aroused by her, and he too plainly knowledge of her failure to arouse him, for them ever to see one another again.

It did not matter to him then that his sleep would be riddled with fitful dreams of the "cool" man, in whom he had seen the end of feeling but felt so secure that he could be openly fascinated, little dreaming that he would later toss and dream of himself immobile under the huge soft hat, and wake intermittently bathed in sweat, hearing himself repeating: "It might be catching! It might be catching!"

It did not matter then, and they left one another with the weary relief of people who share hateful secrets they will try to forget, and who, to accomplish this, arrange, independent of each other, never to meet again.

Fifteen

A COUPLE of nights later, it was on a Wednesday, Kathryn, Hobbes and Ketcham were wandering down Sixth Avenue and quite by chance met Stofsky, who had just been to Agatson's. The hours the four of them spent together that night were aimless, and gave no hint of what was to happen later.

Ketcham often got urges to go abroad in the night (that same restless desire to be among other unsatisfied people that fills the bars of any city), and occasionally he called the Hobbes' from somewhere to join him. This particular night, Hobbes had thrust the phone at Kathryn immediately, hoping she would want a few beers even though she had had an exhausting day, but unwilling to make the decision himself. Seeing this, and desirous of pleasing him, she had gotten dressed again and they met Ketcham on Thirty-fourth Street. From there, they started downtown and reached Twenty-second Street when Stofsky rounded the corner.

"What's this about Verger and that ten dollars?" he began immediately. "Bill was telling me some fantastic story—"

Ketcham gave him ten from his wallet.

"But what did he say?" Stofsky went on excitedly. "He must have given you some message for me."

"He didn't say anything very much. He was drunk and coughing the way he does."

"Paul, you were there. Didn't he say anything at all?"

It seemed crucial to Stofsky that he know everything, and though Hobbes remembered that Verger had said something that he didn't want them to tell Stofsky, so much had happened since then that he couldn't recall what it was.

"No, not a word. What was it all about anyway? Did you lend him ten?"

Stofsky looked oddly bewildered by it all. "Oh, no . . . No, it was for those books . . . But why didn't he explain? Didn't he tell you *why* he was giving the money back?"

"Let's go somewhere," Kathryn put in matter-of-factly at this moment. "I don't want to stand around here in the street. You can talk all you want to when I've got a beer."

"Look," Ketcham said, with a sudden fresh smile in her direction. "Why don't we get a few quarts and go up to Bianca's? It's right around the corner, and I'm sure she wouldn't mind. Is that all right, Kathryn? How does that sound?"

They started for a delicatessen a block down Sixth.

"That's very strange," Stofsky continued to Hobbes. "Bill was saying that he hadn't seen Verger for over a week. Where can he have gone? I called one of May's friends just a few minutes ago, one of those girls that live next to him, but she said he hasn't been in his apartment for six days."

"Oh, he's probably just gone out of town," Ketcham said coldly over his shoulder as they paid for the beer.

"But where?" Stofsky muttered. "That isn't like Verger, just to vanish . . ."

Bianca's studio was cavernous, drafty and up three dark flights. Living alone amid her easels and half finished paintings, she often gave the impression of crouching in the almost furnitureless rooms, aware that the emptiness of the rest of the building (it was to be torn down and she was the only remaining tenant), corresponded to some emotional emptiness in her existence there. She peeked out from behind her door, her small eyes narrowed with agitation, as though visitors had caught her in the middle of some secret activity of which she was ashamed.

Ketcham took one small, limp hand in his.

"How are you? How have you been this past week?" and though this was a standard kind of greeting for him with everyone, something behind his saying of it then was different, and the others noticed, speculated, but kept silent.

Kathryn, who was always uneasy with Bianca because there was something untrustworthy about her perpetual manlessness, asked her if she had seen or heard from Christine.

"No, no I haven't. That is, I see her in the street sometimes, in the neighborhood here. But she doesn't speak to me anymore. She even crosses the street to avoid a meeting. And I heard from the girl next door that she's going to have analysis and that she's pregnant." She glanced at Ketcham with confusion, as a child looks to her father for a sign.

"You mean her trouble with Gene made her sick?" Ketcham asked helpfully.

"What did Gene do to her?" Stofsky broke in, but his question was ignored.

"I suppose it did, yes . . . He . . . he wasn't very kind to her. I mean, from her point of view. I heard she was going to some quack psychologist up on Grand Concourse. And I guess now she's lumped me with . . . with everyone else. Dissipates, you know." She laughed nervously, lighting a cigarette as though to prevent herself from biting her nails. "I'm just glad *Bill* didn't take an interest in her, that's all. Can you imagine what that would have been like? The least she probably would have done was kill herself. She would have been the first one to *actually* kill herself!" The current of quiet bitterness beneath these light remarks embarrassed everyone simultaneously.

They changed the subject as if by previous arrangement, but at the first lapse Bianca asked Ketcham: "I hear he's got a new girl now. May Somebody. From uptown."

"Yes, I guess so. But I don't know her. You know, she hides in the kitchen and won't speak to anyone."

"And she spits!" Hobbes added, thinking it all just a joke.

"That's awful," Bianca went on with surprising seriousness. "Maybe he'll find one some day that won't get like that. I used to feel like spitting at everyone too. I used to get so—. But I suppose she's at the point where she's trying to stop him from drinking. Has she started that yet?"

Though Bianca had lived with Agatson a year before, unlike the girls who had preceded her and all those that followed, when she had moved out she had not left the city, married quickly, or started psychoanalysis, but had taken this large shadowy apartment only four blocks away from him. Ketcham did not feel the embarrassment of the others at remembering this, because it was often close to the thoughts he told no one else, and filled him with helpless anger when he visited Bianca regularly once a week.

To quell this anger, he urged her to show her paintings to Hobbes. Kathryn and Stofsky sat drinking the beer, talking now and then in the stillness, each lost in their thoughts.

"Didn't Paul tell you anything about that afternoon at Agatson's?" Stofsky said at one point. "Just why did Verger send that money back to me?"

Kathryn, who was as troubled by Bianca's remark about Pasternak as she would have been if it had referred to herself instead of Christine, replied: "No. But he doesn't tell me lots of things these days. He's been very strange lately."

"Verger?"

"No, not Verger. Paul. For the last week he's been that way."

"How?" and Stofsky paled slightly, as people do when they know very well the answers to the questions they ask out of tact.

"Oh, distant, preoccupied. And terribly depressed about something. *I* have no right to wonder about it, I guess . . . But you know how sometimes you don't understand people at all, even though you know them perfectly? Well, that's what I mean . . ."

"That's just the way I feel about this thing with Verger," Stofsky confessed almost courteously, as if it would make her feel better. "But as far as Paul goes, it's probably something he doesn't know how to say . . . to you anyway. You know, he has r-e-a-l deep thoughts sometimes! And maybe he's convinced you're not interested."

"If *I'm* not interested, who is? And interested in what?"

"Matters of his soul. I mean, all his big concerns about everything. He doesn't tell them to anyone really. And then you two don't talk to each other about what you really feel."

His earnestness and sincerity in these statements somewhat lessened Kathryn's moment of pique at his candor, and he went on:

"I mean, you never show *other* people that you love one another. Everyone thinks you're afraid of each other. Now, *I* know that you really care about all Paul's intellectual anxieties, and of course they are, actually, very emotional with him, but perhaps *he* doesn't know you care."

"Well, I don't know what I'm supposed to do," she said disconsolately.

"Cultivate him, cultivate your husband! Paul's the kind that doesn't ever say what's really bothering him. He always talks about everyone else, or listens to them talking, or just jokes about things; but probably he writes big confessional journals at night . . . that no one ever sees!"

"Does he have a journal?"

"Oh, I don't *really* know, I was just saying that he's the type who might do it that way. And he's probably been hoping, maybe for years, in fact, that you'll stumble on them and see what he's been thinking about a-l-l this time . . . I'm not joking, Kathryn, Paul's really shy when it comes to emotions, I think he's even ashamed of them. But I can just imagine you two having a big reconciliation after a discovery like that . . . a reconciliation of the heart!"

"And then live happily ever after, I suppose," she replied with a brusque smile to cover the fact that he had set her thinking.

But when the others came back from the farther room and the stacks of paintings there, she found herself looking at Hobbes intently in the light of what Stofsky had said, and wondering if there really might be a diary somewhere in his desk that would open his private thoughts to her. When he sat down next to her, laughing vaguely at something Ketcham was saying, she felt a sweet and melancholy contrition, mostly because of Pasternak, but also because she had just thought of her husband as a lonely and secretive little boy, so proficient at aping maturity that eventually his mother forgets he is only an overly-serious child.

After half an hour of talk and beer, weariness overcame her, and she said that she had better leave. Hobbes got up without a word to go with her, but she urged him to stay, knowing he wanted to be with people, and feeling, in her pleasant penitence, perfectly willing to take the subway alone as long as he was happy.

After she had gone, they finished the beer and put Kurt Weill's "Three Penny Opera" on the phonograph. Bianca hummed along with it, lighting cigarettes one after the other. The records were twenty years old and the music almost obscured by scratch, but they sat listening to the shrill, childish voices and Ketcham made occasional translations of the lyrics to which Bianca would nod happily.

Stofsky seemed depressed by everything, and said to Hobbes once, during a passage scored for a twanging Hawaiian guitar: "It's so strange. How quaint it sounds! And it's all so decadent and sad! What will it sound like in twenty years when the world will be worse . . . or better."

"I suppose we'll be singing hymns by then," Ketcham said sharply.

"Or beating tree trunks and groaning," Bianca put in with a dismal attempt at whimsey.

Then she got up and, turning one of the spot lamps onto the wall, she brought out a crudely carved little puppet and manipulated it before the light so that a distorted shadow danced in angular frenzy along the frame of a painting.

The rest joined in this strange pantomime, standing before the light and throwing huge, menacing images around the little figure. Not a word was said, but low laughter would signify the ingeniousness of someone's action. The music scratched on in the darkened room, and the bizarre ballet of shadows on the wall hynotised them all.

Stofsky opened his mouth, and the shadow-puppet thrust his foot into it. Ketcham stretched out an arm as if to gather the figure in, but with a small, piping laugh, Bianca moved it away. Hobbes for his part made little men of his hands, twiggish figures even smaller than the puppet that jiggled away from them; and finally he made one, with a finger stuck out from it like an oversize penis, at which the puppet kicked violently until it vanished below the light.

But the phone rang to finish the game. Bianca answered nervously.

"It's for you," she said to Hobbes distantly. "I think it's your wife."

Hobbes had no idea what it could be about, because almost an hour had passed since Kathryn had gone home and he had consigned her to bed in his mind, but as soon as he picked up the receiver he felt that something was wrong.

"I just wanted to tell you that I'm leaving you," he heard before he could say anything. "I'm reading your letters to Liza. The *love* letters you've been writing to another woman for three years!"

The voice was so strange, so filled with those bewildered tones of reproach that are beyond mere anger, that all he could say was:

"Oh."

"I don't know how you could have done this to me. I'll never understand it! . . . 'Doomed lovers, you so rare and dark beside me . . .' And *that* was written a week ago in case you've forgotten. Just a week! Well, you can go to *her* tonight, or anywhere, I don't care. But you'd better not come back here, that's all. Because I won't be here if you do."

And before he could get over his shock at hearing her reading that sentence which he had never imagined her reading, before he could utter a word, she had hung up and he was left standing with a dead wire in that empty room amid the idle talk of the others, who (he thought) must surely know that something had happened.

He sat down again. The others talked on unconcernedly, but Hobbes was in such a turmoil that he did not hear. All he could think was: 'What do I do now? What am I supposed to do? . . . It's all over this time, all over! . . . Where will she go? She sounded so funny . . . But she wouldn't try to kill herself . . . No, no. But what do I do now?'

Then gradually all these disconnected thoughts ebbed away, the room and the others there reached his consciousness again: 'I'll take a cab and get there before she leaves . . . Do they suspect that something's happened? Is that possible? How do I get out of here without explanations?'

He could not decide about any of this, and so sat lighting cigarettes, and even trying to smile at witty remarks. He did not know what he was really feeling, and only kept staring at everyone as though trying to ascertain if the sudden flush of heat that had melted through him was noticeable to them.

What to do? What to do?

Now Stofsky was speaking to him, and he was nodding back, and trying to think of an excuse, any excuse.

How had she found out? How?

Meanwhile Bianca was fumbling through a stack of dusty records, Ketcham helping her, and Hobbes got to his feet, eying the door like a fugitive gauging a stretch of open country across which he must get before being challenged.

"I'm going out for cigarettes," he mumbled.

"Here, I've got plenty, Paul," Stofsky shouted after him.

But Hobbes made the door, and ran down the three echoing flights of stairs, hoping they would not hear his hasty steps, wonder what was wrong, and come after him.

PART THREE

Hell

One

ALL the way uptown in the taxi he was filled with anxious misgivings. His intelligence could not seem to catch up to the situation. He kept telling himself that he should be thinking carefully upon everything, trying to anticipate what was to come, but most of his thoughts were hopelessly illogical. He could only feel that the next hours, and even days, would be feverish, full of silence and raving, perhaps insurmountable.

He rushed up the stairs, an incongruous mixture of expectation and apprehension making him weak-kneed. The door was bolted and he knocked instead of using his key, because somehow he was sure she was still there.

The bolt slipped back, but she did not open the door. When he did, and entered, she was walking away into the living room. In her blue kimono and loafers, she looked smaller than he had ever seen her before, and also frail, all gathered tightly together in her body, bracing it from the inside.

When she looked at him, her lips were drawn down firmly, as if at any moment they might start to quiver uncontrollably. In her eyes he saw such hurt, such reproach that at first he did not notice the flashes of bewildered rage there as well. Beside her on the couch lay the folder of unsent letters, some of which went back three years, back to the very beginning.

"What can I say?" he began, and in those first words his voice threatened to crack, as if the emotions that had not come clearly to him on the way home had now, almost against his will, found their way out of him through his voice.

"Don't bother to say anything," and she laid her hand resolutely on the folder. "There are a few arrangements we ought to get straight . . . It's, it's too late for me to go anywhere now, but . . . Why did you bother to come back anyway? I told you not to come back here." This, as if to silence anything he might say. "Anyway I'll try to be out in the morning. I have a *few* things here that are mine, and I'll get them together . . ."

"But where will you go?"

"Don't worry about that! . . . But, now, I think *you'd* better go, if that's all right."

"Anything, but . . ."

He felt helpless, suddenly criminal. If she had started to berate him, to snarl or shout, he would have understood, might have known what to do. As it was, he was completely crushed, and strangely enough, positively frightened.

"But couldn't we . . . talk, honey. I mean—"

"What is there to talk about? . . . I knew you'd say that! I was waiting for it . . . But I don't want to talk. What is there to talk about, after *these*?"

"I don't know, I just thought . . . If only you could understand . . . but I suppose there's no reason why you should. It's stupid of me to even think—"

"Yes, it *is* stupid! What is there for me to understand? Do you think I'm a fool? Do you?" She did not raise her voice, and though it was hard and almost biting, there was a terse censoriousness in it that made Hobbes think that perhaps the greatest injury he had done her was to believe he could dupe her all this time.

"Here, let me read to you. Perhaps you've forgotten your own words! What is there for me to understand about this, for instance? . . . Listen," and she ruffled through the sheets of paper hurriedly. " 'Our marriages go wrong . . . and we have our affairs,' or this, 'one feels trapped' . . ."

She slammed the sheet down abruptly. "I didn't think I was trapping you. I didn't know it had been so terrible for you all along."

"But . . . but it hasn't. That wasn't written about us. I mean, I was just speaking generally . . . about everyone . . . Although that doesn't matter, and I don't want to argue about it . . . But if I could just tell you why I—"

"You don't have to tell me. All this time you haven't told me, have you? Have you? Why should you begin now? . . . That's what I'll never understand. Wouldn't it have been better to leave years ago? If you'd loved me at all—" Then she tried to squash her emotions with a bitter and confused laugh. "But, that's right, you didn't love me. Not all this time!"

Her lips were tight, her eyes shiny as though from anger or the beginnings of tears, and he realized at that moment that, unlike their quarrels of the past, none of his easy logical explanations would reach her, or matter at all.

"I can't expect you to see it the way I see it now. I realize that. It's so funny . . . but I don't feel any connection with . . . *them* anymore. It's like all that, those feelings, whatever they were . . . have vanished and mean nothing."

Somehow it was true, and it so astonished him that he could not describe the feeling accurately, and knew that what he was saying would strike her as being hopelessly contrived. But in that moment, he could not remember Liza with any vividness, nor could he even imagine any of the old, romantic loneliness out of which he had written to her. He could only feel a terrible sense of peril, and know that across from him sat this tiny person who had been with him so long, and whose life (he realized for the first time since the early days) had no pivot any longer, but for him. And he filled with an appalling shame that he could not express.

"It's as though I've been a child about all that, a thoughtless child . . . Do you know what I mean? It was . . . well, all so literary, so adolescent—"

"You're a liar, Paul! Don't try to explain it any other way! Stop treating me like I was an absolute fool! You've *lied* to me for three years! Every day, every hour. You've done nothing but lie! . . . You knew how I hated that. You knew I could stand anything else! But you lied anyway. If you'd told me three years ago, I would have been miserable, but I would have gotten over it . . . I would have gotten over you! But . . . but now I'm . . . I'm twenty-eight and— Don't you understand that you've ruined my life? Because you're selfish, and dishonest, and a hypocrite! Don't you understand that!"

"Kathryn, Kathryn—"

"I may be foolish, a stupid peasant, everything you must have been thinking all this time, yes, yes! But I didn't think even you could treat *anyone* this way! To lie . . . for three years when you knew—"

Two tears fell from her eyes, but she did no rub them away, nor did she sob at all. They ran down her cheeks, and she sat looking at him, without shifting her glance or even blinking, as if the tears had slipped out and she had not noticed. He wanted to rush to her, bury his head in her lap, but some old standard of decorum, some twisted sense of tact that made him feel he had no right to this, prevented him.

"I'm . . . I'm sorry. I really am . . . But what good—"

"I'm sure you *are* sorry now, but it's too late for that!"

"Oh, honey, please . . . if I could only tell you what I'm—" But instead of interrupting him, she simply sat there, looking at him with blank, incurious grief.

"It all started so long ago," he stumbled on, feeling that this was making it worse. "You remember how it was then. I got to know her at Columbia, and . . . and I wrote to her a couple of times. And it just went on. It was a release for me . . . intellectual things, and all my ravings . . . you know. And then I thought I was in love with her, like a kid, like something out of Goethe. Really *because* it was impossible . . . that was really why. And, you know, she didn't even *imagine* she loved me . . . Why, she almost never wrote back . . . and we were always quarreling."

Wildly, he thought that if Kathryn knew that Liza had never approved of his feeling it might ease her anger and pain.

"Are you trying to make me believe you never slept with her? Even now? *Now!*"

"I didn't," he replied simply. "I didn't. You won't believe that, but it was never that kind of thing . . . Why, I haven't seen her for almost two years . . . and I went on writing just out of habit. There haven't been many letters recently, it was getting—"

"What about the one where she's 'so rare and dark' beside you?" and her voice rose with a flare of indignation. "That was written August seventh! One week ago! . . . Stop treating me this way! And how do I know how many you've written since then? How do I know what you do all day?" She lit a cigarette. "And these were only the ones you *didn't* send!"

"Because they were foolish. Even *I* sensed that, though I wrote them . . . I told you it was sort of . . . a carry-over from adolescence. It was a kind of dreaming—"

"I'll never trust you again, Paul," and this was said with painful emphasis, and seemed to have little to do with what he had said. "I might trust you with anything or anyone else . . . but not with me. Never!"

"But what have I really done?" he exclaimed suddenly, unable to restrain his fascination with an idea that had occurred to him, even though he knew it would infuriate her. "I wrote a lot of foolish letters. And, really, it was precisely *because* it was all completely impossible, *because* they were foolish, that I wrote them at all. I see it so clearly now! . . ." He looked earnestly at her. "Do you see? I never *did* anything! Yes, I was foolish, childish. But really all I did was make myself ridiculous!"

"And what about me!" she cried fiercely. "What did you make me? . . . No, no, all that's words, words! You've lied to me for three years. Every time you said you loved me, every time we . . . No, no, I won't listen to you this time!"

"But how was I unfaithful? How? I didn't sleep with her, I swear that! I've never been unfaithful to you, never, never!"

And, unwittingly, these words came out with such self pitying despair that he was fearful lest she would recognize that he was not speaking of Liza, but of his night with Estelle and the way his own body had failed his rueful desire, and been paralyzed with fears ever since.

"What's the difference anyway? For three years you've been in love with another woman! Three years! And every single week you were telling her! Things you never wrote to me! . . . Everything you were thinking, your soul . . . your goddamn soul! . . . Oh, yes, you had sex with me, you wanted me . . . that way . . . But you loved someone else."

Even through his shame and dread, he wanted at that moment to remind her that sexual infidelity had always been the unpardonable crime in her eyes, and that she was guilty of this, and not he; but he knew that her injury was such that no mere consistency of argument could help to mend it.

"But, but what is love?" he said falteringly. "It isn't just . . . well, just letters and all that, lofty sentiments and everything. *You* don't believe that. You never have and you were right. I *lived* with you, didn't I? Day to day, all these years!" He warmed to it, as though seeing a light in his own dark thoughts. "What was . . . the rest of it? Words, words. Just what you said. Isn't that true, honey? I imagined I loved her, I thought it might be romantic and doomed if I did . . . But I *didn't* leave you, somehow I couldn't, even when . . . But what we had was real, *you* could feel it! Don't you see that? You felt what we had. If I'd *really* loved her, you would have known, suspected somehow. But you didn't—"

"Wasn't I a fool though," she replied with wretched sarcasm. "Wasn't I a fool . . . and weren't you clever! I believed your lies, I trusted you. It must have been so easy for you . . . No, no, you never loved me, you were dishonest all along. If you'd loved me at all you would have known that this would kill me! You would have done anything but lie, lie, lie all this time! You would have told me, like a man should! . . . But you thought you could get away with it, and you almost did. But you must have laughed at me, all along, in the letters . . . laughed with her about—"

She broke off with a gesture of impatience at herself, a gesture that told him more than anything else that she did not only want to make him suffer (to pay him back), but that he had torn from her a sense of safety in loving him that was far more necessary to her existence than anything else.

"But I *do* love you, I always have. It was just that I was foolish . . . You must have felt it—"

"I thought I did. I wanted to feel it so much that I thought I did. But that's because I was stupid, because I didn't have anything else . . . because you were, really, the only thing that mattered to me . . . all that I had. Didn't you know that? Didn't it matter that I had nothing else? . . . But what's the use, why should you care about this now! . . . But even without *her,* you had your work, your friends, the kind of life *you* wanted to live. But . . . but what did I have? What? . . . I was the ignorant little wop you married, the peasant and the *wop!* The fool, the drag on everyone! . . . But why did you marry me? Why did you, Paul? So you could hurt me? Is that why? . . . Oh, what kind of a reason is that! I don't understand it, I don't understand . . . the way you do things . . . all of you . . . I'll never understand!"

She turned away and her shoulders quivered tensely, more from her effort to suppress the sobs that were growing in her body, than from the sobs themselves. It was as if some final private pride, of which she had been unconscious all her life, had now become apparent to her and that to humiliate it would be more than she could bear. It had survived all the rich and intolerant schoolmates of her childhood, all the town-boys who had sought to take advantage of her because she was an Italian, all her insecurity and self doubt since marriage, and now her own emotions threatened it.

"Liar! Liar! Liar!" she gasped blindly.

"What can I do! . . . Oh, Kathryn . . ."

She tried to rub the tears away, and not to look at him, but she could do neither and sat, all huddled together, her words broken with the sobs:

"I just thought that . . . I thought everything was . . . better than before. And now this! . . . It's too much. How could you have done it? . . . Why, why? . . ." The tears dropped straight from her eyes, spotting the kimono, but she went on, still gasping: "I always tried . . . I, I know I was terrible sometimes . . . but . . . but I got so tired, so goddamn tired . . . And I *was* interested, I *did* care about everything you were always talking about, but . . . Oh, why can't I stop crying! . . . I hate it . . . I'm sorry . . ."

"Kathryn, honey, sweetheart, please . . . Listen, I love you . . . I *do* love you. You must know that, you must *believe* that," he was weeping himself. The sight of her grief-ravaged face, and the heavy obstacle of his own feeling of helplessness and responsibility, seized him.

He went over and sat beside her, consumed with the same reaction he had had before, wanting to touch her, blot himself out against her, but not daring to.

"Honey, what can I do for you? Please, please, I love you! . . . I can't help that . . . all the rest, what does it matter? It can't matter . . . We can't go on hurting each other . . ."

Something somewhere inside him gave slightly, as though an ominous crack had appeared in the smooth, fragile surface of his heart. "I'll do anything!"

She did not look at him, but the sobbing seemed to have subsided a little, perhaps because his nearness had brought the rest of it back to her. "What's the use of all this? We do this every time . . . I wanted it to be adult, simple, I wanted to get it over without all this . . ."

"What can I do to make you stay? What?"

She took a cigarette and held on to it as if it were something solid, firmly rooted that would support the rest of her.

"If you love me, make me hate you. Make me *hate* you so we can get it over with now."

That thing inside him shattered silently, even without pain. It was as if his very bones had melted into a terrible gelatin from which he could never retrieve their strength. She sat looking at him, drawn, played out and now strangely quiet. Her words had come out without a thought of hurting him, but in the acute moment that had been reached they struck him cruelly.

He put his head down in the pillow and wept shamelessly, feeling, for the first time in his life, that he could not bear himself, that what he had done out of such tragic thoughtlessness would never leave off consuming him.

After an instant, she put a hand on his shoulders, moving him toward her so that he might rest against her, but she did not weep, nor could she have given way again, even at the sight of her abject husband.

"We tried, didn't we?" she uttered softly, almost reflectively, sniffing slightly: "And I understand a little . . . Don't cry, Paul, don't . . . There was just too much against us all the time, wasn't there? . . . No, no, no . . ."

Her sympathy stung through him, he could not understand it. But he knew, with the immediate comprehension of such moments, that it did not signalize any capitulation on her part. Her agony was still there, the wound as fresh and raw as before, but to it had been added the sad recognition that there is no real fatality to life except its end, that her husband was foolish, perplexed, wrapped in his own confused image of himself, and that he, too, felt as lost and done-for as she. They were both suddenly absorbed by this wild feeling of loneliness and terror, and so bent together there, almost impersonally, like two small creatures in a wintry street who crawl to one another only so they will not perish.

After a while, he set up, took a cigarette and knew that the tremor had passed. They said nothing, and only looked before themselves into the room, considering, through their dense emotional exhaustion, something powerful and irrevocable which those emotions had evoked. These were thoughts, secret and complex, that cannot be shared even in the best of moments. But soon weariness drove even these away, and Hobbes turned back to her, full of fear and hope.

"Well, honey . . . what do we do? I mean . . ." He let it trail off, unable to get any closer to what he meant.

She breathed heavily. "Oh, I don't know. I can't think straight anymore . . . I feel half dead."

He felt then that every word was a weight that he must let down gently upon her, and so he stumbled when he said:

"You should sleep, sweetheart . . . don't you think?"

She nodded distantly and got up. He followed her into the bedroom, almost shivering once he got to his feet again. She slipped off the blue kimono and slid into bed. She lay on her back, her hands behind her head, but did not watch him while he undressed, flipped off the light and got in beside her.

They lay there, unable to elude oppressive thoughts in the first moments of darkness; each aware of the other but cut off from the warmth and assurance that being so close had always given them before, no matter how irritated, weary or disinterested they had been. To Hobbes, everything ahead of him, through the deep pit of that night and into the next days, was treacherous and unknown.

He was blinded to everything by her tears and outcries. It did not matter any longer that once he might have felt her unreasonable in her reactions, her angers; the sight of her misery so pained him that it left no room for him to care whether it was sensible for her to be hurt or not. Lying there, free at last from the huge, complicated structure of deceits in which he had encased himself for so long, and crippled by a new and sickening sense of horror at himself, he felt a heaving inside him, a convulsion beyond his control.

His whole body seemed to stir with this ache and heave, as if his flesh itself was somehow incomplete and striving against its own imperfection. He was bathed in a more heightened sexual longing than he had ever felt, and at the same time mortified that he should feel it at that moment when it was so inappropriate.

But when he touched her fearfully, his fingers stiff with the rude want, she was hot and avid and groping, and her body gave itself up into his arms as though she had been fighting that same black battle with herself, and his touch had destroyed her. They writhed together, trying to consume one another, giving nothing, abandoning themselves to silent, fierce demands. In this prolonged and ferocious embrace, Kathryn moaned a single, terrible exclamation of despair and love.

It was a blind, violent act, broken with cries and sobs, and when it was over they fell back into sleep.

Two

THAT night Stofsky finally left Bianca's at one-fifteen. On top of his bewilderment regarding Verger, Hobbes' failure to return to the apartment after the phone call had plunged him into dark speculations. Though he should have been certain that the incident had nothing to do with him, nevertheless he made a dozen imaginary connections, most of which he voiced to Ketcham and Bianca. They became more and more irritated at him, until he was sure their retorts were only thinly disguised insolence. This threw him into consternation, and made him babble on the more, as if he might outwit his growing depression by courting their assurances that it was unfounded. Eventually it became evident to him that they wished to be left to themselves, and with nervous apologies, he fled.

The gloom and emptiness of the dank subways did not help. He felt utterly alone beneath the sleeping city, and even riffled through his address book in the hope of finding someone who would be glad to see him. Then, walking up York Avenue, he thought of Pasternak, somewhere adrift between New York and the glittering, nightless California of his imagination. There, with Hart and perhaps other strange and exciting people, Pasternak was (he thought) whirling in the center of life, from which loneliness, doubt and conflict were banished.

For a moment, as he paused at the entrance of his building and surveyed the empty street, Stofsky was reminded of the hours after the visions. In that bar, just across there, he had tried all his keys, and like tonight, they had fit no door. But then he had known (or thought he had) that all was love, that behind all indifference lay the fear of powerlessness which love alone could allay. But now he felt embittered, almost unable to recall the simplicity of those emotions, and only aware of the way in which his earnest interferences had all, unaccountably, gone wrong.

He climbed the stairways, lost in thoughts of Hart, Verger, Pasternak, and the others, and it was not until he was almost at his door that he discerned that there was somebody lying crumpled up against it. It was so dark that he could not see this figure clearly, but when he drew nearer, and bent forward, he seemed to remember that sunken chest, those wasted legs. Hurriedly, he lit a match and held it forward, until a dim, ghastly glow enveloped the man, who was pressed against the door in a heap and seemed hardly breathing, but was only asleep. To his complete surprise and joy, he recognized him. It was Ancke.

"Albert, Albert! . . . Come on, get up! How long have you been lying there? . . ."

Ancke woke suddenly, as Stofsky shook him, with no intermediate period of confusion. He was totally immobile one moment and the next instant wide awake, and getting stiffly to his feet, but not, somehow, alarmed.

"Hello," he said with a faint smile. "I've been meaning to come around. What time is it?"

"It's . . . it's about— Heavens, I don't know . . . I've been expecting you; I mean, I knew you'd turn up eventually! And I dawdled all the way up the street just now, *dawdled!* But come in, come in!"

Ancke shuffled after him, stood about with curiosity while Stofsky snapped on lights, and then, choosing the couch, he laid himself down on it carefully, and breathed a heavy sigh of relief.

"I must have been out there a couple of hours . . . Whew! My back's throbbing . . . A very cozy pad, David, yes, yes . . . But then, of course, it's my feet more than anything."

He looked down at his feet as though they were not part of him at all, but he felt a distant sympathy for them nevertheless. His shoes were battered and cracked and he was without socks. His ankles were grimy and there were scabby sores along both insteps where the patent leather had rubbed against the flesh. And, indeed, the rest of his attire was just as miserable. The sports shirt that hung around his drooping shoulders was unwashed, wrinkled, out at the elbows. His trousers were torn on one leg, baggy about his lean shanks, and spotted with mud around the cuffs. He surveyed himself with a sort of sorrowful amusement.

Ancke was only thirty-three, but everything about him seemed worn and faded. His head was large for the emaciated, almost girlish body, and his lank brown hair gave the appearance of being dry, even dusty. His skin was puffy, yellowish, and in his whole heavy face, with the wide, soft mouth, the small nose, and the pallid cheeks, only his eyes, that were large, dark and luminous, gave any sign of life. They burned fitfully under thick eyebrows. His thin arms and legs were scarred with the countless wounds of the hypodermic needle which had poured morphine into him for years, and the flesh seemed to have shrunk in upon his brittle bones. He quivered involuntarily every few minutes, as though he had chills. He was extremely dirty and smelled of sweat and decaying teeth. He was, in fact, the wrinkled little hustler that Hobbes had seen in The Go Hole with the "cool" man a few weeks before.

"It's so remarkable that you should have come tonight, tonight of all times!" Stofsky was exclaiming. "It's almost prophetic! But where have you been? Do you realize I've been searching for over a month? I had to see you. Tremendous things have been happening . . . But what's this about your feet? Here, let me— My God, what have you been doing to yourself?"

Stofsky had started to remove Ancke's shoes, but paused in horror at the sight of his bare feet. They were covered with hideous corns and running sores that were black with dirt. His toes were bloody and swollen.

"They've been dragging me for a week or so," and Ancke laughed feebly at his own pun. "I've been walking, you see. I haven't had any junk for ten days, that's why, I imagine. I couldn't seem to score with anyone, not even my usual connection on One Hundred and Third Street. Remember that corner? So I've been getting around, looking . . . But don't bother with them, man. You'll only make yourself sick . . . I just have to rest."

"No, no," Stofsky cried with dismay. "Wait a minute, maybe I have some boric acid or . . . No, I don't . . . But I'll wash them . . ." He rushed from cluttered cabinet to sink. "Really, Albert, it's terrible! You must have been walking around for weeks, even months . . . Watch out now, the soap may sting . . ."

Ancke smiled weakly, almost paternally, as Stofsky knelt at his feet, washing them gently with an old rag, and asking endless questions:

"But where have you been? Do you realize Hart's been here and gone again? Just flew in and flew out . . . like an albatross! And Gene went with him. But we looked for you, almost every night we dug the whole Square. What about Winnie? Have you seen her? And oh, I've had visions . . . actual manifestations! . . . But quick, tell me everything."

And so Ancke began to talk with patient weariness, gazing

now at the ceiling, and now at the eager, intent face before him.

He had been released from Riker's Island almost two months before, and had picked up a few dollars steering second-story men to a friend of his from Chicago days, a fence. This enabled him to get enough morphine to keep "grooved" for several weeks. Jail had, as always, forced him to "throw his habit," and so small amounts were sufficient in the beginning. But gradually he became "hooked" again, and had to hustle about Times Square and Harlem to set up more deals. He bumped into Winnie and "her boy," Little Rock, and they helped him out. Winnie, true to rumors Stofsky had heard, had thrown her morphine habit and, but for a little heroin now and again "just for a lift," was on nothing, and living with Little Rock in a house in Astoria. Ancke "cut around with them once in a while," the evening at The Go Hole had been one such occasion, but preferred staying permanently in Manhattan, where he could keep in touch with all the passers, connections, addicts, homosexual prostitutes, petty crooks and musicians who made up the underground of drugs, crime and craziness which he frequented.

These were his friends from other days in L. A., Chicago, or New Orleans, from numerous jails, tea pads, freighters, bars and cheap hotels; or customers from the year he had peddled stolen prescription blanks on One Hundred and Twenty-eighth Street. Through them he got all the news: who was in and who was out, who was hooked and who was off, what was available and what was going to be hard to get; all the rumors, speculations, gossip, warnings and messages that traveled from mouth to mouth and city to city among the restless, continually circulating fraternity to which he belonged.

Then his money had run out, those few connections who might advance him a little "M" had vanished or been arrested, and for a week and a half he had walked fruitlessly up and downtown, fighting nausea, and the ache and jitter of his body demanding the drug. He had partially thrown his new habit on this trek, slept in bus stations wrapped in newspapers, begged money for coffee and sandwiches, gone from place to place, run down a hundred empty leads, and finally given up, and with the last of his failing strength, come to Stofsky.

"So now I've got to rest. Maybe for quite a while. Take the strain off myself. Perhaps just sleep. Are you alone here?"

"Yes, yes. Hart and Dinah were staying with me, but they've all gone now. All of them. You couldn't have come at a better time. You don't know how I needed you . . . just tonight. You'll stay here, of course, won't you?"

"I'll have to say 'yes' . . . Could I have a cigarette?"

He took it, raised himself only slightly to receive the light, and inhaled deeply, a look of heavy contentment flushing over his features.

"As long as there's no one else around, I'll stay. Because, you know, everyone drags me now. I mean just everyone, anyone, just people. I really prefer to sit quietly alone. Or even sleep. It's not because I'm afraid, of course . . . nothing like that. You understand? It's all just a drag for me now." And his lids fluttered closed.

"But we must talk," Stofsky said eagerly. "I've got to tell you everything! My visions, and Waters . . . Waters went crazy, you know, and had shock treatment and . . . But, that's right, you don't know Waters. And I've huge tidings from Hart, and . . . oh, so much else! Oh, Albert, you couldn't have come at a better time! I must tell you everything."

"All right," Ancke replied with patient forbearance. "Maybe for a little while, and then I'll sleep."

"Oh, and Verger! I wanted to talk to you about Verger . . . Now, Albert, what's this about books? You don't know how I've been involved with those books . . . But first, do you realize Verger's the only one who's seen you since you got out? The only one! Why didn't you come here? I could have given you money. You must have known that. I'm working now; yes, a big job, and . . . But, listen, about the books: now, he *pretended* to understand why you took them. But he didn't really. I mean, not *why* he pretended to understand! It wasn't crucial to him, of course, he didn't really get angry. In fact, I'm sure he's even anxious to see you again, so he can prostrate himself or something like that. But, really, it only set him off on more self punishing thoughts. You know how he is. He doesn't want to believe that he's really very proud, he wants to humiliate himself, to suffer, and your stealing his books played right into that . . . But, actually, he does care a great deal, and struggles with his vanity . . ."

"I'd almost forgotten them. I only took three or four, didn't I? You know, I can't even remember . . . But *you* understand about them."

"Yes, but that's my point, because, you see, *he* doesn't!"

"Oh, man, *don't* drag me about those books, not now." Ancke all but clapped his forehead, but there was no annoyance in his exclamation, only weariness, as though he had been pleasantly slipping into a thick inertia until Stofsky had brought up his theft.

But he went on patiently all the same: "I needed the money to score, you see. I had this load all set up, three fresh caps, stuff right out of Bellevue . . . I knew he wouldn't really mind."

"But, don't you see, really he does! Oh, I know he pretends—"

"But I know all that, man! Don't you think I know all that? What I mean is I knew he wouldn't *do* anything. You see? He wouldn't *do* anything. I had to get enough to function, that's all."

He breathed heavily, taking a deeper pull on the cigarette, but there was in his manner the still watchful relief of a man who had righted himself after almost falling from a tight-rope, but knows he still has a long way to go.

"Just don't put me down about *those* things now. I can't make conversation about those things. I mean, we know all about them. You *know* that I understand that it's just Verger's ego, that he really *wants* to be taken advantage of, that he likes to fester on all that . . . You see, I know about that level. But it just drags me now. Really, I would like to sleep."

"But wait," Stofsky exclaimed. "Of course, I knew you understood Daniel, in that sense. That's all it really is with him, of course. But, you see, I've been tilting with everyone's ego recently . . . like a Saint George! Ever since my visions . . . but I must tell you all about my visions! Do you realize, Albert, that I've had revelations, I've been spoken to, called . . . Don't sleep yet, just a little while longer. I must tell you! . . . Everything is love, love . . . But let me explain it all to you, from the very beginning. Don't sleep yet, you must hear this!"

Ancke seemed willing enough to listen, as long as he did not have to speak. He settled down into the pillows, his large eyes half-lidded, his breathing hardly perceptible, his head wreathed in blue smoke curling lazily in the motionless air.

Stofsky proceeded to tell him everything with minute detail, appending exaggerated comments, and giggling at his own exaggerations. As his account widened to include everyone, as one story overlapped into another and the whole narrative became infinitely complex with his elaborate relations with Verger, Ketcham, Hart, Pasternak and Hobbes, he grew sadder, his voice terse, his gaze fixed and yet bewildered. Ancke only lay nodding dreamily, as if he had heard it all many times before, and it was an old, unfortunate, and yet predictable tale that could have but one ending.

"So something has really gone terribly wrong," Stofsky concluded. "They all mock me, or write these letters. But not that alone, I'm used to that, of course; people have always mocked me, I used to like it you know, even play up to it . . . But they are afraid of me too. And repulsed! Can you possibly know what I mean? . . . But, of course you do, of anyone. That's why I can tell you these things. I've told no one else . . . But, just tonight, Arthur, Bianca, even Hobbes . . . no, you don't know him . . . but they all seemed annoyed with me, and then look what happened with Hart and Dinah! Just because I wanted to love them, to be honest. The truth, the truth! For even now, when it's earned me nothing but contempt, I *do* believe it. Heavens, do they think I—"

Ancke sighed sympathetically, but also with such heaviness that Stofsky broke off.

"Just accept it, man. Don't get all hungup that way."

"Well, maybe you're right. I won't listen to them anymore," Stofsky continued, taking this as the assurance he had courted unsuccessfully earlier. "It's only because they don't understand that they . . . shrink from me. That's really what it is you know. They can't bear me, they pass looks. Oh, I see them doing it!"

"But you shouldn't get hungup on all that, man," Ancke said in such barely audible tones that Stofsky moved closer. "You know how people are. Now, you've got eyes for making things better, for making people get along, and accept one another. That's your trouble. You get all worried about it. You rush around, 'tilting with egos' perhaps, as you said. But that's probably all ego too . . . your ego! . . . Now, don't get angry. Oh, I know when you're getting angry, so come on now . . . But that's just putting other people down, you see what I mean? I mean, that's what they do to you in return."

He smiled benignly and his voice subsided to little more than a weary murmur: "Now don't get all hurt. I really know about all this . . . It's all such a drag. I don't mean that it's unimportant, caring for people, all that concern . . . but you shouldn't get hurt, you know. I wouldn't hurt you, and I understand why you feel the way you do . . . You know, *I* feel sometimes like I'm dying . . . every minute of the day a little more. You see what I mean? I'm being smothered . . . . all these relationships, hangups, conflicts, all that business . . . it stifles me."

He heaved another sigh that seemed to shiver his whole frame. "I've been so tired this time, for instance. Since getting out. Listless, horrified. By the hangups with people. Just anyone. The public. You know, even people you like. You have to smile, talk, arrange to get somewhere. There's hassles about food, where to sleep, news, all that. I used to be able to walk along the street —meeting the people—and get by, laugh, take my time . . . But now it all drags me terribly. I really prefer to sit quietly alone, just to rest . . . And, you know, I really think I'll sleep right now. Why don't I just sleep?" His lids met. "*You* understand."

"Ego? Is that all it is?" Stofsky uttered, asking himself, though speaking aloud. "Is that what it's been all along? Just like psychoanalysis. Maybe that's all it was, even the visions, although I didn't feel that way . . ."

He gazed at the limp figure before him, and there was a wounded brightness in his dark eyes.

"It was probably madness then, as my father said. I should have kissed everyone's feet, or screamed at them. Is that what you mean, Albert? Crushed them for feeling repelled by me? By my very face? Or been absolutely crushed by them. Is that what you mean? . . . Why has it got to be that way? Tell me, suddenly I don't seem to know at all, is that the way things really are?" His stare was more fixed than before, but his lips were trembling. "What if that's the way they really are," he muttered to himself. "Tell me."

"Now look, man, don't be hurt. Don't be crushed . . . and don't crush anyone else either. Don't you see? Don't care about all that."

Ancke had come back once more, as if from the dead. He took another cigarette resolutely, and touched Stofsky's shoulder abstractedly. "But, look, I'll tell you something that happened to me, just a week or so ago. And then I'll sleep."

He cleared his throat, breathed deeply once or twice, took a long drag on the cigarette, blinked his eyes, smiled wanly at the ceiling, and began speaking softly and slowly, with a certain careful solemnity as though to avoid any excitement.

"I was on the Fifth Avenue Bus. You see, I was cutting up to Harlem to see a junkie that Little Rock used to know in Atlanta. It was early evening, and I thought the river might be nice, so I decided to take the bus up the Drive, instead of getting all hungup in the subways. I really just wanted to watch the water and get a look at the George Washington Bridge . . ."

There had been a drunken old woman four seats ahead of him, it seemed. It was crowded, hot, and sitting next to her was a perfectly-coifed young matron with net gloves, in an expensive print dress, and carrying several small parcels from fashionable stores. The drunken woman was fifty or so, ratty, even wizened, and she had a dirty, white linen tam clapped askew a bird's nest of badly dyed hair. Her lean, wrinkled fingers were smudged, her nails bitten and cracked. Her clothes had been youthful fifteen years before, but now they were mournfully jaunty on so withered a figure. There was an underfed scrawniness to her cheeks which made the crude touches of rouge resemble a mortician's handiwork.

"She might have been one of those whores that used to work Columbus Circle in the old days, only since then she's gone to pieces fast . . ."

The young matron pointedly turned away from her into the aisle, but the old woman seemed oblivious of this, and sat picking her nose, mumbling absent-mindedly to herself, and primping her hair as though somehow flattered to be on that bus among all those combed, polished, and dignified ladies. Finally the young matron got up, and with a meaningful look at the other young matrons in the other seats, moved toward the center door. Something in this action infuriated the old woman, for she began to cackle, swear and even spit in her seat. She grumbled to herself, to passing cars, and finally to the others in the bus:

"They're taking over everything! The sonsabitches think they can run everything . . . even the transit system! Well, not while I'm around, the bastids!"

She could not restrain this mounting rage, and went on sputtering and swearing until she had worn herself out, and, noticing the way everyone had drawn away from her and sat peering at her covertly, hopelessness and embarrassment overcame her anger. She was separated, by several seats, from everyone else, for they had edged away as though on the suspicion of disease. She sat on, not daring to look around for fear she would see the pitiless, disapproving glances, and realize that she had cut herself off from the feeling of security and personal worth that being there on the bus amid the colorful frocks, subdued conversations and contented faces, had given her. She sat, flushed and hurt, fidgeting with her clothes, fishing for nothing in her miserable handbag, muttering, and wiping away small, angry tears from her old eyes, while everyone watched and looked at one another with that slight understanding shake of the head that signified all had realized that they had, at least, their disapproval of her in common; and this made them closer to each other, even a little more good-natured than before.

"Everyone was suddenly very sympathetic with everyone else, because they all felt that they might have been rejected, humiliated, anxious or unsuccessful the rest of the time, but now they were the same, for this one moment, simply *because* they weren't like her. You see? . . . But she got all hungup being angry with that woman, and then on being humiliated by everyone else . . . I kept saying to myself: 'What does she care? Why does it matter to her?' I even thought of going up to her and telling her that, but it was too much trouble."

"How terrible! . . . And perfect too, in a way!" Stofsky exclaimed. "But that's what I mean. Why didn't they understand *why* she was injured—I mean, everything you perceived in it —instead of crushing her that way. Why didn't they accept her? Instead of thinking of themselves, their idea of themselves!"

"But, listen, man," Ancke replied, as though he was long-suffering but intended to endure. "Why didn't *she* accept them? . . . They were acting the same way toward *me!* All that time! I'm sure they knew I was completely saturated with narcotics, and had this disgusting skin disease and everything. Why, I had the whole back of the bus to myself! Don't you see? . . . Now, *I* know that's just the way the public is. I realize they think I'm revolting, abhorrent . . . but not only that, I know *why* they think that . . . and more important, I *accept* the fact that they do . . . They're disgusted because they've got to save their own egos, you see? But I haven't got one, I mean I don't care about all that anymore, so it doesn't matter to me . . .I just accept it, so as not to get hungup . . . By the way, do you have a pair of shoes you can lend me?"

Stofsky was stunned and unable to decide on his reaction.

"What a strange idea!" he cried. "The end of the ego, the death of the will!" He was clasping and unclasping his hands. "Maybe that's what I really meant by 'die, give up, go mad.' But what a provocation this is! Do you realize? We should expect people (and ourselves mainly, of course) not only to understand why other people think us abhorrent, unbearable, a contagious disease . . . but to accept it as well! Not even to *feel* humiliated . . . even in the heart!"

Meanwhile Ancke had collapsed from the effort of telling the story, and would only murmur: "It's just a drag, as I've said. Once you know why anyone rejects you or judges you, that it's for themselves and not you, it doesn't matter anymore. But more important, it becomes a terrific, stifling, really death-like drag to care about it . . . And finally you just prefer to sit quietly alone . . ."

He peered at Stofsky, as though checking a final time, and found him lost in calculations there on the floor, his lips drawn, and then breaking into sudden, incredulous giggles. His depression of an hour before had vanished.

"Yes," Stofsky reflected after a moment. "It's a weird perception, almost frightening . . . But it raises many problems. The end of self . . . what a thought!" He turned towards Ancke, his brows pulled together with questions. "But how do you tell people *this*? How can you make them understand *this*? It was hard enough before . . . on the other level. Or is all that—wantting to make them see it—is all that ego, too?" and he mumbled this last to himself, and then looked back at Ancke whose lids had drifted together. "But I've kept you talking too long, eh, Albert? . . . Albert?"

But Ancke was asleep, and had been for the last few minutes; that deep, impregnable sleep that is like a trance, that is almost a rehearsal for death, and from which one cannot be called, but must call oneself.

Stofsky gave a forlorn little laugh under his breath, and getting up, pulled a blanket over Ancke with a careful tenderness of which he would have been ashamed if anyone had been there to see.

"And now I am alone," he whispered.

❊   ❊   ❊   ❊   ❊

But that night he had a dream, without trappings, without symbols; a dream of extraordinary clarity while he dreamt it, but which he could not remember at all clearly when he awoke.

He walked down an inky corridor, much like one of those in Waters' building or in his own, and he was out of breath, as if he had come up many long and tiring flights. The door at the end of that corridor did not surprise him, nor, when he opened it without knocking, did the large, shadowy hall beyond it; a hall such as one can rent for fifteen dollars a night in Harlem brownstones; long, the fancy moldings and dusty crepe streamers giving it a pathetic and abandoned appearance. Nor was he surprised by the throne at one end of it, a throne that was not surrounded by an ambient light, or even very clean and polished, but still somehow regal and entirely proper to the figure sitting there: an aging man of once powerful physique, now vaguely weary, His untrimmed beard fanned out in white folds upon His chest, His eyes shining with muted brightness as only an old man's eyes can shine out of the limpid stillness of an old face. God.

Stofsky approached, without fear or excitement, and found himself on his knees, looking up, still conscious of his breathlessness. He paused for an instant, peering at the face, realizing an old, skeptical curiosity concerning it which he somehow knew would be tolerated; noting the wrinkles, the faint pink glow of the cheeks, the expression of weary passivity.

Then he began to tell all that had happened since the visions, endeavoring to stick close to the facts and keep the report brief and accurate. All the same, it seemed to him to take an inexcusable time to go through it all. Finally, reaching Ancke and mentioning his worry over his future, he came to the end.

"I should have had you here before, I know," God said with an audible sigh. "But then . . ." And He looked down at Stofsky with an expression of such sadness and such resignation that Stofsky was actually embarrassed to have been the cause of such a look on God's face.

"But what am I to do next, Sir?" he managed to say.

At that, he thought that God might lean forward and touch his head with one of those large, veinless hands, so gentle and sorrowful was the light which bathed His Face. But He did not.

"How shall I help them now? You see, I'm so confused and tired—," forgetting that God must know everything.

"You must go back, and even doubt," God said after a moment's pause, "and remember none of this. There's an end which you shall discover. It waits there for you. Without you, it cannot happen. And it must."

"But what shall I do?", wanting, with childlike earnestness, some sign to guide him, to make acceptance easier.

"Being saved is like being damned," God said with thoughtful simplicity, as though it was one of the unutterable secrets of the universe given to Stofsky now because he had been patient, because he had come so far.

Then God did lean forward until His beard fell straight down into His lap and Stofsky could see the wet brilliance of His large eyes. "You must go," He said, "Go, and love without the help of any Thing on earth."

For a second, Stofsky seemed to recall the words; then remembered a line like that in Blake, and thought that perhaps this was not God at all, but Blake himself. But then, looking closer, he knew it *was* God, and thought it wonderful and just that God should quote Blake too.

As he was about to rise, however, a question rose in his mind, something almost irreverent and certainly mortal, and even though he suspected that he had no right to ask it, he could not let the opportunity pass somehow.

"Things are so terrible," he began. "The violence, misery, the hate . . . war and hopelessness . . . I wonder," and he gave one fearful and yet challenging glance into Those Eyes. "Why can't *You* help all that? Do You know how human beings suffer? . . . Can't You help them, Sir?"

God's face grew dim and drawn, as though the question gave Him pain He knew there was no sense to feel, but pain He took upon Himself in spite of that. He seemed for that moment a majestic and lonely man in His rented hall, on His dusty throne, who had received too many petitioners, too long, and understood too much to speak anything but the truth, even though it could not help.

"I try," He replied simply. "I do all I can."

Then Stofsky woke, and it was still dark. He could remember most of it, as though it had just happened, and felt a kind of heavy peace. But very soon he fell off to sleep again, and dreamt no more, and had forgotten when the morning came.

Three

THE next two weeks passed slowly for Hobbes. Nothing had been settled by the fight, and they were not really close for a long time after it. They sat through many boring evenings, listening to the radio and saying little to one another, each knowing that the other was thinking of the letters, both incapable of speaking of them. They watched each other secretly, however, neither wanting to be the first to forget the trouble, but waiting for the other to do so. This uneasy and deceptive calm was shattered by a series of lesser fights that flared up out of nowhere, dredging everything out of them, and bringing the bitterness and remorse to the surface again. Any small disagreement or trivial complaint sufficed to remind Kathryn of the hatefulness of her position, and this inevitably led back to the letters. She could not decide on any course of action, but anger and recrimination freed her temporarily from her desperate thoughts, and letting loose recklessly, she risked his love which was the only thing she really cared about. Hobbes somehow got by from day to day, dragging his guilt along with him, and finding it heavy enough to stifle the objections he felt when she became unreasonable. But for these lapses, they clutched at inconsequential things, like people too embarrassed to mention an ugly smell.

Pasternak came back, having hitch hiked from San Francisco where Hart was living with Marilyn again. No one had been able to find Dinah, although it was rumored she was there. Pasternak was filled with tales of the trip, unaware of everything that had happened since his departure, and glad to be in New York again. Listening to his exuberant stories of the penniless flight across the country in the Cadillac, the wild week in Frisco, and his lonely, haphazard trek home again on the highways, Hobbes noticed that Kathryn seemed to grow less bitter. For the next day or so, they did not fight and things were smoother. They saw Stofsky once, and heard his accounts of Ancke, who was still sleeping, day in and day out, getting up only for bowls of cereal and a cigarette or two. They found it easier to be with people than to be alone, and during the second week they spent several evenings with Ketcham and his friends from Cambridge, Peter and Janet Trimble. Janet had come with Ketcham to the party the Hobbes' had given just before Hart arrived, and Trimble, down from Boston, was a physicist who was contracted to teach the coming semester at Rutgers.

Then Hobbes got a letter from his acquaintance, the editor to whom he had given his novel. It had been over a month since he had delivered it to him, a month during which he had been alternately impatient to hear and full of dread lest he do, and the hope that continued silence left alive be smashed. All that had happened (the turning of his mental phantoms, one by one, into real fears), had driven the book out of his head, and when the note came, saying nothing about the manuscript but only suggesting lunch on the following Tuesday, he was unprepared for what was to occur at that meeting.

The editor was courteous, sympathetic, evasive. They had steaks at a midtown restaurant where publishing and advertising people lunched in talkative groups and drank martinis. The editor, a soft faced man of thirty or so whose rise with the publishing house had been rapid, knew the head waiter, advised Hobbes to have a second martini, but seemed in no hurry to get to his book. Hobbes accepted this as the usual procedure, and after two courses of trivial literary chatter, over dessert, the editor turned to him and said: "And, now, about *your* manuscript."

He talked for quite some time. They had two cups of coffee and another drink, over which they lingered. He spoke of costs, a crowded spring list, and it was only at Hobbes' direct, fretful questions that he allowed himself to discuss the book itself. Hobbes fiddled with his spoon, listening to the relaxed, persuasive voice as it assured him that he had ability, that his book had exciting and even unusual scenes, and that it was obvious he was going to do something "interesting." Then it suddenly occurred to him, what only nervousness and blind hope had prevented him from recognizing immediately, that they were not going to take his book, and that this charming, even-spoken person with whom he was lunching was merely trying to tell him this kindly. Only the fact that the editor had had to get through many luncheons like this with numberless, overly-serious young authors of other "promising, but confused" novels, prevented him from becoming piqued by Hobbes' stubborn insistence that he detail the reasons for the rejection. He was understanding when the questions as to just what was wrong became blunter, more disturbed. He hastily assured Hobbes that his was only one opinion, and it was only after Hobbes had sat lost in thought for several minutes that he saw fit to glance at his watch with surprise, and exclaim: "Look what time it's gotten to! I had no idea!"

Though Hobbes knew full well that the luncheon would become just another item on an expense account, he tried, almost belligerently, to pay his part of the bill. But even in this the editor's suave friendliness defeated him: "Nonsense, let *them* take care of it!" this, as if referring to a common enemy.

They parted in the street, and Hobbes stood in a doorway, watching the unruffled, well-pressed editor walk jauntily away, and knowing that to him the interview was just another unpleasant task brought to a tidy conclusion.

After that he walked aimlessly through the crowded side streets toward Times Square, carrying his manuscript under his arm, drifting with the mobs through traffic, reading the monster billboards automatically, and wondering what to do. Gradually the import of the luncheon settled down on him, and this listlessness disappeared. Standing on the busy margin of the Square that was huge, garish and bright in the sunny afternoon, its millions of bulbs burning, buzzing, going off and on with cheerful regularity, he ceased to believe in his book. He held it before him and seemed to know it for the first time as a lopsided patchwork of influences, wishes and vague intellectual pretensions. Suddenly he was forlornly amazed that he could have written it, and could not imagine what collection of fears and obsessions had kept him from seeing it truly before. He felt exactly as he had when, in the midst of his shame with Kathryn, he had recognized that his long correspondence with Liza had been a childish, fanciful romance in which he had created for himself a stellar part. He realized his book was worthless, and he was shamed by its existence, and yet free from it as well, as he had been free from his image of Liza, once he had known it for an image.

"But what do I do now?" he thought. Kathryn, their fight, the years she had worked so that he might conclude the book, their relationship that was just the reverse of that of other married people: all this swam through his head like some terrible syrup. "What do I do now?" he said aloud, and then realizing it, moved quickly around the corner of Forty-eighth Street and started back toward Sixth Avenue.

The routine of his life, in which he had invested so many

foolish hopes, had collapsed piece by piece without his noticing, like a tenement that is stripped by a demolition crew in no hurry. After weeks of work, glass, sills and cornices are gone, but it is still an angular, ugly skeleton of its former height. Then, with one ponderous swing of the iron ball, the real fragility of its joints becomes apparent, and the whole frame topples with a hoarse roar of crackings and separations; and the beams buckle and descend into a sea of dust in which they disappear.

"What am I going to do? It's been nothing but a dream all along. How can *I* earn money? What job can *I* do? I've never, not in all these years, stopped to think what I'd do if this happened."

He walked across town in the numb bewilderment of these hapless thoughts, the manuscript at his side forgotten, and for once he was unconscious of what passersby might think of him, even unconscious of the passersby. He wandered block after block, unaware of the delicious sunlight that splashed the walks on Fifty-fifth Street where there were a few trees east of Park Avenue, unaware of the tardy lunchers that lounged in that sun talking, loath to get back to their stuffy offices.

In such a mood, he reached his building and climbed the stairs. Almost as soon as he got into the apartment, Pasternak called. He was at the cafeteria three blocks away where they had talked the night he left for the coast with Hart. He wondered if Hobbes could come up there. Resolving that he must not keep the rejection of his book a secret, that he must do away with dreams, and that this was his first test, Hobbes went out to meet him.

Pasternak was sitting at a table by the window with cooling coffee and a notebook before him, in which he was writing leisurely. His air of calm absorption made Hobbes feel even more agitated, but he contrived a sorrowful smile as he sat down.

"What are you writing there, Gene?"

"Oh, nothing. Just scribbling." Pasternak closed the notebook quietly, and gave Hobbes a look of remarkable fondness and warmth and suppressed excitement. "I was really just sitting here considering this great afternoon. Isn't it fine though? Like Paris, only there's autumn in the air."

Hobbes laughed bitterly, but still a laugh. "Sure, sure. But then I hadn't even noticed. That shows the difference, eh?" He looked inquiringly at Pasternak, feeling it another sign of weakness that he could not begin to tell him of the interview immediately, but also conscious that there was a strange elation beneath Pasternak's remark. "Say, what's wrong with you, any-way? You look like you'd just been married."

"Oh, nothing really. I mean— Well, here, let me get you some coffee first!"

And with an embarrassed grin he danced to the counter and brought back a cup. "And here's a Danish too. We'll sit here and enjoy the sun with our aperitifs, American style!"

He studied Hobbes' face for a moment with a look of per-plexed joy. "But say, you look like something's happened to you too. It must be the afternoon, it's a real Christmas of an after-noon! Don't you love the afternoon? I mean, just as a time of day, just any day." He laughed, but then upon noting Hobbes' expressionless countenance, he grew perplexed again. "What's wrong though, Paul? What's happened to you? First you tell *me*, eh?"

"Oh, it's nothing worldshaking," Hobbes began crossly. "Does it show that much? Huh! . . . The publishers turned down my book, that's all. In fact, I just got home from lunch with the editor."

Pasternak circled his cup in the saucer and peered into it gravely. "You mean, just now? Just before I called?"

"Yes, it was one of those long, subtle brush-offs. Oh, they said they liked it well enough, you know what they *say*, but . . . It's the same tiresome old story."

Pasternak nodded vaguely, and continued to stare into his cup, every once in a while glancing at Hobbes with searching, care-ful eyes. "It doesn't mean anything really though, Paul. Just one publisher like that. Look what happened to me . . . But what did they say?"

Hobbes told him the gist of the interview, trying not to spare his own role in it, all the while smiling crookedly and assuming an almost bantering, frivolous tone. But gradually he became aware that Pasternak was hardly listening to the details, but was growing more grave and even embarrassed as Hobbes talked.

"Well, there's no use getting worked up about it, I guess," he finished. "But that's why I didn't notice the afternoon . . . Lis-ten, though, what's your news? Give me a laugh. I can see you're bursting with something."

Pasternak shot him an affectionate, puzzled look.

"Gee, man, I don't know how to say it . . . now. It's such a crazy coincidence, but . . ."

"What do you mean? What's happened?"

"Carr & Horton took *my* book. I got a letter yesterday, and I went and saw the editor, right now. I've just come back, and they're going to give me a thousand dollars advance on it." He rattled this off hastily as though somehow ashamed of it, and then added earnestly: "I came right over here and then I called you. I haven't told anyone else."

"Gene, Gene, that's wonderful! A thousand dollars! My God! Well, what did this guy say? No strings attached?" For the moment, Hobbes was overjoyed, forgetting himself. "You see? You see, I told you they'd take it . . . someone would. Remember? Just after Hart came? You see, it *can* happen!"

"Yah, isn't it funny," Pasternak muttered shyly.

"Right while mine was being rejected, eh? Ha-ha! At the very same instant, I'll bet! You see, for every cradle there's a grave . . . A thousand dollars advance! What did you say when he told you?"

"Oh, I didn't say . . . well, anything, I don't think."

Hobbes sniffed. "I didn't say anything either."

"Oh, yes, let's see, I said: 'It isn't enough to buy a farm with, but maybe next year.' Something crazy like that."

"Maybe next year . . . yes . . . But, my God, Gene, I can see that I made it difficult for you to tell me, didn't I? Just now. I mean, because mine was turned down. And at the very same moment too! Some gets in and some's let out! Ha-ha! I'll bet you weren't even going to tell me, were you? Because you thought it would make me feel worse. Am I right?" Hobbes was snickering and sniffing to himself sarcastically. "But you know what I think of your book. And it even makes me feel better. It really does."

Pasternak could see that Hobbes' excitement was ambiguous, equally sincere and ironic. "Well, Paul, I really didn't know just how to tell you. But I knew you'd be glad . . . And, you see, now I can help other people out. I mean, I can show their stuff to Carr & Horton. They think I'm pretty good up there. It's the funniest goddamn thing. They really do. And, you know, I'll be able to pull some weight with *them*, about your book for instance—"

"Hah! That's how my editor, the one I spoke to, talked about publishers . . . 'them' . . . I guess there is another side of this veil, eh? I mean, one *can* cross over . . ." Hobbes gulped some coffee and then turned a fresh smile on Pasternak, angry at his own fumbling cynicism. "But let's not talk about them! Hell,

I don't care about them! I really don't . . . not any more! What do you feel like? What does it feel like to have a thousand bucks practically in your pocket, and literature shivering at your name?"

Pasternak laughed softly, incredulously, for the first time since Hobbes had sat down, considering those thoughts that had occupied him before Hobbes arrived.

"That's what I was trying to write down. But, hell, I don't know . . ." He looked around the nearly empty cafeteria into which the warm sun fell so pleasantly. "You know, I'd like to lay every woman in sight . . . I mean, I feel I could do it." He looked back at Hobbes and giggled nervously. "Isn't that funny? I don't know what to do with myself. I feel sort of awkward, and yet also wonderful too. But I don't know where to begin—"

"But you don't *have* to do anything! That's it! Don't you see, man, you're safe. A home run! Now all you've got to do is write another one! Ha-ha!" And for a moment, he fell into a silence so deep and reflective that Pasternak's face clouded slightly again.

"Wait'll I tell Kathryn," Hobbes resumed abruptly, because he felt he should not let his own bitter thoughts intrude on this day for which Pasternak had waited so long. "You know, it'll make her really happy. I mean, even with *my* news. In fact, it'll take some of the sting out of my news."

Worriedly, Pasternak studied Hobbes again. "Look, Paul, I meant that. I can show your book to Carr & Horton. And it'll be different than just submitting it cold, you know what I mean?"

"Well, let's not talk about that. Really, I don't want to talk about it!" That was something for the future, and at the moment he did not believe in the future any more than he believed in his book, and he just wanted to forget both. "Why spoil the fact that you've sold your book? Why dirty up this Christmas of an afternoon . . . with all that? The world hasn't come to an end."

"Well, I wanted you to know that I can do it, that's all."

"Sure, sure, I know. Anyway Kathryn will be glad, Gene. Really. She's always thought you'd make it . . . quite aside from anything else." He could not understand why he was torturing himself with these remarks about Kathryn. The parallel between himself and Pasternak, in relation to Kathryn, was too uncomfortably obvious at that moment to be lost on him, but a certain ironical malice seized him. "It's very funny when you think about it, almost like a novel . . . I mean, everything considered . . . At the very same moment, the same instant probably, your book was accepted and mine was rejected, and then just a few weeks ago—"

Pasternak could say nothing, but was only saddened by his friend's words, and so sat there mutely, solidly, fingering the edge of his notebook.

"But, my God, Gene," Hobbes suddenly exclaimed. "You haven't told your mother, have you! Did she know you were seeing Carr & Horton when she went to work this morning?"

"Yes, sure—"

"Well, she's been worrying, man! And look what time it is!" It was already after five, and suddenly he had to be alone for a little while before Kathryn came home and it all had to be gone through again. "You ought to call her, or go home, or something. Don't you think you should start to do something? You're a big author now!"

Pasternak was glad for this new turn in the conversation. "I guess maybe I should. I've really forgotten about everything, like I said. You know, that's what's so funny about it. You'll see, when your book is . . . Well, you'll see, you won't know what to do next."

"But think of your mother, Gene. She's hoping just as much as you were hoping . . . well, just a few hours ago! Go on, go home and tell her! My God, I'd call Kathryn immediately . . . if I had your news. As it is . . . well, it doesn't matter so much. My news will keep. Stale news keeps."

Pasternak got uncertainly to his feet, taking the notebook and following Hobbes out of the cafeteria. He took Hobbes by the arm, a thing he had never done before, and looked earnestly, with a dark gathering of brows, into his troubled face.

"I really want to show your book to Carr & Horton now . . . Just remember that."

Hobbes could not ignore that fond, worried frown that filled Pasternak's face, and for a moment in the street that was golden with the cool twilight and crowded with people hurrying for the subway, he smiled sadly, gratefully, and said:

"Sure, Gene, I know. And I think it's the greatest thing that could have happened. Really. Your book deserves it. I always told you that."

Just before they parted, Pasternak to the subway that would take him home to Long Island a different person than when he had left it, and Hobbes back down Lexington Avenue to the apartment and the next hours that could not help but be terrible,

Pasternak said strangely, with odd emphasis, as if for Hobbes as much as himself:

"You know, you really *can* make a living as a writer. You actually can do it. And I never really believed it before. I mean, a thousand bucks! It's crazy, just for a book," and there was something sheepish in his parting grin.

Four

Hᴏʙʙᴇs' desire to avoid consideration of his position drove him to Stofsky's that night. Kathryn had been thoughtful and not too inquisitive regarding his interview, but their recent difficulties and her own disappointment at his news made it impossible for her to be as consoling as he would have liked. When he said distantly that he thought he might go out for a walk, however, she extracted from him no estimate of the time he would be gone, as was usual.

But at Stofsky's, where his wanderings eventually led him, he found no temporary escape from those thoughts of the uncertain future which the afternoon had revealed to him, for things had altered greatly there in the past weeks.

Ancke was up more often now and pattered around in Stofsky's rose brocade bathrobe in the shortening, yellow afternoons, dusting and rearranging furniture, making curious, twenty-minute perusals of stray books of poetry, or sitting motionless at the window staring leadenly out at the washing and the blunt walls opposite.

During the first week of his stay it had been different. When Stofsky would return from work at nine-thirty in the morning, he would find Ancke curled up, cocoon-like, in the messy, unaired sheets of his bed, behind the faded gauze curtains which had appeared at the door of the bedroom on the second day; then, sinking wearily onto the couch in the living room (which was the only other place to sleep), Stofsky would find, while crushing out a final cigarette, a scrap of paper upon which Ancke had scribbled short thoughts or instructions or messages that had come to him during the night. One read: "Dig vomit-colored leaves on tree in yard, trunk all withered with gonorrhea oozing out of dead earth," this scrawled lazily along the flap of an envelope. Another time he found merely these words: "Pores on cheeks widening, gaping—am slowly being drawn into them." Most often these mysterious little notes (for almost a week they were Stofsky's only contact with Ancke), simply read: "Leave six cigarettes" or "Coffee gone."

Ancke spent all of his time sleeping. His waking hours were only intermissions from his intense preoccupation with it. He was like a tight-mouthed man who tenaciously goes about performing an unpleasant task and gives all his energies to it; in fact, builds his whole existence (time, thought and desire) around its accomplishment. He accepted the need for sleep as a woman, with calm perseverance and a certain savage passivity, accepts labor pains. He slept stoically, in long unbroken stretches during which he did not move, or dream, or (it sometimes struck Stofsky who would stand for minutes at a time peeking through the curtains) even breathe at all. There was something deliberately violent in his surrender to his own exhaustion, but after a little more than a week he seemed to have broken its back, and started to get up, still for only short intervals, in the late afternoons when Stofsky lay half-sleeping and half-musing on the couch. They would talk for a while over coffee, talk of nothing which satisfied Stofsky's eager thirst for more of the mood of Ancke's life, but only of practical, commonplace things; and then Ancke would rise, more easily than before, but still with suggestions of that painstaking concern for his own frame, and drift off to his sanctuary again.

But soon it became apparent that he was up more of the time while Stofsky was working at night, because one morning the furniture was all changed around, the tables and books dustless and neat at last, and the morning after this there was a note reading: "Watch the ashes."

Stofsky grew more and more apprehensive each time he climbed his stairs, wondering what new alterations he would find, because, like most people who care little for comfort, and do not think overmuch about smudged windows, unswept floors or dirty dishes, the sudden tidying of his untidy surroundings annoyed and disturbed him.

The apartment now had a bizarre fastidiousness. The ashtrays were stacked in a pagoda-like heap on the coffee table and a milk bottle cap lay in the top one. Around the Grünewald "Christ" tacked over his mantelpiece were draped three grimy, raveling ties, and the zither which had always lain under the kitchen sink where a long-departed and certainly drunken guest had thrown it, now sat on the top of the bookcase, rows of cigarette butts thrust crazily between its strings. There were even two ice picks sunken into the wall map; one marked New York, and the other, a blank patch of Tibet.

Once, without thinking, Stofsky moved the armchair (on which Ancke had placed a clean dishrag as doily) to face the couch so that he could leave his clothes upon it while he slept, and that evening it was back in place, his trousers crumpled on the floor. Ancke was puttering around in the kitchen, as though waiting for him to awake.

Over the coffee he had prepared, and after the usual talk, Ancke glanced at the chair thoughtfully, and then at Stofsky, and after a pause which was all too meaningful for the words which followed it, he said: "Didn't you like it that way, man? I thought it was better that way, at exactly *that* angle to the desk."

Stofsky took a moment to comprehend this. "Well, sure, I guess so. I just wanted to put my clothes on it. I wasn't thinking about any arrangement . . . But, yes, all right, I suppose it's fine there."

Ancke smiled mandarin-like, adding softly: "Oh, don't apologize, man. Don't apologize."

But there had been changes other than Ancke's settlement in it, by the night Hobbes dropped into the apartment on York Avenue. Winnie and Little Rock had appeared one evening without warning, stayed for an hour or two of talk during which Ancke grew positively sociable, and then, expressing some nervousness about leaving the new Buick, which they had stolen the week before, unwatched in the street below, just as suddenly departed. Their visits thereafter became more and more numerous, and finally they started to leave odd belongings there for convenience: changes of clothes, rolls of quarters tightly wrapped in handkerchiefs, a small supply of crude heroin of which, although they left no instructions regarding it, Ancke took no notice, and a miscellaneous collection of wallets and handbags rigged out with false identities, which they exchanged every few days.

Stofsky did not really mind their being there so often. Little Rock's calculating and indifferent glances, his runtish face that never smiled but would sometimes (in moments of secret amusement) distort into a ragged sneer that was vaguely sinister, his huge wide-brimmed hat, always worn square across his forehead and rarely removed, and which gave him the look of a spindly mushroom: all this fascinated Stofsky. But though he plumbed cautiously for some response that would establish the kind of intimate rapport from which all his relationships were conducted,

Little Rock, without effort or even recognition of Stofsky's interest, evaded it.

With Winnie it was easier, for he had known her when she had been a camera-girl working the dens of Fifty-second Street, and newly arrived from Toledo. Her warm and somehow audacious curiosity, her acceptance of the affectations of intense young men, had quickly made her the comrade of whole hordes of wild students from Columbia who, like Stofsky, played nervously with drugs and lived in a disorderly fashion. More than a few of these were drawn into her life who went out of it frightened by her complicated absorptions. Stofsky had introduced her to Ancke, who in turn had led her into the labyrinths of the underground on Times Square and up in Harlem. Gradually she had slipped down with him, out of the set of youthful roisterers, farther down, as if she had been waiting with quiet female patience, incongruous in one so energetic, for something which she could not have named but which she recognized immediately when it appeared. She started to habituate Eighth Avenue, and soon became intimate with everyone who was a pivot around which that underground swung.

Though Stofsky was somewhat perplexed by her now-thorough commitment to petty crime and Little Rock (for she acted as a come-on for sailors, luring them into drab rented rooms where he would black-jack and rob them), soon he saw that Rock merely allowed her to coddle him, but was unimpressed by her fond and ironic pleasure in the enormous difference in their sizes. In contrast to his impregnable "coolness," she was enthusiastic, demonstrative and of fluctuating mood. She considered Little Rock "a big man," perhaps because he had served four jail sentences for robbery, and felt that she had come up in her world. Though done with times of casual promiscuity and experimentation, she remained affectionately reminiscent about them.

It did not seriously alarm Stofsky that they were carrying out a serious of unclarified, minor robberies on the very nights during which he thought of them, and that when he got home he would find them lounging about in his living room, just back from one of these jobs somewhere in the city: Winnie in only a slip, perhaps smoking marijuana and laughing with Ancke like sister with brother, Little Rock listening and yet not listening to them, crouched in a chair, his hat shading his eyes, and his lips and heart closed against the world that lay outside and tried to trap him into noticing it. But Stofsky never asked them much about these affairs, and knew of them only through fragmentary hints that were dropped in conversation. Little Rock, seeming to snooze across the room, would occasionally interject clipped, ill-tempered comments during these talks, and sometimes he would get up without a word and disappear into the bedroom. Winnie, with a lazy smile, would soon rise, finishing some stray remark to Ancke as she crossed the floor to vanish behind the curtains after him. They would be gone forty-five minutes or so.

Stofsky never knew if they were merely having a nap, or exchanging privacies concerned with future jobs and the small crises of their public life; or whether, there in the dark cubicle, on that disheveled bed, they made silent and strange love (the auburn-haired amazon and the grotesque, inscrutable pipsqueak in the large hat), love that would be complex, perhaps weary, an act performed out of a boredom or a whim that verged on the perverse, an act without passion or reward; a silent, ironical union in which neither sought a consummation other than a momentary indulgence of jaded and incurious sensuality. Ancke would shift his attention to Stofsky during these absences to continue the conversation, and Stofsky never pressed him about them for some reason.

In fact, he found himself incapable of adopting with any of them the same brash, probing manner that was usual to him. Though other of his friends had many more secrecies, and wore a more obvious facade of reserve than Winnie and Little Rock, Stofsky found himself skirting subjects about which they seldom talked, and instinctively silencing questions that rose in his mind. His thoughts became obsessed by their images; once he even found himself repeating while on the subway: "Little Rock is a thread in God's shroud too," but the more he pondered the less was clear and the greater became his obsession. Sometimes he felt trapped among the three of them, his whole routine smashed by their domination of it, but even then he could not shake away the conviction that he must understand them and know where they fitted into the puzzle of his ideas.

It was into all this that Hobbes came that night, seeking to escape from the thought of his own futurelessness. He recognized the three of them instantly from his evening with Estelle at The Go Hole, but the associations connected with that evening, and thus with them (Little Rock's "coolness" in particular) were the very things he was trying to forget, and so he said nothing.

Ancke was remarkably cordial, and told his stories of "scoring" in such places as Oran, Colon and Panama City with graphic and bemused detail, depicting the hunger and degradation of past addictions with the mirth by which a wily buffoon ridicules himself for the benefit of others. He might have been a greying newspaperman speaking from the third stool at the Algonquin Bar, so urbane was his manner.

Winnie subjected Hobbes to a penetrating female stare, her eyes glowing as if they were inwardly laughing at him, but then she turned them on Little Rock, who was standing morosely in the doorway cupping his cigarette as someone does who is used to smoking mostly on windy street corners, and said: "Come on over and sit on my lap, baby," patting her firm thighs invitingly.

But Little Rock only continued to smoke sullenly, and finally swung around with released agility, muttering: "I'm going out to dig the heap." He disappeared downstairs to guard their precious automobile from the gangs of invisible little men like himself who coveted it.

Hobbes had thought at once of stating to Stofsky that his book had been rejected. He felt it was something of a point of honor that he tell everyone about it, but faced with having to do so before the others, he let one lapse in the talk after another go by. He did not pass on Pasternak's good news either.

Ancke was now speaking, with dreamy gestures of his quivering hands, about getting out of the city sometime during the winter. "Perhaps I'll make New Orleans to see Dennison, or even Mexico City. You can get an addict's license down there, you know. Those deals ought to bring in enough for that, eh, Win? And I'll only be needing three caps a day by then, which should leave enough for traveling."

Hobbes, who had said almost nothing up to this point, suddenly heard himself exclaim: "Can you really see ahead until spring? Can you plan, *you*, that far ahead?"

Ancke gazed at him curiously, an almost hurt look, and then made some irrelevant remark. But Hobbes did not hear it, for he was thinking that if people like himself, with order to their lives, with high, though all too often vain, purposes with which they troubled their heads, could not see beyond the treacherous limits of next week, how could Ancke do so who, but for the delights of such harmless dreams, could count on nothing but that he would be "hooked" again in three months and starting to have a hard time supplying himself; who could really plan nothing but that by next spring he would probably allow himself to be arrested again to throw his habit so that he could afford it once more. Hobbes wanted to ask him what he would do in five years, in ten, when his ability to live in a drug-induced state of immediacy, in which tomorrow had no place, had been corrupted by age and the failure of his body. He wanted to see in Ancke's eyes the same fear that made his bright, the same suspicion of powerlessness that made his dart.

But looking back into the room where Ancke and Winnie were lighting up sticks of tea and trading opinions of mutual friends now in jail, he felt that he had dropped into a world of shadows that had drifted out of the grip of time, which was now inescapable to him; a world in which his values were a nuisance and his anxieties an affront. The fact that Winnie would get lax of breast and shriveled of lip, that the nights and the streets would eventually begin to scar her clear skin until it dried and wrinkled away her youth; and that Ancke would one day be devoured by his own idea, the idea that he was slowly disintegrating, until there would be nothing left of him but a scabby, shrunken pod, beset by imaginary flies; the fact that this would relentlessly, certainly occur to them if they did not die first, some death of ironical viciousness in the bitter streets, or the madness of confinement in a cage: all of this was to Hobbes, at that moment, the most useless of insights. For them it did not exist, even as a possibility, for they had never given it a thought, and so to see it in their faces, to hear it like a prophecy in every word they spoke, pained only himself. At the instant of recognizing this, his interest in them turned to horror, and he got up to leave.

Stofsky detained him in the murky hallway.

"Don't think badly of Albert, Paul. His talk about New Orleans, that's my influence. You see, I've been working to get him out of New York, even saving money . . . But you must realize that he never says anything to people he doesn't know . . . and he was going on that way merely for your benefit. It was really quite a strain on him, you have no idea. I think it means he likes you though . . ."

"But are they all staying here? I mean, all the time?"

Stofsky's eyes glowed there in the dark and his voice was little more than a suppressed whisper: "Oh, I know what you're thinking! That I'm going to get mixed up in crime and degeneracy, and . . . and all that! But you must understand . . . They're

like the ancient Jews in Babylon, that's what I keep thinking!
That this is the Captivity, the Punishment! He-he!"

Something weird and impassioned in Stofsky's tone reached
Hobbes and unnerved him.

"They're God's chosen and the world's damned! And who am
I to judge? Who am I? Do you see it? . . . And after all they
may be afraid of me sometimes as well!" He giggled strangely
for a moment at some buried thought, and then went on as if
it had not entered his mind. "You know, they've taken to leaving the spoils in my bedroom. Where I *used* to sleep, right under
the bed! Oh, suits, and radios, and even two fur coats! The stuff
they *take* . . . But I'm going to keep after them, win them
away, deliver them perhaps . . ."

Then he touched Hobbes' arm for an instant and his hand
was shaking. "But I'd better get back now . . . before Albert
starts wondering . . ." And he slipped through the door.

When Hobbes came out into the warm night again where stars
hung far away above the city, he breathed heavily of the hushed
river wind, and a lonely solemnity settled over him, a feeling
of great seriousness at being alone there in the night, something
he had not felt since he was a boy.

Starting downtown, he passed a doorway and out of the corner
of his eye he discerned Little Rock leaning motionless in it, a
mere shadow that smoked contentedly as it watched the street.
It did not stir, but he saw its eyes follow him as he hurried
by not three feet from it, and saw them swing away again to
resume their empty, solitary watch.

Five

Agatson started calling Hobbes at three o'clock one afternoon, very drunk even that early. He wanted Hobbes to come down "to celebrate my last birthday." When he learned that Pasternak was there also, he cajoled the more, but nevertheless Hobbes gave him an indefinite answer. He called again in twenty minutes, insistent, desperate for company, and then wheedling: it was Sunday and he hadn't found anybody else in. Hobbes told him that they would come down as soon as they could, but that they were expecting Ketcham and the Trimbles to drop in first. At this, Agatson shrieked wildly through the receiver, as though he could not believe his good fortune in locating everyone at one crack, and he would not hang up until Hobbes had assured him that he would bring them all down.

Even so, he called twice more in the next half hour, out of impatience and tipsy unawareness of the actual flow of time, until finally, at Pasternak's urgings, they left Kathryn to follow in the Trimbles' car when they arrived.

It had been over a week since the night of Hobbes' visit to York Avenue, a week during which his only activity had been the struggle to avoid the depression he felt potential in everything around him. The time from Kathryn's departure in the morning until her return at night was like the blank sheet of notepaper which the invalid must somehow fill each week with cheerful and diverting sentiments, not so much to spare its recipient as to delude himself. During that week he had taken to buying quarts of beer in the morning, and these turned the afternoons (by far the slowest and most dismal time of the early autumn days) into misty, isolated panels of half drunkenness. At night they spent the hours in bars, or people came over, as Pasternak had done the night before; the same night Ancke had climbed the stairs wearily, carrying a pink portable radio, and wondering if Pasternak would lend him ten dollars on it.

"I can get it back to you tomorrow, man," he had said. "It's just so we can function tonight, you know?", this with a dry wink of understanding. "But, look, Winnie and Little Rock are downstairs in the car, so if you've got the ten—." Pasternak had given it to him, part of the first installment of his advance from the publishers, and Ancke had gone, leaving the radio. Pasternak stayed on, deciding to sleep on one of the couches, which was why he was still there when Agatson began phoning.

Now, as they hurried from the subway to Agatson's place, it was a grey and desolate Sunday afternoon, particularly deserted in that neighborhood. The summer had ended mysteriously, imperceptibly, leaving the great drafty warehouses of Twenty-first Street dry and uniformly grey in aspect; with that blunt, drab greyness of the first cool days of autumn and the deepening last light of Sunday. Something exhilarating and unknown had stirred in them both at Agatson's calls, some secret thrill of apprehension which they could not communicate, and they ran up his stairs, pacing one another.

The next hours were a maze, without center, growing denser the farther into them they wandered, and permeated with a feeling of imminent peril for which there was little tangible cause. They found Agatson squatting in a terrible litter of beer bottles and broken records, staring with mournful, trapped eyes at nothing. But for May, who was also quite drunk and sat in a tattered slip near him, he was alone.

He sprang to his feet as they came in, waving a half-filled bottle, and shouting: "Whoo-oo-ee! Whoo-oo-ee! They came . . . out of goddamn curiosity! . . . Beer for the boys, babe! Come on . . . We're sitting here, you guys, serving tea to friends!"

May rose with that punished, miserable look which all of Agatson's women wore after a few weeks, and, bringing cups, filled them from one of the bottles. They sat about, drinking heavily, and though Hobbes and Pasternak pointedly avoided looking at her, May did not bother to put on more clothes, but with bitter, sorrowful glances at Agatson, drank on.

Pasternak told them about the sale of his book, and at this Agatson paused in his rambling monologue, and a strange mocking paleness spread over his unshaven cheeks:

"So now you're Queen of the May, eh? Ha-ha! Do you hear that, babe? Now he's Queen of the May! . . . Have some more beer, Your Highness!" and, indeed, May seemed to melt a little at this, and looked at Pasternak with taciturn interest, as though seeing him for the first time. But Agatson took no notice, and only slugged regularly out of his bottle. Then, looking back at

Pasternak with a curious glitter in his small eyes, he murmured: "But what about beatitude, eh? Eh?"

At that, he appeared to recover himself from some weighty thought he wished at any cost to ignore, and exclaimed: "That's what Stofsky would say, isn't it? That uptown Augustine! 'But what about beatitude?' . . . Ha-ha! . . . But I don't give a good goddamn about your goddamn book . . . This is a party, a celebration . . . All right, all right, we'll celebrate that too . . . But, look, let's go over and get Bianca. Get everyone!" He did not observe the angry purse of lips that soured May's features. "We'll get everyone . . . Whoo-oo-ee! She's only a couple of blocks away . . . Come on!"

They took one of the opened bottles with them from which Agatson drank continually, brazenly, as he stumbled along in his oversize G.I. brogans. Hobbes and Pasternak always seemed a little ahead of him, as though in fear of some incident which might begin at any moment and from which their distance would disassociate them. And, indeed, as they went through the bleak, nearly empty streets, a remarkable thing did occur.

Agatson plodded steadily along, using the bottle liberally, and getting farther and farther behind them as a consequence. The atmosphere of irresponsibility which was inseparable from him reached Hobbes and Pasternak, and when they turned around at a street crossing, they saw him balanced on the running board of a parked sedan, wrenching at something over the windshield.

A few hundred feet beyond him, in dumfounded amazement, stood an elderly, red-faced gentleman in spats and bowler, whom they had passed a few moments before, strolling in the opposite direction with his faded little wife. They might have been coming from late afternoon services or tea in some sedate parlor on Gramercy Park. Now, perhaps aroused by the wild young man in blue jeans carrying the bottle so defiantly, they had turned, at almost the same instant as his friends, to find him on the running board of an empty car, tearing off the radio aerial, without surreptitious haste, but only with an absorbed and destructive glee. They stood frozen, as though distrusting their own perception, as though what they saw violated in an instant their most commonplace assumptions of the order of reality, for clenched in Agatson's fist, and making his present task the more difficult by their awkward length, were several other aerials torn off other cars he had passed, and forking out of his fingers like Jupiter's bolts of lightning.

The aerial finally came loose, and clutching it with the others, he continued toward Hobbes and Pasternak. The red-faced gentleman was beginning to splutter with shock and bewilderment (the faint echo of his exclamations reached them), but Agatson came steadily, lopingly on, unaware of the consternation he had caused, and Hobbes and Pasternak skooted around the corner and down Sixth Avenue, leaving the elderly gentleman outraged, and just turning to his stunned little wife.

They slowed down to let Agatson catch up with them, titillated and alarmed by his actions. He had a secretive, set frown on his lips that looked as though it forcibly smothered a laugh that would be hysterical or even demented, but all he said was:

"Wands, Your Highness, wands!"

With that, muttered as if it was a justification which he somehow thought necessary, but at the same time considered savagely ridiculous, he plodded on, looking neither to right nor left, past shopkeepers and strollers who stared at him with disbelief; past four smudge-faced urchins, delving in a row of garbage cans, all of whom paused to look with grimy astonishment. Before his steady march the sidewalks seemed to empty, as if he was a personage of dark and terrifying authority.

The three of them reached Bianca's without further incident, and Agatson seemed to quiet down at her first glance, which appraised his condition in an instant and needed no report of the walk through the street to corroborate it. He was brusque with her, giggling, and yet somehow intimate in his half-cruel insistence that she come with them. She opened the bottle of beer which he found in her ice-chest, slipped on a light coat and they left, but only after she had made him agree that they would drive back to his loft in her car, which was parked in the street below.

He joked and drank the whole way there, gripping his aerials in the knotted fist of a small boy, but Hobbes noticed that, even during his most inane, drunken remarks, Agatson was sardonically eying Bianca's aerial, which was just outside the car window. When they got out on his street, he hesitated for a moment, toying with that fatal sense of irony to which he was so often captive, and then ripped it off with a gutteral, wicked laugh.

Bianca was overcome with a fury in which there was no surprise, but only said: "You'll have to pay for that, Bill!"

Kathryn, Ketcham and the Trimbles had arrived, bringing more beer. The maze thickened and an evening began which later all would have good cause to remember on several counts.

May seemed to have abandoned herself to the inevitable as soon as Agatson had proposed getting Bianca, and was by now thoroughly drunk, her sulking young face a mask of clumsy hilarity. She was cordially aloof with Bianca, eying her with suspicion. For her part of it, Bianca was friendly, even sympathetic, although soon May was dancing around in the tattered slip like a poorly-constructed puppet, and was ignored by everyone but Pasternak.

Agatson greeted Peter Trimble with a piercing yell, for they were old friends from Cambridge days. Trimble, though shy and even awkward when sober, speaking then with the rapid, faltering cadences of someone whose special skill or knowledge stands like a wall between himself and everyone else, and who thus always gives the impression of simplifying his conversation so that he may be understood, was, when drunk, given to sudden capering jig-steps, his serious face breaking into boyish grins as he articulated a weird and imaginative gibberish that was usually hidden beneath his rationality. He had the most genuine affection for Agatson that it was possible to have, because unlike most people he felt neither awe nor self-righteousness when with him, but only the unspoken affinity of amiable drinking companions; of people, in other words, who have a cherished vice in common.

They had not seen one another for months, but started immediately to cackle and trot to 'South Rampart Street Parade,' which had been put on the phonograph. Kathryn and Hobbes sat on a mattress with Janet, whose darting, self-possessed glances noted everything. She was of slender, almost lithe body, and possessed of an intelligence that not only enabled her to understand her husband's total concentration on having a good time when he had the chance, but to recognize in Agatson a potential menace to his career and their relationship. Sitting there rigidly, viewing the developing chaos, she remained vigilant, drinking little herself, and even during her remarks to Kathryn, she seemed to be preparing herself for that moment when she would carefully, probably without his noticing it, prevent her husband from getting to where his steps would inevitably lead him.

Kathryn was unhappy there, and when Agatson stumbled up to her and tried to pull her to her feet, she fought back with undisguised distaste. But she drank as much as the others. Pasternak was dancing with May, who gripped him tightly around the neck, giving herself up to him all in a graceless bundle of bare shoulders and disordered hair. Bianca sat by with a sad, unrebuking dismay in her eyes, and Ketcham, who had planted himself beside her and turned away from the rest, was trying to seize her attention. But though she smiled regretfully at him, she kept watching Agatson.

They got progressively drunker. Agatson's occasional mad shrieks and incomprehensible laughter infected them all, setting an ever-rising pitch of noise which Trimble, the physicist fallen among bohemians, endeavored to match. Even for Kathryn, Janet and Ketcham, all there guarding something they considered endangered by Agatson and his wildness, there seemed nothing else to do but drink. The music ground most conversation to bits, and soon everyone was caught up, willingly or otherwise, in it. Agatson was not merely drunk and getting drunker as fast as possible: he was possessed by a demon of fantastic anarchy, and he would leave no one alone. He roamed about, seemingly in a world in which people were mere material objects to be lifted and thrown to see if they would break.

At one point, while he and her husband wrestled about on the floor, Janet said with marked emphasis: "Well, at least there's no broken glass!"

And at this, Agatson got to his feet, glared at her for a moment with positive venom, and suddenly seizing a nearby bottle, smashed it down on the mantelpiece, sending a burst of glass over everything. Then he fixed his grim, challenging stare upon her again, as if hers was the next move.

"Jesus Christ!" Kathryn cried out in alarm. "You might have blinded someone!"

He turned his bright, baleful eyes on her, and tittered crudely as he spat out: "Whyn't you let down your hair, babe, and do us a dance! Go ahead . . . But I'll bet you're cold, common and priggish. Isn't she, Hobbes? How about that, Hobbes?"

But Hobbes had slunk away toward the beer, and Kathryn, at once wounded and furious at this, snapped back: "You'll never find out, damn you!" But with that secretive frown, Agatson lurched off, and beyond him in the smoke-heavy dimness, Pasternak and May were two shapeless silhouettes against the darkening windows.

In an hour, Trimble and Agatson had begun to babble almost incoherently to each other as they searched in dusty piles of records for favorites from the old days. Ketcham had long since slipped away, without a word to anyone, revolted by it all and giving up in his attempt to get Bianca to leave.

She sat huddled on a mattress, her eyes fastened on a book, but every now and again, full of distress and patience, they would dart to Agatson across the room as he struggled with further bottles. Unlike May, who staggered about with Pasternak, gulping from glasses he held before her, and trying for a crude and desperate gaiety, Bianca sat on, with immovable poise, as though certain that it would all come to an end, knowing to what lengths it must go before it would, and content to wait in helpless perseverance until then. But May, whose weeks with Agatson had not yet taught her that all she could do was stay near him, pick him up, nurse him, love him fruitlessly, be unhappy and finally go away, danced on, trying to be as she thought he wanted her to be, and to attract his attention at the same time. But he never looked at her.

By the time Agatson had started to hurl records against a wall, shouting at each succeeding crash: "Goodbye, Berlioz . . . Goodbye, Harry James . . . Goodbye, you all!", Kathryn was very drunk, her lipstick smeared away on glass after glass. She sat on a mattress near Janet, swaying and mumbling: "What's happening? What's happening now? . . . Where's Paul?", for he had kept away from her, making a single-purposed assault on the beer. He could not bear to look at her, as though her blank, afflicted stares would dissuade him from his purpose, which was plainly to tax and abuse his senses until they were numb.

But Janet kept close to her, like an older, wiser sister, saying nothing until Kathryn suddenly cried: "I want him! Where is he? Where's Paul? . . . Oh, God, I feel so sick—"

She sank back among the pillows, her lids pressed shut, her head jerking back and forth as though to avoid blows.

"Don't have any more," Janet cautioned softly, rubbing her forehead.

"Why not? Why not?" Kathryn exclaimed, opening her eyes and trying to right herself. "I want to get drunk! Isn't that what I'm supposed to do? Be just like that . . . that May! He'll think I'm just wonderful then . . . Won't he love me then? Won't he please? . . . Give me a drink then. I can get drunker than he can! Wops are great drinkers, don't you know that? . . . I can go on longer than he can!" But she fell back again, nausea twisting her mouth. "Oh God, God, why doesn't it all stop! Oh, please! . . . Paul, Paul!"

Agatson, also, had passed out, but on the floor. He had simply dropped in his tracks, without warning, without even slowing down. Somehow his jeans had come off, and he sprawled there, his bony legs with a furze of dark hair on them grotesquely askew among the bottles. May, seeing this, tore herself away from Pasternak, and threw herself on her knees before Agatson, like a frightened, trusting child at prayers. One strap of the slip had ridden off her shoulders, her breast was all but bare, and there was on her face at that moment an expression of misery, uncorrupted by self pity. "Bill, Bill, damn you! Get up from there! Oh, please get up!" Then she threw herself upon his prone, unresisting body, and started to moan and coo drunkenly, covering him with despairing kisses, lifting his head and letting it drop, her body writhing against him.

Pasternak gazed at the two of them tangled awkwardly there on the floor, May's blind imprecations and embraces bringing no response from Agatson; and a look of fierce, almost proud, horror filled his dark face. He turned from the sight, and coming up to Hobbes muttered: "Take Kathryn out of this. Take her away, Paul. She's worth ten of . . . It's bad, bad! Don't you see that?"

But before Hobbes could unravel this, before he could be surprised or bitterly amused, Janet was at his arm and saying firmly through the droning music: "I'm taking Kathryn home. She's had enough . . . No, no, it's all right . . . You'd better stay here. But keep an eye on Peter. I'll be back in twenty minutes . . ."

Thereafter the ear-splitting music went on, out of control, whether they listened or danced; and they moved about restlessly, ceaselessly, trying to keep up with it. All but Bianca, who lay in the shadows of a corner, asleep or just averting her eyes. Hobbes stumbled back and forth, emptying glasses at the very moment when he was thinking that he had had too much; noting that with lucid foolishness, as a man does the measurements of a room just before the walls fall in upon him.

The next instant he was confronted by Trimble's shiny, grinning face, full of wild words and motiveless laughter. Then he was laughing too, and heard himself say, without knowing (as he said it) why he was doing so, but convinced that there was a perfectly sound reason which he had merely forgotten: ". . . keep my eyes on you . . . while the women lick their wounds!"

"Like worried sea lions! . . . lick, lick, lick . . ." Trimble said, and Hobbes felt himself to be immeasureably sly for having perceived that Trimble had no idea what he was talking about, and also for not mentioning it.

"Arf, arf!" he replied, certain that this too was uncannily apt. "Yak-yak-yak!" And all the while he was looking past Trimble at Agatson, who was stirring beneath the weight he found upon him. He groped, all blind and pawing, and got up, shedding May like some harmless Liliputian, and staggered a few steps into a patch of light.

His eyes burned right into Hobbes' for a second. But in them there was no recognition, nothing sane or reliable, only an imbecilic steadiness. It was the stare of a man to whom everyone is really a stranger, who passes through fevers and anxieties alone and has never thought to confide or complain to another living soul; a man possessed of a rage that is always frustrated, that has enthralled his waking nature, and which has no object; the sort of rage that only the obliteration of a world could sate.

Seeing this, Hobbes was suddenly frightened and sobered all in an instant; as he might have been if he had been hiding in a closet and seen a bosom friend take a voodoo doll from a bureau drawer, incant *his* name over it, and methodically start to stick pins into its loins. At that moment, he became conscious, as well, that the phone had been pealing for several minutes.

"Tell 'em to bring beer!" Agatson screamed at Pasternak who had picked it up. "May's gonna strip at midnight! Tell 'em that!", and he went lurching about looking for his trousers, stumbling on bottles and crunching over records. "Where'd you hide 'em, you bitch!"

Hobbes and Trimble joined in the search just to keep on their feet, but Agatson with a loud, now somehow meaningless "Whoo-oo-ee!", discovered them under Bianca, who was, after all, awake.

"Come on, babe," he yelled. "Gimme my jeans! . . . Get up and do a dance!" and he pulled her to her feet, squashing her against him, and started to caper and whirl. She let herself be yanked about, her head drooping on his chest, and her small voice saying:

"Let me go, Bill. Let me go. Please."

"Hey! Hey!" Pasternak cried out suddenly, calling for attention, his face drained of color as he slammed down the receiver. "Say, do you know what's happened! Stofsky's been arrested! . . . Arrested! Turn the music down, for pete's sake!"

"What?" Hobbes gasped. "What was that?"

"That's what Verger just said. That was Verger. He says it's

in all the papers. Stofsky, Ancke, Little Rock and Winnie . . .
all arrested!"

Everyone stopped dead, as though a very sober, very disapproving and at the same time commanding stranger had appeared at the door.

"Who's . . . who's Stofsky?" Trimble asked thickly.

"My God, the stolen car!"

"No, not only that, Paul. Robbery too. That's what Verger
said . . . But, Jesus Christ, David wasn't mixed up in any robbery! . . . And Verger was talking about collecting money for
his defense . . . Why the hell didn't he get the story straight!
Just calling up that way!"

His cigarette was quivering between his fingers, and Hobbes,
too, was having a difficult time believing it. "It's in all the papers,
Gene? Is that what he said? . . . My God, that radio! That
must be part of . . . But when did all this happen?"

"This afternoon sometime. Right this afternoon! Just a few
hours ago!"

May was standing near him, her eyes wide and white with fear,
her hands clasped together on her breast.

"See!" she was repeating shrilly. "See, see, see!"

"Maybe it's a misprint," Trimble said quietly, still quite drunk,
and adding with a snigger: "It's a very common name."

Agatson had started to move about relentlessly, searching all
the glasses and upturning the bottles, saying not a word. But
there was palpable in his face some sickening thought, something
inexpressible and black. He looked like a man who is witnessing
the vision of his whole unredeemable existence, seeing it as a
savage mockery; but more, perceiving that *all* of life is a blas-
phemous, mortal joke at everyone's expense, a monstrous joke in
which everything is ignoble, ludicrous and without value or
meaning.

And he seemed to boil up all of a sudden at the thought, and
started to shout thickly: "There's no more beer! We're out of
beer! Come on! . . . Mea culpa! . . . We'll go out and find him,
break him out of jail! Come on. We'll rush the place! Everyone
grab a bottle! . . . Come on, you bastards, mea culpa!"

They shuffled about, not knowing what to say or do, all but
Bianca who came up to May, and ordered: "Get on a dress.
Quick now. We'll get him outside now. Quick. Quick." And May,
with a startled, obedient lowering of eyes, made no reply, but
turned hastily to the clothes closet.

"Come on!" Agatson roared again. "Let's get outa here! Let's go, let's go!"

"I've got to get a paper," Pasternak muttered to Hobbes. "So we'll go downtown with them . . . Jesus Christ, do you think Verger was kidding? He wouldn't kid, would he? About something like that."

They all fumbled down the inky stairways, mostly silent, but for Agatson who was breathing rapidly, and piped out once: "I wonder if they beat him up!"

They milled about on the street, all become conscious now that they were out in the sharp chill of the night that they were drunker than they had realized. May clung on Agatson's arm, her eyes darting back and forth, and every once in a while her lower lip trembled with childish spasms, and she would whimper:

"They'll check on us, I know it! Why did he have to come *here* so often? Involving everyone else!"

"Shut up, little girl! Shut up, shut up, shut up!" Agatson growled as they piled into Bianca's car; but then he seemed to forget her, and sat staring pitilessly out of the window, as though gaping into the maw of hell, his face a mask, his very features too inelastic to mirror his emotion.

But just as they pulled away from the curb toward Seventh Avenue, he seemed to boil over, his shoulders contorting and his mouth torn sideways like a ragged wound. He craned out of the window, far, far out, and started to scream with terrible, piercing earnestness:

"Fuck you! Fuck you! Fuck you!"

Just that snarling curse, shouted over and over again, at everything: the cars, the buildings, the deaf night itself; those two crude words, full of outrage and horror, thrown into the streets like crashing bottles.

"Fuck you! Fuck you! Fuck you!"

Six

ODDLY enough, it was precisely three o'clock when Stofsky left his flat to drive to Brooklyn with the others. The night
before (not three hours before Ancke had come to Hobbes),
Winnie and Little Rock had broken into a house in Jamaica,
bringing back to Stofsky's a cardboard box of plate silver, some
tasteless but valuable jewelry, the pink radio Ancke delivered
later for cash, and a larger better one, a Persian Lamb coat, and
two fairly good men's suits. They knew a fence out in Brooklyn
Heights, and were so badly in need of money that they decided
to dispose of the suits and the coat immediately.

As always, Winnie asked Ancke to come along (as she probably asked him to join them when they went out on a job), but
as always he gave the same answer: "No . . . not today. Couldn't
make it," not implying by even the narrowing of an eye that the
possible danger was deterring him, but only that, even with the
pleasant company and the ease of travel, it would be a drag
for him.

Stofsky's reason for going was more complicated. The night
before, while performing his minor operation in the faultless
machinery of the newsoffice, he had gone through a panic concerning the robberies and "the loot" from them which now over-
flowed the space beneath his bed; a panic brought on in no small
part by that very faultless and impersonal machine of which he
was a part for eight hours out of every twenty-four. That, and
the fact that he had had a difficult time that very evening finding his own cheap covert among the glen-plaids, cheviots and
worsteds that now jammed his closet. In the middle of that panic,
he thought of the journals and letterboxes stuffed in his desk,
and for some reason, lying there in his apartment, they constituted a vague menace, and he resolved to hide them in the most
unlikely and incongruous spot he could think of, deciding on
the house in Flatbush of an aunt whom he had never known
very well, and did not think of more than once a year at Christmas time. Somehow it was the journals and letters which were
the menace and not his guests, but it never occurred to him that,

rather than ask them to stop using his place as a headquarters, he was himself starting a kind of exodus.

And so, a little after three o'clock, they were driving downtown in the desolate silence of Sunday afternoon through which Hobbes and Pasternak were making their way to Agatson's. Stofsky was in the back seat with his papers on his lap and the stolen suits beside him, while Winnie chattered on to him about the job, and Little Rock said nothing, perhaps did not even hear, but sat crouching behind the wheel, the top of which was almost level with his steady, cold and unblinking eyes. He gripped the wheel with both hands, gripped it high, and leaned into it slightly, turning corners with unvarying, mechanical lifts of his thin shoulders. Even when he raced lights, and without a flicker of expression he raced most of them, the only sign of his intention to do so was the extra stretch of his leg toward the accelerator.

"We just kept lugging the stuff out to the car," Winnie was saying. "Baby, here, was set on taking the rugs too, but there wasn't room. You know what he said? I bust out laughing. 'We need a van,' he said. And we could have filled one too. Why, we could have stripped that place naked and taken our time about it!"

Stofsky was aware that reproaches, earnest but firm, reproaches for which he could find no decent explanation, were filling his mouth. Instead of giving them voice, however, he gazed out the window at the pilings of the Elevated that swept past him at an even pace as they drove down Third Avenue, and began to say to himself a verse of Blake that he had memorized a few days before, and which he often found himself repeating like a rosary:

> "Seek love in the pity of other's woe,
>   In the gentle relief of another's care,
>   In the darkness of night & the winter's snow,
>   In the naked and outcast, seek love there!"

The farther downtown they got, the more the shuttered and crooked buildings seemed to crowd in upon the Elevated tracks, until the street was like some dark, uncertain path through a vast forest of brick, a path that becomes a tunnel over which a heavy roof has grown. The pilings were positively trunk-like, and the street itself seemed to deviate from its orderly straightness and swerve a bit to the left, as though it, too, had lost its bearings.

The paintless brick walls, unbroken but for windows blinded with dust, pressed closer and closer until even the patches of bleak sky disappeared, and a queer, underwater gloom suffused everything.

Stofsky, suddenly so hot his glasses fogged over, stared at the two in the front seat, trying to feel that in Little Rock's motionless crouch, in Winnie's languid tea-party chatter about thievery, he had found "the naked and outcast."

And for a brief moment, his heart filled with pity for them, because in their wily innocence they did not know that they were doomed, that they were children of wrath, and that he, despite this, would love and redeem them; it was also a sweet, sad pity for himself, a pity that had only a memory of his old altruism, but it was not love. It would not be love somehow. All these weeks he had tried, filling his head with schemes and lacerations, saving money to get Ancke out of the city, humiliating himself before the indifferent Little Rock, but he could not really love them, and his thoughts had revolved upon that old image of the beast of the universe, now become a huge and aging God, whose anger and whose justice were incomprehensible, yet ordained. Before that image of his mind, he felt wayward, misbegotten and full of half-childish fears. Some light had waned within him, and he sat staring at Little Rock's umbrella-like hat, and thinking hopelessly:

"Seek love there!"

But his gaze constantly drifted to the alley of a street down which they drove, a macabre and silent Chinatown street. Behind every grimy window of the occupied, but strangely lightless houses which leaned together over it, he fancied a face the color of cheap old paper. The few dark figures that wandered in this neighborhood of laundries, upstairs chop suey parlors, and curio shops, seemed to glance at the car with a deferential, yet sinister curiosity, and then hurry on. Everywhere there was an air of spectral and unfathomable mystery, and he thought suddenly, with a flash of cold horror, that God Himself was a Chinaman, with greasy queue and lacquered pipe, sitting at the window of a small room, which was heaped with dusty dragons ensnared by spider webs, overlooking a street of turbulent and frivolous life; and that in that unchanging, Confucian room, He was watching that street, calculating the advent of Judgment Day on the worn beads of an abacus.

"Let's get out of this district," he said.

"We'll take the next left and get over near the Bridge," Little Rock muttered, shifting gears with rapid jerks of one hand.

The next left was a one-way street, going the wrong way for them, but Little Rock pulled into it nevertheless. They were rolling along slowly, and it was not until they were near the middle of the block that they saw the police car. It was idling at the curb, and a corpulent patrolman was standing with one foot on the running board, talking to the officer inside. He looked up just as they got within fifty feet of him, and his round, good-natured face filled with a grimace of amusement and irritation. Saying something to the officer in the car, he started out into the street, waving them back, and puffing a bit in his over-filled uniform.

Little Rock sank behind the wheel, seizing it at the top with a ferocious grip. His shoulders stiffened and his pupils protruded out of his somber little eyes.

"They've spotted us!" he was grunting. "Oh, yeah!"

And suddenly, so suddenly that it might be thought he had no idea what he was doing, he threw the car into high speed as the patrolman came toward them.

"Look out, George!" yelled the officer in the police car, one arm stuck out of the window, pointing at them crazily.

The patrolman jumped aside with amazing dexterity for his weight, his mouth coming open with surprise. They roared past him, making for the corner.

"You almost grazed him, baby!" Winnie gasped.

"They spotted us! I know they did!" and he swerved the car headlong around a corner, almost dumping Stofsky on the floor.

"Take it easy!" he stuttered. "We were going the wrong way, that's all. Slow down!"

But Winnie, who had twisted around and was searching out the back window, suddenly exclaimed: "They're following us! I saw them just coming around that last corner!"

At that moment the inhuman snarl and wail of a siren lifted out of the darkening web of silent streets, pursuing them down short blocks and over the jumble of rooftops.

Little Rock went white at the sound, leaning harder upon the wheel, and snapping: "We'll make the Bridge!", and all but standing on the accelerator.

Winnie kept pushing his shoulder violently, and darting looks out the back window: "Come on, baby! Come on! Faster!"

Behind them, somewhere in the gloomy maze through which

they were rushing, the siren rose and fell with malevolent and relentless stridency. Stofsky cowered in the back seat, barely realizing that he was mumbling:

"God, where will I be tonight!"

And then, abruptly, they shot out of the narrow street into a wide and vacant square, with sections of browning grass and a few stunted, leafless trees. To the left, where this square opened out into a long ramp, the massive, cold arch of Brooklyn Bridge stood high against the dead sky, like the stately open door of a bombed cathedral.

"Left, left!" Winnie was crying, "or you'll miss the approach!"

Little Rock seemed to throw his whole weight onto the wheel, turning it so precipitously that he was slammed hard against the door.

The car responded with dumb and faithful promptness, veering sharply with a shuddering scream of tires. "I'll make it! I'll make it!" Little Rock barked, fighting the wheel; but he failed to release it in time, and the car careened crazily around the curb, lifting off the ground on one side. It could not seem to right itself, and Little Rock was still turning the wheel with helpless fury when it went over.

Stofsky was thrown, head over heels, onto the floor, his journals and letters showering around him. Everything slid onto its side, the front seat oddly vertical, but at first the fact that his glasses had been knocked off confused him more than this. His vision was out of focus, fuzzy-edged, and he groped for the seat to pull himself erect so that he could see around it at the others.

Little Rock was squashed between the wheel and the door, all akimbo, his hat flattened around his ears, and he might have been sleeping heavily. Winnie was sprawled on top of him, crying:

"Where are they, baby? Come on, honey, come on!"

Stofsky struggled with the door above him, trying to peer out of the windows, most of which were streaked with a lacing of cracks. He managed to throw it back, at the same time searching for his glasses among the papers around his feet. But he could not find them.

"Here," he said. "Here, we can get out here."

He lifted himself out through the opening, grabbing Winnie's arm and helping her.

"Are you all right? Are you okay? Rock! Rock! Get up!"

The siren was ominously louder, though still only the disembodied voice of the car which was somewhere in the network of streets leading onto the square.

"Run," Winnie was whispering. "Run!"

"But what about Rock?"

"Run," and already she had swung around and was making off across the nearby grass, running with stilted haste because of her high heels.

"Rock! Come on now! . . . Winnie!"

But she was sprinting across the last open stretch of pavement in front of the houses now, without looking back. Stofsky hesitated, one hand on the bridge of his nose, automatically feeling for the glasses which were there no longer.

Little Rock was still slumped beneath the wheel, his mouth come ajar, one bent leg twitching. When Stofsky turned back, Winnie had disappeared. He started to run after her, aware of the siren again, and, upon darting a breathless look over his shoulder, seeing the police car just pulling onto the square.

He made the narrow street and ran down it, hugging the wall, and expecting to see Winnie ahead of him momentarily. But she had vanished.

He found himself on one of those old cobbled thoroughfares below the Bridge, which burrow among a topple of perishing buildings that once housed generations of clerks and office-boys when commerce kept the sidewalks thronged, but which now stand uninhabited, and wear fading signs which have long ago ceased to refer to anything.

Somewhere nearby was the river, for the distant laments of tugs reached him as he ran, and above the chipped moldings the cordage of the Bridge diced a sky ponderous with rain. Stofsky saw the Bridge and cried. Everything was a dreary and opaque haze to him, and he raced on through a confusion of streets with his hands raised before him fearfully.

At that moment, he longed for something human to appear on those dim sidewalks: a hurrying seaman, a derelict drunk, anyone. But he was alone in all that settling masonry, in streets with brave and homely names out of another century, streets that seemed not to have known the world since then, but down which he must flee alone from the police car, which could barely have traversed them. He might have been the last man in all the city, spared in a general calamity by some witless accident.

Finally he paused at a corner, panting for breath, and looked up with gaping, awesome fright to see, above the heap of rooftops, the clean straight tower of one of the new buildings down near Wall Street; a structure so audacious, cold and irreverent to him at that moment that he said aloud, with an irrational shrewdness, speaking to its distant, topmost windows: "*I see you!*" For there might have been an eye up there, behind binoculars (he thought) charting his flight; a Chinese eye, and by his words he somehow outwitted it.

Then he realized that there was no sense in running that way any longer. And he looked back at the moments just past as though separated from them as age is from youth. He stood, hardly daring to draw breath, listening for the siren, but there was no sound.

He walked on, missing his glasses with that feeling of awkwardness and vulnerability of one who has come to depend on them more than he ever knows. As he walked, he tried to take stock of everything in an instant: where was he, what must he do now, what had happened to the others? Little Rock had certainly been taken. They would discover that the car was stolen. Winnie would head for York Avenue and Ancke; and he must find a phone and call there.

But he could not keep his thoughts this neat. What was he doing down here, lost in these deserted streets, running from a wreck, being pursued? It made no sense to him, and then it did: an inescapable and predestined sense that his mind refused to accept at the very moment of his recognition of it. Why had he not known that this would happen? How had he failed to see? The melancholy ache to be loved which always sweetened his heart suddenly turned sour with fear.

The sense of freedom in his life, the idea of being able to control it, direct it, even waste it, of being able to entertain fancies that were detrimental or exercise a volition that was dangerous: all this suddenly seemed to him to have been the most shameless illusion all along, the idiotic industry of an ant building his hill in the path of a glacier, and imagining that he is free.

"Poor thing!" he sobbed aloud. "Poor thing!"

For it was a dream no longer. He could not wander these streets forever, time did not stop, someone would appear, he could not elude that dread reckoning that awaited him. And immediately he thought of rushing uptown and taking a bus to Hackensack: wanting for the first time in all the last years to be home, to sit among his people without saying a word, without arguing or being ashamed of them; to sit quietly among the neighbors, to sleep dreamlessly in his drab little room, a part of something regular, trivial; and to be, himself, without sin once more. He thought of his mother, who had always been so enigmatically lost to him, whose eyes had held no comfort for him, no assurance that terror would be kept outside until he was old enough to make friends with it.

"She never tucked me in. Where was she every night when I waited?" But he could not seem to remember her.

Then fear swept him again. He would go out to Pasternak's, to Hobbes', or somewhere. He would tell them about everything, get them to swear before God that he had been with them all afternoon, beg them if necessary, promise anything. Or just take a subway, go as far as it went, then walk, vanish for good. But he had no money.

At that, he laughed bitterly at himself, without pity, with an almost unreasoning contempt for his own thoughts. He could not escape the reckoning, the eye, the wrath. No bus or subway, improbable home or foolish deception could elude it. The confines of the trap were infinite and final.

He remembered then, with angry bewilderment, the visions and everything that had happened since then. What had he done wrong? Which action had held the fatal consequence within it like a germ? At that moment he believed in it all, with the same desperate conviction as before, and could see no fault in it but that it had led him here. Love, love! The conflict of the ego!

"I *never* played with it, made gestures! It was them!"

What he had seen was true, what he had done inevitable in the light of it. Then it occurred to him that the wrong-way street, the police car waiting there, and the crash itself were inevitable also. And all the rest (the visions, the interferences, the robberies) was justified because it had led him to this afternoon, and this was where he had to come.

"How powerless we are!" he marveled. "Vain ants! Dear ants!"

But he must phone Ancke, warn him. He hurried on, lighting a cigarette as he reached Fulton Street. A man appeared down the block, and then several more at a cross street; and Stofsky looked at them, without fright, but only with a sad and humble interest, thinking all the while:

"Do you know that I'm a criminal? Do you know that, dear ant? . . . But, yes, everything is God's riddle, even their ignorance . . ."

Then he saw a drugstore up ahead, and remembered that

there was a subway station around the corner somewhere; and that thought was enough for the moment. There was no sense in thinking further than that.

* * * * *

Winnie had called fifteen minutes before, Ancke told him, and he expected her at any moment. "Are you coming back here now, man?" he wondered listlessly.

"But of course I'm coming there! What did you think? Where else would I go? . . . But, look, *they'll* be coming too . . . eventually. So get the place ready . . . do you understand?" He did not pause to realize that he was speaking as though the wire was being tapped. "Get rid of everything . . . and get it ready, Albert. You understand what I mean? . . . And put on some coffee too, why don't you. We'll all have a last pot; for the road, as it were . . . But hurry and get rid of everything . . . you understand me?"

It was only after he had gotten down into the subway, and was succumbing to the dull roar of an uptown express, that it suddenly occurred to him that the York Avenue address was inked in on the front of all the journals and headed most of the letters that he had left in the wrecked car.

"They might even get there before I do! Why, they might be there right now, waiting!"

But then his previous thoughts returned to him, and he could not help but feel that this final irony was only part of the peculiar pattern of justice that was gradually becoming apparent to him. And so he attached most of his worry to the "loot" from the robberies, thinking that at least if they could dispose of that, they would be in a better position.

When he got home, Ancke was stooped over behind a broom, gathering a collection of cigarette ends, used strips of adhesive tape, and bottle caps into a pile in the center of the kitchen floor.

"My God, what are you doing? You didn't have to sweep the place!"

"I just want to get these corners," Ancke replied with a preoccupied smile of greeting.

Winnie came out of the bedroom, just shouldering into her green spring coat. Most of her makeup had worn off, her cheeks were flushed and shiny, and she looked mauled, harassed.

"Where have you been, David? I waited at the Center Street station, but . . . Oh, you didn't find your glasses."

"No, and it took me forever to get to the subway . . . But,

look, look, we haven't any time. I just realized, not more than a few minutes ago, that the address was all over those papers! On every last one of them!"

"Oh, Christ!" Winnie's eyes narrowed and her mouth drew into a serious, speculative pout. "Well, look, then, we all want to tell the same story when they come. We have to get a story worked out . . . Hurry, think of something!"

"Where's the dustpan, man?" Ancke asked distantly, as if he was a servant of the old style who understands nothing his employers ever say in his presence, but those few household instructions directed at him.

"But what are you doing? Why are you sweeping that way, Albert? Did you take care of everything?"

"Hey, I've got it! We don't know anything about the car. That's it. We borrowed it from somebody last night, see? And the stuff was already in the back . . . David, are you listening? We borrowed the car last night!"

Ancke had spread a newspaper on the floor and was carefully sweeping all the refuse into it.

"But what about Little Rock?" Stofsky said. "Maybe he's already told them something different."

"No, no, he'll keep quiet till he finds out what we're going to say. He's got to keep quiet! He wouldn't hang us up like that!" Then she raised her eyes and looked straight at Stofsky with an expression of strange and sudden remorse. "Was he hurt bad? Did you find out if he was hurt bad, David? . . . All I could think of was to run. But he was just out, wasn't he? That's the way he looked, just knocked out . . . And I knew I should have driven! This wouldn't have happened if I'd been . . ." But she let it trail off, her gaze lowering again.

"It would have happened anyway . . . sometime. Don't worry, Winnie. You mustn't worry about all that now. Think of Rock! Think of *him!* . . . Albert, stop sweeping, for Christ's sake! Where did you throw all that stuff? Did you get everything? Did you make sure? . . . All the junk and the tea? . . . And do you know, I had a sort of vision while I wandered . . . an inner vision, and we shouldn't worry because there's nothing that can be done . . ."

While he said this, having no idea of whether they were listening or not, he was getting out three cups and testing the coffee pot with his finger. But it was cold.

"We just borrowed it," Winnie was repeating. "We didn't know the guy . . . he was drunk . . . And you were with us, Albert. Down on Eighth Avenue in a bar . . . Have you got that straight?"

"It just might stick," Ancke murmured disinterestedly.

"Yes, it will!" she exclaimed, as if she had perceived in him an unforgivable lack of faith. "Don't you think so, David? Of course it will! . . . And, you know. I think I'm pregnant too. Really, I think I am this time. It's more than a week overdue."

She gave both of them a quick glance of furtive modesty that implored them not to notice the tiny quiver of shame in her voice. "Do you think that will help? It might make some difference, after all, Albert . . . You know, with the squares. Motherhood, and all that . . . Cause I really think I am. I can feel it in the mornings . . . Isn't . . . isn't that a sign?"

"What's that there! What's that!" Stofsky suddenly cried, for in turning to Winnie he had chanced to look into the bedroom and seen the neatly-folded fur coat that had been lying under the bed for a week. "But you didn't get rid of the stuff in there!"

He rushed into the bedroom and started pulling the stolen clothes out, throwing them in all directions wildly. Everything was still there.

"Albert! Albert! Didn't you get rid of *anything?* What have you been doing?" He threw open the doors of the closet. Nothing had been touched. "My God!" He stormed back into the kitchen. "You didn't touch a thing! Not even one suit, not a button! And they'll be here any minute now. They might be on the stairs this very instant! What have you been doing all this time?"

Ancke emptied his paper into the wastebasket, and then looked up with weary patience. "I've been sweeping, man. Can't you see that?"

Stofsky sank back against the wall. "You've been sweeping . . . Good God!" He felt fatigue lying everywhere about him, and knew that if he noticed it, it would claim him. He tried to rally: "Don't you realize what's happening? If they find all that stuff, it'll make everything—"

"Oh, what the hell, man. Where would I have dumped it anyway? And . . . what the hell. Really . . . How different you look without your glasses!"

Furious, Stofsky started into the living room where the narcotics, in their little Chinese boxes, sat in a row on a book case.

"But, really," Ancke continued, padding doggedly after him. "Why get hungup? . . . Look how clean everything is. I worked all afternoon . . . Now, don't be angry. Tell me about your vision instead . . . Sit down now."

Stofsky swung around with a box in each hand, swung around sharply because there was something faintly cheerful in Ancke's voice. Beneath all the patience, he was strangely good-humored.

"We're going to jail! Don't you realize that? What's wrong with you?" He was nearly shouting. "*So* was Israel carried away out of their own land to Assyria! *Just* like this!"

But Ancke's clear, large eyes had fastened on one of the boxes casually, and he was mumbling: "I wonder if I should have a last fix. One final shot before . . . I guess I wouldn't have time to boil the needle though . . . Oh, well . . ." He sank toward the couch.

Stofsky pushed past him and hurried through the bedroom into the toilet. He emptied all the boxes down the seat, and then he flushed it. He put the boxes under the tap and swished them back and forth in the water; then he raised the tiny window that opened on the air-shaft, and dropped them out. He flushed the toilet again, and went out, closing the door.

"We *could* have just borrowed the car," he heard Winnie say, as he paused in the bedroom where it was hot and smelled oddly of moth balls and unaired bedclothes, peering into the closet at all the suits that hung there, and trying to think where he could dispose of them.

At that moment, he remembered the clothes closet in Water's dirty room, the dark, fearful minutes he had passed in it months ago. Now there was no room to hide, there were too many stolen suits, too little time. And he knew all of a sudden that he wouldn't have hidden anyway, and remembered that the suits were there for a reason, like the last incongruous piece that finally does fit into the jig-saw puzzle after all.

"I shouldn't worry," he thought. "After the captivity and the wandering, comes the punishment," getting his contexts confused.

Winnie was huddled against the kitchen sink, her upturned coat collar prisoning the auburn hair, and she was staring disconsolately before herself, her hands resting gently on her stomach. Through the door into the living room, he could just see Ancke's withered legs flopping off the edge of the couch, and knew that his eyes would be closed, his breathing faint, but that he was collecting his strength, resting from his exertions, and waiting.

They did not have to wait long, for just as Stofsky thought with helpless amazement: "So this is wrath! So this is what it is like!", the door was flung open, almost knocking him off his feet, and three policemen burst in.

Seven

"How do you like my new shoes?"

Stofsky wiggled his feet in the air, and Hobbes, who sat across from him, stared disconcertedly at the stiff brown oxfords with the shiny soles, and did not know what to say. He had not expected that these would be Stofsky's first words upon seeing him after the ten days that had passed since the arrest.

He had not been surprised at the phone call, and the hesitant, almost businesslike voice wondering if he would be at home at two. He had even been eager, concerned, agreeable to anything Stofsky suggested, but he had not expected the bantering, gay tone and the remark about the shoes. He did not know what he had been expecting.

"They're not exactly broken in yet, so . . ." He untied the laces, and eased the shoes off his feet, sinking back with a heavy, comical sigh. His feet were impishly small in the multi-colored socks.

"Well," Hobbes began, with a nervous smile. "How are you?"

"Oh, I'm out on bail. My father arranged it five days ago, and I've been out in Hackensack. I called you once or twice too, but I wasn't sure whether you'd . . ." He interrupted himself with a shy little snigger, a questioning and embarrassed gleam in his eyes.

Uneasily, Hobbes lit a cigarette while he asked: "But . . . how about the others? What's happened to them?"

"Well, Albert's still in jail, just sitting there waiting, I suppose. With his hands folded in his lap, almost as if he were praying, you know? . . . And Little Rock's gone off his head. Yes! They'd taken him down to Bellevue the last I heard. He's a four-time-felony-loser, you see, and stands to get life. And Winnie's going to have a baby," this with sudden intense gravity.

"Little Rock's?"

Stofsky paused with a puzzled gathering of his lips, as though doubt on this score had never occured to him. "Why, yes, certainly! What an idea! . . . Her father's flown in from Toledo, and they're going about bailing her. I think he wants it aborted

". . . Yes, of course it's Little Rock's! . . . But then, heavens, I don't really know. I'm not supposed to know anything about them, you see."

"What do you mean?"

"Well, they've charged me with burglary too, and being a receiver of stolen goods. But the lawyer—my father hired me a lawyer, you know—a regular Broadway Sam with a cigar—well, this lawyer thinks he can get me off on the first count, but I've got to stay away from the others . . . and he won't even tell me what's happening to them."

Hobbes could not restrain his curiosity, even though he felt that somehow it violated a certain tact that had been observed thus far. "But when did this happen? I mean, the burglary itself."

"That Friday night when Ancke was here. Just before that. There I was, sleeping in my apartment, and they were out burglarizing!"

"Oh. Then you weren't . . . I mean, you didn't go with them?"

"Of course not." And at this, Stofsky leaned over and took both his feet in his hands, but his gaze at Hobbes did not falter. "Did you think I had, Paul? You mean, you've been thinking that *I* was involved in the stealing?" He was fumbling with his toes like a perplexed child who can think of nothing to do with his hands. "How funny that you should think that of me! Tell me, did you really think that?"

"Well, that's what it said in the papers. That's *all* it said. And . . . and I didn't know."

Stofsky glanced at him with a hurt, and at the same time gentle, grimace. "But do you believe *everything* you read in the papers?" And for the first time, Hobbes realized that Stofsky was consumed with a feeling of humiliation of which he was, for some reason, terribly ashamed. But before he had time to shift the direction of the conversation, Stofsky had alluded to it:

"But then, of course, why shouldn't you . . . I don't know how to act, you see. I've gotten it all so confused in my head. I keep thinking I should be making jokes about it, or figuring angles . . . And I can't find the right *tone* at all. He-he! It's all the tone, you know . . . But I'm either too serious or too bland."

"Well, you *are* innocent, after all. You weren't involved in the robbery."

"But I *am* a receiver of stolen goods . . . Oh, stupidly it's true, like a fool perhaps . . . but I'm not innocent of that. And how do they know whether I was along during the robbery, after all? How do they know? . . . I keep thinking I should be arranging an alibi . . . And also I'm going up to Columbia to meet my lawyer at three-thirty. We're going to see Bernard, my old English professor. I wrote him a letter two weeks ago, saying that I was thinking of leaving the city, and that may help, you know . . . So will you tell me when it's three?"

"Sure. And that's a pretty good idea," Hobbes said, wondering what help the letter could be to Stofsky, but succumbing to a feeling that his part in the conversation was somehow to avoid the indelicacy of direct questions.

"Oh, and such funny things happened when they picked us up! It was very strange. I took them right into the bedroom, as though showing them where to leave their coats. But instead I opened up the closet and started to pull everything out of it . . . And they hustled us around a lot, of course, jeering at us, because Ancke just lay there on the couch smiling faintly, and Winnie kept saying: 'Be careful of me, be careful of me,' . . . very sweetly really. And she looked so fragile all of a sudden. She kept holding her stomach like this . . . 'Be careful, I'm pregnant!', that's just what she said. And, you know, they actually took her arm and helped her down the stairs."

He laughed gently at the thought of it, but then went on with a manful swallow: "It was so funny, Paul, how womanly she was! She was frightened, of course, but she never broke down . . . I've never seen her that way before . . . But all I could think of was taking some books to read in jail. I held everybody up, choosing which ones to take. I finally took the Bible and the Upanishads. But when we got down to the jail on Sixty-eighth Street, they wouldn't let me take the Upanishads in with me. They said the Bible was all right because it was a religious book. Well, I told them that the Upanishads was a religious book too, but this sergeant sort of sneered and said: 'It's o-n-l-y Indian religion!' . . . And isn't that funny though, that he should have known that? . . . Then I started to insist, and he sneered again and said: 'You want to argue philosophy with me?' It was so strange . . . Anyway, I couldn't take it with me."

Hobbes shook his head. "But the papers said you'd *all* admitted to the robbery."

"Oh, the papers had everything wrong. One of them described me as a 'studious young man with horned rims,' and said that

Little Rock kept me under his influence by supplying me with drugs. But one in Brooklyn had a wonderful picture of us in the patrol wagon. Did you happen to see it? I look very good in that picture . . . But as far as I know no one admitted the robbery. That was what was so funny. I didn't know what any of the others had said, so I tried to just sit tight and say nothing, but they slapped me around and I knew they'd read the journals because they said: 'So you're a big fag, eh? So you like little boys, eh?' "

A look of feverish, profound shame flashed across his face, but was followed immediately by a forlorn half-smile.

"But I kept screaming . . . I mean, mumbling . . . that I wouldn't say anything until I saw my lawyer. It was just like in the movies."

"What's this about the journals? You mean, your journals from the last year or so? Why did they read them?"

Stofsky looked at him with searching bewilderment.

"They were in the car. Didn't you know? . . . Oh, but don't worry, Paul, I . . . I haven't kept one for the last six months . . . There's no reason why they should come here."

He looked away with pained deliberation.

"Mainly there were old records of merchant marine days, and . . . well, quasi-sexual, quasi-religious diatribes to Hart and others. And even a detailed account of the summer I spent in Denver two years ago, when Hart and I drove hot cars up into the mountains. And also a complete list of all the things I stole from the May Company while I worked there. Just little things, trifles, but I listed them all down carefully. And descriptions of heroin and morphine and tea, things like that. And, oh, everything, as though I had confessed. It's so strange . . . and I tried to write a poem while I was in jail too. Did I mention that?"

He stared at the floor for a moment of dazed sadness, during which his pale lips trembled. Then another thought occured to him, and his eyes blazed: "And you know what else happened? They even called up my analyst, and he told them that I was an incurable heroin addict!"

"What? For Christ sake!"

"Yes, that Schachtian! All these months I've been afraid of him, wondering what he was thinking, and then he does this to me! Just because once I told him that I used heroin occasionally . . . and that was just bragging, just boasting really. You'd think he'd have known that, wouldn't you? . . . But then, *everything's* worked out so badly for me. You know, five months ago I would have gotten positively paranoiac about it."

But it was three and he started to put on his shoes.

"By the way, have you heard from Gene? I've been trying to reach him steadily since I got out."

"No, not for the last couple of days, but he may call later on tonight."

Stofsky paused at the door, and his features looked waxen, yellowish as he glanced shyly at Hobbes.

"It's funny, isn't it? I haven't heard from anyone. I can't seem to get in touch with anyone at all . . . Do you think he's avoiding me?"

"No, you know how he is, David. His book just taken and everything. As I say, I may hear from him this evening though."

Stofsky seemed undecided as to whether he should ask, but finally he did: "Could I come back after I see Bernard then? Just in case he calls. I wouldn't stay long. I have to go back to Hackensack tonight anyway—"

"Sure, of course," and as Hobbes closed the door, he wondered why he had not been warmer, less casual, and he sat down, biting his nails, realizing that friendly assurances had occurred to him more than once during the interview, but that he had rejected them automatically, without even a thought, as being somehow unseemly.

How insufferable everyone was, he thought at that. They came to fear emotions, to think of human needs as a sign of weakness, and to view isolation, not as a curse and a blight, but as a protection. For the first time, he saw these attitudes in himself. His book, the letters, Estelle: all were illusions, illusions, and yet even now that they had proved themselves unreal, they held him in the phantom grip of habit.

"And as a consequence, I have hurt my friend," he thought. "And for no reason; not out of malice or dislike or indifference. For nothing, but this frightened egoism."

And suddenly his part in all relationships seemed made up of actions blind and cowardly and base, even though they were unconscious.

These thoughts were still occupying him when Kathryn phoned. He told her of Stofsky's visit, and began to repeat some of what he had said, but she interrupted him immediately:

"Did he take the radio?"

For the first time that afternoon, Hobbes remembered the pink radio, and saw it sitting on the mantelpiece. She had been alarmed about it the whole week, fearful that they would get involved if it was discovered in their apartment, and she had ordered him to give it to either Stofsky or Pasternak the first time he saw them. They had even had a quarrel or two over his reluctance to force it on anyone else, regardless of circumstances.

"No, I forgot it," he said lamely.

"I told you to get rid of that radio, Paul. Do I have to do everything?"

"But he was only here for a little while, honey, and he wanted to talk—"

"I don't care about that! If I had had anything to say about it, it never would have been left there at all. It's his responsibility, and—"

"Look, Gene'll probably call tonight and I'll get it worked out with him, and if he doesn't take it I'll check it myself at Penn Station or something like that."

"No, no, you won't! I'm not going to have you getting involved in all this. Don't you understand anything? It's not your affair . . . if *your* friends—"

"I'll do what I can, Kathryn, and that's all. But I'll do it my own way."

"I want you to get rid of that radio! Do you understand that? My God, don't you ever think of me? . . . Oh, sure, you're very considerate when it comes to thieves and dope addicts and drunks, but that's as far as it goes! . . . But I'm telling you that I won't have that radio in my house any longer. And you'd better do something about it!"

So Hobbes spent the next hour or so wondering what he could do. He could not imagine mentioning the radio to Stofsky under any condition, and waited expectantly for Pasternak to call so that they might make arrangements about it, but finally he resolved that even if Pasternak failed to phone he would say nothing to Stofsky, and explain it to Kathryn later.

But Stofsky did not come. The chilly, clear sky outside the windows darkened; the city, building by building, became studded with lights, and Kathryn opened the door before he had realized what time it was getting to be.

Eight

SHE was pleasant, even offhand. She made no reference
to the radio, noting it with cool detachment as though its fate
had been decided. He realized that she was aware of his nervousness, and that she was pointedly taking no notice of it. She
asked him about Stofsky, and listened with sympathetic interest
to everything he told her, but there was something faintly com-
placent about her comments, something mildly rebuking in her
eyes when she looked at him, as if to say: "Let all this be a
lesson to *you*."

This annoyed him somewhat, and finally he said:

"He's going to drop back again, by the way. When he finishes
at Columbia."

"Oh. All right. He can take the radio then." She got up to
heat some coffee. Her very air of calm assurance was the bait
in the trap.

"Well, I'll see," he replied firmly, stepping into it because there
was no other way. "But I've got to say that I'll only do what
I think best."

She turned to him as though coming out from behind a blind.
"If you don't tell him to take it, I will. I won't have it here another minute! It's not our fault if he's in trouble. And besides,
I don't like the idea of his coming here. What if he's being followed?"

"Don't be silly, he's out on bail."

"That doesn't matter. I don't like it! These people don't give
a damn how they involve everyone else. Can't you see that?"

"He's a friend of mine, and I'll do what I—"

"You're going to give him that radio, Paul, and if you don't
I will!"

Hobbes frowned grimly to himself, got up and stood peering
out of the window. Everything he saw down there in the shimmering street struck him as petty, somehow compulsive in its
continual movement to and fro, and yet at the same time mon-
strously bleak and meaningless. "When will it all be over?" he
thought, but all he said was:

"You will please leave this to me, Kathryn."

"Oh, I'll leave it to you all right, just as long as you get him to take it! Heavens, *I* didn't want to have anything to do with it in the first place."

She poured her coffee with a smile of bitter enjoyment.

"And also I was thinking today that it might be a good idea for you to write one more letter to Miss Liza Adler, one that *I'll* read! Just to tell her that she won't be hearing from you any-more, and that you never loved her, and that it was—"

Hobbes had swung around sharply, and was staring at her with a stunned, almost uncomprehending look of surprise on his face.

"I just want to be sure that nothing's going on behind my back." There was a defiant set to her lips. "I don't see why you should mind explaining to her just what you explained to me."

"I couldn't do such a thing!"

"Well, I'll dictate it for you then . . . And *why* couldn't you do such a thing? You had no trouble doing it *before!* To me! How does it happen that you're so damn considerate all of a sudden? Why is that?" She prepared to goad herself into a fury.

"Do we have to go through all this again? How long do I have to go on paying for it?"

He might have actually struck her by the look in her eyes.

"How long did I pay for it? Three years, three years!"

"I know, honey, I know. Do you think I've forgotten? But I loathe myself enough, I detest myself enough, you don't know . . . And, and do we have to go through it all now? I mean, David will be here in a minute. Why do I have to do the same thing to him too? We could settle it later, couldn't we?"

"I don't know why you're so thoughtful toward *him!* Toward *his* feelings, when he's the one who's responsible for my finding your precious letters!"

He ground out his cigarette with unaccustomed force.

"Well, I should think you'd be grateful to him! I don't see why you're not grateful to him then!"

"For leaving stolen radios in our apartment? For almost get-ting us thrown in jail? Hah!"

"No, for the weapon."

"The weapon?" There was a wild mixture of anger and shock in her voice. "Do you really think I'd rather have it *this* way? Is that what you think? . . . That's all it is to you, isn't it? A balance of power!"

But her anger had been dissipated on so many previous blistering disputes that it could not last long anymore, and gave way to an embittered scowl.

"I wish he'd just leave us alone, that's all. Why doesn't he stop interfering with everyone all the time? Look what he did with Hart and Dinah! His own friends! . . . And he's always talking about love."

Hobbes sighed with heavy submissiveness. "Well, that's the final ambiguity, I guess. To hear you defending Hart! And just to spite Stofsky, poor, frightened little Stofsky, who's on your side if he's on anyone's." He slumped in a chair and said with weary emphasis: "When will it all be over? I really think everything's a sham. Everything."

"Well," she repeated, though not as adamantly as before. "You make him take that radio out of here, that's all."

Just then the bell rang and it was into this oppressive and unhappy atmosphere, of which he was unwittingly the cause that Stofsky came, with an uncertain, bashful look at both of them.

"Well . . . well," he began with an uneasy smile. "But, look, I've brought flowers for the ladies!" With a weary flourish, he brought his hand around from behind him, and held up a rather dog-eared bunch of posies, soggy and drooping over his fingers.

Kathryn gave him a distracted, uncomfortable grin and went to get a glass, while Hobbes bustled him into a chair with an awkward geniality.

"Gene hasn't called yet, but I'm expecting him to at any minute . . . But what happened? Tell me all about it. What did Bernard say?"

Stofsky stared at his new shoes as he said: "Oh, we saw him, and he was very nice, and I guess he'll write a letter or something like that . . . But," and he breathed deeply, soberly, "but such a lot of things happened . . . Naturally everyone knows about it up there, people are talking of nothing else. Rushing around from office to office." He emitted a tiny, sarcastic laugh. "It's just like when Eisenhower was made president!"

"But Bernard agreed to help? He has your letter?"

"Oh, yes. Yes, he had it . . . But, you know, he asked me the strangest question . . . I puzzled about it all the way downtown. I still can't understand."

"Question? What did he ask you?"

"Well, he kept us waiting for a while, loitering in the hallway . . . yes, right in the hall. And the lawyer kept looking at his watch and rustling papers. It really would have been quite funny . . . otherwise. But finally we went in, and the lawyer began to present the case, about the letter. Bernard kept looking at me out of the corner of his eye, without saying a word to me, not a word . . . And, you know, I don't think I imagined that . . . about the eye."

Stofsky kept shifting himself around in the chair, making a concerted effort to keep his report light, to find the tone; but every few minutes, as though in recognition of his failure to accomplish this, he would break out in a bewildered and sheepish smile.

"And the lawyer had everything planned out. I was astounded. I mean, he doesn't tell *me* anything, you see . . . They talked it over, and I felt like some infant. prodigy or something, listening in on a publicity conference! . . . Well, anyway, he plans for me to plead guilty to possession of stolen property, and throw myself on the mercy of the court . . . He told Bernard I might get a suspended sentence that way, or at most just a year in jail . . . Only he told it all at great length, just as if I wasn't in the room. Then he said that he wanted a letter from Bernard about my character and . . . well, all that. He *wanted* a letter! That's the way he put it, his very words! Can you imagine Bernard and this real slick Broadway Sam?"

"But he agreed, about the letter? And what was this question?"

Stofsky was ruffled by Kathryn's return with a glass and the miserable bouquet, and watched her moving restlessly about the room, as he said:

"I'm taking a long time getting to it, aren't I? Good heavens! . . . Well, let's see. Oh, yes, finally the lawyer said, very portentously, almost a threat in fact: 'Are you going to help this young man?' He was really very clever. And then Bernard turned to me and started to chat with me; that's exactly it, we chatted . . . He talked about my satanic attitude, and my . . . my insinuating manner. I think he said insinuating . . . or maybe it was insidious. Anyway it was something evil like that . . . although that was over a year ago, after all," he added softly. "I mean that . . . that satanic business. But, of course, he doesn't know what's happened since then! . . . So I just kept sitting there, and finally he leveled his eye at me and said: 'Now, David, I want you to answer one question,' and then he glanced at the lawyer sort of icily, as though all the rest of it had been somehow beside the point, and he was going to strike right to the heart of the matter, you see? And he said: 'Do you believe in this society?'!"

"You're kidding! He actually asked you that?"

"Yes, yes. Isn't it funny . . . and strange? But, of course, I said 'yes', I said 'certainly'."

"He sounds like an idiot," Kathryn announced gruffly, plunking herself on a couch. For an instant, Stofsky peered before himself almost without expression, and then he looked back at them both timidly.

"And, of course, I do. I think I do . . . I mean, I guess I *have* to, don't I?"

"What else can you do!" Hobbes exclaimed bitterly. "And that makes it clear anyway. The bastards! Anything to protect themselves! . . . But didn't he say anything else? You were one of his favorite students, weren't you? Didn't he even ask how you were? What you were reading?"

Stofsky gave a faint little chuckle. "No, no. But he was busy, I suppose. I wasn't angry, you understand. I mean I can see it, from his position . . . But it was so funny! They treated me just as though I was a communist."

"But the lawyer thinks he can get you off?" Kathryn asked deferentially. "What good would a letter from some old professor do anyway?"

Stofsky turned to her wanly. "Oh, I don't know really. I can't understand what it's all about . . . It seems it's my first offence, and he said something about psychiatric complications. He told me on the way downtown that there's a possibility of a suspended sentence if I agree to have analysis, maybe even go to a city hospital . . . But I don't know. I really couldn't understand most of it. I kept thinking about my father. He's frantic, of course, perhaps even ruined socially. And, you know, he put up a thousand dollars for this lawyer . . . everything he had, his life savings."

"What about your job though?"

"Oh, I was fired. It was very weird when I went to get my last check. Everyone was so nice. I was even a kind of hero to the errand boys! Imagine it. But I was fired, of course . . . And that's what I kept thinking about. Because I've got to get another job, I've got to support myself or I'll come under the complete domination of my father again . . . And I must pay him back somehow, I must! You can see that."

"Well, it won't be easy getting a job, after all this," Kathryn stated firmly. "Believe me."

"I know," he replied with a placid and disheartened smile. "It was never easy for *me* anyway. There are just so many jobs I can do, and . . . well, this doesn't make me any more attractive. But I'll just have to find something."

"You wouldn't *have* to tell your employer about all this, would you?" Hobbes said quickly, with a glance at Kathryn.

"But I intend to. I would anyway. Would you want me to lie? They'd find out eventually. Everything comes out eventually, you know that, Paul? I've discovered that now. All of a sudden I realized that about the police last week, and about everything else."

Kathryn nodded slightly, as if to say: 'I'm glad you've come around to my way of thinking,' but all she said aloud was: "Well, that's good anyway. It's good you saw that."

But Stofsky either did not catch her deprecating tone, or felt that it was warranted, for he leaned forward earnestly and said with unusual warmth: "Yes, yes, isn't it? But when you find yourself thinking of a policeman as God—as a delegated envoy of the Lord as it were—you have to tell him the truth, after all, and that's just what I did."

"You told them about everything?" Kathryn asked suddenly. "Everything? Do they have a list of all that stolen stuff?"

Stofsky was bewildered. "Well, I suppose so. I don't really know. As I said, my lawyer—"

"Because, you know, we're stuck with that radio," she went on obstinately, not looking at Hobbes even when he jumped up.

"Kathryn, for pete's sake! . . . It's nothing, David. You know, it's that radio Ancke left here with Gene. We didn't know what to do about it."

Stofsky looked from one to the other. "Oh, yes, I'd forgotten about that . . . But, I see, you're worried they might come around for it. Is that it?"

"Of course, we're worried! It's none of our affair, and he left it here with Gene, after all."

"But they won't come around! . . . How could they know," Hobbes said excitedly to Stofsky. "It's silly, Kathryn. Really, won't you please let me take care of it? Gene will call and we'll work something out."

"I don't want it here, Paul . . . Couldn't you take it to the police?" she continued evenly to Stofsky.

"Well," he stumbled with shame-faced confusion, staring at her intently, hurtfully. "I don't know about that . . . But, let's see . . . Well, I'll do something about it."

"I won't have it!" Hobbes exclaimed. "I won't have it! Please leave this to me! . . . David, forget about the goddamn radio. I'll take care of it! . . . Kathryn," he implored. "I told you I'd take it down to Penn Station and just check it!"

"No, you'd better let me take care of it, Paul," Stofsky said abruptly, giving him a long and penetrating glance. "Really, it's nothing to me. I'll think of something. I could just leave it in Central Park or . . . But anyway it's no problem."

"I won't have you getting yourself more involved."

"Oh, please, it doesn't matter, Paul . . . And really, Kathryn, you mustn't worry that way. Because no one said anything about coming here that night; believe me, no one even thought of it."

Though he spoke with exaggerated calm and assurance, his bland, half-smiling looks had a strange resignation in them as well.

"You mustn't squabble over this," he went on, taking the radio from the mantelpiece. "You might even keep it, you know. It's a good set, nearly new . . . But, no, we'd better dispose of it. It's better to play safe . . ." He stood there, holding the radio, and absent-mindedly twisted one of the dials.

"You understand, don't you?" Kathryn began in a hesitant, doubtful voice. "We didn't know what to do . . . but if you really think that we wouldn't get into any trouble, why—"

"No," he said briskly, snapping back from his thoughts, and glancing around the room. "No, it's better this way. But you mustn't worry or get excited or fight. Either of you. I'll just give it to some bum in the park. Think of how surprised he'll be!"

His glance caught Hobbes upon whose face there was an expression of powerless anger. "Don't frown, Paul . . . You know, I won't wait for Gene, after all. I'll miss that late bus if I do . . . But don't frown like that, Paul. You look like a walrus! He-he! . . . Kiss your wife now. Go ahead, and listen to her . . . She's right about this. I speak from experience, you know. I have a right to be an old, groaning sage now!"

Hobbes shook his head with baffled sadness. "All right, David. All right."

"No, really . . . But do you have a bag? Just some old paper bag that I can wrap it in? And maybe some string too."

Kathryn got these while Stofsky babbled on with a cheerfulness that only increased Hobbes' desperation.

"Here, here, let me do it. You'll make a mess of it," she said with agitated affection, taking the parcel from Stofsky and setting it right, all the while looking up at him with flushed cheeks, as though he had rightfully reproached her.

They both took him to the door.

"If Gene calls," he said in a voice that was somehow vaguely apologetic. "Tell him about me, will you? You know, I haven't had a real chance to talk to him since his book was accepted . . . I've been so busy." He laughed softly and his eyes glimmered. "You might tell him just that: that I've been busy."

"You be sure to call us," Kathryn said.

"Oh, I will," he replied, smiling at both of them with grave embarrassment at these formalities. "I'll have plenty of time from now on. Goodbye."

And with the radio tucked under his arm, he made his way slowly down the creaking stairs, and he did not look back.

Is it over? Hobbes thought as he let the door close. Is everything over now?

Nine

It was not over. There was one more thing and it happened on another dreary Sunday a week later. Agatson was killed accidentally in the subway. He was very drunk, and had been for days. About noon he started downtown on some pilgrimage or caprice the reason for which was never discovered, but as the train began to pull slowly out of the Twenty-third Street Station, an impulse seized him (no darker than thousands of others that had proved him easy prey in the past) and he tried to climb out one of the windows of the train. But he miscalculated the speed, and before he could pull back, the wall of the tunnel struck his head and shoulders, and he was sucked out of the window, jammed downward among the wheels, and dragged for fifty feet. He was dead when they got him loose, and the trains on that part of the line were held up for thirty-six minutes.

Someone knew somebody who worked for United Press, and the rumor got started even before the item (interesting to outsiders only because it seemed inexplicable) reached the papers. Pasternak called at five o'clock from somewhere in the Village, and told Hobbes.

"Oh, no, Gene! . . . No! Dead?"

Kathryn lowered her newspaper, her eyes widened, and then she gasped: "Stofsky!"

Pasternak said that the rumor went that no one had claimed the body, and that though Agatson had parents somewhere upstate, no one knew where. "But I'll meet you at Haverty's later," and he rang off suddenly.

Hobbes told Kathryn about it and a deep flush spread through her face, and gradually her eyes grew wet. "I suppose we shouldn't be surprised . . . But . . . for a moment I thought it was Stofsky!" She looked away from him. "And then when you told me, I was relieved."

They sat for a while, and neither cared to say anything or could think of anything at all to say. Finally, Hobbes got up, went across the room, and phoned Ketcham and told him.

"Are you sure? . . . How terrible! . . . Did he suffer? But you're sure it isn't one of his ruses?"

Hobbes said simply: "Yes," but he was thinking: "I didn't love him. Did anyone love him?"

Ketcham's voice grew suddenly startled: "I'm going down to Bianca's, Paul. Does she know? . . . I suppose everyone's calling everyone else. But I'm leaving right now . . . Maybe I'll see you at Haverty's . . . don't wait for me though."

They could not sit still, and everything they said to each other was somehow irrelevant. There was no real reason to go out, but they put on coats because it was cold, locked up their door, and went downtown silently, carefully, and did not bother to wonder why. Kathryn sat beside Hobbes on the subway, peeping every now and again at the window across the aisle, and once she said: "The goddamn fool! Look at the size of it."

They walked down Sixth Avenue, hurrying a little, and turned west on Twenty-first Street. Everything was shuttered, chilly, dead. The street lamps glowed feebly, pushing the night away from them. Hobbes paused before the well known building, and looked up at the darkened windows out of which memory would always pour the echo of shrill music and nameless cries; of parties that had had no beginning, but had blossomed in so many nights and afternoons like bright evil flowers, and which had finally ended; of guests who had come from everywhere, full of eager belief in the significance of what was to come or cynically armored against it, and who would never come again; of all the beer, that terrible ocean of it that had been opened, drunk, vomited and flushed away, and that had run out at last.

Then they noticed someone wandering down the sidewalk toward them, and surprisingly enough it turned out to be Verger. The collar of his rumpled tweed jacket was turned up around his throat. He looked gaunt and was actually shivering from the cold.

"I thought there might be some sort of spontaneous demonstration," he said, his teeth all but chattering. "Shall we go to Haverty's?"

They sat in a booth over beer and tried to talk.

"We didn't see you for a long while," Hobbes said.

"No, I was out of the city. I was sick . . . But I guess we ought to do something about Bill, shouldn't we?"

And at that the great embarrassment of death descended upon them all. Everything else seemed intangible but the sickening thought that somewhere in the night, in the city, lay that smashed and ruined body, a body so abused and scarred during its life that any of them could have identified it even if the head was gone, a body now shamelessly exposed in its imperfections to uncaring strangers, empty of the will that had never let it flag up to the very last. All they knew of Agatson lay somewhere unclaimed under a sheet, or in a drawer, and a small tear hung on Kathryn's lid, ignored by the others.

Finally Verger said in choked tones:

"I couldn't claim it. I couldn't bear that, I don't think . . . But what should we do?"

Just then Pasternak hurried in, out of breath, a preoccupied scowl appearing fitfully across his mouth.

"I couldn't find out any more. But somebody down at the Santa Maria said he heard that May was up at the hospital to claim him, but ran away suddenly before they could get her name. And that she's raving around the Village right now, saying she was Bill's wife."

Verger's pale mask seemed to crumple, and his small, dark eyes, which always looked vaguely injured, winced: "I forgot her . . . We had all forgotten her! . . . My God, she must be cold, even hungry. They never had any money . . ."

"I was with Bill last night," Pasternak said suddenly. "But then I lost him . . . She hadn't been there for three days, Daniel. He'd thrown her out . . . But we were very drunk . . . You know, I really think he'd been drunk since that night Stofsky was arrested? . . . Then I lost him down on Bleeker Street. It was crazy."

Verger rose in his chair all of a sudden, and standing back from the table he fished in his pocket with a peculiar, absorbed fumble. He dropped some coins among the glasses with the awkward twist of the hand, so like some clumsy magician, that was typical of Agatson.

"More beer," he mumbled with a strange, shameful smile and a little jig-step. "More beer!" and with that he turned and hurried out the door, a stooped, punished little figure, his head pulled into hunched shoulders, as if in expectation of a more arduous ordeal yet to come.

"He's gone out to find May," Pasternak said blankly.

They sat there saying nothing, but Hobbes, endeavoring to feel no pretty, appropriate sorrow, but only what he actually felt, could not be still.

"I keep wondering if anyone really loved him. Aside from the women, because that never made him happy. And, you know, I can't think of anyone at all."

Pasternak's scowl deepened in consideration of it.

"Verger did. That's what's so funny. For him it's the end of an era."

"That's silly!" Kathryn exclaimed, as if she had thought something horribly indecent, which had frightened her. "You talk about him as though he wasn't real!"

"Oh, Christ, I didn't mean it that way," Pasternak said ruefully.

But Hobbes did not listen as they talked on, because at Kathryn's remark Agatson became simply, terribly dead somewhere and gone from his waking world so suddenly and without reason that for an instant he felt again the trembling frailty of human life, the transparent lacquer of consciousness which was all that kept anyone from the unimaginable void of death. All in a glaring moment, he was swept with mortality, and thought to himself: "He is dead, but I am alive!" And his whole body was crammed with a dense uprush of instincts, hungers, longings and raw appetites. "He is dead, but I am alive!"

He gulped down some beer quickly.

At that moment, Ketcham came in the door, and the Trimbles were close behind him. Hobbes got Ketcham aside for an instant.

"How's Bianca?"

Ketcham's smooth countenance did not actually change in expression, but the expression of heated reserve already there seemed to heighten.

"She'd heard about it when I got there . . . I was too late. Someone had phoned her . . . Oh, she was all right . . . You know . . . What could I do?" But then he turned back to the others and somehow managed not to be caught alone again.

"Have you heard anything more?" Janet was asking Kathryn in a systematic undertone. "You can see the way Peter is."

Trimble would acknowledge some stray remark only with a harried frown, and then fall to staring in front of himself with a sort of omnivorous concentration. He broke out into a wild, distracted laugh every now and again, and suddenly he said:

"Let's go out to Hoboken and have steamed clams!"

There was immediate argument in Janet's face, but she did not articulate it, and they sat there, undecided, until more beers materialized from somewhere. They could not come to an agreement and a tense moment started to take form among them.

In the middle of it, Trimble exclaimed again: "*I* want steamed clams . . . and beer!"

And instantly, Hobbes realized that Trimble, too, had loved Agatson, and so he said:

"Yes, let's go. Why not? Why not?"

And so they went.

Somehow they found Christopher Street, and straggled down it toward the muffled sounds of the river where a few squalid bars forlornly gathered the discontented into gaudy islands of warmth and alcohol.

They reached the great wooden shed of the ferry slip, and sat, chilly and hushed, looking out at the broad, lonely stretch of river that was a wash of feeble lights from the ghostly Jersey shore beyond. The squat, ugly ferry docked clumsily, like some blind hippopotamus, splashing and wheezing. Noisy streams of people crowded off, a few ponderous automobiles.

They hurried on board, making their way to the front and leaning over the railing. Gyrations began somewhere beneath them and the ferry nosed bluntly out into the river. A fierce introspection fell upon everyone during the passage. The fretful motors and the black sounds of implacable water all contributed to a sort of hypnotic isolation, in which thoughts were sharp and inescapable. As soon as the ferry docked, they hastened off and wandered impatiently into the homely streets of Hoboken, looking for the clam house of which Trimble had spoken.

He cantered on ahead of them, stopping at the corner of every crooked alley that led up the hill into the darkness. But everything was closed. They clustered together under a grimy light, suddenly without destination.

"There are some lights down there," Ketcham said. "Look, do you see them? Down two blocks."

"Sure, I remember now," Pasternak exclaimed. "This is River Street, and those are waterfront bars. Where all the Italian ships tie up. I was over here during the war."

"Then this must be the road to Rome!" Trimble cried with ferocious delight. "Come on!" And he set off immediately toward the faint lights with Pasternak just behind him. The others followed silently.

The massive, echoless shadows of warehouses and piers hovered over the river side of the street, and opposite them there was a series of crumbling, vacant buildings with the huge silence of disintegration about them. With their splintered windows and doorless entrances, their gutted hallways and debris-littered stairs, these buildings seemed to belong to some nightmare of a ravaged and deserted Europe. Time and change had passed over them with harsh, swift strokes, and even the rutted side-walk was a profusion of bricks, mortar and glass. Everywhere there were those heaps of rubbish that collect when a building is ignored and begins to die with pitiful slowness; and everything ornamental and impermanent loosens and drops away from it. The very street seemed on the point of disappearing, as though the asphalt and concrete and paving stones were being absorbed by an imperceptible suction in the earth beneath them.

But in the basement of one of these dead houses, there were lights, stifled voices, the scratch of music. A small neon beer sign announced RHEINGOLD, and through the door they could see the dim, reddish glow of bottles and a few motionless figures crouched over the bar.

Trimble and Pasternak led the way. The place was low-ceilinged, indistinctly long, with a paintless shuffleboard alley down one side, and a few tables, empty and obscure at the back. A juke box soiled the walls with shimmering, mustard-colored lights, and purred a sad and throaty blues. There was a buxom, saucy barmaid resting on her elbows and talking to some sailors, who looked up with heavy curiosity and then returned to their whiskey.

As they grouped themselves around the curve of the bar, Hobbes felt an indescribable sense of finality. He was suddenly aware of a desperate thirst, and at the same time, an enormous exhaustion, as though he had just run a mile without stopping to think. It was the profound and heartless exhaustion that comes when a man has risen too far out of the mesh of natural occurrences, and believes he can see their cause and ultimate consequence, but at the same time is powerless to prevent or alter anything. Agatson's death hung over the night, not as a fact to which he must accustom his mind, but as a premonition the meaning of which he could not quite fathom. And so, together with the others, he began to drink steadily, industriously, keeping the barmaid busy.

"How I hate death!" he heard Janet saying then. "And I don't really like to drink either."

"Why do you then?" asked Ketcham.

"To be sociable. Would anyone like me if I didn't?"

"You shouldn't care what anyone else thinks!" he replied with surprising ill temper. "It's foolish to care that much for other people's opinions!"

"Well, we all do anyway."

But just then a queer thing occurred. A man appeared at the door, carrying an accordion without a case; a stooped, bony young man in a shapeless black overcoat that was buttoned up to his chin. His wiry, eccentric hair, and the shrewd, almost contemptuous sneer that curled his pale lips made him look like a misanthropic student, deformed by books and cold and ill-lit midnight brooding, who bitterly rejoices in his degradation. The barmaid, nodding a greeting, snapped off the juke box immediately, and the young man stationed himself beside it. He stared at everyone with icy belligerence for a moment, and then he suddenly commenced to pump the gasping accordion in a frenzied tarantella.

A curious uneasiness seized everyone, even though one of the sailors grabbed the barmaid and began to stumble about in a graceless and obedient dance. Somehow it was this uneasiness which made her hold up her skirts and wriggle her shoulders; and this same uneasiness that compelled everyone else to laugh.

"Whoo-oo-ee!" Trimble yelled, flapping his coattails, and then, pulling Kathryn from her stool, he began to caper and trot, like a blindfolded man running along a precipice.

The dark accordion-player pumped faster and faster, his eyes glittering with unnatural balefulness, and his lips drawn back over yellowed teeth in an avid, mocking snarl.

"No, no," Kathryn was saying. "I don't want to, Peter. Stop it!"

But he was too drunk to notice the intensity with which she said this, and only roared: "Take the hemlock, drink it up!"

Then it was as suddenly over, and the gaunt musician stood, a miserable hat extended in one dirty hand, until Trimble pranced up to him, waving a dollar bill, and crying thickly:

"Can you play 'South Rampart Street Parade'?"

The young man drooped his head slightly in a nod of insolent humility, but then turned, without a sound, and slithered out of the door into the night.

"What a *hell*uva place!" Pasternak mumbled, staring after him. "Imagine Bill in this place."

"This was where he was going when he got off the train!" Trimble shouted rhetorically. "Ha-ha-ha!"

But a strange thing was happening to Hobbes, brought on somehow by the music and its sinister creator. He felt as though he was coming awake. Each word and drink and expression jarred him into a dread awareness of reality, as nausea sometimes seems to make drunkenness real at last.

It was the reality of that shadowy cellar; the centerless, impermanent people there; the desolate, ugly length of River Street; the dark morass of New Jersey that spread tangled and industrial and enigmatic so near by. It was the realization (so strange to him) that all of this had been here always, without his knowing, every time that they had plunged back and forth across the New York night and felt the very world swing upon their dark path. But it was a reality of horror, without meaning, with no certain end.

He fled from his thoughts to the beer, but it was no good.

"Abandon hope," he thought, for actually he was drunker than he realized. "Abandon hope all who enter here."

Then he looked at the others, at the semicircle of intent faces around the bar, and he seemed to see the gnaw of isolation devouring each one. Trimble's exaggerated laughter was actually a mask behind which was hid an emotion of which he was inordinately proud or ashamed. Janet, making a harassed teaparty face, was foolish and brave as she wearied in her contest with fear, but would not relent in the greater struggle to keep this a secret. Ketcham's cool poise was suddenly the emblem of a deep distrust of all confidences, perhaps anger at himself for those he had exchanged to no purpose with Bianca. Pasternak, gloomy and irritated, seemed to be wondering how to fit the joy of his book's acceptance into the dreary facts about Stofsky and Agatson. Hobbes peered into them and knew these things. But it was Kathryn's expression that hurt him most. He seemed to see inside her where even she could never see . . . And then he felt sick.

He got up with sudden violence and stumbled through the tables back to the men's room. He caught a dark glimpse of himself in the shattered mirror over the sink: a drawn, haunted face. The fumes of chlorine, urine and vomit rose from the slippery floor in a thick stink. The walls were sweating, chipped, unwashed. Defaced telephone numbers, obscene drawings, and humorless epigrams were scrawled on them with that desperate and precise crudity of which men are capable only in the privacy of a latrine.

Suddenly he put his head against that slimy wall, and gasped out: "What am I doing here? What's happening? Why is this so?", and felt he could never raise it again, because all the words and faces and nights of the last months were rioting through his mind.

Hart, Dinah, Stofsky, Christine, Ancke, dead Agatson . . . all of them, like children of the night: everywhere wild, everywhere lost, everywhere loveless, faithless, homeless. All with some terrible flaw, a flaw against which even nature rebelled.

"But why did I dignify their madness? And why does everything else seem spiritually impoverished?"

For even the wall he leaned against was crowded with an illiterate testament to the barrenness of the heart. There loneliness scribbled a lewd invitation; desire chalked out a vulgar sketch; frustrate tenderness turned cruel with mockery; ungiven love became a feverish obscenity. All, all . . . blunt confessions of longing, words as would be written on the walls of hell. He was paralyzed by a vision of unending lovelessness.

"This, *this* was what drove Agatson so wild!"

Certainly somewhere, some time this fatal perception must have entered him like a germ and corrupted his heart and mind. And Hobbes suddenly knew that someone who believes this vision is outraged, violated, raped in his soul, and suffers the most unbearable of all losses: the death of hope. And when hope dies there is only irony, a vicious senseless irony that turns to the consuming desire to jeer, spit, curse, smash, destroy.

"I must get out of here!" he groaned aloud. "I must get out!"

Without daring to look at himself again, he returned to the others, to the chatter and the drinks; and the first thing that confronted him was Kathryn's face. He must have appeared visibly shaken for he saw her expression of pensive tipsiness dissolve into alarm. Then she was near him, warm, small, one brown arm about his neck, her flushed, piquant face upturned with worry, as she said:

"What's wrong, honey? . . . Are you sick? . . . You're thinking of Agatson though, aren't you? . . . And that *was* his last birthday, after all . . . How did he *know*, Paul? . . . But hold me up, I may fall . . ."

And she clung to him with a gay, sorrowful little laugh at her own unsteadiness.

"I was just thinking of David too, and wondering where he is, and if everything's all right . . . Am I very drunk? . . . Ah, Paul . . ."

He held her against him, listening to her strange, childlike ramble, and he experienced a sudden emotion of tenderness for her. Sweet, pure remembrances that he could not recognize hung fragilely in the corners of his mind. Like a popular song, he thought with bewilderment, that brings back memories you haven't got . . .

"Let's go," he said to her unexpectedly. "All right? I've had enough." He had to get away or he would drown.

The others seemed to have surrendered to their secret thoughts, and nodded goodbye without questions or regrets. Only Pasternak looked up and perhaps understood, but he made no move to come with them, as if what he pursued in that night lay still a little further on.

And so the two of them stumbled back down River Street alone, holding on to one another in all the dark and ruin around them. Once Kathryn staggered, and giggled blindly in his arms when he recovered her.

The last ferry was about to pull away when they came into the glow of the few failing lights on the pier, but they ran, holding hands tightly, and got aboard just as it cast off.

They stood on the front deck where it was chilly, and a fresh salt wind drove cleanly over the wide blackness of the river. Looking down into the current that swept just below him, Hobbes wondered for the only time in his life if giving up to death was really ignoble, foolish, mad. But then Kathryn, huddled against him, her hair blown soft up into his face, said drowsily:

"You won't let me fall off the boat, will you?"

And he held her closer, and gazed out across the dark, rushing water at New York, a fabulous tiara of lights toward which they were moving. For a moment he stood there in the keen gusts that came up in the middle of the river, and searched the uptown towers of that immense, sparkling pile for the Chrysler Building, so that he might look just north of it and imagine that he saw lights in their apartment.

"Where is our home?" he said to himself gravely, for he could not see it yet.

We've got to revise our opinions—the print assault of the Beat Generation was a joint charge, and John Clellon Holmes and his *Go* was every bit as important to commandeering the bourgeois printing presses as Kerouac's *On the Road* and Allen G.'s *Howl*. (Corso's *Fried Shoes* and *Gasoline* came later, ditto Burroughs' great subversion, *Naked Lunch*.) I never really knew this before, especially before re-reading John's solid, haunting, even at times awkward novel after a quarter of a century of benign neglect. The first time around I felt as many Kerouac fanaticos did—where's the beef, Beat-style? Where's the jazz? The kicks? The lunge and the plunge? Where's that high-rider sass, man?

Well, if you're checking this out after finishing the last page of the novel—that gut-tightening cinematic scene on the ferry back from Hoboken, with Kathryn clutching Paul—you know as well as I that it's all here; even if muted, de-hystericalized, channeled through a more traditional deep leather than Jack's "spontaneous bop prosody." But just as honest. And what different human instruments we're dealing with! J.C. Holmes is almost a compulsive junior priest in his regard for each grain of truth, Kerouac a torrid hot-shot copy writer, but between the two of them we certainly get a dose of late '40s New York scenes.

Of course, my gang in the Village had its own important scene as well; we were the first postwar Village generation of writers, painters, dancers, pioneering serious movie reviewers, etc., but I now feel we were too protected by our anti-commercial elitism compared to the Beat gameness to mix it up. Our elitism and our alienation, I should say, with Chandler Brossard's *Who Walk in Darkness* coming out in exactly the same year as John's *Go* (1952) and preserving in clean post-Hemingway prose how we tried to cope. Albeit with a biblical, doomsday warning that makes Brossard almost as much of a storefront preacher as the young Jimmy Baldwin in *Go Tell It On the Mountain* (1952 as well).

But John shows us things that Brossard's material doesn't quite touch. One is the connection of jazz and the fringe underworld, also the connection of homosexuality and breaking the law, also the great feverish restlessness in New York after the War had ended. ("Everyone traveled ceaselessly from street to street, dive to dive.") Down in the Village, we protected ourselves from a lot of this uprootedness with our own ghetto mentality, in fact we made uneasy jokes about our paranoia when the need for a dollar sent us north of 14th Street into the land of the aliens. We were very cautious and uptight about exposing ourselves to the lurid possibilities of postwar Manhattan (literary kicks with crime, needle-type drugs, apocalyptic visions, as well as holding down nine to five jobs!) that the more unbuttoned Beat experimentalists were open to—no thanks. We Village soul-virgins had our own "uncontaminated" sleep-late community downtown. Were we saner or more selfish?

As for uptown, say around 116th Street and Broadway, it's interesting to note that the funnel for the Beat Generation was venerable Columbia University, where Kerouac (Pasternak) met Ginsberg (Stofsky) and through another ex-student both made the connection with Holmes (Hobbes), who finally seems to have dropped out of the University after returning from Navy service during WWII. Columbia, of all places, where Mark Van Doren and Lionel Trilling were the ruling English Department deities unknowingly nurturing such vipers in their bosoms!

Offstage at this point, as far as *Go* is concerned, are William Burroughs (Dennison) and the mighty imp Corso (nameless because not yet found), but what with Neil Cassady (Hart Kennedy), Herbert Huncke (Albert Ancke) and the death-tripper Bill Cannastra (Bill Agatson), all the rest of the major Beat players are covered. One can see the scrupulous Holmes sitting there, note-book in hand, marking it all down like an apprentice to Charles Darwin on the maiden voyage of the Beagle—the descriptions and action may not be as rapt and rapturous as my friend Kerouac sperms it out, he seems to tell us, but this is something new under the American sun and by putting my ego aside I'm going to get it right, even down to the shoes crookedly lined up under the bed.

And he did. *Go* is a sourcebook, the first entire novel devoted to this new lost (and found) generation, and it will always remain such. In the old newspaper sense, Holmes had a veritably twitching nose for news, of knowing when a big subject was disguised as a minor-league mess. One can say that even though Holmes' writing obviously took on more polish and know-how with succeeding books—perhaps even too much straining ambition with

The Horn, his *Moby Dick*—there is a fidelity about this first one that will inevitably make it irreplaceable with the drip, drip of time.

It has the feel of a true "document" saved from the fire, from the vanished remains of people, places, periods—John, your pluck and doggedness saved it, we want to say with an embrace! (Would have wanted to say, were you still with us).

But then, of course, we pull back. Even though John Holmes was always decent to me the half dozen or so times we met—and never even made an amused, let alone caustic, reference to my painfully thin word-portrait of him in *The Beats*—he was not the kind of man you could easily throw an arm around. John was reserved, his radar dishes were up, his eyes were watching in the night, his brain might be engaged with yours during party small-talk or it might be secretly off on a thousand-mile scouting mission of its own. The cloak of gentlemanliness and quiet amiability was his cover story. One could only read the man through his work, which in a way is as it should be.

So here is the original scribe, the first scribe, of the Beat Generation, meant to be read and not mythologized for himself—but the sweet irony, of course, is that he wrote about myth in its swaddling clothes, in its actual infancy, and can never in future be separated from what he inscribed. The lamp of history will always be lit for him and the new map he so carefully drew.

—Seymour Krim
May 1988

1952 was a great year for American novels, the year of the publication of Ralph Ellison's *Invisible Man,* Ernest Hemingway's *The Old Man and the Sea,* Flannery O'Connor's *Wise Blood,* and Kurt Vonnegut's *Piano Player.* The years immediately before and after were also auspicious: J.D. Salinger published *The Catcher in the Rye* (1951) and William Burroughs Jr, debuted as a novelist with *Junky* (1953). But 1952 was especially important because three novels appeared that year introducing a new topic in American fiction—individuals disaffiliated from the values of conventional society and experimenting with what a reviewer for the San Francisco *Chronicle* summarized as "dope, bebop, and bohemia."

Two of these three novels have slipped into oblivion, alive today mostly on the pages of rare book catalogues: George Mandel's *Flee the Angry Strangers* and Chandler Brossard's *Who Walk in Darkness.* But the third, John Clellon Holmes's *Go,* has been continuously reprinted as one of the classics of Beat literature. What distinguishes Holmes's novel from the others was that it signalled the emergence of a new literary generation, his autobiographical *roman a clef* based on his friendships with Allen Ginsberg, Jack Kerouac, and Neal Cassady. Appearing as thinly disguised "fictional" characters in the book, they became national celebrities after the publication of *Howl and Other Poems* (1956) and *On the Road* (1957).

In 1974, after I wrote the first biography of Jack Kerouac, I began teaching literature at the University of Connecticut, and Holmes became a "neighbor" in Old Saybrook, where he had lived for many years. I had interviewed him for the biography, and later I asked him to tell me how he wrote *Go.* On June 23, 1987, he sent me a letter describing the process:

"I began writing the book when we returned to New York City in August [1949]. So the form—properly a *roman a clef,* I suppose—came of itself, though I had to learn how to use it, and found that simply telling the truth wasn't half enough. It still had to be brought to fictional life. Here my primary influences were the Russians—Dostoevsky above all. . . . I was dealing in extremes of spirit, excesses of behavior, violent emotions or *lack* of them. Dostoevsky is the poet of such states. (Despite saying I was reared on Kafka, James, etc. I was actually in the process of going *backward* from modern literature—being self-educated, I could go where I liked—and was deep in "the great days of the novel" during the writing of *Go*). . . . I didn't think of myself as a "literary historian"; I was already publishing poetry, and everyone wanted to write novels in those days."

Holmes chose the young poet "Stofsky" (modeled on Allen Ginsberg) to be the central character in *Go*; Jack Kerouac has a lesser role as "Gene Pasternak," another aspiring writer. But it is Holmes's own sensibility as the character "Hobbes"—his admirable blend of intelligence, honesty, and decency trying to make sense of his and his friends' chaotic lifestyle in Manhattan after his wrenching experiences as a medic during World War II—that is most memorable in the novel. *Go* dramatizes a six month period in Holmes's life in 1948–49 as he struggled unsuccessfully to finish his first novel and is introduced to a bohemian way of life in New York City that Kerouac characterized as "beat."

Holmes's lyrical aspirations make *Go* a Beat novel, unlike the defeatism of *Flee the Angry Strangers* and *Who Walk in Darkness*. Holmes remembered that he felt an affinity with Kerouac and Ginsberg because they were "Times Square-beat streets types—in other words, 'the real thing' as against 'Bohemian counterfits'! . . . . *Who Walk in Darkness* didn't seem new in any significant ways—Hemingwayesque, tough-guy prose. We were already sniffing down other alleys."

When I asked Holmes why "Hobbes" was so fascinated with the Times Square world of the hipster, the home ground of the Beat experience, his reply was illuminating:

"Why did "Hobbes" yearn to know every aspect of the Times Square world? Undifferentiated reality. That is, life lived moment to moment as it unfolds. Cerebral young men (and women too, I'm sure) are attracted to the spontaneous, the improvised, the random, thus the wondrous. Also, to everything beyond the pale, outside the firelight, everything that has escaped the circumscribed. To "Hobbes," the Times Square world was a gigantic anteroom, off which myriad other worlds opened—hustler, thieves, whores, pimps, lost kids, musicians, etc. A variation on a tag-line for a radio-show of those days: 'There are three million stories in the NAKED CITY. This is one of them.' I was hungry to know everything then. It was a thrill to be young, energetic, imaginative, curious and selfless in the New York of those days. One could entertain the notion that a long, rich, varied shelf of books lay ahead that might start to do for one's New York what Balzac had done so profligately for his Paris. And we were unafraid in those days—alike of such audacious dreams *and* the chancy areas of experience into which we were venturing."

The pseudonym Holmes chose for himself was based on the name of the English philosopher Thomas Hobbes, suggesting his rationality and emotional detachment from the antics of the other characters. Later in *The Beat Journey* (1978), Holmes explained that when he wrote *Go* he wanted "to show the destructiveness" in "some of the Beat stuff too. And of course, Jack [Kerouac] at that point and most of the people I knew who were involved in that really thought it was all upbeat and ongoing and celebratory, while I felt there was also a note of destructiveness and wastage in it." The Dutch literary critic Jaap van der Bent has pointed out the different ways Holmes and Kerouac described the physical appearance of Neal Cassady, the young Denver drifter who came to New York City and was befriended by the group. For Holmes in *Go,* Cassady ["Hart Kennedy"] has "an expression of shrewd, masculine ugliness" and moves with "itchy calculation," while for Kerouac in *On the Road,* Cassady ["Dean Moriarty"] is "a young Gene Autry—trim, thin-hipped, blue-eyed, with a real Oklahoma accent—a side-burned hero of the snowy West."

After Holmes completed the first draft of *Go* in February 1951, he gave the manuscript to his friend Kerouac to read. On March 7, 1951, Kerouac wrote Holmes, "Now I want to write to you about the Beat Generation or simply the Beat Ones—your book. You did the honest thing, the big thing, the good thing. . . ." A month later, Kerouac began the marathon three week typing expercise that resulted in *On the Road.* Unlike Kerouac, Holmes didn't tap into the mythic significance of his material and give new life to an American dream. Nonetheless, in 1952 *Go* signalled the start of something new in American literature. A generation with a new consciousness had found its voice, and that's always news whenever it appears.